THE LADIES ARE UPSTAIRS

Fiction
Angel
Rain Darling
The Colour of Forgetting

Poetry
Because the Dawn Breaks
Rotten Pomerack
Lady in a Boat

THE LADIES ARE UPSTAIRS

A COLLECTION OF STORIES

MERLE COLLINS

PEEPAL TREE

First published in Great Britain in 2011
Peepal Tree Press Ltd
17 King's Avenue
Leeds LS6 1QS
England

'Rain Darling' was first published in the collection
Rain Darling, London: The Women's Press, 1990;
'The Ladies Are Upstairs' was first published in
By the Light of the Silvery Moon, London: Virago, 1994

ISBN13: 9781845231798

Acknowledgement:
Completed with the support of a Summer Creative and
Performing Arts Award (CAPA) from the University of
Maryland

Supported by
ARTS COUNCIL
ENGLAND

CONTENTS

The old stone walls of the building towered above the women as they walked up the hill. They walked slowly, stopping, turning and looking down at the city spread out beneath them. The land stretched like an open palm towards the sea. Blue waters licked the spaces between the outstretched fingers. Buildings looked like they should not have been there, postcard intrusions painted on by a fanciful artist. From where the women were watching, the houses were a mixture of green and red and orange and white and yellow colours, a raging argument painted on the face of peace. In the distance, the sky curved to kiss the sea. Paz was a beautiful city, its name the ironic gift of a lustful conqueror with a twisted sense of humour.

Sister drew a deep and audible breath, pursed her lips and breathed out into the sunshine.

'Somebody down there pushing fire, yes!' she looked down toward Paz, wiping her brow. She took off the wide-brimmed straw hat, stood with one arm akimbo, her mouth half-opened, fanning her face and drinking in the coolness of the temporary breeze.

Ermintrude turned, watched her cousin, put her own hand to her head, but dropped it without removing the soft blue felt hat. She, too, looked down at the outstretched right hand of Paz.

The three women walked, each lost in thought. Unable to keep up the pace, Ermintrude gradually fell back. Usually, she was a good walker, but the sun burned through the felt hat and sent rivulets of sweat down the side of her face, stiffened her legs and prevented rapid progress. The long-sleeved polyester blouse clung to her body. Ermintrude put up her hand and removed the hat after all.

Sister looked back just in time to see the action. She had told her; she had warned her cousin that those clothes, that blouse and that long, thick skirt, would make her steam in the heat. But these people who stay for such a long time in the cold in America always want to wear all kind of long-sleeve when they come on holiday. But Ermintrude should know better. She must be steaming. Not too far now, anyway. And she must be worried about seeing Rain, too. That was another problem.

Sister was thinking about two bags that she had given to the bus driver that morning. Sometimes on these Sunday trips the drivers were so crazy. She just hoped that he had given them to her cousin, Nurse Jones, as she had requested. It should be all right, though; that particular driver was their cousin, too; distant, but a relation. If he hadn't done it, they would have to visit Rain empty-handed – everyone had packed their things in those bags – except for the little rice and peas and chicken she was carrying in the bag slung across her shoulder, and whatever Ermintrude had kept to carry in her own little bag. Sister wondered what Ermintrude would give to her sister at the hospital. Rain didn't like her too much. Rain didn't like anybody too much! Except Cousin Lyris, of course. Poor Rain! She had had a hard life, though. Sister realised that she was thinking about her cousin in the past tense.

'Well!' She said the word out loud, fanning her face against the heat.

Cousin Lyris glanced back at Sister, wondering what she was thinking. She was surprised that Sister had decided to make the afternoon trip with them. She must know that Rain wouldn't want to see her. They hadn't treated her well.

Poor girl! Hers was a hard, hard life. A hard life! People not supposed to have to go through that kind of thing. She wondered how Ermintrude was feeling about this visit. She hadn't said much, but in a way it would have been better for her to go alone. The sisters would need some time to talk. If Rain *would* talk! Still, Ermintrude had wanted them to accompany her. She must tell Sister that they should leave the two alone for a while. She thought about the bags that Sister had given to Maria's son, the bus driver. He was reliable. They should be all right. And a good thing she had done that, too. Imagine walking up this hill with those heavy bags! Ermintrude had shown her two really nice pairs of shoes that she had brought for Rain. And the inevitable grey dresses. Rain should like them – if she looked at them. She glanced back at the others criss-crossing up the hill to make the journey easier.

'You-all come on, come on! We almost there, now. I twice your age, and you letting me beat all-you like that?'

'I don't know where you does get your energy from, non. It must be in the height. You twice my height, too.'

'Well you self, Ermintrude, you have no height at all, so don't talk! At least I in the middle, but you, you nowhere near Cousin Lyris.'

'True, yes,' agreed Ermintrude. 'Cousin Lyris height don't come from the Augier side of the family at all. Mother and Aunt Myra and all of them is a short, short set of people. That must be come from her father people. She like Rain. Is that kind of height.'

The conversation stopped abruptly, the women pushed back into thought. *Oh dear!* thought Cousin Lyris… *The unmentionable… And it just isn't right! It's all that damn man's fault!* Her mother said so, anyway. She had brought up the subject with Ermintrude. Ermintrude had said, 'Well, Aunt Myra is one person inside the family I hear that come out and give me mother right. And Aunt Emma say she don't know, but whatever she do is all right. She do it because she had a reason. And Orilie, I never talk to her about it, but you know what she will feel. I don't like to talk about it at all.'

They went through the stone archway into the wide courtyard. A few people were standing around, talking. Some were obviously visitors, dressed in their Sunday best for the outing; some were patients. Two nurses leaned against the wall; one was looking through the porthole toward Paz and the sea. The other walked up to them. *She really better go alone first*, Cousin Lyris thought.

'Listen,' she said, 'Ermintrude, I think is best if you go in to see her alone, and then we will come afterwards.'

'But...' Both Ermintrude and Sister were protesting.

Sister was thinking, *I sure Cousin Lyris and Ermintrude plan this*. But then Ermintrude seemed genuinely surprised, so perhaps not. Why should Cousin Lyris have taken it upon herself to suggest such a thing? She, Sister, wasn't afraid to face Rain. There was no reason why she should keep away from Rain.

Ermintrude was strangely afraid of facing her sister alone. She didn't want to see the rejection, the resentment on her face. But perhaps Cousin Lyris was right. It was better to face it alone, especially not with Sister. Perhaps it was a good idea after all. Let her sort out things with her sister first. If Rain would let anybody sort things out with her!

'Okay, then.' Ermintrude turned toward the nurse, and Sister shrugged her shoulders.

Cousin Lyris walked to one of the portholes. Sister moved to one of the benches in the courtyard. From the porthole, where in olden times the guns of the fort used to scan the sea, Cousin Lyris could see both sides of the cross. Only one side of Paz had been visible as they walked up the hill, one hand stretching out into the sea. Now, from this building at the top of the hill, the frightening beauty of Paz City was spread out below. From here it was obvious why the Spanish tourists called it Cruz. In the middle, one stretch of land jutted right out into the sea. On it was a large building, with a red roof and grey walls, the old leper house. On the way up they had seen one hand; now the other hand stretched to Cousin Lyris's right, fingers spread. Paz! Crucified and beautiful in the sunshine.

Cousin Lyris turned and looked towards the long, low, new brick building hiding behind these old stone walls of the ancient fort. On the verandah, she could see Ermintrude's felt hat, her left arm on the verandah railing, her face in profile as she talked to the person sitting behind the post, out of sight. Rain, she guessed. Cousin Lyris walked to the bench and sat with Sister.

People said this place up here was haunted. There were all sorts of stories about how in the night soldiers could be heard moving around in search of parts of their bodies, looking for fingers and ears and feet. Some said that at times, on a moonlit night, people could see just a head moving around, looking for the rest. Or just a foot moving, looking for the rest. But the worst were the souls that had lost entire bodies; you heard them when the wind was howling and howling and howling through the mouths of the guns pointing down to Paz.

Cousin Lyris shivered. The wind was cold in this place. There were some things you shouldn't think about even in broad daylight with the sun shining on you.

When Ermintrude came out to call them, they were just sitting there, saying nothing, lost in thought. Sister pushed herself to her feet.

'How is she?'

Ermintrude shrugged. 'She all right. Come, non.'

Rain was standing at the verandah railing, tall and slim. Her shoulders were held straight. She was stately and assured when you saw her from afar, a thick black plait circling her head. She became smaller, somehow, when you tried to look into her eyes. Perhaps she knew this, and so she usually tried to avoid meeting anyone's eyes. Unless she wanted to, and then she had such an intense stare that you felt uncomfortable.

'Rain, how are you?'

Rain stared at Sister. 'Why you want to know how I am? Why you come here? You-all have no shame, you and your mother? She send you to finish me off?' Rain's voice was quiet, conversational. Her liquid black eyes never left Sister's face.

Sister laughed nervously. 'Don't excite yourself, Rain. You know the doctor say you mustn't take things on.'

Rain gave a twist of a smile. 'I not excited, Cousin. I have nothing to be excited about.'

'Your Aunt Orilie dead, Rain. She can't send nobody to finish you off,' Cousin Lyris said, smiling.

'I know she dead, Cousin Lyris. Don't let them make you think I mad; I have me full senses.'

'Yes,' said Cousin Lyris quietly. 'Yes, yes, all right.'

'Don't "all right" me. I not stupid. These people who so wicked in life don't really die, you know. They keep contact with those they want to carry out their deeds here.' Rain looked at Sister, and backed away a step. 'They don't really die.'

Sister looked at Ermintrude, smiled, put a finger to her temple, and shook her head. Rain looked at her sister. Ermintrude lifted her shoulders as if to say, What to do?

Rain said quietly, 'I think I better go inside and lie down.'

Cousin Lyris drew Sister aside. 'You know how it is,' she said. 'I think you better wait outside.'

Sister clenched her teeth and gave a long *stupes*. 'But why she behaving like that?'

Cousin Lyris said again, 'You know how it is,' and inwardly asked Rain to forgive her for pretending.

Sister walked down the steps. Rain watched her go,

watched her turn left and disappear within the courtyard. She turned back to look at her sister and cousin, then moved to sit on a chair. The two women walked towards the long bench.

'How are you feeling, Rain?'

Rain shrugged. 'So-So.' She stared out into the sunshine. After a moment, she added, 'Is just the cough, otherwise I'm all right.'

A nurse came forward with the bags that Ermintrude had requested earlier. She handed them to Cousin Lyris. Cousin Lyris gave one to Ermintrude, the other she kept. Rain looked at the table, where two plastic containers held the rice and peas and chicken that Ermintrude had given her earlier.

'You're ready to eat now?' her sister asked.

'No. Not yet.'

The nurse, who had turned away to the wide front doors of the building, paused to look back. 'She living on air, yes,' she commented. 'She hardly eats anything.'

'Mm.' Cousin Lyris looked at her young cousin. You could see the evidence in those high, protruding cheekbones, no flesh on the face, nothing on the body. The grey dress hung on her frame like a sack. Grey! Rain always asked for grey. It was useless giving her any other colour. She would accept it with thanks, with the same blank expression with which she received all gifts, but it would remain unused. She would never wear any other colour, the nurses said.

Suddenly, Rain started coughing. Deep, racking coughs that sounded like they were pulling her chest apart, tearing up her insides. She was bent double, Ermintrude holding her now. A nurse came to the door, tall, stout, kind. 'All right,' she said. 'All right, Rain. Take it easy.' Cousin Lyris was standing, watching. Another nurse appeared in the doorway. Cousin Lyris walked towards them, drew the younger nurse aside.

'How she doing these days?'

'Very ill, and weak. Sometimes she just sits there dreaming, and talking to herself. One of the doctors was saying the other day that it might be an idea to send her back to the mental home.'

'What! Why? She not mad! Don't send her back there at all! She shouldn't have gone there in the first place; is just that she not talking to anybody. She not mad. And is in there she pick up this germ that have her tearing out her insides there now.'

The young nurse shrugged. Cousin Lyris persisted. 'You know that is inside that cold place she get this TB that have her here?'

The nurse straightened the white apron over her blue uniform, put a hand to her cap. 'Well, Miss, I don't know.'

Cousin Lyris sighed. 'Is not your fault, anyway. But treat her nice, you hear. Is because she have a lot on her mind that she so silent. Life didn't treat her nice. And she don't give any trouble.'

'No. She's no trouble, really. She just keeps to herself, and don't talk to anybody. Bright sunshine, everybody else outside, she want to be inside, alone. She doesn't even sit on the verandah there, non. Inside here, or in her room most times.'

'Yes. Yes.'

'We always make joke and say that perhaps it have something to do with her name.'

Cousin Lyris didn't laugh. Just lifted her shoulders and said, 'Well!' Perhaps it did have something to do with her name. She always wondered what had motivated her cousin Cora to call the child Rain. Her mother said that Cora had been seeing so much trouble with Andrew at the time that when she got pregnant with Rain she thought it must be a blessing in disguise. And Emma, who had her own ideas about the whole business, said she had a suspicion that Rain was conceived one rainy night. She had been born on a day of brilliant sunshine, midday, December 23rd, 1929. Emma and Lyris, standing near to her bedside, had been amazed to hear her whisper, 'I want to call her Rain.' 'Rain!' they had exclaimed together. 'Rain,' she had repeated, and then started to cry. Andrew had left for the States already, the month before. Cora herself left the following year, when Rain was a cheeky, bubbly one-year-old. Lyris shook her head, remembering how much Rain's mother had loved her. She was definitely the spoiled last child. Perhaps it's better to stay with your children, no matter what happens. Ah well! Lyris had been ill when Cora left, and she and her mother hadn't been able to keep both Ermintrude and Rain. Emma left to work in Trinidad soon afterwards. Rain had stayed first with Orilie, and then, when she was about four, with their cousins Zebede and Dinah. When Dinah died suddenly, she went to stay with Orilie again. Everybody in the family said that Orilie was dissatisfied because she thought America should be hers, because she was keeping the child. But perhaps it wasn't easy for her. Who knows? And then the father!

The coughing had stopped when Cousin Lyris returned to the verandah. Ermintrude was holding Rain still, trying to get her to lean her head back. Rain pulled away. She didn't want to be touched. She leaned her head down on the table, breathing deeply, raspingly. Cousin Lyris approached, touched her. Rain stiffened, shrugged her body away. Cousin Lyris spoke. 'You feeling better now?'

Rain looked up briefly, put out a hand, covered Cousin Lyris's hand with her own, and was quiet when Cousin Lyris placed a hand on her hair. After a while, she whispered, 'Take me to my room; take me to my room, please, Cousin Lyris.' And Cousin Lyris held her, wanting to cry for this woman who was still lost in a childhood she couldn't forget.

Because Rain couldn't forget. Most nights, while many of the other patients were asleep, she haunted the courtyard. The nurses didn't stop her. There was no danger. They sat and watched her from the verandah as she covered the distances inside the encircling walls in long, urgent strides. She looked down on the winking lights of Paz from the porthole, disappeared from their sight as she turned and circled the courtyard, came back into view, striding.

Usually, Rain thought of the day that her... And her thoughts would jerk to a stop. She never knew what to call him, really. At the time she called him her father.

And Rain would look around quickly. Had anyone been close enough to see that thought? Sometimes she giggled. Stood and looked at the nurses. They hadn't heard. Suddenly unsafe in the space around her, Rain would stride back towards the verandah. Sometimes the nurses would walk to the room beyond, knowing that this woman, whose pain they shared without understanding it, wanted to be left alone.

One night, at the far end of the corridor, a woman sat, head on her hands, looking intently down between her knees. She wore a dress of fading yellow. Rain sat on the bench, looking at the ear peeping from between the encircling thumb and forefinger of the woman's left hand. Rain leaned forward, right hand folded in her lap, the left hand holding it securely at the wrist, and stared with frowning intentness at the ear. She squinted, trying to see it properly. She began to get agitated.

She leaned forward a little more, releasing her wrist and resting the palms of her hands on her legs. Rain darted a quick backward glance towards the door through which the nurses had disappeared. She didn't want anyone around to hear her thoughts.

Then she saw him – perched on the railing just outside, just ahead of her. The cat paused, a shadowy black outline, looking directly at her. How long had he been looking? Had he heard? Rain burst out laughing, threw back her head and laughed long and loud. He would know then that she didn't care anyway, whatever he might have thought he heard. Rain threw her head back against the grey wall; the thick black plait that encircled her head cushioned it against the wall. Her body shook so much that the bench teetered a little. Rain choked on her laughter.

A nurse came to the door and stood there for a moment looking, shook her head slightly, and turned away. It was after the nurses watched Rain's movements on this strange night and reported to the doctor that he said perhaps she should go back to the mental home for a while.

Slowly, Rain lowered her head, looked through laughter-slit eyes toward the railing. He was gone. Abruptly, Rain's laughter stopped. The nurse peeped through the door and drew her head back inside. Rain looked from one side to the other. Listened. Looked around. Stood up and tiptoed to the banister. Looked down at the ground. Leaned out and looked around the corner. Smiled triumphantly. He was gone. Rain chuckled. She had fooled him.

But then, he had fooled her. She had so looked forward to his coming. She had never known him, really. Not really. He had been back twice on holiday. Once when he came back she must have been... how old? Rain frowned, leaned back against the grey.

'Daddy coming!' she told everyone. That night, Miss Orilie had opened the letter and stretched her mouth long like monkey backside. Rain giggled. Her friend Tisane was always saying that: *Long like monkey backside* – 'But Rain, what do you aunt, girl? How she like to stretch she mouth long like monkey backside so?' 'Aunt? Who aunt you talking bout? Is not me aunt, non!' 'Well whoever aunt she is, she is a aunt with a monkey backside face.' 'Girl, Tisane,

17

what does do you? Is why Miss say somebody go decatché you tail one day.' 'Ah chuts! Miss Mulroon face look like decatché.' 'Girl, Tisane!'

'What wrong wid you? What so good bout the world that you siddown dey laughin like Christ comin? What wrong wid you?'

Rain looked at the mouth stretched taut, at Miss Orilie's thin, long hands resting on the blue and white patterned plastic tablecloth, and wanted to laugh again. When the giggles came was the times that the Devil was around. 'You got the Devil with you?' Whenever she started giggling, they all asked her that. Miss Orilie, Auntie Myra, Uncle Anthony and even Cousin Mildred, who managed to be warm and loving even though she had eight children of her own and three of other people's children living with her. 'You got the Devil with you?' So Rain set her face and stared past Miss Orilie's head straight into the Devil's eyes, daring him to make her laugh.

> *Look de Devil!*
> *De Devil down dey!*

In her thoughts, she sang straight into his face and dared him to come forward. Miss Orilie looked nervously over her shoulder, through the open doorway toward the trees outside. She looked back suspiciously at Rain. Sometimes she felt she really didn't like this child who stared and talked to herself and always seemed to have someone with her. She opened her mouth to ask, 'What wrong with you?' But Rain saw the question coming and knew that it was always followed by the dreaded, 'You got the Devil with you?' She must stop it. She could feel in her bones that that would be unlucky as usual.

Pick up you bat, pick up you bat. Don't let her bowl that ball.

'You get letter from America today, Miss Orilie. Is me mother?'

'Don't be impertinent, child. Speak when you spoken to. Eh, so you smellin yourself, then? You is woman these days? You bigger than me in me own house?'

Rain bowed her head. Under the bench, she rubbed the big toe of her right foot against the hollow towards the back of her left foot.

She dipped her hand into the bowl of water, sprinkled the shirt and looked up just in time to see her spirit slip out of the room to stand shouting under the tree outside; this was its favourite spot for singing.

Boykin oh
Boykin ay
Searching for me boyking
Boykin that cause the girl
To go to the cemetery
Boykin oh
Boykin ay
Searching for me boyking

'You hear what I say?'

'No, Miss Orilie.'

'How you mean, no Miss Orilie? You stand up right inside me nose-hole an you don' hear what I say? I tell you already you will end up in trouble one day, you know. You never know what going on around you.'

Rain crossed her fingers against this curse. *Never*, she said to herself once. *Never*, she said again, looking into Miss Orilie's eyes. *Never*, she said to herself again, still staring at Miss Orilie, pleased that she got through the third 'never' without interruption.

Miss Orilie fidgeted and stupsed. *If I say this child doesn't annoy me, I lie. I don't know where they find her, but she sure as hell got the Devil with her.*

'Is about your father. He say he comin on holiday.'

Lots of things rushed together. The envelope with its red,

19

white and blue border. The red, white and blue dress she had pulled from the suitcase below the bed on the day that Miss Orilie went to market. The red, white and blue dress with the slight stain on the hem because someone in the trace must have dropped something on it as the brown girl swung around the ring tra-la-la-la-la.

'Me father, Miss Orilie? He comin in truth?'

'If he comin in truth? So I dey in little children foolishness, then? I tell you your father comin, you askin me if he comin in truth?'

Rain's big, black eyes moved from the letter to Miss Orilie's face and back again.

'What he say, Miss Orilie?'

'Who "he"?'

'Me father.'

'Is your mother that write. Since when you know your father writin letter? Man doesn't write letter. Everything he have to say to you, your mother say it already.'

Rain thought of the boys who sat in school with her, pretending to write. She looked suspiciously at Miss Orilie. Tisane said that Miss Orilie look like she does make up some good lie sometimes. When she last saw her sister, Ermintrude had spoken of a letter from Daddy. A letter. And a doll brought over by someone on a visit from that magic place called Brooklyn. Bedstuye in Brooklyn.

Two weeks later, a small parcel with a tiny white doll had arrived for Rain. Rain opened the parcel and shouted with joy, challenging Miss Orilie's tight, shuttered face with a laugh that made the lazy green lizard on the window forget the coveted fly and pause to turn its head in her direction.

'She pretty eh, Miss Orilie! She pretty, eh!'

Miss Orilie lifted her head from the letter. 'Your mother send five dollars, too. And she say you must behave yourself.'

That time, too, Rain had asked, 'Me mother? Is me mother that write, Miss Orilie?'

'How you mean if is your mother that write? Look the letter there. It don't have nothing in it your eyes shouldn't see. Read it if you want.'

Her father had visited, but it seemed that he hardly came to Retreat to see them. He stayed most of the time in Victoria, where Ermintrude lived with Aunt Myra and Cousin Lyris. Rain would have liked to stay there, but Aunt Myra wasn't strong, and Cousin Lyris often ill. They couldn't have both children. Father – his name was Andrew, but at that time she always thought of him as Father, or My Father – visited one Monday afternoon when she was outside washing the week's clothes. She didn't often go to school on a Monday, because Miss Orilie wanted her to do the washing then. But she had almost not done washing that day, because the rain kept playing hide and seek with the sun. From morning, one minute it was drizzling, next minute, the sun was shining as bright as ever.

Rain coming, sun shining
The Devil and he wife fighting!

The Devil and his wife must have been having a hell of a fight that day. Rain wasn't sure which one was the Devil, the sun or the rain, and which was the wife, but up to now no one was winning, because it was still drizzle, drizzle, then sun, sun.

Rain looked up when the man came into the yard. She didn't know who he was. The front door was closed, so he'd walked to the back of the house. She looked up from the washing, soapsuds on her hands, wondering if the clothes would be dry in time so that she could iron tonight and so not miss school tomorrow morning. If only the rain would just go away and let the sun shine properly!

'Good afternoon.'

'Good afternoon, sir.'

'Is Miss Orilie in?'

'No, sir. She gone to Paz City today.'

'Do you know what time she will be back?'

'Well, she went this morning early, so she should be back any time soon now.'

She stood there looking at the man, at his cream-coloured shirt and grey pants. His black shoes were shining. He looked like somebody who come from away. He looked nice, too.

'You want to leave a message for her, sir?'

'No. I'll wait a little.'

Rain didn't know what to do. Should she ask him to sit inside? She didn't think Miss Orilie would like that. Tisane, who told her everything that she heard from her mother, had said that she should be careful of strange men. And this was a strange one. She had never seen him around. Well let him stand up there. He walked away from the house. From where she stood, she could see him leaning against the mango tree. She pushed the bucket of water forward a little so that she could see him better. He stood there looking down the gap toward the road, the rough, unpainted board of the kitchen looking even more rough against his smooth, cream and grey neatness. He turned and saw her watching him. Looked at her for a moment. Walked back to stand looking at her.

'What is your name?'

'Rain.'

The man turned and walked back toward the mango tree. He put a hand in his pocket, turned and walked back to her.

'You know Ermintrude?'

'Ermintrude? My sister Ermintrude?'

'Yes. I am her father.'

'Daddy! Daddy!' Soapsuds and everything, she was flinging her arms around him.

'All right, all right! You wettin me all over, man!'

'Daddy! Daddy!' She released him. 'But Daddy, why you didn't tell me? And I leave you standing up outside there. Come inside! Come inside, Daddy! When you come? Where is Ermintrude? She didn't come up with you? I longing to see her. How is Mammie? Why she didn't come with you? I really wish she did come with you. When you going back? Me and Ermintrude could come up and stay in Brooklyn with you-all? You not going back to Victoria tonight? Bring me back there too if you going, eh, Daddy? I didn't know you reach, you know. But Miss Orilie did tell me you was coming.'

Rain was dancing, skipping, laughing, turning back to look at the sober-faced man who was following her inside. And who was actually her FATHER! *He so handsome! Father in you shirt! Wait till I tell Tisane!*

'Miss Orilie?' he said. 'Is your aunt, you know. You calling her Miss Orilie?'

'I don't like her, Daddy. She not nice. She don't like me. She tell me she don't like me. She tell me I growing tall, tall and trampin bout the place like a elephant. She tell me a lot of nasty things. I don't like her at all, Daddy. Bring me back to Brooklyn with you.'

Her father ran his hand along the plastic tablecloth.

'Miss Orilie tell your mother that you very rude. She say that you run away, that you use a lot of bad words and that you very difficult to control.'

Rain stared at him. Was he going to take Miss Orilie's side? Tisane had said that you couldn't depend on fathers, that usually they weren't there and visited only to shout and beat sometimes. Tisane had warned that on the whole children were better off without them. Rain found nothing sympathetic in his eyes; she looked down at the tablecloth.

'You staying tonight?'

'No, I going back to Victoria tonight. I will wait a while longer for Orilie.' He cleared his throat. 'Your mother send you some things.' He picked up the brown bag and opened it. 'Some clothes and toys and books and things.'

Your mother. He didn't show her anything that he had brought specially for her. When Miss Orilie came, they talked a lot. Rain stood in the doorway rubbing her big toe against the back of her left foot while her father told Miss Orilie stories about a train called the A train that they were going to build in New York, and about people in New York that both of them knew.

'Eh! You know I see all-you cousin, Gaiphus, there in New York?'

'Gaiphus? Eh! That alive?'

'Alive and kicking! And mamaguy!'

Rain had never heard Miss Orilie laugh like that before. Laugh and slap the table and choke laughing.

'Well meself I did good for he! Long before I meet him I hear people say that whenever you meet him, he trying to get a few cents off you!'

'Well, since here so he is, you know. And Cousin Melda, he mother, up the hill in the back over there, she like that too, you know! So he ain't take it far. Is like they say, cow doesn't make donkey.'

Rain couldn't help it. *And how your mother manage?* The thought leapt to her head with such force that she looked quickly at Miss Orilie's face. But she hadn't heard, of course. Is strange the way you could just think things about people and they go on sitting down there listening like nothing happen.

'Well Mr Gaiphus meet the right one. Those fellas say when you bounce him up, if he didn't marry last week, he getting married next week, and he asking for a contribution.'

'Oh yes? Gaiphus bright! He ain't fraid somebody bring him up for breach of contract in this New York dey?'

'Well, he ain't giving nobody the chance because he ain't

naming no name! An you know meet I meet Gaiphus, he tell me he getting married, in truth.'

'Woy-o-yoy!'

'Well, I couldn't believe it, you know. I say them fellas did jokin, but Gaiphus tell me he getting married, and he ask for,' Rain's father dropped his voice, 'a little thing, you know. A small forty dollars or so, just to help out.'

Miss Orilie leaned back in her chair, choking with laughter.

'Well you don't know I coulda take Gaiphus and fling him quite in Ohioho! Anyway, I tell him I wan to meet the bride. I stand up there and carry on asking him a whole heap of questions about what she look like, and I say that on behalf of the family, you know, I want to meet her. He leave so fast, eh!'

Miss Orilie actually giggled.

'He must be still in some street in New York trying to get some lady to come and meet me! Me ain't know! That is the last I hear bout the nastiness!'

'Yes! Well that is a good one.' Miss Orilie turned her head to the side to wipe the tears from her eyes, and caught sight of Rain slouching in the doorway. 'Don't stand up there listening to big people conversation, child. Go and find something to do!'

Rain looked at her father. But he said not a word. Just sat there chuckling as he remembered the man in New York. So Rain lowered her head and turned away. She sat on the step and listened to their talk and laughter. Nothing to do with her. He stayed two weeks in the island, but that was the only time he visited her, and it was as if he hadn't really visited her. Fathers were like that, Tisane said. But she heard him talking to Miss Orilie about Ermintrude, about how Ermintrude had grown, about how they were trying to get Ermintrude to go up to the States. He said that Ermintrude was just like him.

'That girl, eh! If you see her play netball, man! Is true she don't have much height but when you see she hold on to that ball on the court, nothing can't get past her, non. The best thing on the court, yes!'

'Mm.'

'She remind me of me in my days, man. I was looking smaller than some of them fellas; some of them big and all six foot and more, but when you see I catch on to that ball, man, ten o them to catch me. Swift, swift on the field, man! And style!'

'Yes,' said Miss Orilie admiringly. 'I always hear you was a good footballer. People does still talk you name.'

'Man, what you mean? I wasn't joking, you know.'

Rain peeped through the door behind Miss Orilie's back and looked at her father. He was looking up at the ceiling and stroking his chin. She almost thought, *Eh! He just think he nice!* But held it back just in time. After a while she stopped hearing what they were saying. She put her head down on her knees and tried to imagine what America looked like. She thought about her mother. She waited for her father to say, 'Rain! Come here, girl! Come and talk to your father.' Then all of a sudden she heard him saying, 'I must really go now, yes. It getting late.' She lifted her head and listened. He didn't even call her. Rain dashed away from the steps and under the house. Miss Orilie called and she didn't answer. And he just said, 'All right, then, tell her I gone.' That was all. 'Tell her I gone.'

She ran away that night. Ran all the way down to Tisane's house in the trace. Stumping her foot against the roots of the trees in the darkness. But she didn't even feel it. She lay down on the bed with Tisane and her brothers and sisters and cousins and listened to them talking and laughing and telling stories for a long, long time. They made jokes about everything, about Old Man Mody who shouted from his verandah when they teased his dog. Mody who stood on his verandah every morning and afternoon to keep watch over his julie and tin mango trees as the school children went by. Some of them defied him, jumped across the drain, seized a fallen mango and ran away laughing while he shouted and the dog barked. They watched the rotting mangoes and wondered why he threatened to poison them rather than allow children to eat them. They decided that he hated children, and invented gruesome stories about his dealings with the devil to explain this hatred. Rain knew that if she hadn't been so sad, they would have compared him to Orilie, knowing that she wouldn't mind. But they didn't want to make her feel worse. And knowing this only made her want to cry more. But it also made her want to stay with them. So she listened and smiled when they talked about Eileen who always talked to herself, and who threatened to send their 'backsides to thy kingdom come' when they passed and hit at the fence in front of her house with thick sticks.

In the midst of the laughter, Tisane's mother called out, 'Rain, time for you to go home now. Miss Orilie must be wondering where you is. One of you, walk a little bit along the road with Rain.' And Rain shouted back without enthusiasm, 'Yes, Cousin Mildred. I going now.'

Then Tisane looked at her friend's face, put a finger to her lips and drew Rain out of the room. The others heard Rain's voice call out, 'Good night, Cousin Mildred.'

'All right, child, say good night for me, eh!'

'Yes, Cousin Mildred. All right, Tisane girl.'

'All right then, Rain, see you tomorrow, eh!'

Two minutes later, both girls tiptoed back into the room. Tisane placed an urgent finger on her lips and motioned to her relatives to continue talking.

Rain was gone early the following morning, before Cousin Mildred was awake. She walked up the hill and into the yard, bold as brass. Miss Orilie decided, 'Well today, today self I killing this child. Rain, where you come from?'

Miss Orilie stripped her naked to beat her with the peas

whip, so that there would be no clothes in the way. Rain took the beating without flinching, making no sound. Frustrated, Miss Orilie screamed at her, 'Little woman like you bringing child in people door-mouth before they know what happening. Eight years you have, and you stayin out already. Oh Lord, I have no children of me own to give me this kind of crosses. Why people don't sit down and mind their children after they make them? Is me they put sit down here to have all this problems with you! Oh Lord me God, well I kill priest? Jesus, deliver me from this burden! I don't want no little whore in me yard, you hearing me?'

'I could put on me clothes now, Miss Orilie?'

'Child, if I say I don't hate you, I lie. Nothing, nothing good could ever come out of you. You curse. Beg God pardon, child, but you well curse.'

And Rain had looked at Miss Orilie with dead eyes and thought of Ben down the road, Ben who walked and dribbled on himself and couldn't even talk properly, and who people said had been cursed by his aunt because he had stolen her clean-neck fowl. And Rain stared at Miss Orilie hard and thought, *The curse will fall right back on you, because God self see I didn't do nothing, and I didn't thief nobody clean-neck fowl! You cursing yourself, Orilie*. And even as she thought it, she called on Papa God to witness it, and to witness that she hadn't done anything, so no curse shouldn't take her.

Later there was Sister. Miss Orilie's only child was born when Rain was nine. Tisane said, 'Rain, girl, everybody wondering where this child come out. Nobody didn't know Miss Orilie in this kind of thing still. I hear Mammie say that Orilie almost hitting fifty.'

'Tisane, girl, they going jail you, you know.'

'Is me mouth they going jail. They won't catch me at all.'

After Sister was born, Rain hardly went to school. She

had to take care of Sister and of the house while Miss Orilie worked. Now, when Miss Orilie was at home, she showered her love on Sister, kissing her, hugging her, playing with her. At first, Rain would pinch Sister and make her scream when they were alone together. Then when Sister was old enough to tell her mother, Rain stopped, and kept the cold hatred inside of her, talking about it only to Tisane.

'Girl Tisane, Orilie think she child is the best thing since fry bakes!'

'You don't find she look like a fry bakes in truth? Watch round she mouth how it does be white. You know when you put the bakes in the hot oil, but the oil not plenty, so round the edge stay white, white?'

Rain giggled. Trust Tisane! And Tisane said, 'Don't study Orilie, girl! That is not people to study.'

Rain wrote often to her mother, and still to her father sometimes. Her mother wrote all the time, sent her clothes that Rain never wore, because there was no place to wear them to. She wrote of money that she sent to Miss Orilie, so that Rain could be properly taken care of. She told Rain she loved her; she told Rain to be good. Sometimes Rain sat staring at the letters and wondering what love looked like; sometimes she took the letters to Tisane; Tisane read them and said, 'You mother love you, girl. She just out there trying to make a better life for you.'

'That is what she say, Tisane. But how she out there could make a better life for me?'

'She going send for you when she could afford. She say that too.'

When Rain was fourteen, she talked to Miss Orilie about going out to look for a job. She wanted to sew, she said. At school, they used to tell her it was her best subject, and Miss Orilie knew that she could sew things well.

'Job? What job? You inside here good, good, helping me

out, now you talking about job? Is hot you little tail hot so, is man you want to go and look for! What job?'

Rain opened her eyes to a face bending over her. 'Move, Orilie,' she shouted. 'Get outa me way!'

The nurse stepped back. Rain focused. 'Nurse,' she said uncertainly. 'Nurse?' Then she smiled weakly. 'Sorry, Nurse. I thought it was a *diablesse*.'

Nurse Jones was thinking about this as she watched Rain's cousin lead her to her room. Was Rain really losing her mind now? She walked quickly ahead of them and straightened the sheet.

'Thanks, Nurse,' said Cousin Lyris.

'I will lie down for a while, Cousin Lyris. I just feeling a little bit weak, but I'll be okay soon.'

'Don't worry about it. Rest yourself. We will stay for a while, because we not getting the bus until later.'

'Stay in here then, for a while, non. I might sleep, but you could stay with me if you want.'

Rain closed her eyes immediately. Cousin Lyris sat on a chair near to the bed, whispering to the nurse that she should tell the others to go ahead and eat. The nurse smiled and left the room. *People always say these nurses unhelpful*, thought Cousin Lyris, *but I must say these here really kind to Rain. And you could see she like them, too*. Cousin Lyris sighed. Rain lived everything so intensely, had so longed for her parents, that Lyris knew that her waking moments were caught up in painful memories. Perhaps she didn't escape them even when she slept.

Ermintrude visited her one day. Rain was always pleased to see her sister, but she never showed it now. Ermintrude was always happy, always bubbling with some story, and Rain's sad eyes made her uncomfortable. Rain always stood straight and tall, staring down into your eyes when you told her something, and she never seemed to see the joke in things.

'Rain,' said Ermintrude, 'our father is coming next month.'

'Our mother said she might be coming. She coming too?'

'No. Daddy said she can't make it. She can't get enough time off from work.'

'Daddy write you?'

'Yes.'

'He does write you often?'

'Sometimes.'

'He never write me, you know, Ermine. Before, it was because you were older and I was very young. But I bigger now. He must know I bigger now.'

Ermintrude shrugged.

'Ah well! I suppose I wasn't even born yet when he leave; so is you he know, really, and not me. You was big already, ent?'

'Yes. I was almost six when he left. Rain, when he visit this time, he will… he might… I mean, he intend for me, for us, I think, to go back with him.'

'To Brooklyn?' Rain's eyes were suddenly alight. 'Ermine, you don't mean he want us to go to Brooklyn? Ermine, you jokin!'

Ermine looked miserable. 'Is true, yes, Rain.'

'But, Ermine, girl, you joking! And you saying that easy so? You ent glad?'

'Yes. Of course I glad.'

'Auntie Myra don't want you to go?'

'Yes, yes. Auntie Myra glad. She and Cousin Lyris say they will miss me, but they feel it have better opportunities for me out there. I will miss them, too, but I really want to see me mother again.'

'Girl, Ermine, I not going miss nobody. Exceptin Tisane. That ole Orilie is a nasty, mean, good-for-nothing, back-side-hole…'

'Rain!'

'Lewwe don't talk bout she, girl!' Rain flung her arms wide. 'Woy! We going America.' Then she looked at Ermintrude's miserable face. 'What happen, Ermine? What happen?'

Ermintrude shook her head. 'Nothing.'

'Is both of us that going, Ermine? Or is you alone?'

'No. Is both of us, Rain.'

Rain told Tisane. 'Me father coming, girl. And guess what, non, Tisane?'

'What?'

'Guess, non!'

'He promise to kill Orilie.'

Rain laughed.

'Well, I don't know what else could make you look so.' Tisane, now in her second year at high school, looked at her friend and hoped it was something special.

'Me and Ermintrude going back with him.'

'You joking!'

Rain danced, circling the tree under which Tisane was sitting in the yard. Tisane shouted. Then, watching her friend, she suddenly remembered the last time Rain's father had visited. 'But anyway, girl, remember to be happy for yourself, eh!'

'How you mean?'

Tisane picked up a twig from the ground and broke it. She couldn't explain her fear, couldn't explain that her friend's eyes sometimes frightened her; she didn't know how to say that she was afraid sometimes, because of the way Rain loved her parents and felt so sure that being with them meant happiness. It wasn't that, really; it was just the way that Rain loved and hated so deeply, and let it into her eyes. Tisane's mother always said, 'Don't wait on nobody to make you happy, especially not no man. Man, them is the most mix-up set of people the good Lord ever create!

Dem does only think about theyself.' And sometimes when she was vexed about something and quarrelling to herself she would say, 'Dem blasted man always thinkin dem is God gift to woman. Never could see further than they blasted nose. The moment you let them know how much you like them you in trouble. Is to keep out of their way and happy for youself. Take you happiness outa de general world and don't wait on no one person to make you happy. Dem!'

'I mean, well, don't wait on nobody else to make you happy; just decide for yourself what you going to do to get happy for yourself.' Tisane hesitated. 'You know what I mean?'

'Girl, is me sewing I like already. I going just do that when I go to Brooklyn. And Ermintrude say it will have opportunities to learn more about it there. And Ermintrude like sewing too, you know. So perhaps we might be able to work together or something. O gosh, Tisane, girl, I can' wait!'

'Girl, I happy for you, girl.'

Lyris's thoughts were on that fateful visit Rain's father had made to Paz. Sometimes, she thought, watching Rain's twitching face, and pushing up her glasses, I believe if we could see the future, we would do plenty things different. But then that is a wasted thought – a wasted thought.

Andrew Darling sailed into Paz City on the boat on a day that was unusually cool for the city – sixty-nine degrees. It was December, one week before Christmas, and shoppers were busy as he drove in his brother's bus through the crowded streets. They drove straight to Victoria, where his brother lived. He stayed a day or two with Anthony, the only member of his family still alive on the island. Then he went to Aunt Myra, which was where he really considered home when he was in Paz.

'You getting prosperous, boy!' Aunt Myra greeted him. 'The stomach pushing out.'

'Is problems, yes, Aunt Myra. Is problems that have it looking so.'

'Come, come, let me pinch you for good luck, so I could get some of this problem. Yes, boy. You looking well good.'

'You must introduce me to this problem and them, boy! You think is today I lookin for some problems so?'

'Lyris! You find them already, girl! How you looking nice so? She getting younger, Aunt Myra? Something, or somebody treatin her well. Watch her, non!'

'I treatin myself well! I not waiting on nobody to decide if they go treat me well! Is why I lookin good so!'

'So where me daughter? Where all-you hidin her?'

'Hm! If we want to hide daughter, we waiting until you pass by here, then? She doing a job for the Sampsons, so she over there. She should be back soon, though. It almost four already. She usually here by half-past.'

'What job is that?'

'Your daughter is a big-time seamstress, yes.'

'Mmm-hmm?' Andrew's eyes were bright with pleasure.

'All kinds of orders coming here for her. She have all the Sampsons' sewing for the holidays, so she there finishing the curtains, I think, today.' Lyris pushed the glasses higher on her nose, placed her arms akimbo again. 'Then last week she was doing the same thing for those fair-skin people up the hill there, the, er, how you call them again? You know who I mean, Mammie. Those that come from England last year.'

'Oh, the Hosein people.'

'That's right. You remember you went to school with some fair-skinned children who used to live along the trace by the standpipe?'

'Er…' Andrew considered.

'Well, the younger ones, the boys, would have been your

age. I went to school with the two girls.' Lyris stupesed and frowned, trying to recall something. 'They had a name they used to call them… Babadee!' she shouted, remembering.

'Oh, Babadee! Little Babadee! And Big Babadee! They here? Ay! Me daughter sewing for these Babadee people an them? I know Babadee, yes. Little Babadee used to play football with me. At least, he used to try.' Andrew chuckled. 'He wasn't in my class at all.' He stroked his thinning hair. 'Yes, man. I know Babadee. Is dem Ermintrude working for?'

'Is not Babadee as you used to know them, non. I hear they come into some good money, so they living in style.'

'Eh-heh? An you ain't find out where they get it?'

'You can't get yours so, boy. Apparently they had family in Trinidad that die out, and leave them well comfortable.'

'Well I wonder if I ain't have a family hide somewhere?'

Aunt Myra shook her head. 'Your race of people never have plenty children. Look you only brother there. Not one. So is only yours to continue the line.'

Andrew stretched, settling back into the armchair. 'Well I really glad to hear me daughter doing so well. She will go far with that over there, too. She don't have to go in nobody house and beg them for their job. I hear Cora saying that she must make inquiries about a place for her, because of what you tell her about the sewing, you know. But I don't think she realise that is high, high level we girl dealing with, you know.'

'So how Cora now, Andrew?'

'Well girl, is one day good, one day bad. She have to go into the hospital all the time for them to put her on this machine, you know. And sometimes she don't leave the bed for weeks. And this new complaint we tell you about just complicate matters. But these last days she been working little bit.' Andrew sighed. 'But to tell you the truth, I don't believe she have long to go again.'

Myra made the sign of the cross. 'God help her! My best niece, yes! A good, good child! Well, we in the Lord's hands. Because when people take with this complaint, is the end, really. God knows best!'

Lyris made the sign of the cross, and kissed her hand. 'Lord spare her! Well, is so it is.' She smoothed the table-cloth. 'If is so it is already.' She lifted her shoulders and tried to change the subject. 'You hungry?'

'No, I eat by Anthony not long ago.'

'You must tell those children, you know, Andrew. We never tell Ermintrude about the mother's illness, and I sure Rain don't know anything.'

'Yes, I will tell her. And,' Andrew cleared his throat, moved restively in the chair, uncrossed his legs one way and crossed them back the other way. 'I have to talk to Rain, too.'

'Yes, you must tell her about the mother. They should know, especially now that they going up, too.'

'Well, to tell you the truth…' Andrew uncrossed his legs, cleared his throat. 'I been wondering if I don't better leave Rain still and only take Ermintrude.'

'You can't do that!' Lyris came to sit in the chair opposite him. She pushed up her glasses, fixing her myopic eyes on his face.

'No!' said Aunt Myra at the same time, sitting on the dining-room chair to his left, her head turned so that she could fix her eyes on his face. One plait was outside the confines of the head-tie, pointing forward over her round face like an exclamation mark. 'You can't do that, my son.'

'She know she going already, you know. That will kill her. And we buy the tickets and get their passports and everything with the money you-all send. What is the prob-lem now?'

Andrew was silent. He sat with his head down, then put his head back and continued looking at the ceiling. They waited for him to speak. Myra watched the dog slinking through the sitting room with lowered head. *What new trouble is this now? They say You don't give us more than we can handle, yes, Papa God, but what new trouble is this now? Or is old trouble that haunting us?*

Myra turned her head to look again at Andrew, watched the way he was staring at his hands.

'You can't do that, son,' said Myra. 'That child living in hell at Orilie. Orilie is my niece, but is not the kind of people you should leave your children by. She not a people person. Everybody have their calling, and Orilie is just not a people person, that's all.'

Andrew sighed, put his head back again and looked up at the ceiling, biting his bottom lip. The women watched him.

'You know some people just don't make for that?' Aunt Myra continued. 'Well, that is Orilie. In fact, now that Emma home, I hear is more so by there Rain does be, and Orilie vex as a result. So is more unpleasantness. You can't leave her there at all.' Aunt Myra pulled the ends of her head-tie, tightening it. 'God go punish you, Andrew. That child grow up by Orilie barely knowing how to read, and she bright, you know. You can't leave her there.' Aunt Myra turned around on the chair, turned back to look at Andrew. 'And she think the world of you, you know. This one here always talking about you, too, and on the few occasions that they manage to get together, when I hear them talking, your name always in the conversation, yes. Is a Daddy this and a Daddy that!' Aunt Myra stupesed, clenching her teeth and pulling air in through the gaps. She stood up and paced to the door. 'What you saying at all, Andrew? What is this at all?'

'All right, Mammie,' said Lyris. 'Remember what the doctor say. Don't get too excited now.'

Andrew sighed, started cracking the fingers of his left hand with the thumb of his right. He drew a deep breath and stood up, walked to the door and put his arms around his aunt-in-law's shoulders.

'Aunt Myra, come and sit down. Sit down here.' He lowered her into the armchair where he had been sitting, pulled forward the straight-backed chair and sat facing her. He looked to the left where Lyris sat in the other chair, shifted his chair around slightly so that he had them both within his range of vision. 'Lyris, you-all wouldn't like this. But I feel I have to say it. Perhaps you hear something already.' And before they could pull their thoughts together, he added, 'Rain is not my child.'

Aunt Myra and Lyris stared at him.

'*Maliwèse!*' exclaimed Aunt Myra, leaning forward closer to his face.

Lyris spoke. 'What you saying at all? What you saying at all, Andrew?'

Andrew kept his head bowed, looking at the brown floorboards beneath his feet. He felt miserable. He had carried a bitterness inside him for all these years. He had quarrelled with Cora about it at first, and then, eight years ago, when she got sick, he had stopped. But the bitterness was always inside him. Even before she joined him in the States all those years ago, he had written her an angry letter about it, and she had returned an equally angry one of denial.

'Where you going with this lie?' asked Aunt Myra quietly. 'Cora tell you that Rain is somebody else child?'

'Aunt Myra, the time when…'

'I ask you something. Cora tell you that?'

'No, Aunt Myra.'

'Well, where you going with this lie?'

'Aunt Myra, you must have known the problems me and Cora were having around that time.'

'Yes, I know you used to beat her,' Aunt Myra said, gripping the arms of her chair. 'I know that she run away more than once to hide from you because those times you had so much hatred in your heart.'

'It wasn't hatred, Aunt Myra. You don't know my side. You don't know who else in the picture. Is problems, Aunt Myra.'

'The problem was both of all-you own. Both of you couldn't find food to put in the children mouth. Is marasma that kill the first little one. I know that. I don't know who and what come in between, but woman doesn't beat man and go on like beast when trouble take them.'

'Me is man, Aunt Myra. Man that suppose to provide, and then with this child – I can't siddown there and let people take me for a fool.'

'You that suppose to provide! You have a daughter now who providing for herself with her sewing. And when man nor woman can't provide, the problem is both of them own. And whatever happen, I don't know where you-all get this habit raising all-you hand on woman. It have all to do with wickedness and nothing to do with providing. But that is not the point. The point is that she run away from you enough times to save sheself, but I put me head on a block to say that she never lie down in nobody else bed.'

'Auntie Myra…'

'And you can't tell me nothing to make me believe that happen.'

'But what it is make you say that, Andrew?'

'Lyris, that was a time that Cora go for three weeks, I don't know where she is. Then soon after she come back, she pregnant. And everybody talking. That child not mine, Lyris. I know.'

'*Maliwèse!*'

'Don't curse me, Auntie Myra! You don't know how I suffer with this thing inside me.'

'You don't know how *she* suffer.' Auntie Myra sat back, turned right and made a spitting sound. '*Maliwèse!*' She placed her hands on the arms of the chair and pushed herself to her feet.

'But Andrew, what Cora say?'

'Is a long time I didn't talk to her about it, but from the beginning I tell her it's not my child.'

'Yes, and you nearly kill her when you tell her that when she pregnant there.'

'So you know?'

'Yes. I know that you beat her until you nearly beat the child out of her. I never understand why she didn't leave you then, and then I thought you change. But now I realise that you can't teach old dog new tricks. *Pa maliwèse*, Andrew Darling!'

'Auntie Lyris! I mean, Auntie Myra!'

'I not your aunt, don't call me Auntie!'

'Mammie! Mammie, take it easy!'

'Auntie Myra, since after those days, I never lay a finger on Cora to beat her. We live good, but she know I never accept Rain as my child. I accept that it might be my fault in a way, that I drive her to it, but I never accept Rain as my child. Since after she sick, I never talk to her about it again, and she don't know that I will tell Rain now, but...'

'That you will what? Andrew Darling, leave my doormouth this minute! Right this minute! Get out, I say!'

'Mammie! Mammie, no! We have to talk about it.'

'Get out!' Auntie Myra was staring at Andrew, her eyes big and round, pointing toward the door.

'Mammie!' Lyris went to her mother, put her arms around her shoulders, drew her away from the door. Andrew stood up. 'Don't go, Andrew. Wait!'

'What!' Myra pulled away. 'So you defying me in my own house, then? Giving the reprobate right to stay?'

Andrew stood with bowed head. Lyris led her mother away. She motioned to Andrew to wait. She sat with her mother on the bed. 'Mammie! Mammie, listen. We can't make him go.'

'*You* can't make him go. Me? I...'

'Mammie, think about Rain.'

'Oh God!' Myra's shoulders shook. She put her face in her hands and sobbed.

'Mammie, this will kill Rain. If he leave her here and then tell her that to boot, think of what going happen to her!'

'We will have to take her. We manage all these years with Ermintrude, we could make it with Rain. We will have to take her.'

'Mammie, we will have to try to make him see he shouldn't tell her that, and that he should take her back with them. Don't make him go, Mammie. Think about Rain.'

So Andrew stayed. He looked ashamed, but it was as if he had to talk about the cancer that had been eating him all of these years. As if he felt he couldn't sit down there and let everybody think him stupid. Later, they sat in the kitchen outside while he talked to Ermintrude. He was so proud of her. He kissed her and told her how proud he was that she was doing so well. Myra couldn't look at all of this, knowing that Rain would have none of it.

'But, Mammie, Rain look so much like his family. The height, the face, everything.'

'Child, you don't hear the worst of it. The person who Andrew believe is Rain father is his brother Anthony. I suppose Andrew feel that with her height and everything, is more Anthony she look like.'

'What! How come you never tell me that?'

'Well some things too bad to repeat. Now remember that Anthony and Andrew is same father, not same mother. All of them grow up in this area here. I never tell you the half of it, but was around the time you were in Carriacou staying that the whole thing develop. When Cora growing up, young lady in me dead sister Alma house, God rest her soul, Anthony start coming round. But Cora never like him, so nothing never go ahead, you know what I mean.'

'Yes?'

'When Andrew appear on the scene, now, like a shot out of a gun, before you know it, she and Andrew pick up and they getting married.'

'So there was never anything between she and Anthony?'

'Not to my knowing. Cora never had time for him. But people say heself never had eyes for nobody else. Now time pass, hard times come and hit the family. Andrew who was so nice before get like beast, and he really used to beat that little girl. Was a shame. That time when Andrew talking about, dey, when she leave his house, is here she did come, because by this time now Alma dead and is me she was closest to. But run she run come here; meself say, well you know is here first he go look for you; this is not place to hide.' Myra sighed, took off her head-tie, replaced it. 'Oh God, eh! Oh Jesus! What trouble is dis now?'

'All right, Mammie. All right. Take it easy.'

'So we talk about it, and the two of us decide that is for her to go some place he wouldn't expect. That time Anthony was moving with Eliza in the trace. I walk over there with her meself; we pass in the back up the hill. Eliza say all right, she could stay there. So is by Eliza she come and end up, stay there three weeks. But I don't know what say, who tell him what. Sometimes I wonder if is Eliza sheself that say thing, you know, knowing how Anthony did always feel about Cora. But when Cora tell me what Andrew think, I say but how is that he reach thinkin dey? You tell him something? Anything happen with you and Anthony?'

Lyris pushed up her glasses, eyes on her mother's face, mouth half-opened.

'And she say to me, never! Not before Andrew, not after! And she put she neck on a block that even if she had that in mind, she wouldn't go in the woman house and take her man from her. And I believe her. I don't know who say what, who put thing in Andrew head, but Cora is the kind of person who never fraid nobody, and if she did ever make mistake do a thing like that, I feel she wouldn't fraid to take her medicine. But, well! Eight years ago, when she know she ill, and they saying she could dead anytime, she write me and say that Andrew still believe Rain not his, but if she dead tomorrow, she want me to know that she never lie down with nobody else, so if not his, is God own. And that is not thing people saying easy.'

'You ever tell him that?'

'Never. This time here is the first time we ever talk about it, because heself never bring up the subject and I don't want to interfere, but Cora tell me in the letter all those years ago that she tell him; she tell him just what you hear she tell me there, but what he have in his head already is that he want to believe.'

'But how? Why?'

'Child, man strange. Pride. Is his pride. He grow up with a big name in this area because of the football. Was a bright young man. One time, before Cora, he used to go with Alpheus daughter, the one that in Trinidad now. She come and get pregnant. Andrew never did want the child, I understand, but he come and accept it, and then when people look at the child, everybody bawl blue murder, because the little girl was the spitting image of Andrew best friend. Nobody didn't have to ask question. Was the stamp of the man. The whole village laugh, and everybody used to tease, say he get a six for nine. I think Andrew never forget that, so anytime it have a shadow of a doubt, I suppose he want to be sure to save face. Is he pride, child. Is nothing but he stupid pride eating him.'

'But to that extent?'

'Man is a strange nation. And Cora self have she ways too, you know. She very secretive. Just through not want-ing to talk about things, she used to keep the stupidest things from Andrew, so he always feel things have more in them than is really there. And I think he only find out where she was afterwards because somebody else tell him. So he must come and feel the thing had more in it than it really had. And you know man. The moment them is friend with a woman is usually one thing they want. And Andrew know heself. So he must be come and feel is only one reason why his brother help out Cora. Child, Cora and Rain just paying for what he feel somebody else do him. That is my feeling.'

Lyris sighed. Rain's face was still twitching, and Lyris knew that hers was not a restful sleep. None of them was feeling restful during this visit. Sitting outside, looking at Sister, who had come back to the verandah and was standing looking out towards the high walls that hid Paz from view, Ermintrude tried to keep back the tears. It hurt that her sister couldn't stand her touch. Her most painful memory was that conversation with her father long ago.

She couldn't believe what he was saying to her. 'Daddy, whatever you do, don't tell Rain that. She always look forward to hearing from you, Daddy. She always wonder why you don't write her, and I never know what to say. The last time, after you write and tell me that you mightn't take her up, I try to tell her, but in the end I even had to lie and tell her she definitely going too, Daddy. I couldn't tell her, Daddy. Whatever you do, don't tell her you not her father, Daddy. It going kill her.'

'Ermintrude, child, try and understand. It hurt me, too, but I have to. I can't pretend so.'

'What Mammie say?'

'Your mother don't know. That is something else I didn't tell you, Ermintrude. Your mother is very ill. She has a kidney complaint. She been like that for a lot of years now. That is why she never take the chance to come out here on holiday. And lately it get complicated with other things. The doctors say she have, er, she have,' he looked at his daughter and lowered his voice almost to a whisper, 'cancer. She not expected to live for long.'

'Oh God!' Ermintrude started to cry. 'Oh God!'

'All right, Ermine. I know how you feel, child. All of us feel like that. But I couldn't tell you before.'

'And Daddy, you going tell Rain all of that? You so wicked? You going tell Rain all of that?'

'Child!'

'No. No. No! Daddy, you so wicked? Oh God, no!'

'Ermintrude! Don't pull away from me, Ermintrude. Listen, baby. Dry your eyes. All right! All right!' And he put his arms around her, rocking her quiet. 'All right, baby. Everything will be all right. I know it will make you happy, so Rain will go up with us, then. But she have to know the other things, Ermintrude. She have to know.'

Aunt Myra said afterwards that Rain died inside that December of 1944. Andrew said she took it well. After she heard what he had to say, she just sat and stared at him. She stared at him and was almost straining to hear his voice because the rain was beating so hard against Miss Orilie's galvanise. December was always like that, very cold and lots of rain. It was the time when things were really bearing. Rain looked out of Miss Orilie's window at the trees growing at the side of the house. The green peas were ready now for eating. Miss Orilie would have a good crop this year. Rain asked Andrew Darling one favour. Not to tell Miss Orilie. He assured her that he had spoken only to Ermintrude, Aunt Myra and Cousin Lyris. He would tell no one else.

Rain did not even go to say goodbye to Tisane. Tisane couldn't believe this. She knew that something was wrong. She didn't go to Miss Orilie, but wrote afterwards to Myra Augier, of Victoria, putting in brackets after the name, Ermintrude's aunt, just in case that wasn't really the surname. Myra answered the letter, saying that Rain had specially asked her to say goodbye to Tisane, that she was sure Rain would have wanted to say goodbye herself, but that something had made her very unhappy before she left.

Myra and Lyris would never forget Rain's eyes those last days of December, when she should have been happy about celebrating her fifteenth birthday. She had returned with her father to stay for three days before their departure. She greeted Ermintrude as though she wasn't really seeing her. When she inclined her head and said, 'Good evening, Aunt Myra,' her eyes remote and looking just beyond her great-aunt's ear, Myra burst into tears and pulled the child into her arms.

'Come, child. Don't believe everything you hear, you see? Is not true, child. Your mother tell me is not true, and I believe her. And anyway it don't matter, Rain. Who you is, is who you is. Always remember that. Rain, my child, it don't matter. Is not true, and we don't love you no less.'

'Is not true, Rain,' Lyris repeated. 'Whatever your father believe because he and your mother was in confusion, it have nothing to do with you. Is not true.'

When Myra drew back and looked into her niece's face, it was as if the child hadn't heard. Her eyes were remote. 'Rain,' she said, shaking her slightly. 'Rain, child.'

'Is all right, Auntie Myra. Is all right, you know.' Rain's voice was soothing, as though she were consoling her great-aunt about something else. *Perhaps she is*, thought Myra. *Who knows? Perhaps she is*. Myra stood at the door and looked over far away at the hills behind Clozier. The tops of those mountains seemed to have absorbed all the mist from the Grand Etang lake this morning.

'Lord,' Myra said, 'I wish sometime you would explain the trials and tribulations you bring to bear on us. But that must be too much to ask, Lord. This time, though, I have to say that I don't understand your ways. Forgive me,

Lord, but like Thomas this time I have to say, "Help my unbelief".'

Before they left the house, Lyris heard Myra speak quietly to Andrew. 'Andrew Darling, tell me one thing. After Cora reach back to your house that time, you didn't have any dealings with her?'

'How you mean, Auntie Myra?'

'We is big people, Andrew Darling. You sleep with your wife in those days? You have dealings with her? You make love to her?'

'Auntie Myra, Cora is me wife. I love her then and I love her now. We sleep together, yes, if that is what you asking. We do what man and woman does do, if that is what you asking.'

'And still you saying what you saying?'

Andrew looked uneasy. 'Auntie Myra, Cora stay away from me for three weeks. You know she never even tell me where she was? I take a lot. I take the blame because I did treating her bad. But nobody not making me look like a fool.'

'And that is all that making you say what you saying? The fact that she stay away from you for three weeks?'

Andrew sighed. Auntie Myra felt that there was something he wasn't saying, that somebody had poisoned his mind. *Whoever it is*, she thought, *going to have to answer to God*. Watching them, Lyris crossed her fingers, knowing that her mother wanted to curse Andrew again. Myra opened her mouth as if she would tell Andrew never to cross her doormouth again, but must have changed her mind and decided not to add to the hatred that was touching so many things already.

Myra and Lyris went to see them off. The last thing Rain said to her aunt and cousin was, 'Auntie Myra, Cousin Lyris, if you ever see my friend Tisane, tell her for me I say goodbye.' She turned back to say, 'Tisane really nice. Don't forget to tell her if you see her, eh.'

Myra and Lyris were crying too much to respond as the three walked up the gangway and into the ship. Ermintrude and Andrew turned and waved. Myra and Lyris did not return the wave. They were waiting for Rain, walking behind the two, straight-backed and tall, to turn and wave. Rain walked into the ship without a backward glance.

Two months later, there was news of Cora's death. Myra wrote to say that perhaps Rain should come home. She could stay with her and Lyris.

Ermintrude answered. Rain said that she would stay; one place was as good as another, she said. No point in going anywhere. 'Auntie Myra, I don't know what to do with Rain. She just sits in her room all day, or sleeps.'

A few months later, Ermintrude wrote to say that Rain was working, that they had found her a job as a maid with a family in New York. Then she lost the job, or in fact she left the job. One day, she just didn't go back, and didn't answer when Ermintrude asked her why. Ermintrude wrote to say that Rain just stayed at home, not bathing unless you told her to, hardly eating, and sometimes talking to herself. 'The two of us living together now, Auntie Myra. Daddy moved out. He and Rain never get along. They don't even talk to each other. I think Rain better go home, you know.'

Then Rain found another job, but didn't stay. 'Auntie Myra, when I start to quarrel with her, she asked me, "What is the point, Ermintrude? Where it leading? What we doing it for?" Auntie Myra, I don't know what to do.'

For a long time, Lyris and Myra had no news. Rain had been in Brooklyn for almost five years when there was news that she was in the psychiatric ward of a Brooklyn hospital. For the next eight years, Rain was in and out of hospitals, never seeming to adjust to life in Brooklyn, never doing the sewing she loved, working as a maid in the homes of various families. Then a letter from Ermintrude said that Rain had been placed in an insane asylum.

'I don't know what to do, Aunt Myra,' Ermintrude wrote. 'Is not that Rain is mad, really, but there is no one to take care of her. She doesn't like Brooklyn, especially when it's cold. She is always shivering. Recently she got a job again working as a maid with a family, but they say she never does anything, and so she lost the job. At home, she just sits all the time, and it is a problem. She doesn't eat, she won't bathe, or anything. Just stares and doesn't say anything.'

Myra said she should be sent home. 'Don't leave her in any New York asylum. Send her home.'

For weeks after Rain returned, she stayed with her aunt and cousin. Then Myra died suddenly of a heart attack. When Rain knew, she became hysterical. When Sister entered the house, someone said she was Orilie's daughter. It was the first time Rain was meeting Sister since her return. She started throwing everything in sight. Cups, plates, glasses, everything she could put her hands on was thrown in Sister's direction. She could not be calmed. The doctor committed her to the asylum in Paz.

The women walked back down the hill towards Paz, in time for the evening bus back to Victoria.

'A wasted life,' said Cousin Lyris. 'What a waste of a life!'

'Well,' Sister shrugged and opened her hands, palms upward. 'What to do? Rain too bitter. I never do Rain nothing in my life. What she and Mammie have, that is their business. I don't think I was even seven years yet when Rain leave this country, non, and Mammie never speak bad to me about Rain. Not really, except to say that she was rude, and all children does be rude.'

'She had to take care of you, and she wasn't happy in that house, to tell you the truth,' said Ermintrude. 'She had a hard life, a hard, hard life.'

'I don't think she have long to go again, non,' said Cousin Lyris. 'She light like a feather. She not in this world at all.'

49

'Rain take things too much to heart,' said Sister again. 'Is not so people suppose to live. You can't take every little thing make you whole life so. Who could live like that!'

Tisane, on a visit from her first year of graduate studies at the University of the West Indies, went to visit her friend at the asylum. For the first time, the nurses saw some sign of life in this strange woman whose eyes held them in thrall with their unspeakable sadness.

Rain smiled when the two met. 'I believe they think I'm mad, Tisane. They gave me shocks. They force me to eat through tubes.'

Tisane had resolved not to cry. She couldn't help it. The sobs just came. Rain touched her gently, hugged her.

'Don't cry, Tisane. You never used to cry. I'm not mad. I just don't want to live.'

'I'm sorry, Rain. I shouldn't be crying like this. A real monkey.'

Rain smiled gently. 'No. That is Orilie. You forget?'

Tisane smiled through her tears. 'But what you doing here, Rain?'

'Well, I don't eat, I don't do anything for myself, so I can't stay by anybody. Besides, Auntie Myra dead, Cousin Lyris sickly, Auntie Emma living in Orilie yard now and the sight of the house and Sister would make me go really mad!'

Rain laughed, touching her friend's hand. 'Don't feel sorry, Tisane. It don't have nowhere else for me to stay. I don't have to talk to nobody here. Here I could just stay sane watching people being mad, and wondering why.'

'You must get out of here, Rain. You can't live in the past. I always used to try to tell you it's no good to live on dreams, Rain. Face life, love.'

'Don't try to get me out, Tisane. This is the only place I sane, because everybody in here supposed to be mad. I like them; is the sane people I fraid. I happy here.'

Tisane's tears were threatening to fall again. Rain looked at her quizzically. 'People does grow up funny, in truth. You never used to cry before. Is either you getting wise, or you getting stupid.'

Tisane shook her head at her friend's attempts to make her laugh. Rain was comforting her. 'What happened in Brooklyn?'

Rain smiled, her eyes becoming remote. 'I'm a sunshine child, and I couldn't stand the rain.'

Tisane shook her head again. 'So you getting poetic!'

'How is university? Imagine! University!'

The friends talked for hours. Tisane told Rain about her daughter. 'She's five. And Rain, she doesn't have a father.'

'She...?' Rain frowned, looking at her friend.

'No. Not Virgin Mary style or anything.' Tisane laughed. 'She doesn't have one who wants her. He didn't want to know. I've told her about it already. I'm not sure she quite understands yet, but she'll be able to deal with it. I'll see to that.'

'You not by any chance trying to give somebody a message?'

Tisane smiled. 'Not any message I haven't given before.'

Rain hugged her friend. 'Girl, you mother make you kind of all right. You not too bad at all, you know.'

Tisane wondered if she should tell Rain what she had named her daughter, but decided not to. Not yet. She would bring the child to visit her friend. She talked to her, though, about her last little brother, who had been born some time after Rain went away.

'He was really cute, Rain. He looked like Mammie. He was really mischievous and everything, too. We think he was poisoned.'

Rain said she had heard about this. She had heard someone say it may have been Mody's mangoes.

'Yes,' said Tisane, 'the doctors say it was "causes unknown". But that little boy was really writhing in pain and holding his stomach. Rain! I don't like to think about it. Mammie was really ill afterwards. I thought she was going to die, too.'

Rain touched her friend's hand, and sat there not saying anything, just looking deep into Tisane's eyes as though she were trying to understand how one dealt with things like that. Tisane shook her head. That was always Rain's way, trying to understand so much that she forgot everything else. After a while, Tisane grinned. 'Life goes on, Rain,' she said.

Rain smiled. 'Tisane,' she said, 'you're my best, best friend in the world.'

Tisane knew she couldn't answer without crying, so she just hugged her friend, holding her close.

Afterwards the nurses talked to Tisane. This was the best they had seen Rain. What did Tisane think? But Tisane was non-committal. Rain had chosen her asylum, and would not want to be anywhere else. By the time Tisane was ready to leave, Rain had gradually withdrawn into her distant stare, and did not turn to say goodbye. Tisane saw her four more times before she left the island, but never again did Rain talk so freely.

The following year, when Tisane visited, Rain was in hospital, dying, they said, of tuberculosis, probably picked up from the cold walls of the asylum. A sunshine child, thought Tisane.

Tisane visited Rain this time with her six-year-old daughter. Tisane was saddened at the sight of her friend. Rain's eyes were glazed, distant. She sat in her room with bowed shoulders, a tired old lady just thirty.

'Rain. Rain, you hearing me?'

Rain smiled, nodded.

'Rain, I want you to meet my daughter.'

The little girl moved forward, peeped into Rain's face.

'Hello,' she said to this silent woman. 'Hello, my mommy says you have the same name as I do. My name's Rain. I'm six. What's your name?'

'Rain, my name's Rain.'

They looked into each other's eyes. 'Don't look so sad,' said young Rain.

Rain looked at Tisane. 'You know, Tisane, you're wonderful. I'm not sad anymore, Rain. I'm all right now. My voice is like this, low and breathless, because I'm sick. Thank you, Tisane, I'm all right now.'

Rain lay back, closed her eyes. Tisane! Tisane! She wondered if Rain had been born on a rainy night, or on a day full of sunshine. And then everything got mixed up in her mind, and she was remembering that day when her father had come and she had run away to Tisane in the trace. Tisane was putting her fingers to her lips and pulling her into the room. Any Rain would be all right with Tisane. Any Rain. Tisane, bending over her friend, watching her lips move, wondering if she were asleep, wasn't sure whether she was muttering 'Rain' or 'Tisane'. She put her hand on her friend's for a moment, and then tiptoed away with Rain.

The gravestone paid for by Cousin Lyris, Tisane and Ermintrude told a brief story:

RAIN DARLING
1929–1960

DOUX STORIES

MAPPING

When Mr Moses shows them the map of Paz, she thinks the island looks like a leaf, a long, scraggly leaf, drifting to the right-hand side when you hold it up in your hand. Her friend Sharpey says the island is like a yam. It does look a bit like a long yam when you pull it out of the ground, before you peel it and cut it up to put in the pot. But yam makes her think brown, and the map Mr Moses shows them is all green, with place names written in black all around, and a black PAZ in the middle.

When Mr Moses brought out the map to talk about the geography of Paz, what she thought of was the way her mother said, when she was talking to herself sometimes, 'Nothing to show for it, but I map this country with my work. I walk from stem to stern, working for high-up people and dragging my children with me. Name the place in this Paz, I work there!'

Where they are now, Providence, is just below the word Paz, under the middle on the right-hand side. She can't find the exact name of the place where her grandmother lives, Hideout Hill, but she knows it is right near that place called Leaping Lift, at the top of the map. Leaping Lift is the capital of St Camillus, and that is her grandmother's parish. The capital of the country, Paz City, is on the left-hand side near the bottom, near the squiggly part where you could put your fingers to hold up the leaf, or grip the yam. She has never been to Paz City, but she knows that the high-up people live there, the Governor and people like that. Her mother says that she used to work with a family in Paz City once, before

Doux was born. 'Nothing to show for it, non, but I map this country with my sweat and my tears. You never know how life will meet you.'

Doux looks at the spot named Providence, the place her mother is mapping with her work now. Her mother goes to wash their clothes in Providence River and sometimes, when her mother can't go, she, Doux, takes them there. For some reason, her grandmother, Mama, won't keep her in the house in Hideout Hill like she keeps the other two sometimes. So wherever her mother works, she is like a dress-band dragging behind. That is what her mother says. 'Wherever I go, you like a dressband dragging behind me.' Doux looks at the map of Paz and imagines her mother walking across it, with a dress-band trailing behind her. Mr Moses pulls the map to one side, and begins to talk about something else. About goats, and a ledge.

Doux is big for Standard Two. Most of the other children in the class are eight, or some even nine. Her best friend, Sharpey, is nine. Sharpey was born in 1922, two years after Doux.

For a change, this time, her mother has all her children living with her. She is a baker for Mr Jimmy's shop right here in Providence, just down the road from the school, and she has a whole house to stay in, so all of them can stay together. Her mother, Mr Jimmy's baker, sells bread to all the shops in the area, and sometimes, on a Saturday, she and Sister carry baskets of bread on their heads to the other shops. One good thing this time is that she, her sister and her brother go to school every day. Sometimes her mother can't manage to buy the books, but she thinks children must go to school, so she doesn't keep them at home. Her mother says, 'You have to show me real evidence that you dying, for me to tell you stay home. And if you dying,' she says, 'we could call somebody to make the coffin. I want you children to go to school and see if you could find out how to put money in your pocket! It have a secret there, and I want you to get it!' So now, even on Monday and Friday, Doux is at school. Trying to find out secrets about how to put money in her pocket.

'Doux! Doux Thibaut! You with us?' Mr Moses is standing over her desk, tapping in the palm of his left hand with the long ruler he holds in his right. Doux sits up and glances across at her friend, Sharpey. Mr Moses is asking a question. Sharpey's finger lingers under the title of the lesson. Mr Moses asks, 'What did I say the homework is?' Sharpey's finger is right under a sentence.

'Two goats met on a narrow ledge, sir!'

'Good!' Mr Moses swings away, looking for another victim. Over his shoulder, he says, 'Pay attention, Doux!'

'Yes, sir.' Doux smiles gratefully at Sharpey.

Mr Moses is the Standard Two teacher. Today he gives the class reading to do for homework, reading and spelling, because usually the spelling goes with the reading. Doux doesn't have *Royal Reader Book Two*, the book with the homework, but Sharpey has the book. The lesson is about two goats. Two cabrit, one child giggles, because that is what they call the children from the Catholic school, *français cabrit*, french goat. And the Catholic children call them *cochon*, pig. *Anglais cochon*, they say, English pig. In the first part of the story, Sharpey explains, the two goats meet on a narrow ledge over a high cliff, and there isn't enough room for them to either turn back or go on together. But they are nice to each other. One of them lies down to let the other one pass, and then that one gets up and goes over, so that both goats end up bounding about the meadow and enjoying the sweet grass. Two Catholic goats, they giggle, enjoying the sweet grass. They have to read the second part of the lesson and learn to spell the words for Monday. Right after school, Sharpey lets Doux write down the homework from her book. In exchange, because she is good at plaiting hair, Doux promises

Sharpey that she will ask her mother to let her go up the road to Sharpey's aunt's house this Saturday, in the evening, after she carries the bread to the shops. She will plait Sharpey's hair in cornrow. She writes down the lesson on both sides of her slate.

> Two other goats had left the valley, and climbed far up the mountain. At length they met on the banks of a wild, rushing stream. A tree had fallen across the stream, and formed a bridge from the one side to the other.
>
> The goats looked at each other, and each wished to pass over first.
>
> They stood for a moment with one foot on the tree, each thinking that the other would draw back. But neither of them would give way, and they met at last on the middle of the narrow bridge!

Even though she is writing small on her slate for the homework to fit, Doux has no more room after that, but Gift, her brother, is waiting, and she borrows his slate to write the rest.

> They then began to push and fight with their horns, till at last their feet slipped, and both the goats fell into the swift flowing stream, and were lost in the waters!
>
> Both might have been saved, if either of them had known how to yield at the right time.

On Saturday morning, Doux doesn't have to wash in the river. Her mother says she will have Monday off from the shop, so she will wash then. After Doux and her sister Selma finish cleaning the house and helping Gift to sweep up the leaves in the yard, all the children do their homework. Their mother believes that children must always have enough time to do their homework, so she doesn't mind. That is another thing Doux likes about staying with her mother. Her mother understands things that other people she stayed with couldn't understand. Her mother doesn't think Doux is idle just because she isn't doing something in the house or cleaning up the yard.

Doux learns to spell the words Mr Moses told them to underline – 'stream', 'length', 'bridge', 'horns' and 'ledge'. If Mr Moses calls her to read, or to spell, she will be ready. She has to give Gift his slate for school on Monday morning, so she learns by heart the part of the lesson that she wrote on Gift's slate.

> They then began to push and fight with their horns, till at last their feet slipped, and both the goats fell into the swift flowing stream, and were lost in the waters!
> Both might have been saved, if either of them had known how to yield at the right time.

When she is done, Doux goes up the trace to Sharpey's aunt's house and keeps her promise to plait Sharpey's hair. Later that evening, she and Selma help make up the baskets and carry bread to shops in the area. Selma makes two trips, but then she is tired, so Doux continues alone for two more trips, one to a shop on the Providence Main Road, and another one to a shop just lower down, off the Providence Road and along a track.

First thing when it is time for Reading and Spelling on Monday morning, Mr Moses calls on Doux to read. She picks up her slate, relieved because the part he has asked her to read is the part she has on her slate, and not the one that was on the slate she has returned to Gift. She learned that part off by heart, it's true, but at least she has this one here on her slate to read.

Mr Moses says, 'Child, put down the slate and read the lesson.'

Doux stands with her mouth open and the slate in her hand.

Mr Moses says, 'Young lady, I'm waiting.'

Doux lifts the slate again and stands looking at it. She opens her mouth. Mr Moses says, 'Put down the slate, child, and pick up your book.' If Sharpey weren't at home sick today, she would just pick up Sharpey's book and read from it. Mr Moses is walking towards her. Doux can see him out of the corners of her eyes, but she doesn't look up. She stands there, still, looking down at her slate. She is suddenly feeling very tall, very big and stupid, with all the little children turned around in their seats, looking back at her, waiting to see what will happen. The cut of the whip across her back surprises her. She jumps and cries out because it hurt through her thin dress and because she is surprised. Mr Moses always threatens, but he is not a teacher who beats much. And besides, she has done the homework. Doux puts the slate down on the desk, puts her hands up to her face, and begins to cry.

Mr Moses picks up the slate and stands looking at it. He looks for a long time, as if he can only read slowly. He turns the slate over and reads the other side. He pulls a breath deep into his lungs, holds it, and stands there with his eyes closed. He opens his eyes and stands for a moment looking down at the head of the sobbing girl, at the two big plaits, the print dress, the hands held to the face in shame. He looks up at the eyes fixed on them, around at the silent, waiting faces, at the apprehensive looks that say, *I hope is not me next*.

Mr Moses says, 'Come, child, come outside.' He touches her arm to guide her, and then turns away, walking toward the door. Her hands still up to her face, the child follows him, sobbing, walking slowly. The slate still in his hand, Mr Moses walks to the door at the right-hand side in front of the class. He walks through the door, watches her follow him through, leans back inside and says, 'Learn your spelling. Kenneth, you're in charge. Make sure there's no noise while I'm out here.' Mr Moses pulls the door almost closed behind him, and then he goes to stand by the railing. He looks at the little girl still sobbing with her hands to her face, and he pulls in his lips, biting the bottom one as if he, too, will start crying. He puts the slate under his arm, puts both hands on the railing and stands looking down into the empty schoolyard. When he looks back, she is wiping her eyes with the palms of her hands. She jumps and takes a step back as he turns.

Mr Moses says, 'I won't beat you. I shouldn't have hit you. I didn't know you had done the homework.' She sniffs, stands looking at him.

He is looking down at the slate, turns it over and reads. He asks, 'When did you write this?'

'Friday, sir. I borrow Sharpey book and I write out the lesson.'

'Where is your book?'

'Sorry, sir. My mother say when she get some money, when Mr Jimmy pay her, she will buy a book for me, but she don't have it yet.'

Mr Moses looks at the child for a long time. He looks at the faded red and white print dress with one band trailing, at the four big plaits of hair arranged neatly on her head, down at her bare feet, back at the face streaked with tears. He puts up his hand and seems to be trying to loosen the knot of the red, white and blue tie lying against his white, short-sleeved shirt. He turns away and stands looking away into the distance, the slate under his arm and his hands in the pockets of his dark brown pants. He turns back, clears his throat and says, 'Child, I would not have hit you if I knew you had the lesson on your slate. I thought it was just defiance why you weren't answering. And I remember that last week you weren't paying attention. Why didn't you tell me?'

'I didn't have a book, sir,' she tells him, as if this explains everything. The tears are in her eyes again.

Mr Moses says, 'It's alright. After school today, come to the staff room and I will give you a book that you can use for the rest of the term. Okay? Tell your mother that she won't have to buy a book for you. And – Doux – child, I'm very sorry. I didn't know.' And then he asks, gently, 'You know the spelling words?'

'Yes, sir.'

'Okay. Stop crying. Go back to your seat now.'

'Yes, sir.'

When she goes back into the class, heads turn. The children watch Doux's face to see what they can read there. There is a general murmur and Kenneth, the little Indian boy sitting at the front of the class, lifts his voice and says, 'Sir say stay quiet!' The noise dies down. Doux goes to her desk, sits down, puts her head on her hands and sits looking at her slate.

Mr Moses actually said he was sorry, and teachers supposed to beat, so they don't tell children they are sorry! Mr. Moses said he was sorry!

When he comes back into the class, he doesn't ask her to spell a word right away. But before the bell rings, he asks her to spell 'ledge'. Doux doesn't even stumble over the spelling like some of the other children have done. She just spells it right out, one letter after the other, her voice confident and strong. Mr Moses says, 'Very good.' And then he says to the whole class, 'I made a mistake when I hit Doux. I realise now that she really knows her homework.' And all the other children turn around and look at her. Mr Moses tells them strange things sometimes, like when he said he doesn't really like to beat, but this is the strangest of the strange. Mr Moses seems to be saying he was wrong, and they don't know what to do with that news. It is a good thing the bell rings right at that time. Doux runs out to go and find Selma and get something for break.

She cannot forget that Mr Moses said he was sorry. She wonders now if she should tell him that every time he brings out his map and talks to them about what the country looks like, she thinks about her mother. She wonders if she should tell Mr Moses that her mother says she maps the whole country with her work, from stem to stern. She tells Selma and the two of them use the dictionary Mr Moses leaves on his desk to find out what 'stem' and 'stern' mean.

Doux says, 'From just how she say it, I know it was two different end, but I didn't realise it had to do with boat.' Selma says, 'I thought it had to do with a flower, but Paz in the middle of the sea, so is like a boat in truth!'

Mr Moses finds them there, laughing at their discovery, leaning on the desk during the break, looking at his dictionary. They jump when they see him, and look ready to run away, but Mr Moses says, 'It's alright, it's okay. That's why I have the dictionary there, so you can find out the meaning of words.'

Their mother always warns them, 'Don't fight in school road.' She says, 'I sending you to school to learn, not to fight.' Doux doesn't want to fight, but she thinks, *I ain't dead yet, and if anybody hit me, I don't see how I could walk away.* She doesn't see how she could let somebody trouble her in the school road and get away with it. She knows that sometimes this thinking gets her into trouble. Her sister Selma, who is older than she is, and so might be expected to set the example for behaviour, doesn't have any problem walking away. Selma doesn't stand up to anybody. She starts running away the moment she realises that the person walking in her direction is someone who likes to fight or to tease. Even if she doesn't know, she seems to be always poised, waiting to run away from an attack. Doux, now, would think, *Hit me and you will see how I buss up you face!* Selma tells her that when the desire to hit back comes to her, she should remember what the Sunday school teacher said, ' "Vengeance is mine," saith the Lord.' Their brother, Gift, is little, and he isn't a fighter either. Their mother says she doesn't know where Doux got this fighting habit from. Once when she said that, their grandmother, Mama, was there and she didn't say anything out loud, but Doux could see how Mama looked out from under her eyebrows, as if *she* had some idea where Doux had taken that attitude from.

It seems to Doux that something is always happening on a Friday in the Providence school road. Doux thinks that perhaps she is not lucky with that day. It was a Friday the first time Mr Moses walked up to her in class and she wasn't paying attention. Friday is a day to watch.

That's what she thinks when she sees the children walking up to her, grinning. *I don't know what they planning, but today is Friday. Help me, Lord Jesus!* The little boy with the khaki shirt and pants, hair red like red mud and teeth yellow in his grinning face, puts one stick on her shoulder and runs across to put one on the shoulder of the big boy on the other side of the road. Doux knows that boy, or at least she knows about him. They call him Armstrong.

Armstrong is the badjohn from the Catholic school on the hill, and, just because she is bigger than the other children in her class and doesn't take nonsense, they called Doux the badjohn from Anglican. Doux doesn't like the name. She knows they gave it to her because she is eleven, big for Standard Two, and because, although she doesn't talk a lot, the children have learned that they can't hit her and get away with it.

Selma takes off running. Doux knows that Selma is going to run down to the shop where their mother works and tell her that she, Doux, is fighting in school road. Gift holds on to Doux's skirt. Doux puts up her left hand and pushes the stick off her right shoulder. A girl with a faded green shirt and the blue skirt of the Catholic school, with her hair plaited in cornrows and a red ribbon in the centre of her head, rushes up to Doux. She picks up the stick, and runs along near Doux, trying to balance the stick on her shoulder. It is a stick with a crook at the end, and the cornrow-head girl tries to hook it on to the cloth of Doux's red bodice so that it will stay. The other children from the Anglican school are around her, some wearing the brown school skirt, most wearing anything they have. They walk with her, some of them egging her on to fight, because they want to find somebody who could be a champion against this Armstrong, the badjohn from the Catholic school. Doux's friend, Sharpey, walks on the other side of Gift. She says in a low voice, 'Don't study them, girl. They just trying to provoke you.' Doux pushes away the stick a second time. A short boy, hardly bigger than Gift, in khaki pants and a grey shirt and with no shoes on his feet, just like Doux and most of the other children, runs up to her from the Catholic side and tries to put the stick back. He tries to hold it in place for a while. Doux can hear the Catholic children starting to shout.

'Woy! Armstrong boy, she fraid you, boy!' They are egging him on.

One little boy is walking alongside Armstrong, too, like his lieutenant, Doux thinks, holding the stick on Armstrong's shoulder, so he can walk with it. Armstrong makes no effort to push it off. The boy removes his hand and the stick falls. Armstrong continues walking. The boy picks it up and runs to catch up. He puts it back and Armstrong leaves it there.

'I thought she did bad. She doh bad. Armstrong is king, boy! You is king of Paz, Armstrong!'

'You see she walking, dey, she fraid like cat. You doh see she can't even watch him?'

Doux can't say how the stick comes to be on her shoulder again and who put it there. They keep putting it back and she keeps pushing it off. It doesn't stay, because she is walking, and moving her shoulders so that it will fall. It falls each time, and if it doesn't, she pushes it away, but they put it back, insisting. Now somebody is walking alongside her, too, to hold it in place. Doux can't say if it's a Catholic hand or an Anglican hand holding the stick there. Children from both sides want the fight. She pushes it off again. As fast as they put it back on her shoulder, Doux pushes it off. She doesn't want to fight. Sharpey turns to the other side of the road, looking across at Armstrong and his army. She shouts, 'Leave the girl alone, non! You don't see she don't want to fight? What do all-you? Leave her!'

Doux can see Armstrong out of the corner of her eye. He

is on the other side of the road, just at the bottom of the hill under the Catholic school, his little army around him, and every so often looking across at her.

All of a sudden, he changes direction, turns, and now he is walking straight toward her. He must feel sure now that she is afraid of him, and so he is coming for her! Doux moves her head around a bit and she can see the cross over the Catholic school rising tall over his shoulder. Her heart beats fast. She doesn't want to fight. The Catholic children, shouting, whooping, rush across to circle around in front of her, stopping her, forcing her to face Armstrong.

She turns, and she watches him come. He is wearing black three-quarter pants that look as if they have been cut from longer ones. His khaki shirt is open at the neck and the ends are flapping over his pants. He is a big boy, tall and strapping, her mother would say, with his hair big on his head. Sharpey and Gift stand up with her, watching him come. They hold hands, the three of them. She is holding Gift's right hand and Sharpey is holding his hand on the other side. When Armstrong is almost up to them, Doux pushes Gift aside. 'Stay over there,' she says. Sharpey pulls Gift away, surprise and fear on her face, because now it looks as if a fight is really going to take place.

Before Doux can catch her breath, Armstrong lowers his head. He moves in with speed. His bull's head hits her in the stomach before she knows his intention. The butt lifts her off the ground and flings her away. She falls into the muddy drain and scrambles around. Her back is hurting, her body aching. She stands in the shallow drain at the side of the road, the children shouting, still egging them on. She is ashamed, not shame like earlier in the week when Mr Moses beat her just because she didn't have a book, but a shame full of rage. With that rage inside her, she is scrambling about trying to keep her balance. She doesn't say anything. She can't speak, because if she opens her mouth she will cry and she doesn't want them to see her cry. She turns her head and looks around for Gift. Sharpey is holding on to his hand. Doux beckons to him with her right hand, opening and closing it toward her. *Come!* Sharpey lets go of Gift's hand. Doux can see Sharpey taking one little step forward as if she is wondering what she should do. She stops and Gift walks towards his sister. He reaches her. Doux hauls his slate from him and pulls out the wooden frame. 'Go back,' she tells him. 'Go back to Sharpey.' Gift's slate is broken. It got broken one day when it fell on the road on their way to school. Doux grips the smooth part where the piece has been broken off. She holds the slate like an axe.

Armstrong is standing with his arms out at his sides, like a fighter sure of himself, a fighter who knows he has the upper hand, a fighter with all the bets in his favour. Around him, she can hear his army chorusing.

'Woy!'

'I thought she did bad. You doh see how he lif er up?'

'Anglican doh have no hero!'

'*Anglais cochon!*'

Her side of the road is silent. The other side has Armstrong. Sharpey's voice lifts itself above all the others to shout.

'*Français cabrit!*'

Armstrong begins to move forward again, his band of backers in a semi-circle behind him. They advance on Doux with open mouths, grinning teeth, shining eyes. Armstrong makes a sudden rush forward, coming in for the kill. Doux is afraid, and what goes across her mind is, *Either me or you to be dead today, so I go make sure is not me*. What goes across her mind is, *If you is bull, come! Tomorrow is Saturday; they selling meat in the market; I chopping you up in fine pieces for people to buy*. What goes across her mind is, *I don't do you anything, but if you figure you want to kill me, well, the best one win*. She lifts the slate, and steps back. All she knows is her fear and Armstrong's strength. Armstrong is taken off guard for a moment. He lifts his head slightly. And in that instant Doux brings the slate down on his forehead. The blood gushes out. There is a moment of shocked silence among the children. Armstrong puts his hand up to his head and steps back. Doux can see the shock on Armstrong's face, the surprise in the 'O' of his open mouth. His backers from Catholic find their voices and they are shouting.

'She show him he blood, *oui*.'

'Well is now self he go kill her!'

'*Anglais cochon!*'

'That girl playing she bad!'

Suddenly, Doux is calm. She feels no more fear. She grips the axe handle of the slate. She is thinking, *If one of us have to die, it won't be me! I not letting you kill me at all! If you is bull, come!*

There is excitement among the children from the Anglican school now. From all sides, voices are egging on the fighters. Doux waits, feet apart, slate ready in her hand.

But Armstrong has his hand up to his bloody face. And now he is backing away. Doux moves forward two steps, waiting for him. Armstrong turns away. Doux watches his bull back with the khaki shirt stretched across it as he walks to the other side of the road. One boy, probably the one who was his lieutenant, tries to touch him, but he shrugs away. He keeps walking toward the big grey and white Catholic school near the white Catholic church on the hill. His backers follow him, looking back at her over their shoulders. All those eyes that were shining when they were coming up to her before are looking back at her now, wary, no longer shining, as if they would like to fight her but they are not sure of her any more.

'*Anglais cochon!*'

And now her Anglican school watchers get the spunk to shout from her side.

'*Français cabrit!*'

'Girl, you don't jokin girl!'

'She bad in truth, *oui!*'

'You don't see how she chop him up!'

On the hill opposite, Doux can see two people who must be teachers, a man with a tie round his neck, and a woman in a white bodice and a long green and white skirt, walking quickly down the hill. She doesn't know if either of them was around when Armstrong rushed her, and when they were fighting. Other children must have called them, and now one of the teachers is holding on to Armstrong, helping him up the hill.

Doux picks up the pieces of frame from the ground. Gift walks over to her, his eyes big and fearful. She fits the pieces of frame back on to the slate and hands it to him. She holds his hand and they take off down the road. Now she is walking fast, almost running, dragging Gift with her. Sharpey is running alongside.

'You all right?' Sharpey asks. 'He didn't cut you? You body hurting you?' Doux doesn't answer. She is thinking of home, afraid of what is to come.

The children walk along behind them, eager to tell Doux's mother what has happened, ready for another exhibition. Doux knows that, as an example, her mother will beat her right there, in front of everybody, because she has warned her time and again not to fight in the school road. Selma would have told her that Doux was fighting, and other children may even have told her that Doux had a fight and drew blood. She knows she is in for it!

As she turns the corner, she can see that her mother is standing by the roadside at the next corner, in front of Mr Jimmy's shop, a thick guava whip in her hand. Yes, someone has given her the news about the fighting, of course, and she is waiting. Mr Jimmy is probably not there. He usually comes by the shop later. Afterwards, she knows her mother will say, Thank God Mr Jimmy wasn't there to see all this nonsense and all this waste. Her children making her waste his time! He would be out in the land somewhere now, picking his cocoa or his nutmeg, or down by his other shop perhaps, and it looks like her mother is alone in the shop here, waiting to sell drops and penny bread for children who come in with their tuppence after school. And now she, Doux, is making her mother waste the man's time! She is standing up outside of the shop, and the shop door is pushed closed behind her, so people can't go in. Doux knows she will hear about this later. Now Gift starts to cry.

'What you crying for?' Doux pulls at his hand and mutters under her breath. Why should he start crying now? She doesn't want to have to begin worrying about him now. She has herself to worry about. She turns to him, and gains some time by leaning over him, careful to stand behind him and keep him between her and her mother, still some feet away. She straightens his khaki shirt, pushes the shirt-tails into his washed-out blue short pants. She rubs her hands across his white knees. She lifts his head and wipes her hand under his eyes, trying to dry his tears. She bends down again and whispers to him fiercely, 'Hush you mouth!' Then, bending briefly right over him, trying to be sure no one else but he and Sharpey can hear her, she says, 'Is me she going beat. She won't do you nothing. Hush!' Gift pulls the back of his hand across his eyes, pulls his palm across his nose. He gulps and tries to swallow his tears.

Doux holds her brother's hand and they walk, moving closer to the shop. 'Evening, Mammie.' Sharpey moves restlessly near her. Doux can feel her friend wanting to say something.

'Evening, Mammie?' Her mother lets the guava whip fall onto the ground near her. She lifts her hands, puts them behind her back, looses the strings of her red and white apron, takes it off, folds it and puts it on her right shoulder.

It is as if she wants to put it out of the way of all the confusion. Now she stands with arms akimbo, watching her children. The band of school children stand on both sides of the road, some in the drain at the side, leaning on each other, lounging against the hillside, pushing at each other to get a better view, waiting. Doux's mother puts a hand into the pocket of her blue and white print skirt, pulls it out. She is holding something wrapped in a paper. She stretches it out toward Gift. She says, 'Come, Gift. Go down home. Give that to your sister. Tell her to give you a piece of it and to make some lime juice.' Gift takes the paper from his mother and walks away, down the hill behind the shop.

Doux's mother puts her arms akimbo, looks at her daughter. 'So, Madam! Instead of coming home with your sister and your little brother after school, you in school road fighting?'

Sharpey says, quickly, as if to avoid interruption, 'Is not she fault, non, Miss Thibaut. Armstrong from the Catholic school rush her and he push her in the drain. She didn't do him nothing.'

From the road, one of the children shouts, as if trying to help, 'And she buss he head. She draw blood.'

Another agrees. 'Yes, she draw blood.'

'You draw blood?' Doux's mother looks at her questioningly. Then she removes her hands from her waist, bends down, picks up the whip, and takes a step forward. There is excited scrambling among the spectators in the drain. 'So you in school road becoming professional fighter while I here bussing me tail to try and make a life for you? What I sending you to school for?'

Sharpey moves away from Doux's side, but she is still looking straight at Doux's mother. She begins to talk again, sounding anxious, lifting her voice a little, as if she wants to be sure it will climb over others that might try to say something. 'He hit her first, Miss Thibaut. Armstrong hit her first; she didn't do him nothing. He run up to her and he lift her up with a butt and he throw her in the drain.'

Doux's mother pauses, taking in this announcement, looking from Doux to Sharpey to Doux again, with a question in her face. Doux can sense that her mother's blood is rising at the idea that someone, some human person, took it into his head to butt her child like a bull. And that makes Doux start to hope.

There are some mutters from the children, perhaps from the Catholic children in the drain.

Not true.

Not true.

Doux says nothing. The audience is too big. She can defend herself if she has to, but all this attention makes her tongue-tied. She watches the guava whip in her mother's hand, preparing herself for when that hand goes up.

And then, from behind her, another voice says, 'Why are you children waiting to fight every Friday afternoon, instead of going home like decent children? What's wrong with you? Go on, now. Go home.'

Keeping one eye on her mother, Doux turns to watch Mr Lord, the tall, light-complexioned teacher from the Catholic school. His people weren't white, but he was high colour. People say that his grandfather was a full white man, a long ago man from England. The children start to slink away along the drain, along the side of the road, giggling, muttering things under their breath. They know they will meet Mr Lord in school on Monday. Those from the Anglican school know that Mr Lord and their teacher, Mr Moses, are friends. Mr Lord says again, 'Go home.' Then he turns to face Doux's mother.

'Good afternoon, Mrs Thibaut,' he says, inclining his head slightly as a sign of respect. 'Good afternoon, Ma'am.'

'Good afternoon, Teacher,' Doux's mother says. She is still holding the guava whip.

'The child was only defending herself, Ma'am,' Mr Lord says. 'She didn't start it. The little boy attacked her and she had to defend herself. It wasn't her fault.'

Suddenly, Doux's eyes are brimming with tears. She doesn't want to cry but her eyes are stinging and she can't keep back the tears. She puts her hand up to her face and wipes at her eyes. Across the road, she can see Sharpey, standing far away but still not leaving, pulling her hand across her own eyes in sympathy. *One day if I have a lot, a lot of money*, she thinks, *I will give Sharpey some*. Her mother looks at Mr Lord and says, 'Oh, is so?'

Mr Lord smoothes his blue tie and smiles, almost looking as if he wants to apologise. 'Sometimes these children don't do the right thing, Ma'am,' he says. 'The little boy from my school, the Catholic school on the hill there, is always teasing her. I heard him myself one afternoon. This afternoon, I was on the hill, not near enough to stop him, but from what I could see, he left his side of the road and rushed in and attacked her. I was hurrying to a meeting and I thought it was over, but then I heard that afterwards he tried to attack her again. It's really not her fault, Ma'am.'

Doux's mother looks at her and from her to Mr Lord. 'Thank you, Teacher,' she says.

Mr Lord says, 'Perhaps if I wasn't there it would be worse. He was attacking her and she had to defend herself.'

Doux thinks that Mr Lord made it sound as if his being there had saved her. If that was true, Doux hadn't been aware of it. As far as she knows, she could be mincemeat now if she hadn't called Gift and taken his slate, but she doesn't say anything. She is glad Mr Lord is explaining to her mother. Her mother looks at her and says, 'Go on down. And go inside.'

Mr Lord turns around to look at the few stragglers still waiting, apparently anxious to see something. 'Go home,' he says, and his voice sounds more severe now. And as they start to move away, Mr Lord calls again, 'Why you calling each other "Français cabrit" and "Anglais cochon"?' He steps forward, looks around, 'Who is French?' he looks from one side to the other. There is no response. 'And who is English?' There are giggles in the drain. A brave voice mutters, 'You, sir.' There are more giggles as they walk away. Mr Lord shakes his head from side to side and turns back to Doux's mother.

Sharpey calls out, 'I going see you Monday, eh, Doux?' Doux still doesn't trust her voice to say anything. But she lifts a hand so that Sharpey could see she is pleased to have the support. Her mother looks at her and says, 'Go on, go on down.' Doux keeps her head down as she walks past her mother, because, still, you never know. She walks past, and down the hill to the house behind the shop.

For a long time they stand there talking, Doux's mother and Mr Lord. Selma, Gift and Doux stay inside looking at them from behind the curtain their mother has put on two rods, top and bottom, across the room window. They stand there in front of the shop, the *Français cabrit* teacher and the *Anglais cochon* mother, and Doux is thinking that her mother is missing sales in the shop, and she wonders if they are talking about the way children could make people sin their soul.

Mr Lord leaves and Doux begins to turn away. But Selma calls her urgently back to the window. 'Come, come!' Their mother is outside of the shop still, her hand on the door as if she is about to go in, but she has paused to talk to no less a person than Armstrong, who seems to have materialised from nowhere. He has a bandage around his head and two books in his hand, tied around with a piece of string. They can hear their mother because she is talking loud. 'Your arm strong, and mine weak. But when you see my child passing in the street, leave her alone for me, please. I not sending her to school for cow to butt her.'

Armstrong mutters something. Doux imagines he says, 'Yes, Ma'am.' He walks past the shop, and around the corner, as if he is the meekest *Français cabrit* there is.

After that, Doux is always expecting trouble. On the way to school, she is always looking back, wondering if Armstrong will come from down the road, ready for revenge. On the way from school, she and Sharpey keep one eye on the Catholic school across the street. One afternoon, Armstrong is there, walking on the other side. Selma looks ready to run. Gift, who is walking in between Doux and Selma, grabs Doux's skirt and holds on. Doux can see some children looking from one to the other, but Armstrong keeps his eyes straight ahead. Sharpey, who is walking on Doux's left, nudges her. 'He won't take chances with you, girl.' Doux doesn't laugh because she doesn't want Armstrong to hear laughter and think they are laughing at him. But she thinks, *So now I could walk the road in peace because you know I won't give way when you push me because I'm not afraid of you! Eh bien, oui!*

YOU SHOULD SEE THEM IN CHURCH
WITH GLASSES ON!

When Miss Diana asked if she had seen her grandmother's glasses, Doux had to hold on to her temper, but perhaps that was only because she and Miss Diana were the same age, sixteen. *You're not in my bracket,* was what ran through Doux's mind, *you higher than me, so you could ask me whatever question you want.*

'No, Miss Diana, I haven't seen your grandmother's glasses.'

'She is so forgetful, you know. I just wondered if you might have come across them.'

'If I come across them, Miss, I would tell the Madam for sure.'

'I know that, Doux. I don't even know why I'm asking you.'

I don't know, either! You should know better! Mr John and Mr Peter would never ask me that.

When Mr John came up the steps on to the verandah, he smiled, said, 'Good morning, Doux, how are you?' and looked at her from under his eyebrows in that sheepish way he had. Whatever he was thinking, he knew better than to ask her something like that. And he was Miss Diana's father. Why couldn't she take example from him? Asking about her grandmother's glasses! And Mr Peter acted just as you would expect Mr Peter to act. He was younger than Mr John but he was the take-charge one, and always with old jokes. He slammed his car door, and came up the steps two at a time. He was dressed as if for tennis in his white shorts and white tee-shirt. Perhaps he had just come from tennis because he couldn't be going to play in this hot sun at almost midday. Soon, the sun would be right overhead. Doux hadn't prepared lunch for them so she hoped they weren't planning to stay and make her cook for them. She hoped they would just find the lady's glasses where she had put them and go back to their homes. Well, it was their place anyway. But she was the one with the work. Still, you couldn't be vexed with Mr Peter. Even as he was bounding up the steps he was shouting, 'Mother, where are you? What's going on with these glasses now?' He paused on the verandah, as Doux straightened from arranging the phone books beneath the small table in the corner and said, 'Good morning, Mr Peter.'

'Morning, Doux, how are you?' he said, watching her beat the leaf-green cushion between her hands. He grinned. 'Work as usual?' He pushed the shades up onto his fore-head, glanced quickly toward the door, lowered his voice, and said, 'So I hear you're spiriting away glasses, girl! Always thought there was something a little bit odd going on around the place! Vangie teaching you some spirit tricks?' Doux was too angry to think it funny, but when she kept her face serious and just looked at him with a question in her face, Mr Peter laughed out loud and walked toward the door of the living room, calling for his mother again. 'Mother!' He turned back to say, in a lower voice, 'Take it easy, Doux. We know you didn't steal the glasses. My mother knows too, believe me. She's just annoyed it's you and not your mother here to take care of her. And she's losing her senses, you know, poor thing.' He turned as his mother came through the door from the dining room. 'Mother! How are you?' He walked up to her and kissed her. 'That pastel colour suits you, Mother. You should wear it more often.' His arm around her shoulders, he guided her back through the archway.

But Miss Diana just wouldn't leave her alone to do her work. She was behind on it already because of all the fuss the lady made this morning. Now Miss Diana had her witnessing her search as she looked in the garden for these glasses her grandmother said she had lost. Miss Diana looked inside of the rose bush, bending down and peeping through the prickles, even pushing a stick in there to shake the bush. She would know what o'clock it was if the rose pricked her finger. Miss Diana had better not get hurt, though, because it would be she, Doux, running to find a bandage! Now she was all around the poor bouganvillea, poking it, pushing aside the leaves, saying 'Come, help me, Doux,' as the thick bouganvillea dropped its red flowers and put prickles in the way to resist her manhandling. Miss Diana lifted up the thick fern in the big flowerpot in the middle of the garden, put in her hand, softly patting the dirt right around the inside of the flowerpot, apparently to see if the glasses were there. Now who would she be thinking put them there? Her grandmother might walk in the garden, but she didn't do any gardening. There was a yard boy for that. Even she, Doux, didn't work in the garden, so if she was thinking she might have taken them, why would Miss Diana think she'd put them there? This whole thing was a waste of time. Why didn't they stay in their house instead of coming here to waste people time? Miss Diana wasn't thinking. Miss Diana touched the white queen of flowers with her hand, looking up at the tree as if she was asking it to say something. She even tried to push aside the two big flowerpots on either side at the bottom of the steps to look under them, although the only thing she would find there would be crushed glass. Doux pretended to be looking instead under the flowerpot with the yellow shrub they called bread-and-cheese, because she wasn't going to try pushing aside those heavy flowerpots unless Miss Diana asked her directly. Miss Diana looked behind all the flowerpots going up the steps to the verandah. She looked inside the hanging pots on the verandah, standing on the small stepladder and pushing her hand through the curling vines, although all she could possibly find there was the damp soil from this morning's wetting. She picked up the cushions Doux had just shaken and checked under them.

Doux said, 'Miss Diana, I just finish cleaning here, you know. I shake all these cushions.'

'I know, Doux, I'm just trying to satisfy my grandmother. And I want you here as a witness that I looked everywhere.'

Who you witnessing to? I'm sure your grandmother wouldn't need a witness. And what you want me witnessing for? I suppose when you is Boss, or Boss daughter, same thing, you could ask people to do all stupidness!

Miss Diana looked under the living-room sofa, where she couldn't even find dust because Doux had given the place a good cleaning as usual. She looked on top of the grandfather clock, under all the cushions on the living-room chairs, she put her hands down behind the side tables, she looked inside the vase on the centre table, she asked Doux to help her move the big standing mirror in the corner and she looked behind there.

She stood back and looked under the dining-room table, made a show of pulling out the heavy dining-room chairs and looked on them, staring at the seats as if she expected to see the glasses rise up from somewhere inside them. She looked questioningly up at the china cabinet, stood on tiptoe, put her hand on top of it, and stretched to run her hand further in, along the top.

'Come, Doux,' she said. 'Just pass your hand along here to check.'

'Miss Diana, your grandmother says I took her glasses, so if I find something, she will just say I found it where I put it.'

'Oh, Doux, she doesn't really mean that!'

Doux said nothing. She wondered if Miss Diana would release her now, so she could get back to her work, but Miss Diana said nothing about that. She kept looking, and Doux watched her look. Miss Diana looked under the bed in the spare room; Doux watched as she pushed her hand in between the headboard with carvings of horns from Africa. She passed her hand under the pillows, stood on the small bench in front of the bureau and reached on top of it. In the big bedroom, she looked under her grandmother's bed, asked Doux to bring a small stool from the bathroom so she could climb and run her hand along the top of the closet. She opened her grandmother's clothes closet and touched the dresses, put her hand into the pocket of a red dressing gown, felt the pockets of a blue dressing gown. In the bathroom, she looked in the cabinets, shook the shower curtains, untied the bow of the outer curtains and knitted her brows anxiously, as if she thought the glasses might just fall from behind that big blue bow. In the little cubicle near to the shower, she looked in the space behind the toilet.

In all the rooms, she lifted up the ends of the rugs and looked under them. *She know the thing*, Doux thought. *That is where the devil used to put things to test me in the beginning, when I just come to work here!* Miss Diana even climbed and put her hand high up on the window-sill, on top of the kitchen cupboards, she pulled out the kitchen drawers, looked through the cutlery, looked under the kitchen towels. Doux watched as she looked in the cabinet with the wine glasses, over by the sherry decanter, everywhere.

Doux looked on, annoyed, bored, not contributing to the search. She was still remembering how the old lady wound up the arm of the telephone, how she put the thing to her ear and said, 'Yes, dear. I'm glad I found you. That girl took my glasses! They have disappeared! She steals like a cat! Anything I put down, my money, my jewelry, everything disappears. You'd better come right away. I don't want her here anymore!'

Once before, the old lady had accused her of stealing a ring. The same Miss Diana had found the ring where her grandmother had put it, under her mattress, down inside of a glove she had worn to church that morning. So now Miss Diana's father and her uncle left it to her to search. Miss Diana's mother hadn't even come with them. Something told Doux those two didn't get on too well. That time with the ring, the lady had called them right after the Sunday morning mass, after they had dropped her home and gone away. But Miss Diana had remembered seeing her grand-mother wearing the gloves, and Doux was away in her room that morning, because she had the half-day off, so the devil had miscalculated that time! This time, she had pulled them all from home on a Saturday morning, when Doux was staying in and working for the weekend, and when the lady knew Mr John and Mr Peter would most likely be relaxing at their homes.

When Doux had first come to the Great House in Bakersfield, the madam used to put pennies under the carpet, with the edge outside. At first, Doux would pick them up. When she handed them to the lady, the lady would just look at her from under those yellow-brown eyebrows and say nothing. Sometimes she would put a florin, once she even put a guinea. Every time, Doux would pick them up and hand them to her. Afterwards, when Doux realised that these losses were no accident, she stopped picking up the money. She would sweep, dust, clean the carpet, watch the edge of the money peeping out and leave it right there. She said to herself, *Not a bit of it! Pick it up yourself!* When the lady realised Doux wasn't bringing the money to her, she said, 'I had a florin somewhere around here,' the white skin of her forehead wrinkled and disapproving, 'and it disap-peared. I know you took it.' And Doux would say, 'It's right there where you put it, Ma'am,' and she would add to herself, *playing hide and seek on the carpet*. Then the lady kept putting things at one end of the carpet or the other, but stopped asking Doux about them. When Doux didn't bring her the money, she would say, 'You didn't sweep; I put the money there, and you didn't see it. That means you didn't even sweep. I told my sons they were paying you for nothing. You are a good-for-nothing child. You didn't even see it.'

Time and again, Doux reminded herself of what her mother always said: 'Drink vinegar if you have to, just beat your lip and look as if you enjoy it. Pretend you think is honey. Then, when water more than flour and you can't make good dough, when you can't take any more, leave the work. In these days, high-up people in charge. Learn how to handle yourself.' But this wasn't her mother's day. This was nineteen thirty-six, modern times – today, not yesterday. Doux knew she wasn't being polite enough and the lady would want her to go.

Still, she was hanging on by the tips of her fingers, making dough even when the water was too much for mixing, because she didn't want to leave the work. It was her first real little job and, bad as it was, it was a way of getting something to help her to live. She had to admit, though, the lady was a devil. She was always bothering Mr Peter and Mr John. She complained that Doux was nasty, that she didn't do any work, that she was stealing her things. Doux could often hear her on the telephone, because she made no effort to be discreet. And now, with this glasses episode, she was sitting out there on the verandah and telling them again, not minding if Doux heard her, that her glasses had disappeared, that she could have nothing in the house because since that girl started to work here, things keep disappearing.

Considering all of that, Doux really didn't appreciate Miss Diana asking questions about her grandmother's glasses.

She said, 'Miss Diana, I have to continue my work. I want to go and prepare something to drink because I don't have anything prepared yet.'

'All right, Doux. I can't imagine where these glasses are!'

Ask your grandmother to imagine for you!

Mr Peter and Mr John left their mother leaning back, dozing on the cane-bottomed chair in the verandah, and they went out to the kitchen to talk to Doux.

Mr John pulled on the seam of his pants, worried his red earlobe with his finger, and looked embarrassed. Mr. Peter pushed his hand through his brown hair, grinned, and sat on the chair at the kitchen table in the corner.

'Doux,' Mr John said, 'I know you haven't done any-thing. For whatever reason, my mother is against you, and when she is against you, it's difficult.'

Doux said, 'Thank you, sir.'

I wish you would tell your daughter not to ask me any question, and to look for her grandmother's glasses herself.

Mr Peter said, 'Our mother is getting senile, you see, and it's a real problem, but we know it's not you.'

'Thank you, sir!'

Senile? She just wicked!

She had never done that lady anything, but right from the beginning the lady hadn't liked her. Perhaps she was just too disappointed Doux's mother hadn't taken the work. Her mother had worked for this lady once, when the husband was still alive and Mr John and Mr Peter were little boys. And she had worked for her again when Doux was a little girl, and the lady was living in Grand View, and everybody said the lady never thought anybody was as good as Evangeline, that Evangeline was totally committed and you could ask her to do anything, and that's who she wanted to work for her. When they asked, Doux's mother said she couldn't come, and Doux had asked her mother to recommend her for the work instead. Her mother hadn't wanted to do that. She'd wanted

Doux to learn to sew. 'Stay and learn to sew with your aunt Jeryl.' But Doux had already stayed six months learning to sew with Aunt Jeryl, and she complained that all she had done was hem and wash dishes. She wasn't learning to sew, and she wanted to make money. 'You can't handle all this work yet, child,' her mother said. 'Those people make you work hard,' she warned. 'You could never do enough. And the moment you have somebody of your own to see about, they get antsy. You have to hide your own business and see about theirs. When you have to take it, you take it.' And that was why she wasn't going back to work in these people's houses now that her children drink water already and were big enough. She didn't think it was a good idea for Doux to start on that journey. They'd got Selma already. Doux's sister was working as a maid in Paz City, the capital. 'Learn to sew, Doux,' her mother advised. But there was no money in learning to sew with Aunt Jeryl. The lady would pay her, Doux argued, and money was what she wanted. She had to find money now that she was big, to buy clothes and the little things she wanted.

Eventually, her mother gave in. When Mr Peter drove his car all the way up to her house on Hideout Hill to find out if she had thought about it and if she would take the job, she asked him if Doux could take the work instead. He said he would have to discuss it with his brother, but as far as he was concerned, yes, if Doux could do the work and she wanted it, it was hers.

Mr Peter and Mr John were the ones who paid her – sometimes one and sometimes the other. They started off promising to pay her eight shillings a month. Mr John was the older one, but Mr Peter was the one who handled the business more. Her mother said Mr Peter was the one who was more comfortable dealing with people. When they saw how she worked, Mr Peter gave her twelve shillings – time and a half. 'I feel like a king,' Doux told her mother. Mr Peter had said, 'We decide to give you twelve shillings, Doux. You didn't work like a child. You deserve full pay.' Doux could buy her own clothes and even give her mother a change. Her mother had worked hard, baking for people, washing, cooking for people, and always Doux had to be behind her or off staying with other people when her mother couldn't keep her on the job. So Doux was glad of the money. She knew she had worked for it, and now this devil...

Mr John and Mr Peter went back out to their mother. Doux was in the kitchen making sandwiches for them when she heard their voices raised in laughter and comments she couldn't make out. Mr Peter was laughing out loud, and when she went out through the dining room she could see Mr John on the verandah, leaning back against the wall and holding his head in both hands. Doux turned and went back into the kitchen. She supposed they had found the glasses where the devil had hidden them. Let them rejoice. She didn't want to rejoice with them.

The granddaughter, it seemed, had asked her father to bring a stepladder inside. She had climbed again and stretched her hand to feel about on top of the closets in all the bedrooms. On top of the big closet in the spare room, she'd found a little parcel wrapped up in cloth. She pulled it out, brought it down and opened it. And there they were, the glasses well wrapped up in paper, and tied around with an old white vest.

So this is what being senile could do to people! Make them wicked enough to plan something like that? Fling them where you think nobody will ever put their hands on them? She's stronger than I thought, though. Those hands not so weak, after all, for her to be able to hold back her hand and fling the glasses up there. Wickedness make her strong!

Miss Diana came into the kitchen, and stood looking at Doux, smiling. She said, 'Don't worry. We found them.'

Doux lifted her eyebrows. She said, 'Yes, miss.'

I knew you would find them if you looked hard enough –
unless she flush them down the toilet!

When Doux went out to the verandah with the sandwiches, the devil was sitting on the cane chair with her
hymn-book on her lap and a blue and white fan in her hand,
fanning her face and looking as if she didn't understand
anything that was going on. *Senile, my foot!*

When she saw Doux come in, she said, 'You put them
there! I know you wanted my glasses. You always wanted
them.'

Mr John and Mr Peter said, together, 'Mother!'

This time Doux couldn't help it. She answered. After all,
she wasn't dead yet! Why would she steal that old woman's
glasses? She might steal a piece of bread if she was hungry
enough and she got the chance, but glasses?

'Madam,' she said, 'what would I do with your glasses?
I'm sixteen years old. You are an old lady, and I'm a little
girl.'

The lady sat up and said, 'Yes, you would want my
glasses, yes. Of course you would want them. When you
grow older, they would fit you beautifully. You should see
the niggers in church with glasses on!'

'Mother!'

'Grandmother!'

Perhaps when you're getting senile, thought Doux, all
the wickedness that you hide before starts coming out. Mr
Peter and his brother and their family had never shown her
anything racial, but you could never tell, because their
mother had enough to say all the time. Still, it wasn't fair to
judge the children by their mother, and they had never
shown her that.

And even after all this, she couldn't say she was sorry
she'd taken the work, because it had given her a start. She
was too big to be going to school; there was nothing more
for her to do there, and she had to find something to do.

This lady was a devil, yes, but she still had to thank the Lord for small mercies.

But Doux knew it was the end. She couldn't stay on after this, and she knew Mr Peter and Mr John would think so too.

In spite of that, when they told her, shamefacedly, that they would have to let her go because their mother didn't like her, it felt as if they'd fired her. She cried afterward, not for them to see, but after she left the house. She had wanted the work, not that one specially, but the opportunity to work, and this one was right there, not far from her home on Hideout Hill.

It was hard, because aside from a place where her mother had given her the opportunity to fill in for a maid for a few months during the holidays when she was about fourteen years old, this had been her first real job. It felt as if she had failed. But God is good. Everybody among the high-up people in Paz knew her mother. And, like her mother would always say, 'There's a plan that we don't really have all the pieces to understand. Give God a chance to work on it.'

The Dumbarton house has three bedrooms, a verandah right around, a dining room, living room and, inside, toilets that can be flushed. The workers aren't allowed to use the toilets upstairs, but the one right downstairs is a flush toilet as well, and the workers don't mind. It is expected that you would have some division between one kind of people and another.

The people of the house – those who own it, that is – have their water supply in a tank, not a government tank, but something they have built for themselves, or, rather, hired workers to build, and they get water when it rains. It rains a lot, so the tank doesn't run out of water. But most times the workers have to go to the standpipe outside to get their water, so they put containers outside to catch water when it rains, as well.

Doux likes it here, in Dumbarton Cocoa. Everybody calls it Dumbarton Cocoa because it is a cocoa estate. It's always cool, not only under the cocoa trees, but throughout the place – on the verandah, in the boucan where the bananas are put to get ripe, on the hillside behind the house. It's as if the cocoa spreads a cool blanket over everything, so that even on the days when she leaves Hideout Hill and it's really hot up there in that nutmeg place that is her home, down here under Dumbarton Cocoa, it is cool and breezy.

She likes the big board house, with its shutters and shingles. She likes it when she goes down to the kitchen and Miss Melvina gives her a little edge of tart, when Miss Melvina teases her about the dry-foot yard boy and the way he looks at her. As if Doux would find herself taking on the yard boy! She's doing well here, in Dumbarton Cocoa, and in spite of the fact that his mother used to say nasty things about her when Doux worked taking care of her, she gets on well with Mr Peter. In fact, she knows that he likes her, likes the fact that she speaks her mind and doesn't take nonsense. And the madam likes her work, too, she can tell, even though she is more serious and she doesn't make ole talk like Mr Peter would make ole talk. Miss Melvina says that usually when you're working in these people's houses, the women are more circumspect with themselves. Miss Melvina says you have to understand that, because the same boss man that is so nice and so friendly, if you give him a chance he will get too friendly, and the madam knows that, so she can't be too friendly with every and anybody. Sometimes the same person that you're so friendly with in the kitchen, you come and discover is somebody that is making a child for your husband, willingly or otherwise, that's what Miss Melvina says. So sometimes you find that the women appear more sour than the men, but that's with a reason. Is something they say come down from slavery days, Miss Melvina says. But anyway, slavery or no slavery, Miss Melvina says, woman always have to be on the lookout, because man ready to make you feel shame without thinking twice, and you mouth on the ground with every and anybody before you well realise it. The madam right, Miss Melvina say. She know how life is and she living to suit.

Miss Melvina says that man, whether they high or whether they low, wasn't made to be any woman's trusted companion, and most women know that by the time they drink water. Watch yourself, child, Miss Melvina is always telling Doux. Never forget that you are somebody, and don't let any man make you think otherwise.

But in spite of all the things to worry about, Doux is comfortable here. She likes it, and she works hard. They are always praising her work, the way she cleans the rooms, how she makes up the beds, the way she keeps fresh flowers from the garden in the house without anyone having to tell her, the way she keeps the bathrooms clean like a whistle, the way when company comes they don't even have to ask her to work late after they asked her the first time and told her it would be expected. They know she can work, so much so that she felt good enough to ask Mr Peter for a raise just last week. She asked him for one shilling more, and he only gave her sixpence, but that is still something. In fact, it's a lot. Mr Peter is something else.

When she asked him for the raise, he said, 'Doux, you don't know trouble. You think things easy?'

Doux had to laugh to herself. She thought, *Imagine Mr Peter sounding as if he is my mother. Things not easy for my mother, but Mr Peter?*

She told him, 'I know trouble, Mr Peter.'

And he said, 'I manage my brother's estate, so I'm working for somebody, too. I don't know when last *I* get a raise.'

She said, 'Well, sir, perhaps you don't need one, so you didn't ask for one.'

Mr Peter laughed, cyah cyah cyah! He said, 'Yes, girl, you could argue your case! So you think I don't need a raise, eh?'

Doux said, 'Well, sir, if you need one, ask him, sir! If your work is good, he will give you one.'

Mr Peter said, 'Girl, you think things easy, in truth? Things not easy at all. The cost of everything gone sky-high.' Mr Peter was like that. When he was ready, he would talk just like youself that working for him, as if he is one and the same with you.

Doux answered, 'If you saying that, Mr. Peter, what you leave for me to say? That is not for people like you to say.'

Mr Peter laughed, a little laugh for him, and he said, 'So you think I can't have money trouble, eh, Doux? Bigger the man, girl, bigger the trouble, bigger the trouble.'

Anyway, he gave her the raise, and that was what she wanted.

Doux had thought a lot before she asked them for the job, but short of going and work for black people – and nobody would want to do that, of course, because, as her mother said, when your own colour trying to be high they treat you worse than anybody – short of that, she had to turn back to these same people. But Doux likes people to pay her for the work that she does, and when she heard what Sharpey's aunt was getting for working with Mr Peter's brother-in-law, she knew they were still underpaying her and that she could get more. She might be young, but she was doing the work.

It is a sweet thing to have your own money, to be able to spend money on clothes, to be able to dress. Last week, when her brother Gift came home from his union organising all over Paz, he told her that these days she was dressing like queen and acting as if the world belonged to her. 'Of course it belongs to me,' she told him. 'Who does it belong to if it's not mine?' Trust her mother to come in and remind her that it was God's world. But her mother understands. Her mother is the one who taught her that if you don't have strong eye and realise the world is yours, people will walk all over you.

Doux thinks about how it is when you don't have and then you start to work. *Believe me when I tell you*, she says to herself, *that it is a wonderful thing*. Every payday, after she takes out the money for her grandmother's tobacco, she buys something – a dress, a bag, a pair of shoes. And it's a sweet thing to be able to go home and say to her mother, 'Look, Mammie, I'm giving you this change specially so you don't forget to buy tobacco for Mama.' Last time when she did it, she could see Mama looking at her, as if she was waiting to see what she planned to do. But even though she knows her grandmother never liked her, Doux is not planning to do anything more than buy her tobacco, buy the little things she needs to make her happy. She doesn't like what she sees and hears now. Her mother and aunts still hide things from them as if they're not big enough to know what's going on, but anyone can see that Mama, her grandmother, is not well. She gets thinner every day, and Doux is sure she heard her mother and aunt whispering that, 'Is just a matter of time.' She doesn't want to think about that. She wants to have the opportunity to show her grandmother that she was wrong about her, that really she is a good person, that there is no reason not to like her just because she wasn't pleased with Doux's mother when she was born, just because she thought her daughter looked too low when she looked at Doux's father. Doux would like to be able to build her grandmother a little house one day, or do something to show her that she doesn't have her in mind for the way she couldn't stay in her house for long when she was little, the way she always favoured Selma and acted like Doux was nobody. Once, she couldn't understand that. But she knows now. She still thinks that people shouldn't make children pay for what big people take it into their head to do, but perhaps Mama didn't know better, and, yes, she wants to show Mama that, in spite of everything, she is not bad, in spite of everything Mama used to think.

It is good that she is off again. She is going home to spend the weekend with her mother, and with her grandmother. It doesn't ever get stale, she thinks, this feeling she has because she is big. All of them are big people now, all the unpleasantness is over, and she is going home to the house where her mother and her grandmother are waiting. Her last weekend off, Selma wasn't at home because she was working with a family over on the other side of Paz, but she might be at home this weekend – and her aunt might even come by the house.

Doux knows she is looking good today. She holds her head high because she feels like a queen in her white dress with the red buttons down the front. Her aunt Jeryl made the dress. Nobody has to tell Doux she looks good. She knows. She can see it in the yard boy's eyes, although *Who he think he looking at like that?* She doesn't have time for that kind of person. The yard boy is the lowest of the low and Doux has more ambition than that. She can see it in the eyes of the boys liming on the bridge, she can hear it in their whistle, but she's not going to stoop to them because she won't let anybody take advantage of her. She wasn't going to end up with a child people didn't want to keep in their house if she had to go somewhere. Doux notes, without seeming to, how the women doing the work in the garden look at her as she walks past. 'Good afternoon,' she says demurely, and she hears one woman ask another one, 'Who is that one?' She doesn't hear what the woman's companion says in answer, although she's trying to hear, but she can imagine the answer: *She working in Dumbarton Great House. I believe her people from Hideout Hill up there. I suppose is her weekend off and she going up.* And she knows they're thinking: *A nice young girl. You don't see that head of hair? It don't look as if she have Indian in her, but she must be have good quality somewhere. A nice, full head of hair.*

Doux likes herself, and she knows she has to make sure, as her mother always says, that pride doesn't go before a fall. She knows that she is not fair skinned like Selma, so she has nothing to fall back on. She used to think at one time that it was because of this their grandmother liked Selma better, but even though she is not fair skinned, she knows she looks good, and anyway she wouldn't want to be Frighten Friday and never have courage to do anything, like Selma. Sometimes she thinks it's because she's had to fight more for herself and for her corner in the world that she has more courage than Selma, but she likes to be this way, with courage to fight her battles. She lifts her head and smiles as she walks. Her mother always says that life is a battle, so you better prepare yourself.

She walks along the back roads. She always walks here, because it would take too long to go all the way down to Heaven Junction and then up again through Carawa and Boli and Belmont Pass, up to Hideout Hill. The walk in the back through St John's is long, but it's not that bad, and anyway unless you are jefe in this country, walking is what you have to do, unless you want to wait forever and waste your money on bus, and anyway Doux likes to walk.

She hasn't been walking that long – she doesn't think so, anyway – and here she is going down St John's Hill already. She likes the quiet of St John's River. When you're walking down the hill near the houses at the top, you can't hear the river at all, but when you turn the corner at the bottom of the hill it will be there, peaceful and quiet because the rain isn't falling, and there's no noise coming from the mountain. She likes the evenings, the way the sun warms up the day and now leaves the afternoon cool and full of breeze. She likes St John, but she likes Attaseat better – the way the mountain sits up there over Hideout Hill, quiet and green like the whole island of Paz, sheltering her grandmother's house. Mama, her grandmother, says that once she, her mother and her father used to live up there in Attaseat Mountain. When her grandmother mutters this, it sounds as if she is regretting that those days are gone. Perhaps it is true what her mother says, that Mama has come down in the world, that she used to live high-up and pectus with her parents, but then, when their father died and the son and heir divided the land, the girls didn't get much, so that is why Uncle Big has a lot of land and Mama has nothing but a little one-room board house with an acre behind it to leave to her children.

Doux looks across and smiles at the man sitting on the step to her right. This is a St John's man, not an Attaseat man, she thinks irrelevantly, so she doesn't know him that well. She remembers his name, though.

'Good afternoon, Mr Littleman,' she smiles at the man sitting on his step.

He looks at her. She can see Mr Littleman taking in that she looks special. She can see him wondering who she is. She remembers him, though, or about him. Mr Littleman was a big man already when she was growing up. She wasn't in the Hideout Hill area that much growing up, but she remembers him. She has seen him, too, since she left school and came back to Hideout Hill. He might not know her, because she was always out with her mother when her mother was working in all those different places all over Paz, because she couldn't stay with her grandmother. She knows Mr Littleman, but big people never know who children are after they grow up. They are always wondering, *Which one is this again?* She can see Mr Littleman's forehead and the little wrinkles running across it. She waits for the question, because she knows it will come.

'Who you?' It is almost as if Mr Littleman wishes he didn't have to ask, as if he asks the question grudgingly. His shoulders are hunched and he sits forward on his step, looking up at her from under his eyebrows.

She says, 'Miss Thibaut in Hideout Hill is my mother.'

He considers that, his eyes intent on her face.

He asks, 'Which one?' And, before she can answer, he asks again, 'Miss Golden is your grandmother?'

Ah, now he knows who her people are.

'Yes.'

'Which one? Which one is your mother?'

'Vangeline.'

Mr Littleman stands up on the step. He is taller than she is now, and he is looking at her searchingly. There is a story here, his eyes say. Oh, yes. Everyone would know the story of Evangeline, how she got married, how her husband died soon after the marriage and the birth of a little girl, how, instead of keeping herself quiet like the child of decent people would, Evangeline shamed herself and her pectus mother afterwards by getting a belly about a year after the husband died. The glee of discovery is starting to glow in Mr Littleman's eyes. He lowers his head as if he is preparing to rush forward. The sun makes a sudden dive and a cold breeze blows across St John's Hill. Mr Littleman is smiling. He looks at Doux's hair, how it curls prettily on her shoulders, because when her hair is pressed it is very long. She wonders if it's her imagination that Mr Littleman drags his eyes down across the bodice of her white dress, as if he is looking with scorn at the little red heart-shaped buttons. It might be her imagination, but Doux feels a cold breeze blow across her skin.

She remembers that her mother always warned her to be polite, but to walk her way and not stop to take on people, not to fight in school road, not to give people a chance to run their mouth on her. She lifts her hand to say goodbye as Mr Littleman turns and spits over the side of his step. She remembers her mother saying, 'You play with puppy, puppy lick your mouth.' Doux starts to move away, but the question stops her.

'Who is your father, chile?'

She says, 'Mr Princeton Henry.'

Mr Littleman says, 'Mr *Princeton Henry* is your father?'

She says, 'Yes.'

He says, 'So you about twenty, twenty-one?'

'Yes, nearly twenty-one.'

Mr. Littleman nods. He says, 'Mr Princeton Henry knew you before he died?'

She knows she doesn't have to explain, but perhaps she is trying to claim something when she says, 'Yes, and I used to live in his house with his family after he died.'

Mr Littleman laughs. 'So the wife take you in?'

Doux says nothing. She turns away. She should go now.

99

Mr Littleman says, 'You so don't count, you know.' Mr Littleman stands tall now, arms akimbo, on the step in front of his house. In case she didn't get the point, Mr Littleman leans forward to explain, 'Children like you, you don't count.'

At the bottom of the hill, Doux looks down at the river. The water is dirty. Perhaps it has been raining in the mountains.

The bridge she stands on has been built to help the river control itself when the rain is too heavy in the mountains. When that happens, the river frightens the people of both St John and Hideout Hill, and it divides the two villages. No one likes that. People on the two sides don't always agree, but they are one people – at least to the extent that they don't want a raging river between them. When the river behaves like that, they call it 'Mr River' and get together to talk about it.

When Doux gets home, she tells her mother that Mr Littleman told her she doesn't count. She tells her mother the whole story. Her mother says, 'Don't bother with Mr Littleman.' Doux says, 'I can't bother with Mr Littleman. I have my life to live.' Her mother says, 'I don't know why you stand up at all to say anything to Littleman. Is not any and everybody you stop to talk to. You give older people respect but you keep yourself at a standard where they don't have anything to say to you. You might think you know everybody, but not everybody is people who want the best for you.'

And suddenly her mother is talking a lot, more than she talked the day Doux was thirteen and her aunt Geraldine, her mother's sister, told her why her grandmother didn't like having her around. 'Is due to your father and the fact that your mother splice in there between your father and his wife.' Her mother says now, 'I make my mistakes and is me and my God alone to have conversation about it. Littleman have a nerve.

Littleman didn't even go to school. He don't know what inside the schoolhouse look like. Littleman can't write ABC. Is crazy Eliza crazy that she go and put herself with Littleman. For fifteen years, she sit down there making children with Littleman, one every year, and he keep his married in his pocket like is something too precious to share with her. So what he think? Because Eliza could read and she have a little colour, his children count? He know my child don't count, but he not even putting his woman and his children in line for them to count? What make him figure they could count, and my child can't count?' And then she ends with, 'Remember what I tell you. Play with puppy, puppy lick your mouth.'

'Life gone,' Doux's mother says, 'but life is to come. Life is to come. And you count.'

Doux opens her bag and says, 'Look Mammie, I get pay today. Take this and buy tobacco for Mama.'

BIG STONE

When they asked her to explain exactly what happened, she said she knew she was tired that evening, so she couldn't swear about anything, but what she was saying was what she remembered. She had been called to the house for a delivery since midday. The child didn't make her appearance until just after one o'clock the next morning. Yes, the last she heard, both mother and child were well. She had been afraid that she would have to get the mother rushed to the hospital for a Caesarean section, because she was quite old to be having her second child, yes, over forty, but she, Nurse Chalmers, had managed to turn the child around. She had shown her the way so that she could come into the world on her own. Well, sort of on her own. With all of that, though, she wasn't able to get away until after six, when the little girl finally made her appearance.

Yes, January twenty-second. She supposed that meant the child's sign was water, Aquarius, but she didn't pay a lot of attention to those things. Yes, the husband had a car – a Hillman Hunter, she thought that was it, not that she knew that much about cars – and he said he was going to take her home, but the tyre on the car was flat when they went out and when he checked the spare was flat, too, so there was nothing he could do. No. She didn't think the family was being selfish, she wouldn't say so at all. And no, she didn't think it was strange. The car tyre had a hard time in these roads, and, like everybody else in this area, the Johnsons weren't rich people, they just had enough, but you couldn't expect them to have a trunk full of tyres waiting. It was understandable. And in fact, they had tried to get her to stay overnight, but she hadn't planned for that. Her son had to sit the scholarship exam the next day, so she wasn't comfortable staying down there. And it wasn't that late, when you think about it; she felt she could walk home comfortably. Ordinarily, Giles, her husband, would have come for her, but he was giving extra lessons in school that day, and when that happened, he didn't get home until about six or a little later. She was often out late, delivering little ones, and you never knew how long that would take. Sometimes the little ones surprised you.

No. She had never delivered a baby of the kind they were talking about, not that she knew about, anyway. And no, she didn't believe in such things. No, she couldn't explain it. She hadn't been drinking. On the job or not on the job, she didn't drink strong liquor. No, she hadn't stopped to buy any rum; she didn't know anybody along the road sold bush rum. It wasn't that far away, she said, the place where Jeremiah and Doux Johnson lived, just a little more than a mile – perhaps about a mile and a half – from their house to hers. It's just that theirs was in the bush on that old estate road, and she never liked to walk that road at the best of times. A lot of things that aren't so nice happened in those old estate places long ago, and things stayed in the air, you know, so she wasn't happy being in those areas late. At night, well, it made her sound superstitious, perhaps, but she didn't think it was fanciful to suggest that those places always made you wonder if there were people from long ago who wanted to remind you of how things were. Well, no, not to stay in the past, but just to remind you that even when times got better for you, there were always others outside. Well, yes, she agreed that sounded fanciful, and she wanted it to be clear, she wasn't really the superstitious kind.

Their house, where she delivered the child? As far as she knew, it used to be an old boucan, a place where the estate would put cocoa and that kind of thing, so they could get dry. The Johnsons had bought it from the estate, moved it higher up the hill, and put an extra piece on to it, so that they could get a bedroom for themselves and one for their children. It was a nice spot, really, where they were. It looked right down to the sea, like one of those modern spots people like so much these days. It was on the old estate land, but with a good view of the sea in the distance.

What kind of night? Well, you know how those old estate places were. Those places used to have a lot of pain and wickedness in the past, but she wanted to emphasise that they were not like that today. And it was an ordinary night. She was just thinking about the child and the mother, not about the past and all that kind of stuff at all. And the Johnsons were nice people. Mr Johnson was telling her a bit about his life. Yes, of course, as everybody knew, he was a master carpenter. He was doing really well, and had added those rooms to the boucan himself. He used to be working in the land in the old-time days and he said that at one time he thought that was what he wanted to do; that's why he'd moved to the old estate. Yes, he knew a lot about land; he used to work in the land once, he said, in fact, in the early days, he even used to be a yard-boy, a long time ago, so he knew about right around the estate house – somewhere up in the country, but that is far, far back. He'd been a trades-man for a long, long time, in Paz City and around the place, so that other experience was well in his past. Well, even if they used to see hard times once, that was not their life then. Carpenters were doing well, actually. But why are they asking her so many questions about the Johnsons? They only came into the story because she helped them bring their beautiful little girl into the world. A real pretty little child, and the Johnsons were an ambitious family, so that child would be all right in the world. You could tell things like that. Not her business, of course, but she always thought about things like that when she delivered a baby. That was just her way, but, anyway, the Johnsons didn't have anything to do with what happened. The only way they came into this at all was that it was through them she was out in the road at that time, through having to deliver their child.

To be fair to them, they hadn't let her walk out there all alone. That's not what happened at all. No sense trying to give them a bad name because of that. The husband – Mr Johnson – walked with her part of the way, along the darkest part of the road. He had a bottle-light and a flashlight, and he walked with her to help her to see along that road. Yes, it really is a shame that, in this modern day, nineteen sixty-two, the Joie de Vivre road is still in such a terrible condition. Really, she wasn't joking, she had to lift her feet high off the ground and put them down carefully, trying not to trip herself up in the darkness. It really was time for the government to get rid of all those stones and make that a paved road. You can't blame England for everything. They were still in charge, yes, but now the country had its own council down there in Paz City, and Chief Minister and Ministers here and there, so why couldn't they see to a thing like this? Anyway, this is not the time nor the place. That is another story. On the road, her shoes were good and thick, but they felt heavy and clumsy as she walked. Even then, even before it all happened, she couldn't say she liked the walk. It wasn't a walk you could like! You do it when you have to. And she was anxious to get home after a long day. And, as she kept saying, she didn't like the Joie de Vivre road in the daytime, much less in the dark. A little moon was starting to come up, she remembered; she noticed the moon, because it gets dark quickly in this area. It wasn't a full moon. Perhaps it was third quarter. And she hadn't liked the way the cocoa trees leaned across the road, touching each other, their leaves rustling against each other in the late evening breeze. That road was really dismal, and there were hardly any houses around.

When you turned right at the end, down the road from the Johnsons' place, there was Jane's little house, and only one light from a little lamp at that hour. People went to bed early, she told the reporters, still trying to put together a story after all this time – why wouldn't they leave it alone? And even if people weren't in bed, those little lamps didn't give off a lot of light. Perhaps Jane only had a small lamp in her house. She remembers wondering, as she always did, how Jane could feel safe staying alone like that in Joie de Vivre cocoa. Hardly any houses around except for the Johnsons' way up the hill in the middle of that old estate, and then the people in the estate house on the other side. Things were changing, it was true, and other people were talking about building there under the cocoa trees, especially now that the estate land was getting parcelled out, but it couldn't have been easy to be the first. Although she didn't tell them, Nurse Chalmers remembered that she had said this to Jane once, when she came to the surgery, 'Why you alone living in that dark place, you not afraid?' And Jane, in her usual quiet, almost surly way, had answered, 'I not afraid of spirit, Nurse. Is living people that frighten me.'

What Nurse Chalmers told them was that sometimes people said they are more afraid of the living than the dead. If you looked at it like that, Joie de Vivre was a safe place, because living people in the area those days didn't go around hurting each other, not physically, anyway. Not like the books say happened long ago. And people from outside the area didn't know enough about Joie de Vivre to just visit the bush for no reason. Though it's near to Paz City, well, that is not a factor, really, because crime was not something the area heard a lot about. And she, Nurse Chalmers, well, she didn't live down there, and least said soonest mended.

When she and Mr Johnson reached the corner near the

river, they hurried past. No. They hadn't seen anything. It was just that there were lots of stories about that corner, and she had grown up in the area, so she knew the stories. Well, she knew that there used to be an old water mill right there, on the corner by the river, that at one time, perhaps long ago in the days of slavery, there used to be people working in that mill, and sometimes even now people said they heard sounds there. No, there had been no mill there in all the days she knew it, just the old wall, ruins. She was born in the area, not down there, but near enough, and she was almost forty and she had never known a mill there. But no, they hadn't heard anything. She didn't know about Mr Johnson, but she knew that *she* walked quickly because she never liked that corner. And as soon as you go past that corner, there is the river. She had heard stories about mermaid and River Mooma combing her hair on river stone, so, to tell the truth, the river is not a thing she liked to be around in the night, but no, she hadn't seen anything, not then, not at any other time. It was just a superstition she knew about, and one that she paid attention to, especially at night, because you know how it is with night. Not that she was superstitious, just – well, human, she supposed.

No, Mr Johnson hadn't said anything. To tell the truth, they didn't talk a lot when he was walking out on the road with her. She was anxious to get home and he was anxious to get back to his wife who had just had their second child, so both of them were preoccupied, she would guess. She remembered that Mr Johnson held the masanto high as they hurried past the corner and the river. Not that she believed or anything, you understand, but you can't help thinking about stories you have heard all your life. Strange, though, that she didn't think about it at all then, but no, she didn't.

They went past the river. 'The river quiet,' Mr Johnson had said as they started up the hill. 'No rain falling in the mountain,' and she agreed, 'Yes, the river really quiet,' and

107

'No, no rain in the mountain.' They went past the golden apple tree on the left, and the stinking-toe tree over the road on the right, and then they started to climb further up the hill.

As they got to the first house, Mr Johnson said, 'Well, I will leave you here now, Nurse, because I want to get back to Doux and the children.'

And she'd said, 'Of course; this is good. You walk me more than half the way, and we're past all the darkness. There are houses along here now, and it's brighter. No more cocoa trees. I'll be all right. I'll be home soon. You don't have a telephone down there, so I can't say I will call to let you know, but I will be all right. I know you want to get back to your wife. Good luck. Your wife and your baby are fine. They will be all right.' She said she remembered that was exactly what she told him.

And Mr Johnson had said, 'Yes; yes. Thank you very much, Nurse. It was good of you to come. Thank you very much.' And then he'd told her, 'Take the flashlight with you,' and he unhooked it from around his waist where he'd secured it, and handed it to her. He said that he would stop by the surgery and get it during the week. She remembered that he turned the masanto, the bottle-light, to feed the wick with kerosene, and the light got brighter, and she remembered, too, that she saw that Mr Johnson had painted a cross on the bottle. She remembered that because afterwards, when she talked about it, someone told her that people often did that because they walked with these lights in the night, and the cross gave them protection. So she'd remembered that Mr Johnson's had the cross and she'd realised why. In fact, because the light was so bright when he'd fed it with kerosene, and not because of the cross, for a moment she'd wondered if it wouldn't be better for her to take the masanto, but then she didn't have far to go, and anyway, she could handle the flashlight better. So she just said, 'Good night, Mr Johnson.'

And he said, 'Good night, Nurse,' and she'd walked away holding the flashlight to help show her the way.

She didn't have far to go, as she said, and she took off walking fast, anxious to get home. She had to go just around the corner, past the spot everybody called Big Stone, and then straight up the hill to the police station, and her house was on the corner there.

And then, just around the corner, on the ground near to Big Stone, the little girl was sitting. It was at a place where the road made such a wide curve that the one road became like two roads, one leading downhill, from where she was walking, one going uphill, where she had to walk to get home, and then the other one, sort of leading downhill on the right in front of her, under the road below these two. Yes, just there, at the curve, where the other road comes from below to meet these two, that's where the child was. The road? What was it like there? The condition? Well, she was coming from downhill, and that was rough road, but not too bad by the time you got to that spot. On the main path leading uphill, the stones in the road were almost the same as where she'd been coming from, a little bit bigger, perhaps, more sturdy, closely packed. When you walked there, it wasn't smooth, but it felt like road, as if you were walking to some real place, not like down inside Joie de Vivre. That main path, one side of the curve, was the one that led up to the police station, and the school, and the Catholic and Anglican churches and the Main Road where you can take a bus into Paz City, and her house. Yes, that's right, it was the dirt road that comes uphill to meet the curve, so that the effect was of three paths meeting. So yes, you could call it a crossroads. Right there, at the place where the paths meet, a huge stone is set in the ground. People were up and down there now, to see the spot. She wasn't sure where that stone came from. She grew up knowing it there. Centuries ago, she supposed, it might have fallen from the hillside above the curve. Because the thing is, all that part of the road used to be the Joie de Vivre estate in long-ago days – no, not in her day. She only knew that because of stories her father and her grandmother used to tell. Not in her day at all. Anyway, however that stone got there, and however long ago, it had become a boulder marking the crossroads, and as far as she knew, that was what gave the crossroads its name – Big Stone.

So the little girl was right there, sitting on the ground at Big Stone, and she had her right thumb in her mouth, and her eyes were wide and filled with tears. At first, she was alarmed, and then concerned. Who could have left their child there, crying like that in the night? It wasn't quite night yet, but it was almost that; it must have been about seven o'clock in the evening, and people would have called their children inside earlier, when the dew started to fall. And certainly you could see the leaves of the soursop tree just below the stone in the crossroads wet with dew. The road is lonely there, yes, not as lonely as Joie de Vivre cocoa, so not so frightening, but lonely still, and mainly because people went to bed early. Yes, there was lamplight in that house on the corner but it must have been a small lamp for the children to pray by, because she could remember seeing it through the window curtain, but just a little glow. The river? Yes, she could hear the sound of the river below the road there, but not loud.

Yes, of course she wondered. She'd stopped and waited, looking around, thinking perhaps this little girl's mother must have been down the path, relieving herself in the bushes. But to just leave the child there, like that! And yes, she did think, 'These people!' Sorry to have to say it, but yes, she was thinking that some people were really careless with their children.

She'd asked the child, 'Little one, you could talk?'

And then she thought, almost as if the child had answered – no, she'd only thought that afterwards – almost as if the child had answered, she'd thought, of course she could talk. Those were the eyes of somebody who could talk, somehow. Those eyes looked at you so hard it was difficult to look anywhere else but deep inside them. And the child's eyes were blue. And then, yes, perhaps it was then she realised the child's dress was blue, too, and the neck all buttoned up under a thin, bony face.

But she'd asked again, 'Can you talk?' And the child had nodded; yes, of course she could talk. She kept saying that because that was the answer that came to her in her head, 'Of course'.

And to tell the truth, she'd thought that the child must belong to that Riviere girl, the youngest one. Yes, she didn't like to talk about people, and she was only saying this so people would understand how she was thinking, so she hoped they wouldn't go and write anything contrary, but, to tell the truth, like everyone else, she had heard that Pa Riviere's last daughter, the one that wouldn't talk to anybody because she was so – well, so sort of what people called high and mighty – and she wasn't trying to bad talk anybody, understand, just explaining because of how things had happened – she too had heard that the last Riviere girl had come back from Trinidad with a child and people were saying how that young Riviere spirit like it had gone restless and roving. So yes, she'd thought this must be the child that the Riviere girl had come back from Trinidad with. She liked the Riviere family, you understand, she was just saying what she had heard and what she was thinking, so that people would understand why she acted that way at Big Stone. And well, sometimes it was good to talk things out so that they don't remain a stone on your conscience.

So yes, she'd asked the child, 'Where is your mother?'

The child's eyes were brimming with tears. The child lifted one hand up to her head, and she passed that hand over

111

the short black hair – yes, it was like an ordinary little thin baby girl's hand – and short black hair like – well, like short-hair children – no, not soft and curly like Indian or anything, as far as she remembered, nothing out of the ordinary, not that she could remember, just ordinary black people hair when it short – anyway, the little girl wiped her eyes with the inside part of her arm, never taking out the thumb of the other hand from her mouth. Yes, a little suck finger, that was all she thought.

Then, yes, she'd moved closer and bent down to the child. No, she hadn't felt strange. She'd just wondered if she should stay with her a few minutes until the mother got back. And she supposed she'd been getting annoyed, too, wondering why these people would have children if they wouldn't take care of them. Yes, to tell the truth, she'd been getting vexed more than anything else.

She'd lifted her head and called down the hill, 'Hello?… Hello?' hoping that the mother, even if she were hiding to – well, to relieve herself – in the bushes nearby, would rush out to get her child. So she waited, yes, and when there wasn't any answer – they were laughing now, but it wasn't a joke – when there wasn't any answer, she started to feel uneasy. But she was more uneasy and *annoyed* than uneasy and *afraid*. She must say, all of that time, she wasn't afraid at all. She just knew she couldn't leave the child there, and perhaps that was her training, she didn't know, but she was thinking, too, that she had to get the job done and get home. So she stood up from in front of the child, looked down the path again, in that dirt road under the curve, and when she saw no sign of the mother, she turned back to the child, wondering what to do.

She'd asked the child, more for something to say than anything, 'Child, where is your mother?'

The child shook her head as if to say she didn't know, and sort of lifted her little shoulders and fixed her wide blue eyes on her face. And *that* was when – she remembered well – that was the first time a sense of anything strange started to settle on her. But still, not so much that she was frightened. It was just that those blue eyes started somehow to register. And – well, she was so sure that it was that Riviere girl's child, that she'd just asked herself who that girl had this child for, because it was a little strange to see those blue, blue eyes against that dark skin. But then, too, she'd thought that Trinidad, where they say the girl went, was a mixture, so anything was possible. Anyway, the Lord said you should help those who couldn't help themselves, so she'd decided she had to take the child with her because she couldn't leave her there. No, nothing else went through her head, just that.

So she'd leaned down to the child, stretched out her arms and picked her up. Yes, she remembered well what she said. 'I'll take you up to the surgery and let the doctor have a look at you. The doctor won't see you tonight because he's gone already, but there's a nurse there overnight, staying in the surgery, so you could stay there until your mother picks you up.'

Then she'd thought that she would stop by the police station and let them know she had the child at the surgery. No, she hadn't thought the mother had abandoned her child or anything like that; you didn't usually find things happening like that in this area here; if people couldn't take care of their children, there was usually another family, or there were neighbours to give them a little something, but yes, she had thought it was carelessness, all the same, to leave the child like that there in the dark and go God knows where. She was more vexed than anything, to tell the truth. No, she wasn't afraid at all. She supposed she was kind of thinking that this mother needed to be taught a lesson.

When she'd picked the child up, all she could remember was that the legs and the little frame felt bony against her, and the little thing was as light as a feather. Yes, sorry, but she had to keep doing that, yes, trying to brush something off, because she couldn't forget that this child had been on her shoulder. And yes, she'd thought that the child was mal-nourished, for sure, and that had to be carelessness, because Pa Riviere wasn't that badly off.

She remembered saying to the child, 'You're light as a feather.'

No, it didn't stay that way. When she went past that first house on the corner, the one with the little lamplight, the child was feeling heavier already. Well, she knew she was tired, and she thought she didn't have too much stamina. Then she'd said, 'You not as light as you seem,' and she'd eased the child up a little bit on her shoulder. By the time she was past the third house up the hill, right by where the track goes down the hill to join the dirt road a little lower down, the child was noticeably heavier and she, Nurse Chalmers, was really breathing heavy. That was when she said, 'Wait, go down. I can't carry you. Walk.'

And yes, that was when – it gave her the shivers to talk about it – but she felt she had to and to be totally honest, so that if anybody had an answer or knew what to say to her, it would come out – that was when, as if on cue, from the bushes just past the house and under the road there, a voice called, 'Ajakbé, where you dah go?' And yes, she can't keep still, she has to walk about, because just to tell the story now is to bring everything right back.

The child just lifted her head, suddenly active, and the head turned toward the bush and the child called out in a strong voice, 'Me na-a know, Mama. Ce Missis wey dah say ah sick, she ah bring me go doctor.'

And no, to tell the truth, she couldn't move. She'd just stood there, as if somebody had planted her in the ground, and she stared down at this thing in her hand. It turned its head toward her again, and it yawned, so that she could see

114

a mouth full of teeth and way down inside of a – in fact, all of a sudden it was as if it was only a yawning throat she had in her hand, and all she could remember is that she just fling this thing away. She just knew that she was flinging her hand out, flinging away whatever it was on her shoulder, flinging, flinging, and with her other hand she was grabbing at her shoulder and flinging – in her head, she supposed she was trying to get rid of anything else that might be there, and she didn't wait, she just knew that she was running up the road.

And all around her, it was as if the whole air was suddenly full of people or whatever it was laughing as she ran. And yes, she'd heard this voice calling out, in a kind of song, behind her, 'Ou tini bon chance, ou! Ou tini bon chance, ou! Ou a parti!' Yes, her mother spoke Patwa, because they were from the country, so she knew that meant something like, 'You're lucky. You escape!' And that voice still rings in her ears, 'Ou tini bon chance, ou! You're lucky! You want to take care of child? Mine is child too, you know. It outside, but is child. Ou tini bon chance, ou! Ou a parti?' And then there was the laughter.

And no, she can't forget. Those blue eyes, that yawning mouth and the sound of that laughing, chanting voice, they go with her everywhere. And yes, yes, yes, she wouldn't mind hearing from anybody who has an explanation, because that voice is in her head: *Ou tini bon chance, ou! Ou tini bon chance, ou!*

Jericho should have guessed something the moment he picked her up by the river. He said so afterwards, but that night he wasn't thinking straight. He and the boys were liming in the corner by the shop in Fortuna and the lime was good. With Guinness and Heineken to sweeten it, nothing was missing. Keeperman from up the road in the cocoa behind Miss Icilda shop, that man could talk nonsense. Keeperman was in form and man just drinking Guinness and bawling. Keeperman stories not good for man nor beast to repeat, and if Miss Icilda didn't have strong eye for sheself, she put them out of that shop long time! But when Joe Brain said, 'Miss Icilda, I sure you want us to go,' all Miss Icilda said was, 'I tell you I want you to go? Who taking you-all on? Sit down and talk you nonsense and live you lyin dreams on the bench right there, I don't care! You want me to push you out into the night drunk for you to go and do somebody mischief down the road? No, I not selling you any more drink because you have enough inside you already. Buy salami and bread and salt nuts to cut the drink if you want, or buy nothing, but no more drink! Sit down there and talk it out, I don't care.'

So they sat, and Keeperman talked. Keeperman told them about a pretty, pretty young lady he met in the road one night when he was just out of school, and had to carry the clothes his mother ironed for the people up on the hill. And Pell said, 'Just out of school? You leave school since nineteen nought!' But Kenneth decide to stand up for Keeperman on this one. 'Is the rum have his face so,' he explained. 'He leave college the year before me – nineteen eighty-six. Not ten years yet. Is the rum mess him up. Tell you story, man.'

And because carrying clothes for people seemed to him like a long-time story, the kind he heard from his grandmother, Jericho said, 'In this day and age you carrying clothes for people?' And they looked round at him and Pell said, 'Town boy! Away boy! New York boy! What you know?' And Miss Icilda said, 'What town boy? What New York boy? His people from right up the road in Hideout Hill there.' And they looked at him sitting there smiling with the bottle of Guinness in his hand and they know he have big work as some kind of accounting man in that firm that just open up in Mango Village and Pell said, 'Well is long-time country story he know. He don't know anything about up here in these days.' And Miss Icilda said, 'Well, look where he is sit down with all-you. He don't fall far from the tree. Leave him alone. It in his blood.' And that had everybody quiet for a while, and perhaps they were thinking about blood and wondering if that really say anything about anybody and if it had anything to do with the story.

Anyway, they more interested in the fact that Keeperman stories does be dirty, so man waiting to hear thing. But Keeperman surprise them. Keeperman say this young lady, a high brown from out of the area with pretty, pretty cat eyes and a smooth face and soft hair well pressed and bobbing round she face, say to him, 'Keeperman, is a long time I looking at you!'

Man shout, 'Lie!'

Keeperman say, 'Serious thing!' And Keeperman pause, his face quiet and considering. Man looking at Keeperman now, and man don't know where the story going.

So town boy or not, Jericho interested, and he pushing again. He ask him, 'So what happen next?'

'Boy,' Keeperman say, 'is a story to live and not to tell.'

But they waiting to see if he would tell. But it was like Keeperman really couldn't tell this one. 'Boy,' he say slow, slow, his face still serious and considering, and then he take a shot of the Heineken in his hand, and he put it down on the counter, and still he considering. 'Boy, all that happen is that one thing become another, and I tell her I see her too and I find her attractive, but I didn't know how to talk to her and...' – man waiting – Keeperman say, 'and that was all.'

Man scratch their head and say, 'Boy...' and Keeperman say, 'Then eventually she crook her arm in mine – like this – and...'

But man couldn't let it go so. Pell say, 'Wait, Wait, Wait. Go back to the part where one thing become another and tell us, what thing, and what it become.'

Man laughing and giving bait, but Keeperman for once not biting. Keeperman say, serious like, 'Nothing. Nothing. Eventually, the young lady just crook her arm in mine, and she tell me, like, walk her up the hill to the house where she staying with her friends.'

'Wait. Wait. Up the hill? Is the same house your mother was working in?'

And Keeperman say, 'Allyou man want to know too much! The wire bend, and the story end!'

And man shout, 'Is a damn nanci story in truth! Wire bend, yes. Do better than that, Keeperman. You think is so-and-so little boy you talking to?'

And Miss Icilda say, 'The moment you-all start to use word, pack up and leave my shop, eh?'

They murmured agreement, and point out that they just say 'so-and-so' and they leave the word alone, but Miss Icilda not buying it and they say sorry, because they would always keep it clean out of respect for Miss Icilda.

Keeperman throw his head back, draining the last of the beer, and Miss Icilda lean on her counter looking at them and she pass her hand across the counter, wiping out some dust that they can't see, but then by this time they not seeing much anyway. Then Miss Icilda say, 'OK, you want me to give you a cup of water to throw on your face outside there, so you-all could reach home? All Fortuna asleep already. Only this shop awake for you-all to sit down here and talk foolishness. Go home.'

That's when Jericho asked for two bread and some salt salami. Jericho stood up, biting into his bread and salami. These men just have to walk up the road there, but he had to jump in his car and drive all the way down to Mango Village, which is where he living now, although is true he grow up in Paz City and driving down to Mango Village not feeling like a good thing to do this time of the night after all that Guinness. Anyway! The salami would settle him.

Joe Brain said, 'Give me a lift up in the cocoa, non!'

But Jericho wasn't buying that. 'Man behave yourself, non, man. You just going behind the shop there…'

'Let the man go!'

And Miss Icilda asked Jericho, 'You still have people living in Hideout Hill?'

Jericho said, well, some cousins and distant family, but he didn't know too much about it. His father would know, and his grandmother, of course.

And Miss Icilda said, 'Say hello to your grandmother for me, when you talk to her. I know Doux well.' And Jericho said yes, he would do that.

So now there he was, past Sweet Song, driving down the hill, and right there, on the corner by the bridge, she stopped him. He thought afterwards that if she had been sitting on the bridge he wouldn't have stopped. But it seemed that she was just walking quickly past the bridge, and as the car lights picked her up, she raised a hand as he was about to pass and the sea green of her dress just catch the corner of his eye. It was his soft heart that made him stop, he thought afterwards. His sister Mireen went to party sometimes and stayed late, and he had heard her talking about having to walk all the way from Paz City into the bush near Joie de Vivre there, and how the drivers were so wicked they never even stopped to give her a lift. Perhaps it was because of that he stopped to pick her up. And perhaps, too, with the Guinness in his head, he just wasn't thinking straight. And perhaps, too, after those years in New York when nobody would stop and pick him up like this, he get stupid, so that now he picking up everybody he see and some he can't even see properly.

She came around behind the car and got in next to him. Afterwards he was explaining how when you give a person a lift you don't really look in their face to see who it is, you just make sure they pull the car door and then you take off again – well, he didn't look, anyway – if he was in New York, yes, but not in Paz; here you don't really look too close into the face of a person you giving a lift. Somebody want a lift you give them a lift. That was how he explained it. And you have to think he knew what he was saying, because he used to live in Brooklyn, so it not that easy to make a fool of him, or so he believed. Paz in the nighttime is different from New York at night, he said. They told him that was just the problem. He underestimate Paz because he live in New York.

Whatever it was, suddenly he was uncomfortable. When he was telling Miss Icilda afterwards, he say he turned to look at the woman he had given a lift and realised he couldn't see her face. She must have put on the hat after she got into the car because she certainly wasn't wearing a hat when he stopped for her. He wouldn't stop for a woman with a hat. Not in the night! But then as he see the hat, he realised what he was thinking and he rushed to talk, so that he would stop that kind of thinking.

'How far you going?' he asked her. 'Where you want me to drop you?'

And she said, still not turning so that he could see her face, 'Just around the corner; not far.' And her voice was quiet and musical and he wanted her to talk again so that he could figure out if she was talking like Paz people or talking *English* English because he wasn't sure or perhaps he just wanted her to talk again for talking sake.

'Not far,' she said, through the side of the hat covering her face, and he straining, waiting for her to say more, but that was it. 'Not far,' and she finish, with that *far* word hanging in between them.

So now he was thinking that he wasn't stupid. He wasn't drunk, either; he was sure of that. Not any more, even if he was before, and he didn't think he was before. He put his foot on the gas, and he going down there, wishing for traffic, but is night – it must be about eleven, twelve? – and not a car on the road. Why Miss Icilda must stay open so late just because man in the shop drinking? Let them go to a club! Miss Icilda acting as godmother to all those men around the place, keeping them off the street. That is craziness. He had gone up there just to meet some old-time friends and to visit Miss Icilda because she was the mother of an old friend in New York, but he had really stayed too late. All these thoughts going through his head while he trying to figure out who this is, what else to say to make her talk, and how he get himself into this and when this woman will drop out of his car. He usually wouldn't think of himself as a person at a loss for words, but all of a sudden he has no idea what to say to a woman who is sitting in his new Honda Civic and this in itself keeping him really agitated. And then sudden so, just after he leave Sweet Song and he entering Kumar, he see a light under Canute shop door and he see one door open and he swerve sudden and stop in Canute yard without even thinking and open the door and out of the car before you could say Jack and he shouting out for 'Canute! Canute! You there?'

He pull open the door with the light under it and Canute and Christopher sitting inside the shop enjoying a quiet drink and looking up, surprised.

'Jericho? What happen, man?'

'Hey, hey, hey,' he stuttering. 'I glad to see allyou, man.'

'You stay up the road late? You going down Mango now?'

He looking back outside through the door, and he telling them, 'Come, come and check out something here with me.'

Canute lift the flap and come from behind the counter looking apprehensive and Christopher get off his seat, pulling his vest down over his protruding belly, and together they walk to the door. All three of them trying to get through the door together because Jericho stand up there and is like he afraid to go back outside although he calling them to come out.

'What happen?' Canute say. So now Jericho step out into the yard and stand up there watching his car. They follow him into the concrete yard and Jericho watching the car with his mouth open.

'Come,' he tell them, and they follow him to the car and stand up there with him, looking at the car and wondering what wrong. And Jericho looking at the car, sort of peeping at it as if he couldn't see too well, and then turning right around to look to all sides in the darkness.

'Come,' he tell them again, and he moved closer to the car. They watch as he open the door, and stand up there looking at the empty car. He turned and looked right around again, and they looking around, too, wondering what this is about.

Jericho say, 'You see anybody in the car?' and Christopher and Canute glance at each other, wondering now what going wrong with their friend.

'How you mean if anybody in the car? You can't see nobody in the car? Who you leave there? What happen to you?'

'Come,' he tell them again, and they follow him to the back of the car, looking right around at the night because he himself was looking right around, too, and they watching while he open the trunk and lift up the spare tyre. He close the back, lift his head and turn around in the yard, looking to all sides.

'You back door open?' he ask Canute.

'How you mean if my back door open?'

'Around the side where you have the toilet customers use sometimes. It open?'

'No; that close long. What happen to you? You don't know the time? Why the door would be open at this time? That close long. What going on?'

'There was a woman in the car.'

'A woman? Who…?'

Then Christopher say, in a low, urgent voice, 'Look, look over there.' They turn to look where he was watching, because Christopher have enough sense not to point. And across the road, through the trees, they could see a woman's shape in a dress blue-green like the sea, and a slanted wide-brimmed hat, going through the trees, walking kind of hop and drop, as if she walking on one good foot, and the other one not so good. And afterwards all of them swear she didn't go up, she didn't go down, and as far as they could tell, she didn't continue going straight ahead. She just disappear like that as they watching her, becoming one with the green of the trees across the road, just sort of fade into the trees, and she wasn't there any more.

THE LADIES ARE UPSTAIRS

Moonlight tonight.
Tantie Mary, thread the needle
Ring ting, thread the needle.
Thread the needle, let me see you
Ring ting…

'Moonlight tonight. After one time is another. I can't hear one little voice outside tonight. And I inside here waiting for them to bring on *The Young and the Restless*. My granddaughter out there, looking up at the sky. Moon full, yes, she saying, as if she surprise. Is like that. When night dark, we waiting and hoping for moonlight. And when it come, so swift and so sudden, is a surprise. You even forget what darkness was like. But when darkness there, you never forget what moonlight was like.

'Moonlight tonight. I sitting here with the television watching me, what you think I remember? Miss Mary. Look at that, eh! After all these years I talking to myself? Well, with these years on my head, is all right to talk to myself sometimes. Seventy years I making this Christmas. So is to be expected.

'Go back and watch you moonlight, child. Go back… All right, then, let me tell you if you want to know… It look like they push back this programme well late tonight … Leave the door. Leave it open.

'Is Miss Mary I remember this moonlight night – Miss Mary and Belmont River. I was walking home from by your aunt in La Poterie. I stay late. Moon full and lighting up the road bright like tonight. And reach I reach by Belmont bridge, what you think I see in the river? I shouldn't say what, non. Shouldn't call people what no matter the state that they reach. Who? Is who you think I see in the river?

'Miss Mary. Sitting down on river stone in the middle of the river.

'To understand what a shock that was, you have to know who Miss Mary was, and the height these people reach in the place in those days. You don't remember I tell you about Miss Mary, long time ago? You probably forget.

'But anyway, see I see this figure in the river; I say, Lord have His mercy! La diablesse! Or River Mooma! What you closing the door for? Big, hard-back woman like you, you still fraid la diablesse story? I was thinking, moonlight and la diablesse combing she hair on river stone like mermaid. I was thinking, River Mooma come for food and is me alone in the road.

'I stand up there paralyse. Ready to run, if the truth be told. Ready to run. Then la diablesse stretch out she two hand wide and turn round on the river stone. And that is when I realise. Miss Mary, yes! Oy o yoy! After one time is another, in truth.

'Miss Mary and she sisters grow up pectus pectus in the house on the hill. Was a house everybody in the village could see. Bigger than everybody own. Fly couldn't touch them. My sister used to say, is like they messin ice cream. If wind blow too hard and ruffle them little bit, Madam, their mother, would employ the whole district to take care of them. My aunt Geraldine was the one who used to take their clothes every week to wash in the river. And their father was a very drastic man, a big shot, a big jefe, and he never had a pleasant word for nobody. And those little girls, Miss Mary and she sisters, fly couldn't touch them, I tell you.

'So now look at this. Imagine my shock!

'I call out, "Miss Mary! Miss Mary!" Miss Mary turn

125

round. Stand up on the river stone. And stay there rocking on the river stone and waving. She squint up she eyes and then she recognize me. "Bella!" she shouting. "Bella-a-a!" Like me is a long-lost friend. Everybody else call me Doux, but you know, some of these high-up people don't like to use home name. "Bella," she calling.

'I don't want to laugh, non, child, but after one time is another in truth. I telling you like this now; it sounding simple, but you could never imagine what it was like in those days.

'I remember one time, after my mother find a little work for me in their house – Miss Mary mother and father house, that is – because my mother used to work domestic there for a long time, you know, so after I get a little work there, teenager still in school, about fourteen, perhaps fifteen, I used to go every weekend, and sometimes Mondays if they had washing, and sometimes on a Friday, for cleaning and dusting and so on. So one day, I remember, a lady pass selling fish – was small jacks.

'Madam, Miss Mary and Miss Margaret mother was upstairs. I know I did hear Madam say she would like to buy some jacks. I hear the shell blowing and the jacks person shouting out, so I know she was down by the gate. Then the dogs start to bark and when I look outside, the yard boy was holding them back and standing up down there by the gate talking to the lady with her basket on the other side of the gate. So I tell Cook, and she tell me to go and ask Madam if she want any jacks. Same time she push out the window and call out to the yard boy to let him know Madam might want jacks, so he start to secure the dogs so he could open the gate for the lady. And me self, I run inside, and I call out to Madam upstairs.

' "Madam! Madam! A lady in the yard with jacks!"

'Well! Madam appear at the top of the stairs. Is as if I could see her now. Standing up there in a kind of soft gold-colour dress with she hand on the banister. "What's that, child? Why are you shouting? Haven't I told you not to shout?"

"'Sorry, Madam. Is a lady, Madam. A lady in the yard with jacks and Cook tell me to come and ask you if you want."

'Madam raise her hands and then she rest one on the banister. "A *lady* in the yard with jacks?" she ask me. And then she raise the other hand and point back upstairs, back to the bedrooms and the upstairs sitting room and so behind her. "The *ladies* are upstairs."

'You laughing? So you understand what I tell you about how I shock to see Miss Mary in the river? I tell you, is a good thing Madam dead and gone before Miss Mary reach river stone. I tell you is God that know what he doing. People say was always a sadness in the family that they never have any boy children to carry on the family name, but the Lord knows best. Must be better so.

'Was Paz white, you know. The boss man was black, but Madam was white. Why you surprise? I tell you was the boss; I didn't tell you he was white. His family was black people of substance from long time. People with property, you know. I can't tell you where the money come from, but wasn't poor people. So he had the name already and then he come and marry this white lady. Well, people say she had black in her, but nobody know that for sure, and when you look at her is white you seeing. Perhaps people say she had black in her because the family didn't have a lot. People say her family was family with name but without the means, but the two put together now, so, well, matter fix. His family had three boys and all of them make good marriage; none of them marry black.

'And then, I don't know how it happen, but people say boss man, the black one now, the one with colour like me and you, Miss Mary father, he, too, come and lose his money, and the family – yes, Miss Mary family, that is – after a while, well, they come and fall. Everything, all property they had, had to sell to pay debt. One of his brothers buy the house so they could still have it to stay in, but they couldn't even afford to keep it up like before. You know what I mean? Grass start to grow high in the yard that was pretty lawn and nobody not working for them any more. I tell you, child, money is king, yes. You could take over the place, but if you can't keep it up, say what?

'Then the boss man come and dead, one lick. I don't really know what happen to him, but after money disappear they say he only keep to his room and one day I hear Aunt Geraldine telling my mother, "The boss-man dead, yes. They say his heart give out for lack of sunlight." And I remember my mother making the sign of the cross and she say, "Poor thing. God rest his soul and welcome back his son into the fold. What a ting, eh!"

'So after the boss man dead, now, the big daughter – well, it had two of them; I think they say one was a cousin, but she was there like one of them – I don't really know what the inside story is, because I didn't grow up staying in Hideout Hill too much – I remember one was Mavis, one was Margaret, and then the one I was telling you about, Miss Mary. Well, after the father die, Mavis go and work some-where in town – in a store or something in Paz City, one of those high-class places – and she take the mother to town with her. I hear after that the madam waste away, die talking foolishness, not knowing nobody, thank God, because by this time Miss Mary self, alone in this big, dying house, start roaming the street. Eventually, I hear Miss Mavis went away, after the mother died – to England, I think, and she get lost over there – and I don't even know what happened to the other one, Miss Margaret. Perhaps she went to England too. I don't know. Meself, I was away when all of these changes taking place. And when I come back from Maturin in Venezuela and see Miss Mary walking the streets, I tell

128

you, I couldn't believe. I just couldn't believe was the same little girl I did know.

'My mother have a word she used to say, "How have the mighty fallen!" The boys in the area used to hold Miss Mary's hand and drag her in the bush all over the place, do what they want with her. And all of them still calling her "Miss Mary", you know, from habit, but doing just what they want with her. And then the children start to call her Miss Mary Zagzo – I suppose because she was so thin and so zagzo, non, so po jab and so wasted. And the worthless boys passing down the road, shouting up the gap, "Miss Mary Zagzo, you want to go under the cocoa with me?"

'Well, well, well! After one time is another! Just like that, because of the devil called money, the world turn upside down. But you know, still, when I think of it, I always make the sign of the cross, because this world so round, and spinning so steady, you never know what will happen when the wheel go round again. Today for policeman, tomorrow for thief, as they say. Jefe as boss-man and his family was jefe in their day, I could never rejoice. I was never high like them, is true, but still sometimes when they dragging Miss Mary down under the cocoa, I used to find myself thinking, there but for the grace of God… I tell you, in those days, I was about twenty-six, twenty-seven by that time, and I born 1920, so you could work it out, but as long as it might seem, is not so long ago, and I used to watch those things happen and the state of Miss Mary, and think that it was the ending of the world.

'That night, eh, child, when I see Miss Mary in the river, I sit down on the river-bank and call out to her to tell her to come out of the river.

'Yes, that time all those things had start to happen already, although it was in the early days. I call out to her and I say, "Miss Mary, come out of the river, because you never know, rain might be falling in the mountain and you never know if the river will come down all of a sudden. It late, and getting later. Come out of the river, Miss Mary!"

'What a thing! Push the door close little bit, you hear, child. The breeze blowing cold.'

'Miss Mary down there dancing on the river stone and looking up at me and laughing. "Bella!" she calling. "Come here, Bella." And I saying, "Miss Mary, come out of the river, non." And Miss Mary look down at the water, then she stretch out her hands and turn right around on the stone, then she looking up at me, and laughing.

'Then she stand steady and look up at me and call out, "I see you come back to Paz and build block house, Bella? You know the song, Bella?"

'Now I listening, because my mother had a board house when she used to work for them, the same board house that my grandmother used to have, and is only when I come back from Maturin in Venezuela I build a block house on the same spot. So I know Miss Mary know what she saying, and I ask her, "What song, Miss Mary?" And still she turning round on the stone so that I shout out, "Careful, Miss Mary. Miss Mary, you will fall in the river, you know."

'And she stop again, with those hands stretched out in the moonlight, and she look up at me to say, "The song about:

> *Those far-away places*
> *Where the strange calling names*
> *Far away, over the sea."*

And she giggling, but was a serious word she tell me there, you know. Was a song I grow up hearing. A song I used to hear in their house a lot, because boss-man was the only person in that area up there that had radio. Sometimes he used to play it loud enough, when the good mood take him, so people could hear it from the road down below.

> *"Those far-away places*

130

> *Where the strange calling names*
> *Far away, over the sea."*

'So I shout down to Miss Mary, yes, I know the song. And she stand up in earnest now, talking to me, looking up at me. "Well," she say to me, "look you go away and come back to build block house. I want to go to one of those places, Bella, those far-away places, where the strange calling names."

'And then Miss Mary throw back her head and laughing so much, all call I call her she wouldn't stop. It getting late and just us two woman in the moonlight there, you know, near the river. It didn't have anything much to be afraid of in those days, though, except for Miss Mary and those worthless boys who everybody know what they doing. I keep calling her to come on, come on out of the river. But eventually I just leave her there, balancing on the river stone in the moonlight and singing:

> *"Those far-away places*
> *Where the strange calling names*
> *Far away, over the sea."*

'Moonlight tonight, eh. And nowadays, no little children out there singing like in long-time days. Even not so long ago, the little ones would be out there singing. You know the song that go, "Tantie Mary, thread the needle"? Yes, that's right. That is it.

> *"Ring, ting, thread the needle.*
> *Thread the needle, let me see you*   ·
> *Ring, ting…"*

'Go and watch your moonlight, you hear, child. It don't look like *The Young and the Restless* coming on tonight. Look how after all these years I remember Miss Mary in the river – after all these years.'

She was coming from Paz City that morning. Her son Gellineau had sent her a barrel from New York, so she had spent the whole morning at the customs house, running up and down with forms, finding people to sign and answering this and that question before they could feel satisfied and let her carry away the few things the boy had taken his time to pack for her – a few dresses, some panties, half slips, toilet paper – the thick kind that would cost the earth if she had to buy it here – oatmeal, condensed milk, rice, sugar, some window curtains, things like that. She always told him not to worry, that the time he was taking to buy things and pack barrel, he might as well send her the money to buy the things here, but he had this idea that things were a lot cheaper in America, so it would be better to send a barrel. She wasn't so sure. There was so much up and down she had to do to get this barrel that she wasn't sure it made a lot of sense, but anyway, that was her morning. She asked Jemmot, the truck-driver living not far from her, to bring up the barrel for her when he finished his day. She cleared everything in the customs and gave him the paper to pick up the things so he wouldn't have any trouble and that was that, she could give a sigh of relief. Jemmot wouldn't take the whole amount for hire, because he would drop off the barrel on his way home. That was what she hoped, anyway, although with Jemmot you never know. So perhaps if you don't count her time and the help those fellars around the customs house give her to fill out the forms, without charging, and the fact that Jemmot won't take the whole amount as if is a real hire, perhaps it make sense, but she still not so sure, because you have to give everybody a little something out of barrel, because you can't be too selfish, but anyway, the boy heart good, so thank the Lord for that!

So now that set of foolishness was over, and she was on her way home, walking through Joie de Vivre and Beau Soleil, and thinking about how after one time is really another, even though there is nothing new under the sun.

It was when Hurricane Ivan visited them and did all that damage that she started to think seriously about what life was saying to them in this country. She was thinking how Ivan had stripped the hills bare, how the trees had bent down but some of them still didn't break, how the mountain ended up protecting the houses that had been built under it. So although people had enough to say about how old people planting and keeping bush and big tree around the place for generations, Hurricane Ivan came and explained in his rough way that they really needed the bush and the mountain, that those things were not just there wasting time, that, believe it or not, the bush and the big tree was serving a purpose.

And as that came to her mind, she was thinking that it would be such a pity if those who had land in the places around there – although they were now living in far country, in England and America and where not else, and were not really there to understand what is what – it would be such a pity if the dollar and the pound and other things tantalised them so much that they decided to sell land in order to get pounds and dollars, and that was possible, especially in these times when things so hard. Because, face it, although 'away' people act sometimes as if hard times don't touch them, life is life anywhere you living it, and hard times might put on a different face, but it not hard to recognise it when it pinching you and staring in your face. But sometimes, when people not there to see for them-

133

selves that land without house have a point, they could end up trying to make money off every little slip of land in the place, and not even realise that they clearing the way, making space for hurricane to enjoy itself and cause more destruction in the place when it decide to come again. In fact, not only those away, but those right around here self could end up making that decision, because hard times and the thing they call 'want more' hit everybody same way, no matter where they live.

But people away have a special problem. Even when you hearing on the news that hard times all over the world, that even rich America feeling a serious pinch, people coming back from New York wearing plenty pretty clothes, renting car and living nice, staying in hotel, and looking as if America is the only place in the world that hard times don't touch. What to do! That is how life is already. Things always better on the other side, even if they have to go back and cry over their credit card.

And all of a sudden, with these thoughts going through her mind, and the walk along that long road through Joie de Vivre and Beau Soleil feeling short because she thinking so much, she look up and realise that she was going round the corner in Beau Soleil, right by where she notice the week before that they cut down about six huge trees that must have been there since long before, when King Hatchet was only a little jookootoo hammer. As she was coming up to these trees, right at the corner by the old mill, she could see a woman with a parasol under each tree, about six of them line up like is a modelling competition. She stop, of course, because that was a strange sight. She didn't hear anything on the radio but it look like they were having some function right on the ground there, not so far from her house, and to think that she hadn't heard a word about it! The Old Mill, as they call that spot, is not a place you would expect to see something like this. This is a place where, long ago, they used to make sugar, so up to recently you had all the different vats in there for the molasses and so, and school teachers used to make trips to show children what it was like in slavery days, and even long afterwards, how they used to transfer the juice of the cane from one vat to the other in the process of making the sugar, and then how afterwards they had stopped making sugar and used to make rum, and the teachers would show the children where they put the cane into the chute, and explain how it was possible for people to get their arm dragged into the chute sometimes when they were pushing in the cane, and long-ago stories like that. Sometimes the teachers would even bring children to show them around the place where some farmers still plant cane for this selfsame mill. But those days gone, of course, the days of the mill and the sugar, that is – and even the rum – even though people still planting cane, so the mill just there now to make people remember. Up to a few years ago, when Mr De La Mothe was alive, the mill was working and producing rum with the same cane and using the same old vats, but then Mr De La Mothe died, people in different places bought different parts of the mill, and everything changed. There was just the old broken-down building there now, and the cane farmers trying to take their cane to a mill somewhere else before that one disappear too, so it stand to reason that the old mill here – the building – would be gone soon, because they have to clear it away to make room for – well, for the future, you could say, for new houses and business places and things of that sort.

She had heard that Mr Johnson's son in America – Mr. Johnson and the wife, Doux, the son that grow up right there – well, all of them grow up right there – just up the road there in Joie de Vivre, he and a lady in England bought some of this land around there and now he and the lady – she wasn't sure if they were working separately or together, but both of them had bought land right in this area, people said – were clearing it to build. As far as she had heard, Mr Johnson's son was putting down two establishments there – his house and a big business place. So that was why there was so much clearing going on, and so many old trees getting cut down, and a bulldozer had arrived to get the old mill out of the way.

But now what was this? It looked as if there was some kind of social thing going on, and it must be a modelling competition because the women were in that spot where they had cut down the trees, and they had these long umbrellas that looked like long-ago parasols. It was like a scene from that movie she had seen once in the cinema in town – *My Fair Lady*. She wondered how come she hadn't heard anybody in Beau Soleil talking about this event.

Last week, when she realised the silk cotton trees were gone, the hog plum trees gone, and even the mango trees get axe, she couldn't believe it. There used to be a bois canot tree just in front there, and two big Julie mango trees. She couldn't believe they were gone. At least they could have saved the Julie mango. Who in their right mind would cut down Julie mango trees? You know how many times those trees save her from serious hungry going home on an evening? And it was a real nice Julie. Somebody could at least have put in a good word for them and the bois canot. None of the people who bought land on the ground there were people born away. Yes, they had spent years in England and America, but that couldn't make them forget what mango tree is, and how good bois canot is on boundary line. Of course you could cut a bois canot tree when you had too many, but if you have one bois canot tree on your boundary line, you don't just cut it without reason.

Well, perhaps, she shouldn't think that way. Perhaps they had reason and her reason is not other people reason. So now it look like they were having modelling competition. She wondered who these women were. They looked like movie-star ladies. She couldn't see their faces, but those long dresses and the shape – that kind of bottle shape like Hollywood. And this man coming up the road now, she supposed he must be the director for the show. Perhaps it was something like long ago when people said they had filmed the movie, *Island in the Sun*, over there in Grenada and some of it even right here in Paz, but she hadn't heard anything about a movie. She wondered if they had come with their own stars or if any local people were involved.

He was coming toward her, a short man with a rolling kind of walk. For a moment she thought it was the man who used to live in the little board house opposite the mill. She looked up toward where the house used to be. There was nothing there now, of course. That house had been moved. The land was sold, she had heard, and the house moved somewhere else. The man who used to live there had been squatting, really, since he had no title to the land, and now that the old sugar mill was sold, he couldn't stay.

He was still walking toward her. He looked too local to be a big movie director. At first it looked as if he was coming to say something, but, as he moved closer, she realised he wasn't looking in her direction at all. He was walking with his head down. His face looked old, tired. He wore khaki shirt and pants. Somehow, it looked like a face she had seen before. She couldn't quite place it, though. He looked a bit like Mr Dorcas who used to be Mr De La Mothe's watchman when the sugar mill was still working. But he wasn't looking at her. Now he had turned his face right away from her, and was looking at the mill. Was it Mr Dorcas? But Dorcas knew her; he wouldn't keep his head turned like that when he must have seen her. No, he must be a bit shorter than Mr Dorcas. And anyway, Mr Dorcas was dead, wasn't he? Suddenly, she couldn't be sure. He had gone away a long time, to another part of Paz. She believed she had heard he was living somewhere in Beausejour. But had he died?

She couldn't remember. He was muttering as he passed her, but she heard clearly:

> 'They cut me down'

And then:

> 'I have no crown
> I don't live in country
> I don't live in town
> They cut me down
> I have no place that is home.
> You see?
> They cut me down.'

He went past, still muttering, not looking at her. She turned her head as he went by, shivered. She turned back and, slowly, started moving forward again. She wasn't sure how long it was before she realised that although her feet were moving, she wasn't really advancing, not going anywhere along the road. Slowly, as if moving under water, she turned around and saw the man now leaving the road. He turned right to go down through the track as he went past the mill. She could hear his words even more clearly than when he was walking past her.

> 'I don't live in country
> I don't live in town
> They cut me down.'

She waited in a kind of daze, watching for him to appear just under the road where the track continued. People always used that track, and, once they left the road, after they went past the trees, you could see them appear again under the road, cutting across there to come out on the other side, by the other silk cotton tree in the distance. She was still trying to figure out who he was. She waited, and there was no sight of him. Where had he gone?

Still with that under-water feeling, she turned back to

look at the women. It seemed they hadn't moved. They were there, in the same spot, backs to her, holding the pose. Then something changed in the afternoon air. Or it must have been that she became more aware of her surroundings. She wondered why no cars were coming, not from up Joie de Vivre side, nor from lower down Beau Soleil. It was as if time had stopped at this spot near the old mill. She tried to move her legs to walk again, and abruptly remembered what she must have forgotten, although it had happened just a moment ago. She was walking but not moving, not advancing. As she started to move her feet again, she saw the man walking towards her, just as he had been walking towards her moments before, with the women outlined in the background. Then, perhaps because they made some slight movement, she saw them all more clearly – six women, all similarly dressed. Long blue and white dresses, with wide-brimmed straw hats perched on the left side of their heads.

Suddenly released from the under-water feeling, she made the sign of the cross and started moving backwards, away from the man coming toward her. As she moved back, his pace increased. He was walking faster, muttering, 'They cut me down!' Now he looked as if *he* was moving under-water, quickly but not quickly. The women's hands started moving upwards, each woman pulling the dress up along her left leg, as if in rhythm to the man's chanting.

She turned, unable to scream, running back past the spot where the man had turned right down the track, past the standpipe, toward the house on the corner. Around her now was a definite chant – women's voices crooning and a man's deep bass.

> 'You see?
> They cut me down
> I have no crown
> I don't live in country
> I don't live in town

They cut me down
And now I have no home
I don't live in country
I don't live in town
They cut me down.'

She ran, the voice choked inside her, the chant consuming her, echoing inside her head.

She counted, one, two, three, one, two, three, one, two three. She made the sign of the cross three times. Past the standpipe, she turned right, flew past the mango tree in the yard, up the gap to Emelda's house. She ran up the steps, pounded on the door.

'Emelda! Emelda! Open the door.'

'Jewel? What happen? What wrong?'

She fell through the doorway, past a startled Emelda, and collapsed on the seat just inside the door. She turned, lifted the curtain. She saw nothing outside.

'Lajabless,' she stuttered. 'Lajabless down the road by the mill.'

Emelda sat down on a red, patterned chair opposite.

'You see it too? Since they cut down the trees, people seeing all kinds of things down there.'

Emelda made the sign of the cross.

'Big bright evening so? How I will go home?'

'Is okay. When the others come home, we will walk down with you. People have to walk together round here nowadays. They don't come out when people walking together. Is like long time when the land was restless. You remember revolution time in Grenada, before nineteen eighty-three and all that confusion, before all those people get killed on the fort and then they had the US invasion? Remember we used to see all kind of thing over here in Paz that time? That is the kind of time we're having again.'

'Mr Dorcas that used to be watchman at the sugar mill, he die, not so?' Jewel asked her friend.

140

'Yes; you see him, too? Plenty people say they see him recently.'

'Oh my God, yes. So was him in truth? He walk right near to me. And I suppose that…!' Now she knew what she had recognised in his face. It was the familiar absence that she saw all the time on the faces of the dead at the funeral home. Her father had looked like that. He had features she had known, and she was not afraid, but she remembered how his face when she touched it in death was leathery, lifeless, features she knew, but features not now connected with the living person. It had been clear to her that she was looking only at a container. The real person was gone and the leather left was empty of anything but the power to make her remember.

She could see Emelda's mouth moving but she could no longer hear what her friend was saying. She was thinking that she had seen all of that performance before. She wasn't sure if she had dreamed it but she had seen it once, long ago, before it happened.

HE BRINGS HER WARMTH

She fingers the thick sheet on the bed. Always, he brings her something. When it's just a visit for the week, or for the month, he brings bread, juice, fruit. Once, he used to bring oranges, but she told him the acid wasn't good for her stomach, and now he brings watermelon. Always, he brings bananas, because he knows she likes to have them with her oatmeal. For birthdays and Christmas and New Year, he brings something warm. Last September, he brought this sheet, thick enough to warm her body when the real cold started. The year before that, he brought her this little blanket that she covers her feet with in times like this, when the winter comes and it's snowing outside.

She hears his voice in the living room and wonders if he let himself in with his key, because, as far as she knows, Sarah is not yet home. Sarah is never at home, always running here, there and everywhere with those two children, dropping them off, picking them up, and, if not that, at work doing something. Sarah doesn't seem to remember she is alive, she thinks sometimes. And even when she's at home, she's resting, forever resting, or cooking, or doing whatever it is she does. When she thinks of how hard she worked with her children, how hard her own mother worked to map a way of life for herself, she wonders if these children think *they* are the beginning, if they know the sacrifices…

'Ma?'

This one, her son, he knows. He always brings something to warm her body.

'Ma?'

'Yes, I hear you. I'm down here. Come down, non?'

'OK. I'll be down in a minute.'

'Sarah up there?'

'No, I just getting something to eat up here. Be down in a minute. I see Sarah cooked and left food.'

One good thing, they get on well with each other, all her children.

He sits on the bed and hugs her, kisses her on the cheek. Sarah never does that, as if she doesn't want to be near her, as if there is something eating at her, that child. She stays upstairs there in her place as if it's a trouble to visit, even just down the stairs. It wasn't like this before, when Sarah was up here in America and she was down there in Paz. They could see eye to eye then, but from the time Sarah brought her up here, she could feel the change. And it's not as if she interferes. She could see that Sarah wasn't going the right way with these children, yes, letting them do just what they want, but she tries her best not to say anything. Only when water more than flour, when the children look right in her eyes and you have to ask them to say good morning, only then she might say something to Sarah, but usually, she makes sure not to interfere. She might shout at the children now and then, to make them have some respect, to pull them away from this constant television, but nothing much. So what else? Why Sarah should be so sour she has no idea. One thing, though, thank the Lord for small mercies, Sarah gets her everything she needs, and she cooks for her every day, but what a sour face!

He lifts her foot and presses a finger into the flesh around the ankles. 'The foot doesn't look too bad today?'

'No. Sarah took me to her doctor and he changed the medication. He told me to keep the feet up, and that is really helping.'

'Yes,' he agrees. 'You can see the difference.'

He says, 'I will be here next week, to spend Christmas day. Sarah will cook. But I know they said we're expecting snow this week, and you said it is cold here sometimes, so I brought you your Christmas gift.' He pulls something out of a big packet. 'An electric blanket,' he explains. He plugs it in and spreads it over her from the waist down. In a few minutes, he tells her, she will feel the difference. He turns on the television, and watches for a few moments one of those games in which men are pushing each other every which way.

'What kind of enjoyment they get out of that?' she asks.

'It's football,' he explains. 'American football.'

After a while, she says, 'Yes, I feel it. It's warm!'

'Good,' he says. 'Use it, you know, when you start to feel cold.'

It means electricity, she thinks, but she doesn't say anything. Sarah wouldn't mind, anyway. Though she talks about money sometimes, she would be pleased to know she is comfortable.

'What about Junior?' she asks him.

'Jericho? He's okay. He's enjoying Paz. He doesn't call himself Junior any more. He is claiming my name – and his – Jericho. These children who grow up outside of Paz claim the country easier than us. That's where he wants to be. He's doing all right.'

He has brought her groceries, too. 'I have some watermelon for you,' he says, 'and some bananas and pawpaw. I put the bag on your kitchen table there. I will cut up the watermelon and put it in your fridge for you. That is all right? You need anything else?'

No, she doesn't need anything else. 'I'm grateful for you, son,' she says. 'Sometimes I look at you and I say I know you didn't learn to take care of your family like that from your father. Wherever you learn, I'm grateful you learn.'

He says, 'Daddy wasn't that bad, you know, Ma. He met a different life, and…'

She says, 'He met a different life, and he didn't know what it was to honour his wife.'

He says nothing.

'Wherever you learn,' she says, 'I'm glad you learn. I'm proud to see how you act with your son and with your daughter. It do me heart good.'

He goes to the door and looks through the peephole. 'It's snowing outside,' he says. 'It's warm in here, but it's snowing outside.'

She looks back to see if she might catch a glimpse of the grass or the snow, but the shades are down over the tiny basement window, and she can't see anything outside. It's all right, though. Thanks mainly to him, it's warm inside. He always brings her warmth.

His father, now... his father...

When he visits her at night, it is as it always was. They are going somewhere and he stands near the car outside by the guava tree, waiting, or she is in the kitchen and he sits in the dining room nearby, looking through the window at the golden-apple tree and the mango trees on the hill. The last time he visited, he disappeared somewhere in the house, and she kept calling for him. He wouldn't answer but she knew he heard her. It was the house at Joie de Vivre before the children made changes to it, with the big living room that used to be the whole boucan – before they had cut the bedroom from it – directly opposite her, the dining room on her left-hand side when she sat in the living room, and their bedroom on the left, next to the dining room. She knew he wasn't in the kitchen, which was on the far side, through the dining room, although even there he would be able to hear her. Of course, he could have gone out through the bedroom and be sitting there in the bathroom, where he often went to spend holidays, but even there he would be able to hear her. She kept calling, and eventually he came.

She had no idea what door he came through, but all of a sudden he was there, looking at her. She seemed to remember that he wore faded blue and white pajamas. He didn't say anything, just stood looking at her with that long face of his all serious, as if he were asking, *So what you calling me for?* As if he were impatient and waiting to hear what she wanted.

So nothing had changed. He used to do that long ago, not

answer when she called and then just appear to stand there, looking at her, and waiting for her to say something. Life as usual was what it felt like.

She woke then, and woke laughing, as if it were a joke. It took her a moment to realise what had happened. She stretched out her hand to turn on the lamp on the bedside table, because of course it was night and night in this basement room was more night than ever. For a moment she couldn't remember where she was – Brooklyn or Boston, with Sarah or with Jericho or with Carl. She fumbled as she tried to find the lamp switch on the nightstand, and the picture frame with her grandchildren leaned to one side. She straightened it. She turned on the light and asked out loud, 'So where you going? I not calling you at all, so don't imagine I calling you. Stay on your side over there! Don't find a reason to come and visit me! I'm not calling you.'

She looked at the clock. It was twelve-fifteen. She leaned over and picked up the flashlight from the floor near her bed, felt around to find the church calendar, peered at it. She just wanted to make sure. Yes, it was Wednesday March 11, 2009, so today would be thirteen years since Jeremiah died. So that's why he woke her. Last night, Trudy, Jericho's wife, said she was making a mass in the church right there in Brooklyn for him, and she and Jericho and the three children would be going. That's why she was thinking about Brooklyn. She had talked to Trudy on the phone. Trudy wanted to know if she would go too, up there in Boston, if her knees felt up to it, or if Sarah was making a mass. Trudy was like that. She wouldn't forget. Not like Sarah, who might remember or might not. And anyway, Sarah was in church one minute, not there at all the next, and not even sure which church she was following, or if she was following one.

Jeremiah had appeared as soon as the day started. Well,

whatever he had to say, he'd better realise this was her territory now and that he was settled in another place. And what did he mean by coming all the way here to Boston to visit her? She didn't like Boston, a cold, cold place. Brooklyn, now, Brooklyn was good. Everything was right around. Even though her knees weren't as they used to be, she could take her time and walk with the stick – or with the cane, as they say – out there to the church, out to the shop on the corner to get a little deodorant or a pair of stockings. Nothing was far away in Brooklyn, and somebody from home was always dropping in to say hello. Maisie's grand-children had come to see her, Carl's little girl – well, not little girl now – was starting college and her friends always dropped in to say hi. In Brooklyn she could see her people. Here in Boston with Sarah, she didn't see anybody. If she wanted something, she had to wait until Sarah was going out and go with her. And Sarah was always busy. She definitely didn't like Boston. Brooklyn was like home. You could meet people all the time without bothering anybody. The neighbour on the other side of Jericho and Trudy, when they lived in Brooklyn, was from the Dominican Republic or somewhere like that, and that neighbour's wife was from St Vincent. Not her own Paz people, but still not too strange. So that was good. She had spent her life in Paz, up there in Joie de Vivre, because of Jeremiah – Jeremiah and his fascination with land – and she had no intention of going back there if she could help it. But here he was, acting as if he had only come because she called. *Let me make it clear; I'm not calling you, okay?*

She moved, turned so she could ease her legs over the side of the bed. *These knees*, she sighed. She had to put her feet down on the floor and wait for a while, so that the brain would catch up and realise the feet were there and wanting to move. She put her hands down on the bed and tried easing herself up. She put one hand up to the dressing table

148

and pushed, taking purchase so that the table could help make the knees realise she needed their support to stand. 'Yes, Sweetie,' she said out loud, 'after one time is another. Once upon a time, you moving vroop vrap all over the place, running from stem to stern; now, look at you! Ah, Papa God, you know the reason.'

That's what he used to call her, Sweetie. Doux, he said, means sweet. That's what he called her in the beginning, and even afterwards, when things weren't so sweet between them again, the name stayed. Doux stood up, waited again for the brain to catch up and tell the feet it was alright to move, then she put one hand on the walker, shuffled two steps forward, reached with her left hand for the overhead light. She needed as much light as possible in the place to make Jeremiah realise that she was on one side and he on the other. Her hand fell away from the light switch and she muttered again, 'I didn't send to call you, so keep your side!'

She supposed things were good, in a way, in these dark underground apartments in Brooklyn and Boston. What to do! You reach a stage where the choice is not really yours, and you have to say please and thanks for the piece of food. When she was with Sarah in Boston, she had her own kitchen, her own bathroom, food put on the table for her every day. True, sometimes Sarah was running too much to remember to buy bananas or apples or something in the supermarket, but then Jericho would remember to stop by with some shopping. But they don't have time for you, these children. Sometimes, if she didn't make strong eye and say she wanted to go somewhere, they would be rushing to work, to the supermarket and to wherever else all the time and forget that even old clothes need to air out sometimes.

Doux flushed the toilet and looked toward the sound of water rushing down the bowl. She straightened her clothes, shuffled two steps to the sink, let the water run over her hands. One thing she could say for Jeremiah, much as he liked the ladies, it was always people his age he was after, not the nastiness on the television now, with big men running after little children. Thank God that wasn't his style. The television is company, but sometimes, she thought, if you take it on, you live in fear all the time. She wondered if the world as bad as the television saying?

She put her hand on the walker, eased out of the bathroom door, turned for a moment to look to her left. She shuffled a few steps past her door on the right and the door of the washroom on her left, leaned forward over the walker and looked up the stairs. No light. The ladies upstairs must be in bed. They had remembered to turn off the light tonight. Always talking about expenses and yet always forgetting to turn that light off! This modern generation, they knew nothing about expense and about trouble. Working, she was sure, for more than she could ever have dreamed of making, in those days when she was working for Mr. Peter and his mother the devil, and still they never had money. *It's not my fault, though. I teach them all I know about how to spin things out and make what they have work. What they learn about wasting, they learn somewhere else. Not my fault at all.* She paused, listening, suddenly wondering if they were even there. Suppose they had... but would Sarah have gone out and left the little girls upstairs alone? Had she taken the twins out, perhaps, to some sort of get-together at their friends or something like that? *I tell you, you kill out your soul working for these children, and then they take their life and speed off with it, like you had nothing at all to do with it. After all, I'm not dead yet. They could tell me what they doing. If the car isn't in the garage, that could mean...*

Doux turned the walker, limping with the turn, listening and waiting as her knees became accustomed to the movement. Every time she stopped for a while, those knees would freeze up on her. She moved toward the door, going past the dining table, the refrigerator on her left. She put up her hand and touched the doorknob. She pulled. It was difficult to open the door these days. Sarah said it was because it was raining so much this March. Not usual, but that was it. The seasons were getting completely messed up, Sarah said. Global warming, or how they say the thing. The door, Sarah said, was swollen, so that it didn't open easily. *What foolishness is this? So I'm a prisoner inside here, then?* Doux pulled again. She couldn't take purchase properly, didn't have the strength to get a good grip. Frustration with her situation made her stronger. She tugged and the door…

She jumped, fumbling with the walker. Behind her, there was a shrill noise. The alarm! In this place, you couldn't even open the door without… The thing could make your nerves give out completely. She didn't know it was…

She could hear the feet pounding, coming down the stairs. She stood there, caught by alarm and pounding feet.

'Mom, what is it? There's a problem? What happened?'

'I…'

'Did you open the door? Why did you open the door?'

'Yes. I opened the door.'

'Cara, go and turn off the alarm. Put in the numbers.'

'Grandma, you opened the door?'

'Go! Kandia, turn off the alarm.'

The children go.

She could see them clearly. It was strange. Sometimes she could see things clearly. And hear well enough to know that Sarah didn't really believe that her sight and her hearing were as bad as she said they were.

Both Cara and Kandia were wearing pink and green pajamas. A pink top, green shorts with pink dots. They were stylish, these ladies. They turned off the alarm and Cara came quickly back down the stairs. Doux was pushing her walker toward the room.

Cara asked, 'Grandma, why did you open the door?'

That child talks as if she is in charge, as if I have to explain everything to her. Young people nowadays just don't know their place. If I tell that child how much life I see already!

'Cara, leave it alone.'

'Grandma…'

'Cara!'

'Sorry, Mom.'

'What happened, Mammie? Everything alright?'

Should she say she'd wanted to see if the car was there? Sarah would take offence.

'Yes, it was a little hot in here, so I was just opening the door for a while…'

'To get some breeze?'

'Grandma! The alarm…'

'Cara! It's all right, Mammie. You didn't know the alarm was on. I didn't realise it was so hot down here? I don't think it's that hot. You feeling hot?'

'It's not hot, Grandma.'

'So I can't open this door? I didn't realise the alarm was on. I didn't know you put this thing on so that I can't even open the door. I usually go out early and take a walk, so…'

It was true. It wasn't walk time, though. Still, early in the morning, she would push the walker out through the garage and around the cul-de-sac. A person needed some exercise in this place. You were locked inside the house day in, day out, you and the television. Sometimes she would even walk upstairs, but not much these days. It was too much trouble to drag herself up the stairs, even holding on to the banister, and, anyway, in her own little corner down here she didn't have to bother anybody.

'It's around one o'clock in the morning, Mammie, even earlier than that, not twelve-thirty yet. I usually take off the alarm about six, and I know you don't usually go out there until after six.'

'Well…'

'It's alright, Mammie. Not to worry. You couldn't know the alarm was on.'

She couldn't.

'Goodnight, Grandma.'

'Goodnight, Mammie. The alarm will be off before six. You could walk outside after six without a problem. Come. Let us see you go back to the room.'

They walked with her to the door, waited while she got into bed, turned off the light.

'*I'll* turn off this one on the table.'

They said 'Goodnight', pulled the door behind them, and walked away upstairs.

Doux lay there looking up at the shades over the basement window. Beyond that, across the lawn, was the garden. She wished the basement had a window that she could look through. True, it wouldn't be the bouganvillea back home in Joie de Vivre, not something she could pull down to trim the branches, but at least she would be able to see something. To tell the truth, though, she couldn't say that she missed Joie de Vivre. Every time she thought about that place, what she remembered most was work, not relaxation. It was his choice to live in that place behind God back, not hers. Still, it would be nice to be able to work in the garden. Even if she walked upstairs, though, it wasn't easy to move over that bumpy ground up there. Even if she were in Joie de Vivre, the time for working in the garden outside was probably gone. Eighty-nine she would be this year, so those days were over. She wasn't longing for them; she had worked enough in her life. She was content now to do nothing and wait to be given a piece of food – except for when her grandchildren wanted some fry bakes, or saltfish souse, or something like that. She liked to make those things for the children. But they didn't really have time to take her on these days, only every so often…

Doux closed her eyes, drifting back into sleep. He didn't wait for her to call out to him this time. He appeared immediately. He was outside, standing on the other side of a stream of clear water running between them. He was pointing down at the stream, showing her where to cross. But she stayed on her side looking at him, thinking to herself, *You better keep yourself quiet. Since when you so anxious for my company? I will come when I'm good and ready.*

Merle Collins was born in Aruba to Grenadian parents who returned to Grenada soon after her birth. She had her primary and secondary education in St George's, Grenada. In 1972, she graduated from the University of the West Indies, Mona, Jamaica, with a degree in English and Spanish. She then returned to Grenada, where she taught English and Spanish. She has also taught in St Lucia. In 1980 she graduated from Georgetown University, USA, with a Masters in Latin American Studies. She was involved in the Grenadian revolution and served as a Coordinator for Research on Latin America and the Caribbean. She left Grenada in 1983. In 1990, she graduated from the London School of Economics with a Ph.D. in Government.

Her first collection of poetry, *Because the Dawn Breaks*, was published by Karia Press in 1985. At this time she was a member of African Dawn, a performance group combining poetry, mime and African music. In 1987, she published her first novel, *Angel*, which follows the lives of both Angel and the Grenadian people as they struggle for independence. This was followed by a collection of short stories, *Rain Darling*, in 1990 and a second collection of poetry, *Rotten Pomerack*, in 1992. Her second novel, *The Colour of Forgetting*, was published in 1995, and a further collection of poetry, *Lady in a Boat*, in 2003.

She currently teaches Caribbean Literature at the University of Maryland. Her critical works include 'Themes and Trends in Caribbean Writing Today' in *From My Guy to Sci-Fi: Genre and Women's Writing in the Postmodern World*; 'To Be Free is Very Sweet' in *Slavery and Abolition*; and 'Are you a Bolshevik or a Menshevik?: Mimicry, Alienation and Confusion in the Grenada Revolution', in *Interventions*.

Lady in a Boat
ISBN: 9781900715850; pp. 84; pub. October 2003; Price: £7.99

In poems that express an oblique and resonant disquiet ('people dream of a lady/ in a boat, dressed in red/ petticoat, adrift and weeping') and a sequence that addresses memories of the death of the Grenadian revolution, too painful to confront until now, Merle Collins writes of a Caribbean adrift, amnesiac and in danger of nihilistic despair. But she also achieves a life-enhancing and consoling perspective on those griefs. She does this by revisiting the hopes and humanities of the people involved, recreating them in all their concrete particularity, or by speaking through the voice of an eighty-year-old woman 'making miracle/ with little money because turn hand is life lesson', and in writing poems that celebrate love, the world of children and the splendours of Caribbean nature. Her poems take the 'new dead ancestors back to/ mountain to feed the fountain/ of dreams again'.

Angel
ISBN: 9781845231859; pp. 320; pub. June 2011; price: £12.99

First published to great acclaim in 1987, Merle Collins' novel covers the years in Grenada from 1951 when the workers revolted against the power of the white owners of the sugar and cocoa estates, to 1983 when the Americans invaded to put an end to a radical experiment that turned violently in on itself. At the heart of these events are Angel, headstrong, self-assured, looking for personal as well as national liberation, and her mother Doodsie, who greets the overthrow of the old, corrupted leadership with as much enthusiasm as her daughter.

When the populist Chief and the vanguardist ideologues of the Horizon movement start to fall out, Doodsie knows instinctively where she stands, but Angel is altogether more conflicted about the rights and wrongs of the situation.

What makes *Angel* such a rewarding novel is the seamless movement between the warmth and tensions of the family life it portrays and the seriousness with which it deals with the political conflicts that tear long-term relationships apart, provoke fratricidal killings and provide the excuse for an outrageous breach of sovereignty.

In this new edition of *Angel*, Merle Collins seizes the opportunity to revise and expand the last part of the novel, not to arrive at different conclusions, but to deal with episodes that at the time of the novel's first writing, proved too raw to deal with as effectively as she wished.

Robert Nye in *The Guardian*, praised *Angel* for "...a richness, a thickness, a stinging slangy that-there thingyness of observation and detail..."

SWAY

SWAY

The Irresistible Pull of Irrational Behaviour

Ori Brafman and Rom Brafman

Published by Virgin Books 2009

2 4 6 8 10 9 7 5 3 1

First published in the United States by Doubleday, an imprint of The Doubleday
Publishing Group, a division of Random House, Inc., New York

Book design by Chris Welch

First published in Great Britain in 2009 by
Virgin Books
Random House, 20 Vauxhall Bridge Road,
London SW1V 2SA

www.virginbooks.com
www.rbooks.co.uk

Addresses for companies within The Random House Group Limited can be found at:
www.randomhouse.co.uk/offices.htm

The Random House Group Limited Reg. No. 954009

A CIP catalogue record for this book
is available from the British Library

ISBN 9780753516829

The Random House Group Limited supports The Forest Stewardship Council [FSC], the
leading international forest certification organisation. All our titles that are printed on
Greenpeace approved FSC certified paper carry the FSC logo.
Our paper procurement policy can be found at www.rbooks.co.uk/environment

Printed in Great Britain by CPI Bookmarque, Croydon, CR0 4TD

TO NIRA,

FOR ALWAYS BELIEVING IN US

Contents

Contents

Contents

SWAY

Preface

A little house on the Tel Aviv prairie.

Asbestos and open-heart surgery.

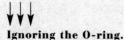

Ignoring the O-ring.

Diagnosing the wrong patient.

Where psychology and business collide.

When we were growing up, our mother had two idols she hoped we would try to emulate. The first—and there was really no competition there—was Laura Ingalls of *Little House on the Prairie* fame. In our mom's eyes, she was the picture of perfection. We'd talk back to our mom, and she'd sternly ask, "Would Laura Ingalls ever talk that way?" We'd forget to do our homework, leave dirty dishes in the sink, or generally cause trouble, and Laura Ingalls would travel from the nineteenth-century American prairie to 1980s Tel Aviv and admonish us to get with the program.

The second heroic figure was our mom's cousin Reli, a hotshot lawyer who was valedictorian at Harvard Law. In our eyes, too, Reli could walk on water.

Although Ori thought about law school when he was in

eleventh grade, neither one of us took up a legal career. But if you count Reli in, we form the Jewish mother's equivalent of the holy trinity: Reli, the lawyer; Rom, the psychologist (we'll call him a doctor); and Ori, the businessman.

In a way, this book was born from our different paths in life. While Rom was completing his PhD in psychology, Ori was getting his MBA. On day one of business school, expecting to find himself immersed in a sea of finance, economics, and accounting, Ori realized in his first class, with Professor Roberto Fernandez, that this would be no tranquil sea. Fernandez had a voice that could project from here to the moon. He had that larger-than-life aura about him that made you sit on the edge of your seat. "I have some news for you," he told the class of eager MBA students that first day. "People aren't rational." And with that, Fernandez turned on a grainy film, shot in the 1950s, of open-heart surgery. "See that white stuff they're pouring over the guy's heart?" Fernandez narrated. "It's asbestos." People gasped, unsure of how to react.

"I'm serious," he boomed. "Unsurprisingly, the patients administered the asbestos started dying off." But the hospital had continued with the procedure. How often, Fernandez asked the class, do we turn a blind eye to objective information?

Then he shifted gears and passed around copies of a table featuring mechanical engineering data about a synthetic rubber seal called an O-ring. "Take a look at this chart," he said. "It represents the likelihood of a mechanical failure as temperatures drop." The data showed that at around 32°F, the O-ring would lose its pliability and malfunction. None of the students knew where this was going.

It turned out that the O-ring in question was part of the design of the Space Shuttle *Challenger*. The night before the launch, engineers from the company that had built the O-ring recommended that the launch be delayed because they did not have conclusive proof that it would hold up in the cold weather predicted for the next day. Despite their concerns, however, management decided to proceed with the launch.

As Ori's class listened, mesmerized, Fernandez launched into similar stories of irrational behavior: movie executives bullied into hiring an actress who was obviously wrong for the part, a manufacturer that knowingly produced airplane brakes that caught fire, and more.

Fernandez's point was that although most of us think of ourselves as rational, we're much more prone to irrational behavior than we realize. It was a point that stayed with Ori long after business school, and it made us realize that our future professions had a lot more in common than we might originally have thought. Fernandez became a regular part of our vocabulary. Referring to someone who was obviously acting irrationally, we'd say: "This is a total Fernandez situation." And we found such situations everywhere we looked: in our own lives, in stories we read about the missteps of Fortune 500 companies, and in the actions of politicians.

Meanwhile, while we never quite lived up to the Laura Ingalls standard, as fate would have it, we did both become writers. The true genesis for this book came after a dinner conversation Ori had with a doctor who had been practicing obstetrics for the better part of thirty years. Dr. Jenkins possessed all the qualities you'd hope for in an OB/GYN—he was patient, he listened, he was smart, and most of all, he was experienced. You could count on him to make the right decision.

The conversation drifted to group dynamics and how emotions play a major role in decision making. Without thinking, Ori said, "I'm sure it's very different in your profession, where you're all scientists."

The doctor's face took on a serious expression as he explained that doctors are by no means immune to irrational forces. And because lives are on the line, the repercussions of irrational behavior can be devastating.

Take what happened to ER doctor Brian Hastings, who shared a story of how irrational behavior can derail even the most professional of physicians.

A few weeks earlier a woman had arrived at the emergency room in a panic. Her two-year-old daughter, Amy, she said, was experiencing severe stomach pains. Abdominal pains might signal a condition as benign as indigestion, but the woman was worried it might be something more serious. Normally, doctors would start running tests and evaluating Amy's symptoms.

Dr. Hastings paused in his story and quickly enumerated a litany of procedures the ER physicians could have performed. Rather than focusing on Amy, however, the doctors focused their attention on her mother: she was flustered and anxious and appeared overly concerned—basically, she seemed to be the type of parent who'd overreact. The physicians made a judgment call to send Amy home.

The very next day Amy and her mom were back in the emergency room. Physicians know that when treating toddlers it's absolutely vital to listen to their parents, who usually have an acute sense of when something is wrong with their child. But at the same time, the doctors now had even more evidence that Amy's mom was overreacting: here she was again at the hospital, showing all the signs that she was the kind of hypochondriac they refer to as a "frequent flyer." Once more the doctors sent Amy home without running any tests.

The third day started out pretty much the same way as the previous two. Amy and her mother returned; the doctors became even more convinced that the mother was overreacting. It was only when Amy lost consciousness that the doctors realized something was terribly wrong. But by then it was too late. Dr. Hastings shook his head as he recalled, "We lost her."

Had they considered the situation fully, the ER doctors would have recognized the need to keep Amy under observation. But instead they ignored the warning signs and repeatedly sent the toddler home. The moment the physicians labeled Amy's mom a "frequent flyer," they fell under the spell of an irrational force we call the *diagnosis bias*—in other words, the moment we label a person or a situation, we put on blinders to all evidence that contradicts our diagnosis.

Why would these skilled and experienced physicians make a choice that contradicted their years of training and ultimately cost the life of a child? We wanted to understand what was going on in this situation and the countless others in which people are swayed from the logical path.

What psychological forces underlie our own irrational behaviors? How do these forces creep up on us? When are we most vulnerable to them? How do they affect our careers? How do they shape our business and personal relationships? When do they put our finances, or even our lives, at risk? And why don't we realize when we're getting swayed?

In this book we'll explore several of the psychological forces that derail rational thinking. Wherever we looked—across different sectors, countries, and cultures—we saw different people being swayed in very similar ways. We're all susceptible to the sway of irrational behaviors. But by better understanding the seductive pull of these forces, we'll be less likely to fall victim to them in the future.

Chapter 1

ANATOMY of an ACCIDENT

Taking off at Tenerife.

The oversensitive egg shoppers.

The lure of the flat rate.

Would you like insurance with that?

So long, Martha's Vineyard.

The passengers aboard KLM Flight 4805 didn't know it, but they were in the hands of one of the most experienced and accomplished pilots in the world. Captain Jacob Van Zanten didn't just have a knack for flying. His attention to detail, methodical approach, and spotless record made him a natural choice to head KLM's safety program. It was no surprise, then, that the airline was keen to show him off. One magazine ad featuring the smiling captain captured it all: "KLM: from the people who made punctuality possible." Even seasoned pilots—not exactly the type of individuals prone to swoon—regarded him as something of a celebrity.

On the flight deck of the 747, en route from Amsterdam to Las Palmas Airport in the Canary Islands, Van Zanten must have felt a sense of pride. Today's trip was moving along with the smooth precision that had become his hall-mark. The schedule was straightforward: land in Las Palmas, refuel, and transport a new set of passengers back home to Holland.

But then Van Zanten got an urgent message from air-traffic control. A terrorist bomb had exploded at the airport flower shop, causing massive chaos on the ground; Las Palmas would be closed until further notice.

The captain knew that at times like this the most important thing was to remain calm and proceed with caution. He had performed drills preparing for this kind of situation countless times. In fact, Van Zanten had just returned from leading a six-month safety course on how to react in exactly this kind of situation.

Following standard procedure, the captain obeyed orders to land fifty nautical miles from his original destination, on the island of Tenerife. There, at 1:10 p.m., his plane joined several others that had been similarly diverted.

Now, you don't need to be a seasoned airline pilot to appreciate that Tenerife was no JFK. It was a tiny airport, with a single runway not meant to support jumbo jets.

With his plane safely parked at the edge of the runway, the captain checked his watch. Seeing the time, he was struck with a worrisome thought: the mandated rest period.

The Dutch government had recently instituted strict, complicated rules to which every pilot had to adhere. After getting in touch with HQ and performing some quick calculations, Van Zanten figured the latest he could take off was 6:30 p.m.

Flying after the start of his mandated rest period was out of the question—it wasn't just against policy; it was a crime punishable by imprisonment. But taking the rest period would open its own can of worms. Here in Tenerife there would be no replacement crew to take over. Hundreds of passengers would be stranded overnight. That would mean the airline would have to find them a place to stay, and there weren't enough hotel rooms on the island. In addition, a delay here would initiate a cascade of flight cancellations throughout KLM. A seemingly minor diversion could easily become a logistical nightmare.

It's easy to imagine the stress that Van Zanten was experiencing and why he became so determined to save time. It was like being stuck at a red light when you're late for a big meeting. Try as you might to stay calm, you know that your reputation is on the line; your frustration grows, and there's really not much you can do. But there was one thing Van Zanten *could* do: the captain decided to keep the passengers on board, so that when Las Palmas reopened, he could get back in the air immediately.

But the air-traffic control personnel who worked at Tenerife tower were of a different mind-set. Here was a small airport on a tropical island, now inundated with planes from all over the world that had been diverted because of the Las Palmas explosion. Not only was the tower understaffed, but the air-traffic controllers were in no hurry to get planes out of the gate; they were, in fact, getting ready to listen to a live soccer match on their transistor radios. Twenty minutes after landing, Van Zanten received word from the tower that he should let his passengers off: it looked like they would be here for a while.

From there, events at Tenerife continued to move forward like molasses. Twenty minutes turned into an hour. The captain spent every moment thinking of ways to minimize the delay. He held a strategy session with his crew. He called KLM headquarters to find out exactly how much time he had left before the mandated rest period kicked in. An hour on the ground had turned into two; then the captain came up with another idea. He decided to refuel at Tenerife and thus shave half an hour off the turnaround in Las Palmas.

But this time-saving idea backfired. As soon as Van Zanten started refueling, word came from Las Palmas that the airport had finally reopened. But it was too late to stop the thirty-five-minute refueling process.

Finally, just when it looked like the plane was set to go, nature threw its own wrench into the plan: a thick layer of fog descended upon the runway.

Kicking himself over his decision to refuel, Van Zanten became even more intent on getting under way. With the fog growing thicker, visibility dropped to just 300 meters—so poor that gazing out the cockpit window the captain couldn't see the end of the runway.

Van Zanten knew that every moment the fog got worse made it that much likelier that the Tenerife tower would shut down the airport. He saw that his window of opportunity to get out of Tenerife before an overnight stay was closing. It was now or never—time to go.

But what the captain did next was completely out of character. Van Zanten revved up the engines, and the plane lurched down the runway.

"Wait a minute," Van Zanten's copilot said in confusion. "We don't have ATC clearance."

"I know that," replied the captain as he hit the brakes. "Go ahead and ask."

The copilot got on the radio and received *airway* clearance—approval of the flight plan. But the tower said nothing about the vital *takeoff* clearance. And yet, determined to take off, Van Zanten turned the throttles to full power and roared down the foggy runway.

The jumbo jet was gaining momentum when, seemingly out of nowhere, the scariest sight Van Zanten could have imagined appeared before him. A Pan Am 747 was parked across the runway, and Van Zanten was approaching it at take-off speed.

There was no way to stop or swerve. Instinctively, Van Zanten knew that his only chance was to take off early. "Come on! Please!" the captain urged his plane. He pulled the aircraft's nose up desperately, dragging its tail on the ground and throwing up a blinding spray of sparks.

The nose of Van Zanten's plane managed to narrowly clear the parked 747. But just when it looked like he was in the clear, the underside of Van Zanten's fuselage ripped through the top of the Pan Am plane.

The KLM plane burst into a fiery explosion as it hurtled another five hundred yards down the runway.

Van Zanten, his entire crew, and all of his passengers were killed. In all, 584 people lost their lives that day.

The aeronautical community was stunned. It was by far the deadliest airplane collision in history. An international team of experts descended on Tenerife airport. They examined every bit of evidence, interviewed the eyewitnesses, and scrutinized every moment of the cockpit recorders in an attempt to pinpoint the cause of the accident.

The experts quickly ruled out a mechanical failure or terrorist attack. Piecing together the events of that day, it was clear that the other plane on the runway, Pan Am Flight 1736, had missed a taxiway turnoff and ended up in the wrong place. The thick fog contributed to the disaster. Van Zanten couldn't see the Pan Am plane, the Pan Am pilot couldn't see him, and the tower controllers couldn't see either one of them. On top of that, the tower was undermanned and the controllers were distracted by the day's events.

Despite all these factors, though, the tragedy would never have occurred if Van Zanten hadn't taken off without clearance. Why would this seasoned pilot, the *head of safety* at the airline, make such a rash and irresponsible decision?

The best explanation the investigators could come up with

was that Van Zanten was feeling frustrated. But that didn't quite add up. Feeling frustrated is one thing; completely disregarding protocol and forgetting about safety is another.

Clearly, Van Zanten was experienced. Clearly, he was well trained. And clearly, he was good at what he did. How could he cast aside every bit of training and protocol when the stakes were so high?

The aeronautical experts turned over every stone in their search for an explanation. But there was something in Tenerife that remained completely hidden. Alongside the rolling fog and crowded airfield, an unseen psychological force was at work, steering Van Zanten off the path of reason.

A growing body of research reveals that our behavior and decision making are influenced by an array of such psychological undercurrents and that they are much more powerful and pervasive than most of us realize. The interesting thing about these forces is that, like streams, they converge to become even more powerful. As we follow these streams, we notice unlikely connections among events that lie along their banks: the actions of an investor help us to better understand presidential decision making; students buying theater tickets illuminate a bitter controversy in the archeological community over human evolution; NBA draft picks point to a fatal flaw in common job-interview procedures; women talking on the phone show why a shaky bridge can be a powerful aphrodisiac.

Charting these psychological undercurrents and their unexpected effects, we can see where the currents are strongest and how their dynamics help us understand some of the most perplexing human mysteries. These hidden currents and forces include loss aversion (our tendency to go to great lengths to avoid possible losses), value attribution (our inclination to imbue a person or thing with certain qualities based on initial perceived value), and the diagnosis bias (our blindness to all evidence that contradicts our initial assessment of a person or situation). When we understand how these and a host of other mysterious forces operate, one thing becomes certain: whether we're a head of state or a college football coach, a love-struck student or a venture capitalist, we're all susceptible to the irresistible pull of irrational behavior. And as we gain insight about irrational motives that affect our work and personal lives, fascinating patterns emerge, connecting seemingly unrelated events.

Let's examine the first of these streams, to help us solve the mystery of what happened with Captain Van Zanten. We find our first clue in an unlikely place—the egg and orange juice aisles of our neighborhood supermarket.

Professor Daniel Putler, a former researcher at the U.S. Department of Agriculture, has spent more time thinking about eggs in a year than the rest of us spend in a lifetime. He carefully tracked and studied every aspect of egg sales in southern California. Looking at the data, he found some interesting patterns. Egg sales, for instance, were typically higher during the first week of each month. Not surprisingly, they were abnormally high in the weeks leading up to Easter, only to experience a sharp decline the week after.

That was all well and good, but Putler's next discovery wasn't just of use to the USDA and Al the grocer. Poring over cash-register data that reflected egg-price fluctuations, Putler identified what is referred to in economics as an "asymmetry."

Now, *traditional* economic theory holds that people should react to price fluctuations with equal intensity whether the price moves up or down. If the price goes down a bit, we buy a little more. If the price goes up a bit, we buy a little less. In other words, economists wouldn't expect people to be more sensitive to price increases than to price decreases. But what Putler found was that shoppers completely overreacted when prices rose.

It turns out that, when it comes to price increases, egg buyers are a sensitive bunch. If you reduce the price of eggs, consumers buy a little more. But when the price of eggs rises, they cut back their consumption by *two and a half times*.

Anyone who's made a shopping list with a budget in mind can tell you how this plays out. If the price drops, we're mildly pleased. But if we see that the price has gone up since last week, we get an *oh no* feeling in the pit of our stomachs and decide it's cereal for breakfast that week instead of scrambled eggs. This feeling of dread over a price increase is disproportionate—or asymmetric—to the satisfaction we feel when we get a good deal.

We experience the pain associated with a loss much more vividly than we do the joy of experiencing a gain. Sensing a loss as a result of the high price, the shoppers can't help but put the carton back on the shelf.

And it's not only egg buyers who are affected by the pain of a loss. A group of researchers replicated Putler's study among orange juice shoppers in Indiana and arrived at the exact same results: Midwest OJ drinkers are just as finicky about price increases as are Los Angeles omelet makers. Regardless of geography and breakfast preferences, losses loom larger than gains.

Putler's research illuminates a mystery that economists have been grappling with for years. For no apparent logical reason, we overreact to perceived losses.

This principle is key to understanding Van Zanten's actions. But before we return to Tenerife and the investigation, it's important to see how our aversion to loss plays out in our own decision making.

Think about the seemingly straightforward decision we make when we sign up for a new phone service. After wading through the phone company's electronic menus, we're presented with a choice: we can either pay for service by the minute or opt for a flat monthly fee and talk till the cows come home. Chances are that the pay-as-you-go plan is our better bet. Most of us just don't talk enough to justify a flat-rate plan.

But at this point loss aversion kicks in; we start imagining ourselves gabbing like teenagers into the night. The fear of a monstrous bill looms, and we sign up for the unlimited plan "just in case."

Economists can scold us for making a poor choice, but in deciding which service to sign up for, we're willing to sacrifice a little bit to avoid a potential loss.

AOL stumbled upon this same phenomenon when, after years of charging clients by the minute for their dial-up Internet access, it introduced a flat-billing option. The results were catastrophic, but not in the way you'd think. As AOL's CEO explained, the flat-pricing plan was "working too well." New customers were signing up in droves, and for three months AOL's servers were completely jammed. As with the phone service, Internet users wanted to avoid the perceived loss associated with pay-as-you-go.

The word *loss* alone, in fact, elicits a surprisingly powerful reaction in us. Companies like Avis and Hertz, facing the challenge of selling a product that is both useless and overpriced, have capitalized on this powerful effect. When we rent cars, our credit cards—not to mention our own car insurance—automatically cover us should anything go wrong with the vehicle. But the rental companies push additional coverage that not only is redundant but would cost a whopping $5,000 on an annual basis. Normally, we'd scoff at such a waste of money. But then, as the sales rep behind the counter is about to hand over the keys to that newish Ford Taurus, he asks whether we'd like to buy the *loss damage* waiver.

When we hear those words, our minds begin to whir: What if I have bad luck and end up in a wreck? What if, for some reason, my credit card won't cover me after all? Normally, we'd never dream of taking out an extra policy at an astronomical rate just to be doubly safe, but the threat of a loss makes us reconsider.

Looking at the larger picture, the behavior of the supermarket shoppers, phone customers, Internet subscribers, and car renters is strikingly similar to that of Captain Van Zanten. The losses that Van Zanten was trying to avoid were all the downsides of the mandated rest period: the cost of putting up the passengers, the chain reaction of delayed flights, and the blot on his reputation for being on time.

Van Zanten's desire to avoid a delay started out small enough. At first he simply wanted to keep the passengers on board to save time. But as the delay grew longer, the potential loss loomed larger. By the time an overnight delay seemed almost inevitable, Van Zanten was so focused on avoiding it that he tuned out all other considerations and, for that matter, his common sense and years of training.

Of course, there's a big difference between signing up for a phone service and causing the tragedy at Tenerife. Needlessly spending a few dollars is one thing; taking off without tower clearance is another. You would think that in such a situation, with hundreds of lives on the line, the captain would have exercised greater caution and acted even more deliberately than he would have under normal circumstances. That brings us to our second clue. As Columbia Business School professor Eric Johnson explained to us, the more

meaningful a potential loss is, the more loss averse we become. In other words, the more there is on the line, the easier it is to get swept into an irrational decision.

If anyone knows about having a lot on the line, it's Jordan
Walters of the Silicon Valley branch of the investment house
Smith Barney. Jordan is exactly the kind of person you'd look
for in a financial planner: he's calm, he's thoughtful, and he
always takes the time to listen. As we sat down in his office
and sipped from the minibar-sized can of apple juice he'd offered us, it was easy to forget that just outside the door associates were calling in millions of dollars in stock trades.

The thing about Jordan is that he isn't just a numbers guy.
He genuinely cares about his clients, and when they make
bad decisions, it bothers him. He remembers one client in
particular. "A fellow comes in," Jordan recalled. "He had a
business he'd started, a biotech start-up that got bought over
by a public company—and he's made! They were going to
retire! In Martha's Vineyard!"

That "fellow" was clearly on a high. He'd probably told
everyone—from the gardener to his kids' teacher to his old
college buddies—about his windfall.

But Jordan pointed out to his new client that investing the
vast majority of his wealth in his biotech company stock
would be putting all his eggs in one basket: "Oh my gosh, it's
such a big concentration—we need to find a way to wean
ourselves out of this." It would have made a lot more sense
to diversify, and Jordan came up with a solid plan: Sell a pre-
determined percentage of your holdings every quarter, he

advised his client, "so you take the emotion out of the decision."

But the investor wanted to ride the stock even higher. He had just sold his company. He'd made it big. Why stop now? "Well, what happened," Jordan recalled, "when he came in and the stock was at $47, we sold maybe 10 percent of his total position."

Shortly after that, the stock began to drop. "The stock was down to $42 and he says, 'If the stock goes back to $47, I'm going to sell.'"

Sensing that money was starting to slip through his fingers, the client developed an aversion to loss that was strikingly similar to Van Zanten's. Like the captain who was preoccupied with getting back on schedule, the investor was blindly focused on getting back to even.

Jordan realized that his client was so eager to make up for a loss that he was becoming oblivious to the risks he was taking. "What about the downside?" he asked the client. Now, from Jordan's rational perspective, there was nothing magical about the $47 stock price, and there was no guarantee that the stock would get back up there. On the flip side, the stock was liable to slip even further. But for the client, selling at anything less than $47 represented a loss—a bogeyman to be avoided at all costs.

"Well, the stock goes down to $38," Jordan recalled, "and the investor says, 'You know what, if it goes back to $44, I'll sell it then.'" Stock traders call this kind of behavior "chasing a loss"—when investors ignore the current data, put on blinders, and proceed with singular purpose to recover as much of their loss as possible.

Jordan explained to his client that holding on to the position in hopes that the stock price would recover was much too risky. But the client would have none of it, and took matters into his own hands. He ignored Jordan's advice and kept his stake. "[The stock] ended up at twelve cents," Jordan said. "The only thing he got out of that, the only value, was the initial 10 percent [he sold up front]."

Painful as it might have been, the investor could have sold at $42, perhaps giving up the dream of the fancy yacht but keeping the majority of his assets and realizing his plan to retire to Martha's Vineyard. Likewise, Van Zanten could have accepted the small blot on his reputation for punctuality and spent the night at Tenerife. Surely it wasn't worth it for either man to risk everything—be it a huge nest egg or the lives of his passengers—just to avoid a potential loss. You'd think that with a great deal on the line, people would play it safe. But, as Jordan explained, "You may not see that the stock is going to go into a tailspin. I would say you may misinterpret it." That's when this hidden force takes over.

So now we have two important clues. First, Van Zanten overreacted to a potential loss. Second, because so much was on the line, he was even more susceptible to taking a dangerous risk. But there's another missing clue. In order to get to the bottom of the Tenerife mystery, we'll need to visit the Swamp.

Chapter 2

↓

The SWAMP of COMMITMENT

Playing not to lose.

Fun-n-Gun.

↓↓↓↓

Only the Gators walked out alive.

↓↓↓

The $204 twenty-dollar bill.

↓↓

The end of the Great Society.

↓

"We don't even know where the tunnel is."

Kayaking on the University of Florida's Lake Wauburg can be a disconcerting experience. The scene is quintessentially southern. The lake, or should we say swamp, is surrounded by wild marsh grass and a canopy of towering trees draped in thick Spanish moss, their roots dipping into the warm water. Insects buzz day and night, and the mosquitoes can drive you mad.

The romance quickly fades away, though, when you see a pair of reptilian eyes staring up at you from the water. True to the school's mascot, the lake is full of alligators. It's said that they don't attack adults, but, paddling along in a plastic kayak, you're not so sure.

Lake Wauburg is home to many an alligator, but it's not the most notorious swamp in Gainesville. That honor goes to

UF's football stadium, affectionately dubbed "the Swamp." Each fall an army of campers, RVs, and SUVs descends upon the campus, and grown men walk around clutching stuffed alligators as game time approaches.

Amidst all this hubbub, with the excitement of an upcoming game in the air, lies the final missing piece of the Van Zanten puzzle.

Even in the chaos of a campus gearing up for a Gators game, Steve Spurrier felt right at home. He grew up in the South and played for Florida as a star quarterback, winning the coveted Heisman Trophy. Twenty-three years later, he returned to UF's football stadium to coach the team.

The most flattering way to describe the Gator team upon Spurrier's arrival in 1990 was as a "fixer-upper." The team had never won a conference title; in fact, it was on probation because of allegations of rule violations by the team's former coach.

To say that Spurrier had a job on his hands is an understatement. Against all odds, though, the coach led a turnaround so dramatic that it still lives on in the memory of fans years later. Spurrier's charisma, his rapport with his team, and the new player talent he brought in all helped put the Swamp on the map. But Spurrier's most important move was to identify a weak spot in the strategy employed by his opponents.

For years the teams in the conference had adhered to a "war of attrition" game strategy: they called conservative plays and held on to the ball for as long as they could, hoping to win a defensive battle. The idea wasn't necessarily to score a lot of points. It was to wear down the opponent and eat up time. In other words, the coaches were playing not to lose.

When you think about it, the conference coaches were acting a lot like Jordan Walters's investor who lost his windfall from the biotech company: rather than focusing on maximizing their gains, they concentrated on avoiding losses. It was exactly this mentality that opened a window of opportunity for Spurrier. In the simplest terms, Spurrier came to dominate the conference by playing to win, by introducing what he called the "Fun-n-Gun" approach.

When we caught up with Spurrier, he explained that, like all coaches, he had his list of conservative plays: "You know, like little screen passes, little short passes behind the line. You got a chance to have a surefire completion." But Spurrier also mixed things up with a generous helping of "big chance plays, where you got to give your players a shot." In other words, Spurrier's team passed more often, played more aggressively, and tried to score more touchdowns.

The Fun-n-Gun strategy took the Southeast conference by storm. UF's stadium earned its nickname, "the Swamp," because "only Gators," it was said, "walked out alive."

And here's where the first of our two hidden forces or sways comes into play. Spurrier gained an advantage because the other coaches were focused on trying to avoid a potential loss. Think of what it's like to be a college football coach. As you walk around town, passing fans offer themselves up as instant experts on the game—never afraid to give you a piece of their minds on what you did wrong in yesterday's match-up. You make one bad move and you get skewered by fans and commentators alike. Meanwhile, ticket sale revenues, your school's alumni fund-raising, and your job all depend heavily on the football team's success. All of that pressure adds up. Just as with Putler's egg shoppers, the losses loom large. As Coach Spurrier explained to us, "What coaches start thinking is, don't do anything to lose the game."

You'd have thought that after losing a few games to a team like the University of Florida Gators—much less having a losing season—the coaches would have reevaluated their war-of-attrition model.

But they didn't.

And so Spurrier and his Gators continued to dominate former powerhouses like Alabama, Tennessee, and Auburn. Over the next six years, the coach and his team went on to win four division titles, culminating in the national championship. All the while, opposing coaches continued to stick with the old model.

The coaches fell victim not only to loss aversion, but also to another closely linked sway called *commitment*. In other words, they had used the grind-it-out-and-hold-on-to-the-ball strategy for so long that it was simply hard for them to let go. They were committed to continuing down the road they had always walked. They were so committed, in fact, that it was virtually impossible for them to take a different path. Trying to avoid potential losses led the coaches to adopt a war-of-attrition model, and commitment to what they'd been doing for years made them unable to react to Spurrier's superior strategy.

We've all experienced the pervasive pull of commitment in some form or another; whether we've invested our time and money in a particular project or poured our energy into a doomed relationship, it's difficult to let go even when things clearly aren't working. As difficult as it can be to admit defeat, however, staying the course simply because of a past commitment hurts us in the long run.

Independently, each of these two forces—commitment and aversion to loss—has a powerful effect on us. But when the two forces combine, it becomes that much harder to break free and do something different.

It's precisely because of the compounding effect of these two forces that students in Max Bazerman's negotiations class at Harvard Business School would do well to hold on to their wallets when he introduces his "twenty-dollar auction." They say it's easy to take candy from a baby; Professor Bazerman has found that it's just as easy to take money from Harvard MBAs.

On the first day of class, Professor Bazerman announces a game that seems innocuous enough. Waving a twenty-dollar bill in the air, he offers it up for auction.

Everybody is free to bid; there are only two rules. The first is that bids are to be made in $1 increments. The second rule is a little trickier. The winner of the auction, of course, wins the bill. But the runner-up must still honor his or her bid, while receiving nothing in return. In other words, this is a situation where second best finishes last.

Indeed, at the beginning of the auction, as people sniff out an opportunity to get a $20 bill for a bargain, the hands quickly shoot up, and the auction is officially under way. A flurry of bids follows. As Bazerman described it, "The pattern is always the same. The bidding starts out fast and furious until it reaches the $12 to $16 range."

At this point, it becomes clear to each of the participants that he or she isn't the only one with the brilliant idea of winning the twenty bucks for cheap. There is a collective hard swallow. As if sensing the floodwaters rising, the students get jittery. "Everyone except the two highest bidders drops out of the auction," Bazerman explained.

Without realizing it, the two students with the highest bids get locked in. "One bidder has bid $16 and the other has bid $17," Bazerman said. "The $16 bidder must either bid $18 or suffer a $16 loss." Up to this point the students were looking to make a quick dollar; now neither one wants to be the sucker who paid good money for nothing. This is when the students adopt the equivalent of football's war-of-attrition model. They become committed to the strategy of playing not to lose.

Like a runaway train, the auction continues, with the bidding going up past $18, $19, and $20. As the price climbs higher, the other students don't know whether to watch or cover their eyes. "Of course," reflected Bazerman, "the rest of the group roars with laughter when the bidding goes over $20."

From a rational perspective, the obvious decision would be for the bidders to accept their losses and stop the auction before it spins even further out of control. But that's easier said than done. Students are pulled by both the momentum of the auction and the looming loss if they back down—a loss that is growing greater by the bid. The two forces, in turn, feed off each other: commitment to a chosen path inspires additional bids, driving the price up, making the potential loss loom even larger.

And so students continue bidding: $21, $22, $23, $50, $100, up to a record $204. Over the years that Bazerman has conducted the experiment, he has never lost a penny (he donates all proceeds to charity). Regardless of who the bidders have been—college students or business executives attending a seminar—they are always swayed.

The deeper the hole they dig themselves into, the more they continue to dig.

We've already seen how Captain Van Zanten was affected by the power of loss aversion: it was incredibly important for him to avoid the mandated rest period. But add to that the force of commitment and you have a situation that could sway even the most experienced and capable of professionals.

By the time Van Zanten reached the end of the foggy runway, the pain of his potential losses seemed so massive—and he had already committed himself so firmly to getting off the island—that in his mind he could not seriously entertain any plan other than taking off.

This same compounding effect of loss aversion and commitment repeats itself time and again—even in the highest echelons of American government.

If 1950s politics was like an episode of *Survivor*, LBJ was surely the hands-down winner.

It's hard to find an instance when LBJ wasn't being strategic. There's a thin line between determination and intimidation, and LBJ had no trouble skipping between the two. When he was elected to Congress, he'd call fellow legislators at all hours of the night, just to catch them off guard. Later, as president, during official White House meetings he'd shock and intimidate visitors by announcing a swimming break, taking off his clothes, and jumping naked into the pool.

But he didn't employ these tactics for kicks alone. LBJ had a cause that was close to his heart. While other politicians hailed from a world of privilege, LBJ had grown up surrounded by poverty. He had seen firsthand just how difficult life could be for poor people in the South.

"Some men," LBJ once said, "want power simply to strut around the world and to hear the tune of 'Hail to the Chief.' Others want it simply to build prestige, to collect antiques, and to buy pretty things. Well, I wanted power to give things to people—all sorts of things to all sorts of people." Specifically,

LBJ was dedicated to easing the plight of the poor and giving African-Americans and other minorities the rights they deserved.

He made it his mission to complete the work started by FDR during the Depression. Johnson admired the social progress that had been achieved through the New Deal but felt that FDR's ultimate goal of realizing social change was still unfinished.

LBJ used his bulldog strategies to launch the most important campaign of his career: the war on poverty. Towering over others at six foot three, he would literally get in people's faces, encroach on their personal space, and bulldoze allies and enemies alike into submission. With the passing of the Civil Rights Acts, the establishment of antipoverty community programs, and the launch of Medicare, Medicaid, and federal education funding, the "Great Society"—one of the biggest social reform programs in American history—took shape.

In 1964 LBJ was at the height of his political prowess. America had begun to recover from the JFK assassination. Congress was heavily Democratic, Johnson's approval ratings were sky-high, and most legislators were either sympathetic to his cause or too intimidated to oppose him. "I knew Congress," he later reflected, "as well as I knew Lady Bird."

But just as his lifelong dream of enacting massive reform—from making urban ghettos a thing of the past to providing universal health care—was beginning to materialize, LBJ unknowingly became a participant in Bazerman's auction.

There are three essential elements to the auction. There's the $2 phase—where with wide-eyed optimism everyone's banking on winning the equivalent of a free lunch. And there's the final phase—where participants are bidding upward of $20, digging themselves deeper into a hole, but are unwilling to let go. But the most interesting phase is the middle stage, at $12 to $16, when it first becomes clear where the train is heading. And it's here that loss aversion and commitment meet.

LBJ entered his auction in much the same way that Bazerman's students did. But instead of a $20 bill, the prize dangled in front of him was the opportunity to stop the spread of communism in Southeast Asia.

To the president, the North Vietnamese communists seemed like weak opponents. They lacked a powerful army, sophisticated technology, money, and broad international support. LBJ cast his first bid—the equivalent of $2—by launching an aerial bombing campaign in 1965 aimed at eroding support for the communists. With the United States fighting against a less powerful enemy and with a massive arsenal at its disposal, things looked promising—as is always the case in the first stage of the Bazerman auction.

But just a few years later LBJ was already deep into the third stage of the auction. With more than 500,000 troops on the ground in 1968 and tens of thousands dead, LBJ was long past the $20 mark. He lamented, "Light at the end of the tunnel, hell, we don't even have a tunnel; we don't even know where the tunnel is." Like the coaches in Spurrier's conference, the president was getting beat but could not bring himself to change course.

In the end, Johnson lost more than just Vietnam. The war cost him the full realization of the Great Society, his approval ratings, and ultimately—when he decided not to run for another presidential term—his political career. Many years later he reflected, "I knew from the start that I was bound to be crucified either way I moved." He explained, "If I left the woman I really loved—the Great Society—in order to get involved with that bitch of a war on the other side of the world, then I would lose everything at home. All my programs . . . all my dreams to provide education and medical care . . ." But he also recognized, "If I left that war and let the Communists take over South Vietnam . . . there would follow in this country an endless national debate—a mean and destructive debate—that would shatter my presidency, kill my administration, and damage our democracy."

Ironically, that's exactly what happened anyway. But it is what went on at the second stage of the auction—the $12–$16 phase—that is the key to understanding how Johnson was swayed in his decision making. On the one hand, LBJ could see where the war was headed. A phone conversation the president had with his national security advisor in May of 1964 is incredibly telling. "I just stayed awake last night thinking of this thing," LBJ confided. "The more that

I think of it I don't know what in the hell, it looks like to me that we're getting into another Korea. It just worries the hell out of me. I don't see what we can ever hope to get out of there with once we're committed . . . I don't think it's worth fighting for and I don't think we can get out. And it's just the biggest damn mess that I ever saw."

But on the other hand, just a few moments later LBJ acknowledged his fear that "if you start running from the Communists, they may just chase you right into your own kitchen."

Driven forward by the momentum of the "auction" and the dread of capitulating to a loss, LBJ abandoned the possibility of retreat. And that's what happens in the $12–$16 stage. Oddly enough, the convergence of the two undercurrents brings about exuberant optimism. When looking a potential loss in the face, we hope against hope that everything will turn out okay.

In fact, if you listen more closely to LBJ's speeches, the exuberance, the determination, and, for that matter, the entire approach start to sound eerily familiar. LBJ's message, and even the specific words he used to describe Vietnam, bear an uncanny resemblance to George W. Bush's remarks about Iraq.

"There is no easy answer, no instant solution," declared LBJ. "There is no magic formula for success in Iraq," proclaimed Bush.

These similarities in thinking aren't the product of shared personality or political ideology but rather of a common dialect; both men are using the language of the Bazerman auction.

Both presidents showed strong commitment and resolve to stay the course. LBJ stated, "We will not be defeated. We will not grow tired. We will not withdraw, either openly or under the cloak of a meaningless agreement." President Bush asserted, "We will not fail. We will persevere and defeat this enemy and hold this hard-won ground for the realm of liberty."

And then there's the optimism. As the Vietnam situation grew increasingly out of control, LBJ declared, "There has been substantial progress, I think, in building a durable government during these last three years." Similarly, when it became evident that the Iraq war wasn't going to result in an easy victory, Bush boasted, "Iraq has a new currency, the first battalion of a new army, representative local governments, and a Governing Council with an aggressive timetable for national sovereignty. This is substantial progress."

Nobel Prize–winning economist Daniel Kahneman, who, together with Amos Tversky, first discovered and chronicled the phenomenon of loss aversion, offers a telling reflection of our psychology during such situations. "To withdraw now is to accept a sure loss," he writes about digging oneself deeper into a political hole, "and that option is deeply unattractive." When you combine this with the force of commitment, "the option of hanging on will therefore be relatively attractive, even if the chances of success are small and the cost of delaying failure is high."

Aversion to loss, on its own, is strong. But when it converges with commitment, the force becomes an even more powerful influence in shaping our thinking and decision making.

As we'll soon see, commitment is often bolstered by yet another force, one that will take us on the ultimate quest: the search for the missing link.

Chapter [3]

The HOBBIT and the MISSING LINK

The real-life Indiana Jones.

The hunt for the missing link.

The Stradivarius on the subway.

What's in a five-cent hot dog, anyway?

Homer Simpson and Piltdown Man.

Can a discount drink decrease IQ?

Shakespeare was wrong.

A paleontological lineup.

t was one of those moments you see in the movies—just add the Indiana Jones theme music to complete the picture. In the fall of 2004 Dr. Dean Falk, an anthropology professor and forensic expert, was sitting at home next to her computer. When the phone rang, the first thought that crossed her mind was, "I hope it's not a telemarketer." She never imagined how much that call was about to change her life.

"Hi," said the man on the other end of the line. "My name is David Hamlin, and I'm with the National Geographic Society." As if reading her mind, he quickly added, "I'm not selling magazines."

Hamlin could barely contain his excitement. "I've been dying to talk with you for at least two months. I haven't been able to because what I'm about to tell you was embargoed until right now; but the embargo just lifted, so now I'm free to talk about it."

"Are you putting me on? Is this real?" Falk asked.

Hamlin laughed. "I can assure you it is. I just returned from Indonesia, where we filmed for National Geographic television," he said. "I'm calling you because Mike Morwood, the discoverer, recommended you."

Hamlin started to tell Falk about an unexpected find made by Morwood, at the time a little-known Australian anthropologist, on the remote island of Flores in the Java Sea.

The interesting thing about Flores and islands like it, Falk later explained to us, is that when it comes to evolution, they are great equalizers. Small species grow larger, and large ones become smaller—converging, more or less, at the size of a German shepherd. Nobody knows exactly why this island-effect phenomenon occurs, but scientists speculate that it's a result of genetic adaptation to an environment with relatively few predators and a limited supply of resources. Indeed, over the decades anthropologists working in Flores have discovered bone remains that could have belonged to creatures from *Alice in Wonderland*: from six-foot-long lizards to giant rats to dwarf elephants.

But also amidst these bones were found sophisticated stone tools, some dating back hundreds of thousands of years, tools that—it was thought—could have been made only by humans. The catch, though, was that humans hadn't arrived on the island until forty thousand years ago. "There are no hominids for a long, long time," Falk explained to us, "just tools." Someone had to have fashioned those artifacts, someone possessing both intelligence and manual dexterity. Yet there was no archeological evidence to indicate who that someone might have been.

This is where Morwood's discovery comes in—a discovery that was, anthropologically speaking, mind-boggling. The finding purported not only to solve the mystery of the sophisticated tools, but also to shed new light on a branch of our evolution.

Falk didn't suspect that along with a significant discovery she was about to encounter a psychological undercurrent that had swayed the anthropological community a century earlier. Not only does this force regularly alter our perceptions of other people and our experiences, it caused hundreds of people to ignore a violin prodigy giving a free concert, imbued an energy drink with the power to alter students' IQs, and played a role in the biggest fraud in scientific history.

Although she didn't know it yet, Falk was about to witness history repeating itself. Back in the 1850s, the scientific world was in the midst of a revolution. When bone remains of an ancient hominid were found in Germany's Neander Valley, scientists struggled to make sense of what this creature could have been. Its features closely resembled ours, but something about the skeleton was not quite human. It had a more pronounced nose, a thicker skull, and a squatter body shape—in other words, it looked like what we now think of when we imagine a caveman. At first the scientists figured that the remains belonged to a Russian soldier who had met an untimely death in the Napoleonic Wars. But Darwin's *Origin of Species* cast things in a whole new light. When viewing the remains through the lens of evolutionary theory, the scientists surmised that they must have belonged to a recent ancestor of modern humans—an entirely new species we know today as Neanderthal.

At the time, evolution was believed to be a linear progression (whereas the modern theory sees evolution as resembling a much more complex family tree). Following this logic, scientists felt there was an obvious gap in the progression from apes to the more humanlike Neanderthals. This "missing link" became a holy grail for European scientists.

But you can't go searching for a missing link without having *some* idea of what you're looking for. The scientists developed the equivalent of a police sketch of this mysterious creature: they figured it would have a big brain but the physical appearance of an ape. With that, they started digging.

During that same time, a precocious young Dutch student named Eugene Dubois was becoming fascinated with evolution. Indeed, later in life Dubois would make one of the most important finds of all time—one that would have surprising implications for Dean Falk and the Flores discovery in the twenty-first century.

By the time Dubois was twenty-nine, he had earned his degree in medicine (finishing at the head of his class), gotten married, had a baby daughter, and taken on a university professorship. Over the years the scientists in Europe had continued to dig, but they had little more than piles of rocks to show for their efforts. The missing link remained elusive.

After spending months reviewing all the literature and theories on the subject, Eugene Dubois concluded that the scientists were looking in all the wrong places. He decided to quit his professional career and move his young family to the East Indies, where many prehistoric ape remains had been found over the years. There, Dubois was certain, the missing link was waiting to be discovered.

Since he had minimal funding, no government backing, and no organizational support, life for Dubois and his family was anything but easy. Dubois came down with malaria, and he and his wife lost a newborn child to tropical disease. The work was grueling—exploring dense, uncharted territory, descending into unexplored caves, even confronting tigers. But three years into the search Dubois hit gold. In October 1891, his team was exploring in a region called Ngawi, colloquially known as the "hellhole of Java." The place was hot, desolate, and known for ancient lava eruptions.

The day seemed like any other until the team happened upon what at first looked like a coconut shell. A closer look revealed something much more spectacular. It was a skull. "Near the place on the left bank of the river . . . ," Dubois reported, "a beautiful skull vault has been excavated." The skull was certainly not that of an ape: "As far as the species is concerned, the skull can be distinguished from the living chimpanzees: first because it is larger, second because of its higher vault."

Near this find Dubois discovered a leg bone that clearly belonged with the skull. But the femur looked like it had been severely injured, as if struck by an arrowhead, and subsequently healed. This was significant because it showed that the individual must have been cared for and treated by her community—untended, the injury would have immobilized her and she wouldn't have lived to see the bone heal.

Dubois knew he was onto something momentous. All the pieces pointed to one conclusion: a new prehistoric species, more advanced than apes but not quite human. And this evolutionary link was a lot more like us than anyone had imagined. She even walked upright. "It is obvious from the entire construction of the femur," Dubois wrote, "that this bone fulfilled the same mechanical role as in the human body." The only major difference was the structure of the skull and its size, which was smaller than that of modern humans. Rather than having a big brain and apelike physique, the missing link turned out to have a humanlike body and a smaller brain.

Dubois was elated with the find. He documented all the facts, drew comprehensive sketches, and carefully verified his results. But the reaction Dubois received from the scientific community was not what he expected. One expert took issue with the skull size and dubbed the finding a modern victim of microcephaly (a neurological disorder that causes reduced brain size) "of an unusually elongated type." Another thought the fossil was that of a "giant gibbon of some kind." Yet another insisted that the skull and femur were completely unrelated. Dubois tried to defend his find, but for years the discovery remained largely ignored.

When we look at this story in light of what we've learned about commitment, it's easy to understand why the scientists dismissed Dubois. The anthropologists at that time were committed to a certain view of evolution. A hominid with a small brain who walked on two legs and belonged to a community simply didn't fit this view. It was much easier to dismiss Dubois's find as an abnormal human or a strange gibbon than to change their theory of human evolution.

Still, Dubois was perplexed and offended. He prided himself on being a man of science, and he expected other scientists to respect his rigorous methodology. After all, he had carefully documented every aspect of the dig and included elaborate sketches of his find. But the fossil of what we know today as *Homo erectus*—one of the most momentous discoveries in anthropological history—remained stashed in Dubois's house for decades.

The way in which the scientists responded to Dubois in the nineteenth century is critical for us to understand, because it sheds light on the next force we'll encounter. While a part of their dismissive reaction can be explained by their commitment to a previously held belief, there was also another force at play. Here's where commitment merges with the sway of "value attribution": our tendency to imbue someone or something with certain qualities based on perceived value, rather than on objective data.

To understand how value attribution works and how it swayed the anthropological community, we'll need to fast-forward to the present day and journey beneath the streets of Washington, D.C. On a January morning in 2007, L'Enfant Plaza subway station was about to be filled with music. At exactly 7:51 a.m., during rush hour, an ordinary-looking man dressed in jeans and wearing a baseball cap noncha-lantly took out his $3.5 million Stradivarius violin and got ready to play. The man was Joshua Bell, one of the finest violinists alive, who regularly performs to sold-out crowds in the best concert halls. Unbeknownst to any of the com-muters, Bell was taking part in an undercover field study conducted by the *Washington Post.*

Bell's subway performance started with Bach's Sonatas and Partitas for Unaccompanied Violin, one of the most challenging pieces ever composed for the instrument. Over the next forty-three minutes the concert continued, but on that January morning there was no thunderous applause. There were no cameras flashing. Here was one of the best musicians in the world playing in the subway station for free, but no one seemed to care. Of the 1,097 people who walked by, hardly anyone stopped. One man listened for a few min-utes, a couple of kids stared, and one woman, who happened to recognize the violinist, gaped in disbelief.

Now, the commuters might have been in too much of a hurry to pay attention to Bell. But clearly, had there been news cameras present, or had people known this man was a virtuoso, at least a *few* more people would have stopped to listen. But think about how Joshua Bell appeared to the subway riders. He wasn't dressed in formal attire; he stood on no stage. For all intents and purposes, Bell looked like your average, run-of-the-mill street performer. Even though he didn't *sound* like a mediocre violinist, he looked the part. Without realizing it, the commuters attributed the value they perceived—the baseball cap, the jeans, the subway venue—to the quality of the performance. As they passed by Bell, most subway riders didn't even glance in his direction. Instead of hearing an outstanding concert, they heard street music.

The D.C. commuters who dismissed Bell's performance were swayed by value attribution in the same way that anthropologists were swayed to ignore Dubois's discovery. Everything associated with the fossil of *Homo erectus* was perceived by the scientific community as having little value: Dubois, its discoverer, was a virtual no-name; the European scientists looked down their noses at the prospect of the "hellhole of Java" being home to a human ancestor; and the fossil's brain size was too small to fulfill anthropological preconceptions of what the missing link would look like. It was as if Dubois were holding a Stradivarius in his hands but no one paid attention because he was wearing a baseball cap and jeans and standing in a subway station.

It's easy to understand, though, why the scientists and subway riders reacted the way they did. Value attribution, after all, acts as a quick mental shortcut to determine what's worthy of our attention. When we encounter a new object, person, or situation, the value we assign to it shapes our further perception of it, whether it's our dismissal of a curiously inexpensive antique we find at a flea market or our admiration of a high-priced designer bag in a chic boutique. Imagine, for instance, stumbling upon a discarded armoire on the street. Do you see it for the rare treasure it might be? Or is your knee-jerk reaction that *something* must be wrong with it? In the same way, value attribution affects our perceptions of people. We may turn down a pitch or idea that is presented by the "wrong" person or blindly follow the advice of someone who is highly regarded.

That is not to say that a person's title doesn't count for anything or that a product's price doesn't often give you a good idea of its true value. But when we apply that price tag (be it real or metaphorical) too broadly, we compromise our rationality. Take what happened when Coney Island visitors encountered entrepreneur Nathan Handwerker's new food stand. When he went into business in 1916, the Polish immigrant decided to undercut the competition. Everyone else was charging ten cents for the classic Coney Island meal— the hot dog—so Handwerker priced the dogs he made from his wife's old recipe at a mere five cents. Despite the fact that Handwerker's hot dogs were every bit as delicious as the competition's (and were made from real beef), he attracted almost no customers. Visitors to Coney Island viewed these mysterious half-priced hot dogs as inferior and wondered what cheap, substandard ingredients went into the recipe. It didn't help when Handwerker offered free pickles or free root beer to hot dog buyers. Sales remained flat and, if anything, giving away freebies only further cemented the value attribution.

It wasn't until Handwerker came up with a clever new ploy that his hot dogs really started selling. He recruited doctors from a nearby hospital to stand by his shop eating his hot dogs while wearing their white coats and stethoscopes. Because people place a high value on physicians, customers figured if doctors were eating there, the food had to be good. So they soon started buying from Handwerker, and his "Nathan's Famous Hot Dogs" took off. It makes you wonder just how many times we miss out on something worthwhile because of our preconceptions about its value.

But preconceptions go both ways. As we'll see, the very phenomenon of value attribution that worked against Eugene Dubois led the same community of scientists to wholeheartedly embrace an unscrupulous charlatan. After Dubois's discovery, other hominid fossils were found throughout the world. But England had remained discovery-free—that is, until Charles Dawson came along.

Unlike Dubois, who was an unknown Dutch scientist, Dawson was British, respected, and well known and had been elected to a fellowship in the Geological Society of London. The tale he spun to his fellow scientists was this: He had been strolling along a dirt road outside of Piltdown Common in Sussex when he happened upon a piece of flint. The flint was obviously out of place, so Dawson asked some nearby ditchdiggers about it. They confirmed that they had unearthed the flint and discarded it along the dirt path. The conversation that followed supposedly went something like this:

"Say, did you happen to find any skulls in the course of your dig?"

"No."

"Well, let me know if you do."

According to Dawson, he visited the laborers every now and then, and, sure enough, during one of the visits they had something for him: a hominid skull. Over the following months, more pieces of the skull mysteriously turned up, including a remarkably well-preserved jawbone. It was with these alleged artifacts that Dawson marched into London's British Museum (Natural History). For good measure, he threw an authentic ancient elephant tooth into the mix, presumably from a prehistoric inhabitant that must have roamed the British savannah.

It's important to understand how crude Dawson's specimen (dubbed *Piltdown Man*) was. The skull had belonged to a medieval man but had been dunked in a bucket of brown paint to make it look older. The jaw had come from a modern orangutan whose teeth had been filed to make it look more or less human. You didn't need to be Sherlock Holmes to realize the specimen was a fraud.

The best way of describing the physical model that was constructed based on Piltdown Man is to note its striking resemblance to Homer Simpson. As the curator of the British

Museum (Natural History) wrote, Piltdown was "perhaps ungainly, and may have walked with a shuffling gait, but his brain and skull were essentially human, only with a few ape-like traits." Seeing the diorama of Piltdown in the British Museum, gently polishing a stick tool, you almost expect him to exclaim, "D'oh!"

But when the British scientists looked at Piltdown Man, they didn't see a crude specimen. They marveled at the new find, because it confirmed two cherished beliefs. First, Piltdown Man proved that civilization had indeed originated in England. One anthropologist boasted, "It bucks me up to think that England is coming up trumps." The scientists felt a sentimental connection with the fossil. He was seen as an ancient forefather, "indeed a man of the dawn." A pillar was erected at the site of the ditch where Dawson claimed to have found the bones. The inscription proudly announced, "Here in the old river gravel Mr. Charles Dawson, F.S.A., found the fossil skull of Piltdown."

Piltdown Man also confirmed scientists' assumption that the missing link would have a humanlike brain and apelike features.

If only Dubois's *Homo erectus* fossil had received half the fanfare. Instead, few anthropologists accepted it as authentic. Piltdown, on the other hand, was embraced by the vast majority of the scientific community. Only decades later, in 1952, did scientists finally—and cautiously—debunk the great hoax.

Why would the scientific community dismiss Dubois's authentic discovery and embrace Dawson's forgery? Once again, it comes down to value attribution. If Dubois was dressed in metaphorical baseball cap and jeans, Dawson was decked out in full concert regalia—tails and all. In other words, Dawson was perceived as distinguished and reputable and his findings were considered to be of high value. Moreover, Dawson alleged that he had found his remains on British soil, rather than in the hellhole of Java; and the Piltdown specimen's brain was large, in contrast to the relatively tiny (and apelike) skull of Dubois's find.

Now, while most of us would like to think we'd be able to tell the difference between a real fossil and a skull dipped in paint, let's put ourselves in the British scientists' shoes. Every major institution deemed Dawson's discovery genuine. The press was in a frenzy and the head of the British Museum supported the find.

Once we attribute a certain value to a person or thing, it dramatically alters our perceptions of subsequent information. This power of value attribution is so potent that it affects us even when the value is assigned completely *arbitrarily*. To see this process in action, let's visit a group of economists who set up a clever experiment using SoBe Adrenaline Rush, a beverage that claims to increase mental acuity. To test acuity, the researchers developed a thirty-minute word jumble challenge that was administered to three groups of students.

The first group, a control group, took the test without drinking any SoBe. The second group was told about the intelligence-enhancing properties of SoBe, given the drink, and asked to watch a video while the tonic had time to take effect. These students also were required to sign an authorization form allowing the researchers to charge $2.89 to their university account for the SoBe. We'll call this second group of students the "fancy-shmancy SoBe" drinkers. Finally, a third group of students was given the same spiel about SoBe but was told that the university had gotten a discount and that they would only be charged eighty-nine cents for the drink. We'll call them the "cheapo SoBe" drinkers.

Now, the results of the experiment were surprising. The group that drank the fancy-shmancy SoBe performed slightly better on the test than did the group that received no SoBe at all. But before we rush out to buy SoBe, with its acuity-enhancing powers, it's important to note that the students who drank the cheapo SoBe performed significantly worse than either the fancy-shmancy group or the SoBe-free control group. Given that exactly the same SoBe beverage was served to both groups, we can only conclude that it was the *value* the students attributed to the SoBe that made the difference in their test scores. Strange as it may sound, fancy-shmancy SoBe made the students smarter, while cheapo SoBe hindered their performance.

"The intriguing idea," Dan Ariely, one of the study's authors, told us, "is that expectations change the reality we live in." The value that we attribute to something fundamentally changes how we perceive it. "When you get something at a discount, the positive expectations don't kick in as strongly." And once we attribute a certain value to something, it's very difficult to view it in any other light.

When Joshua Bell dresses up and plays at a concert hall, he's regarded like fancy-shmancy SoBe—and his talent more than merits his audience's appreciation. But when Bell plays the same instrument and music "at a discount" at the subway station, he's perceived like cheapo SoBe. Whenever we're called upon to make judgments, value attribution plays a role, often altering our reactions to a person or thing. Who hasn't had their views about a movie shaped, even before they watched it, because they heard or read the opinions of critics? Even when it comes to our own enjoyment or entertainment, we're not immune to the powerful influence of value attribution. It turns out that Shakespeare was wrong after all: a rose by any other name really doesn't smell as sweet.

Columbus, Ohio, home of Ohio State University, isn't the kind of place where you'll find glitzy Broadway-style theater. Still, students and community members alike had long appreciated the Ohio State theater department's productions. For $15 any theater aficionado could buy a season pass and gain access to all ten shows in that semester's scheduled lineup.

Unbeknownst to the first sixty people who purchased a season pass one year, they were about to play a key role in an economic study. "After the person announced his or her intention to buy a season ticket," the study's authors explained, "the ticket seller sold the purchaser one of three types of tickets, which had been randomly ordered beforehand." One-third of them received a regular, full-priced, $15 ticket; one-third received a $2 discount on their tickets; the rest received their tickets at a discount of $7.

Those receiving the bargain tickets were told that the discount was being given as part of a theater department promotion. Regardless of the price of the ticket, however, all subscribers had equally good seats.

It turns out, though, that the price we pay for a ticket affects our enjoyment of the performance. Although it's difficult to measure how highly audience members value a play—we don't know how enthusiastically everyone clapped or how hard each laughed—we can track whether they return for subsequent performances.

As the researchers pointed out, given that the attendees all held the same ticket books to the ten plays in the series, from a rational economic perspective, all the theatergoers should have been equally likely to attend subsequent plays.

But those who paid full price attended significantly more shows than did those who received either the $2 or the $7 discount. One explanation is that the full-price ticket holders perceived that with each show they attended they were recouping a part of their initial investment (i.e., the price for the season pass). Thus those who had paid full price went to more shows because their investment was higher. But there was virtually no difference in attendance levels between the two discount groups. If the desire to recoup their investment were the only force at play, you'd expect that the group that received the $7 discount would skip more shows than did the group that received only a $2 discount. But this wasn't the case. The amount of the discount didn't matter—what swayed the attendees was the very fact that a discount was given. Value attribution kicked in when they received a *discounted* ticket: Regardless of the size of the discount, the patrons regarded the tickets and the productions as inferior.

Knowing how value attribution affects our judgment—and with our anthropologists, the subway riders, hot dog buyers, SoBe drinkers, and theatergoers in tow—we're ready to return to Dean Falk and to the remarkable discovery on the island of Flores. A lot has changed in science since the time of Dubois and Dawson, but as we will see, despite the Piltdown fiasco and the technological advances that followed, modern anthropologists still get swept up by the same force of value attribution.

The groundbreaking news that David Hamlin of National Geographic had to share with Falk was that Mike Morwood had discovered who had crafted the stone tools found on the island of Flores. It turns out that the island effect wasn't just limited to lizards and elephants. Just as there were miniature elephants roaming the island, there were also miniature hominids. It was this previously unknown species that had used the mysterious tools to hunt ancient dwarf elephants.

If the existence of this new species, *Homo floresiensis* (nicknamed "the Hobbit"), could be verified, it would have huge implications: scientists had never before come across any hominid or apelike species that had undergone the island effect. A miniature hominid would constitute a category all by itself. But even more interestingly, the discovery would also add another twist to the unfolding human evolution story: humans and *Homo floresiensis* coexisted as recently as twelve thousand years ago, long after all other hominid species, including Neanderthals, became extinct.

Although Falk was feeling excited, she knew that she had to approach the mystery cautiously and objectively. As she told National Geographic, "It's too important not to do right." Falk joined the rest of the team in St. Louis, where the work of investigating the Hobbit began.

At the center of the inquiry was, once again, the brain. Falk hoped to get to the bottom of things by taking what's called an *endocast* of the skull. "An endocast," she explained, "takes up the impressions that the brain left on the walls of the brain case." This cast of the brain captures detailed impressions, which, Falk said, "can be really important and telling."

Though not all skull remains retain enough details to make a good endocast, fortunately, Falk told us, "Hobbit made a gorgeous endocast."

You can almost imagine the scientists holding their breath when the completed endocast came in. The most surprising part of the little brain mock-up was "right at the tip of the front—which would be right where your forehead is, above your nose, an area that is called Brodmann area 10," Falk said. This was an important discovery, because area 10 "is really a very highly advanced part of the brain in living people," Falk explained. "It's where taking initiative happens, planning ahead, silent thought, and daydreaming." The fact that the Hobbit had a complex and well-developed area 10 meant that it was capable of abstract thought.

Falk was amazed: "I've not seen a combination of features like that in any brain, so our interpretation is that it is definitely a small brain, but it's a fancy brain." This was a promising revelation. But the team still hadn't fully verified the existence of a new species. To do so, Falk said, they'd have to compare the Hobbit endocast with every possible alternative: "a human pygmy woman, a chimpanzee female, a normal woman, an adult female *Homo erectus* specimen, and even a human microcephalic—because some people have suggested Hobbits weren't real but pathological *Homo sapiens*."

It came down to a police lineup of sorts. "I could see all of them together and Hobbit in the middle," Falk said. "It looked a whole lot like a *Homo erectus,* which was very exciting. It also shares some features with another group of early hominids. I remember showing that to David Hamlin, and it was this great moment."

Falk and her team took measurements, ran some statistics, and got ready to write up their first paper, which was accepted for publication in *Science*. With the rigorous tests completed and all the alternatives eliminated, Falk was finally convinced. "Based on further studies and also other people's studies of the body," Falk said, "what I think is that the discoverers are correct, that it's a totally new species in the genus *Homo*, that it is a so-called insularly dwarfed species." In other words, it got smaller than its ancestors because it lived on an island. Falk couldn't help but get excited.

"The form of its body is unique; the form of its brain is unique. *Nothing* has been seen like it before."

But rather than embracing the find, modern anthropologists from universities and museums in Australia, Indonesia, and the United States became swayed by value attribution. Taking a page from anthropological history, they doggedly opposed the validity of the Hobbit. They insisted that it was nothing but a microcephalic human. The situation was a replay of what Eugene Dubois had encountered more than a century earlier. "I was a little surprised," Falk recalled, "because I guess I kind of thought, 'Oh well, it's 2004,' and I thought, 'Well, this is a modern day; we've learned a lot since Neanderthal.' So I was surprised at the extent of the acrimony, and the debate—which has gotten quite nasty at times."

Now, it's understandable that anthropologists would have questioned the new findings. Even Falk herself was scientifically cautious before accepting the claim that Hobbit was a new species. But these anthropologists have held out, even in the face of hard data. Meanwhile, the research continues to mount. "We recently did a study on microcephalics," Falk said. "We figured, that's how we'll answer them. We'll image their brain cases, we'll compare Hobbit to them, and we'll *show* that it is not shaped like a microcephalic. And we did that." The study, which used highly advanced statistics, bolstered Falk's previous data.

But despite the new evidence, some scientists still couldn't shake their value attributions. "What they said," Falk recalled, "was, 'Oh, well, your sample size wasn't big enough. We want a bigger sample size of microcephalics.' Well, our sample size was statistically significant and the statistics take sample size into account."

At a certain point, Falk saw that these anthropologists had abandoned science altogether: "Just arguing, 'I don't believe! Maybe there's something out there no one has ever heard of'? It's just not scientific." Falk recalled, "They said, 'Maybe there's some weird form of microcephaly out there that no one discovered yet.'" She was dumbfounded. "How can you argue with that?" Value attribution is such a strong force that it has the power to derail our objective and professional judgment. Simply put, this faction of modern-day anthropologists wasn't thinking scientifically.

If they had been, explained Falk, they would have had to come up with a falsifiable hypothesis. For instance, if the hypothesis is that all tomatoes are red, you can disprove the hypothesis by finding a yellow tomato. "What I said in my paper," Falk told us, "that [the Hobbit] is not a microcephalic, can be falsified with one specimen from a proven microcephalic whose virtual endocast looks identical. And that is scientific."

In the end, it all came down to how the anthropologists ascribed value: an unknown anthropologist, bones from Java, and a too-small brain. Like their predecessors, they couldn't shake the notion that the discovery was too "low-value" to be the real thing.

When the undercurrent of value attribution takes hold, it completely distorts our decision making. And as we'll soon see, it's closely related to another powerful sway—one that can make or break a basketball player's career, win or lose an MIT instructor the favor of his students, and even make us fall in love.

Chapter 4

MICHAEL JORDAN and the FIRST-DATE INTERVIEW

The curse of the low draft pick.

The "cold" professor.

What lovesick college freshmen have in common with HR managers.

When a pretty face equals a higher interest rate.

The "mirror, mirror" effect.

The Joe Friday solution.

t was like picking teams in P.E. Only instead of playground bragging rights, millions of dollars were at stake. And instead of anxious elementary schoolkids, the athletes waiting to be picked were some of the world's best. Welcome to the NBA draft, where choosing the right player can make all the difference.

Pick early and wisely and you can grab a future superstar. That's why NBA teams strike complicated trade deals with each other, vying for the best draft position. It was in just this enviable place that the Portland Trail Blazers found themselves in 1984. They'd finagled the number two position in a year that was especially rich in talent; four of the draftees would later be listed among the top fifty basketball players of all time: eleven-time NBA All-Star Charles Barkley; Hakeem

"The Dream" Olajuwon, who led his team to two back-to-back NBA championships; John Stockton, holder of the all-time NBA record for steals and assists; and a player who needs no introduction, Michael Jordan.

When it was the Blazers' turn to pick, Olajuwon was already spoken for. But the team passed over Michael Jordan and all the other future all-stars, instead selecting Sam Bowie, a talented seven-foot-one player who had shown a lot of promise in college but, because of injuries, would never go on to become an NBA superstar. Since then, Portland has gotten its share of flak for passing on Jordan. They'd visited the biggest candy store in the world and left with a stick of celery.

But before coming down too hard on the Blazers, it's important to realize that the draft is—at its core—educated guesswork and speculation. If we had a time machine, we could go back to the 1980s, load up on Microsoft stock, and give the Blazers' scouts a heads-up about Jordan. Lacking a crystal ball, though, the Blazers did the best they could with the information they had at the time. When it comes down to it, a team can never be exactly sure. Who knew Michael Jordan would become *Michael Jordan*? The draft is just a selection process.

Or is it?

Although none of the participants realized it, the teams were being swayed by the draft long after the selection process had been completed. The evidence is all there, thanks to the league's data collecting practices, which would make the most obsessive accountant proud. From the moment a new player walks onto the court, every aspect of his game—from points scored to number of rebounds, turnovers, fouls, minutes played, and assists—is meticulously recorded. These statistics are a boon to announcers, broadcasters, and fans alike. Buried within this mountain of data, though, are patterns that caught the eye of two economists: Barry Staw and Ha Hoang.

You don't expect economists to sift through sports stats for their data, but there's a lot more going on in the NBA draft than first meets the eye. Staw and Hoang's analysis reveals one of the most alluring sways we've encountered, one that begins at the same source as value attribution, but that diverges from it, pushing us even further from the shore of rationality. Our exploration of this current will help us see how our first impressions of a person can be altered by a mere word, why interviews are a terrible way to determine a job candidate's future performance, and why, sometimes, a pretty face is all it takes to create an offer you can't refuse.

But first let's get inside the heads of basketball team managers. Because so much rides on which player is on the court, it's pretty clear that owners and coaches want to give the most playing time to the most skilled athletes. After all, this isn't elementary school P.E., and you don't have to worry about anyone's mother calling to complain.

Staw and Hoang developed a clever empirical method for judging who the best players are. Dissecting the statistics of 271 new NBA players, they were able to distill all the numbers into three distinct categories that measure skill: *scoring* (points per minute, field-goal percentage, and free-throw percentage); *toughness* (rebounds per minute and blocks per minute); and *quickness* (assists per minute and steals per minute).

If a player is quick, tough, and high-scoring, you'd expect to see him out on the floor a lot. Indeed, when Staw and Hoang ran the data, they confirmed that an athlete's scoring contributed to how much playing time he got. No need to call *Sports Illustrated* with that nugget of data. But the weird thing was that the other two performance factors, toughness and quickness, "had virtually no relationship to the number of minutes a player got to play." Instead, a wholly different, hidden force overshadowed all three of these relevant measurements.

It all came down to that P.E. class moment when players got selected by their respective teams. Staw and Hoang found that the variable most responsible for an NBA player's time on the court—"above and beyond any effects of a player's performance, injury, or trade status"—was his *draft selection order*. Even after controlling for all other factors, in a given season "every increment in the draft number [e.g., getting drafted ninth instead of eighth] decreased playing time by as much as 23 minutes." Incredibly, draft order continued to predict playing time all the way through a player's fifth year in the NBA, the final year measured in the study.

But draft order had even deeper implications. Being picked late in the draft increased a player's likelihood of getting traded to another team and ultimately affected the longevity of his career. "A first-round draft pick," found Staw and Hoang, "stayed in the league approximately 3.3 years longer than a player drafted in the second round."

Now remember, Staw and Hoang had isolated draft order from all the other variables. That means that if you have two players with the exact same toughness, scoring, and quickness record, the one picked earlier in the draft would get more playing time, be much less likely to be traded, and have a longer career than his counterpart, who—although he turned out to be just as good—had the misfortune of being picked later in the draft.

Let's pause here. Are Staw and Hoang saying what we think they're saying? If we think about this rationally, once a player is picked, his draft order shouldn't matter. After all, coaches and managers should only be interested in a player's level of productivity on the court and his overall fit within the team. Once the draft is over, the draft number becomes an arbitrary statistic that gives no indication of how he'll actually perform on his new team.

But here's where value attribution meets up with a sway called the diagnosis bias—our propensity to label people, ideas, or things based on our initial opinions of them—and our inability to reconsider those judgments once we've made them. In other words, once a player is tagged as a "low pick," most coaches let that diagnosis cloud their entire perception of him. It's as if each athlete wears a permanent price tag on his jersey. Score points, catch a lot of rebounds, block shots, and make steals, and it still won't affect your playing time as much as your draft order does, even years down the road.

None of us is immune to falling into the same trap that snared the NBA coaches. Imagine, for example, that you needed to hire an attorney and had a choice between one who'd finished at the top of her class and her classmate who'd finished sixth. The top-ranked one would be much more appealing—even if the sixth-ranked one was equally competent and might end up being a better fit for your particular needs. Even after you made the hire, it would be impossible to let go of your awareness of class rank and keep it from affecting your perception of the lawyer's competence. Every time something seemed to be going wrong, in the back of your mind you'd think, "I bet the top-ranked one would have done things differently."

We are so susceptible to this diagnostic sway, in fact, that even a single, seemingly innocuous, word has the power to change our opinions. To see this in action, let's head to MIT, where the students of Economics 70 thought they had reason to relax. They had just been seated when a college representative walked in and told them that their professor was out of town that day. But before they had time to pack up their books, they were told that a substitute instructor would be filling in, an instructor they had never met. The representative from the college explained to them that "since we of Economics 70 are interested in the general problem of how various classes react to different instructors, we're going to have an instructor today you've never had before." At the end of the period, they would be asked to fill out some forms about the sub. But first, to give them a sense of who this mysterious guy was, the students received a brief bio describing him.

What they didn't know was that there were actually two different bios being handed out. Half the students received this version:

Mr. —— is a graduate student in the Department of Economics and Social Science here at MIT. He has had three semesters of teaching experience in psychology at another college. This is his first semester teaching Ec 70. He is 26 years old, a veteran, and married. People who know him consider him to be a very warm person, industrious, critical, practical, and determined.

The second half received a nearly identical bio. Only two words had been changed:

Mr. —— is a graduate student in the Department of Economics and Social Science here at MIT. He has had three semesters of teaching experience in psychology at another college. This is his first semester teaching Ec 70. He is 26 years old, a veteran, and married. People who know him consider him to be a rather cold person, industrious, critical, practical, and determined.

The difference, of course, is that half the bios describe the professor as "very warm" while the second half describe him as "rather cold." Remember that the students were under the impression that they had all read the same description. Now enter the substitute, who spent the rest of the period leading a discussion about material the class had recently covered.

At the end of the period, each student received an identical questionnaire about the sub. Upon seeing the results, you'd think the students were responding to two completely different instructors. Most students in the group that had received the bio describing the substitute as "warm" loved him. They described the instructor as "good natured, considerate of others, informal, sociable, popular, humorous, and humane." Although the second group sat in the exact same class and participated in the exact same discussion, a majority of them didn't really take to the instructor. They saw him as "self-centered, formal, unsociable, unpopular, irritable, humorless, and ruthless."

This one word, "warm" or "cold"—albeit irrelevant in the larger scheme of things—made students assign a high or low value to the professor. Like the NBA teams with the draft order, once the students read the substitute's bio, their opinions of him were set.

In other words, a single word has the power to alter our whole perception of another person—and possibly sour the relationship before it even begins. When we hear a description of someone, no matter how brief, it inevitably shapes our experience of that person.

Think how often we diagnose a person based on a casual

description. Imagine you're set up on a blind date with a friend of a friend. When the big night arrives, you meet your date at a restaurant and make small talk while you wait for the appetizer to arrive. "So," you say, "what do you have planned for this weekend?" "Oh, probably what I do every weekend: stay home and read Hegel," your date responds with a straight face. Because your mutual friend described your date as "smart, funny, and interesting," you laugh, thinking to yourself that your friend was right, this person's deadpan sense of humor is right up your alley. And just like that, the date is off to a promising start. But what if the friend had described your date as "smart, *serious,* and interesting"? In that light, you might interpret the comment as genuine and instead think, "How much Hegel can one person read?" Your entire perception of your date would be clouded; you'd spend the rest of dinner wracking your brain over the difference between Heidegger and Hegel and leave without ordering dessert.

Interestingly, even when we're not given a clear-cut value tag, we are so eager to assign a value that we create our own diagnostic labels. Most of us simply can't stay neutral for long, which is why we're so susceptible to following the siren song of the diagnostic bias.

Each day we're bombarded with so much information that if we had no way to filter it, we'd be unable to function. Psychologist Franz Epting, an expert in understanding how people construct meaning in their experiences, explained, "We use diagnostic labels to organize and simplify. But any classification that you come up with," cautioned Epting, "has got to work by ignoring a lot of other things—with the hope that the things you are ignoring don't make a difference. And that's where the rub is. Once you get a label in mind, you don't notice things that don't fit within the categories that do make a difference."

What Epting is saying is that all of us put on diagnostic glasses when we encounter new people. When we meet someone at a party, for example, we quickly diagnose him or her as "approachable" or "standoffish" before deciding whether we want to engage in a conversation.

But we pay a price for these mental shortcuts, explained Epting: "The baggage that comes with labeling is the notion of the blinders, really. It prevents you from seeing what's clearly before your face; all you're seeing now is the label." An NBA player is labeled as a low draft pick. Thanks to our diagnostic bias, it doesn't matter whether he plays his heart out: he'll always be viewed as subpar. Once a professor is described as cold, his personality and teaching ability cease to matter: his students dislike him anyway. The diagnosis bias causes us to distort or even ignore objective data.

No one knows about the power of these diagnostic distortions better than Professor Allen Huffcutt, who for the better part of twenty years has studied one of the most important diagnostic moments we encounter: the job interview.

When you think about it, the standard job interview is a lot like a first date. As Huffcutt explained, "You don't have a clear format to follow and you just let the interview go as it will." Sitting across from a candidate, managers try to form an impression: Does the candidate share my interests? How's the chemistry between us? Is there a connection? "If you look across all industries," Huffcutt told us, "this unstructured interview format is by far the most dominant form of applicant selection."

It's easy to understand why companies would be so drawn to the "first-date" interview format. After all, a manager will be spending a lot of time with the person they hire; they want to make sure the person is a good fit. And, Huffcutt explained, "We have a notion of the ideal employee that we want to hire."

Ideally, of course, companies would have a magic box that could perfectly predict a potential candidate's performance. Drop in a few facts about a hire, add a sampling of their skills and—voilà—out comes a score indicating how good an employee the candidate would be. As it turns out, this notion isn't as fanciful as we might think.

There's a whole segment of academics fascinated with hiring practices. Every year, Huffcutt makes a pilgrimage to a conference where he and his colleagues review all the latest studies about hiring practices. Over the years, Huffcutt and his colleagues have examined a host of specific selection criteria and determined their relevance to actual job performance—and through this process, they have, in essence, created the elusive "magic box" of job candidate competence.

The contents of this box, assembled through meticulous research, would be a gold mine for anyone making a hiring decision. But when we look inside, what we see comes as a complete surprise. Explained Huffcutt, "Your typical unstructured interview"—the common "first-date" method—"just doesn't do well. We have a long history of research confirming that."

Just how "not well" is surprising. When researchers conducted a meta-analysis—a broad study incorporating data from every scientific work ever conducted in the field—they found that there's only a small correlation between first-date (unstructured) job interviews and job performance. The marks managers give job candidates have very little to do with how well those candidates actually perform on the job.

It all comes back to the dating analogy. "How many people go on a first date," Huffcutt reflected, "get a certain impression, keep dating the person, and then, over time, see the reality of the person? That first impression can be totally wrong. You later wonder, 'What in the world was I thinking? How did I not see these things?' Well, the same thing happens in the interview. You've got a very limited time exposure, applicants put on their best show, managers put on their best show, and—not surprisingly—you just don't see the realities of the person in twenty minutes."

In this way, professional hiring managers have a lot in common with college students sitting in their dorm rooms, daydreaming about their girlfriend or boyfriend. As two Canadian psychologists, Tara MacDonald and Mike Ross, recently discovered, students dismiss objective data when the information doesn't fit what they want to see. In their study,

MacDonald and Ross talked to college students during one of the most exciting times in their lives: as college freshmen who'd recently become involved in a new romantic relationship.

The researchers asked the students to assess the quality of their relationships—everything from trust to commitment to communication to overall level of satisfaction. Then they asked each student: Do you think you'll be together with your partner in two months? How about in six months? In a year? In five years? Do you see yourselves getting married? Do you think you are going to be together for the rest of your life?

Now, we've all been there: in a new relationship, head over heels in love, feeling on top of the world. Of course the students tended to be optimistic about their relationship's prospects. But then, continuing with the inquiry, the researchers asked permission to reach out to each student's roommate and family and ask them what *they* thought about the quality of the relationship and how long it would last. These people were observing the relationships from the outside, without new love's rose-colored glasses. Indeed, across the board, students were more optimistic about the relationship's prospects than were their roommates. Least optimistic of all were the parents.

A semester of college life passed by—classes and parties were attended, fights were had. When MacDonald and Ross revisited the students six months later, 61 percent of them were still in the relationship. Six months after that—a year after the original interviews—the number of students still involved with the same partner had further decreased to 48 percent.

When they analyzed the results, MacDonald and Ross found that judgmental roommates and nosy parents really do know best—well, sort of. Roommates and parents were far better than students at predicting a relationship's longevity. But, surprisingly, what MacDonald and Ross discovered was that even when the students predicted their relationships would be long-lived, their assessments of the *problems* in their relationships were right on the money. The students weren't blind to the issues that were already putting strains on the relationships; they simply ignored them when it came to making predictions about the future. Overwhelmingly, whether students detected the early warning signs or not, they overestimated the relationship's longevity. This dismissal of the facts is the first of three types of mistakes, or traps, we all fall into when we diagnose.

It's a trap you might be familiar with if you've ever been in the market for a new home. You see an ad for a house in a neighborhood you love, maybe on a tree-lined street you make it a point to drive along on your commute. You make an appointment with a real-estate agent right away, convinced that *this* is your dream home.

When you actually see it, the house turns out to be a little less dreamy than you'd originally imagined—the bathrooms need to be gutted, you've seen closets bigger than two of the bedrooms, and the backyard looks like a jungle. But given that you've already judged it a dream house, are you more apt to focus on the house's faults or sigh over its spacious front porch, shiny hardwood floors, and Jacuzzi tubs?

It's understandable that lovesick college students would twist information to convince themselves that their relationship is going to last or that prospective homeowners involved in the emotionally charged process of buying a new home might behave less rationally than usual. But you'd expect professional managers selecting new employees to be more level-headed. As it turns out, however, Huffcutt explained, managers are especially prone to ignoring highly relevant information when it comes to hiring. While the infatuated students are blinded by optimism, hiring managers, according to Huffcutt, "just ask poor questions."

The standard job interview questions are familiar to all of us. But they make Huffcutt cringe. During our conversation with him, he shared a list of the top ten most commonly asked questions during an interview. You'd think that, given the frequency with which they're asked, at least *some* of them would be useful. But of the whole list, Huffcutt gave a passing mark to only one question. See if you can guess which one it is.

1. Why should I hire you?
2. What do you see yourself doing five years from now?
3. What do you consider to be your greatest strengths and weaknesses?
4. How would you describe yourself?

5. What college subject did you like the best and the least?
6. What do you know about our company?
7. Why did you decide to seek a job with our company?
8. Why did you leave your last job?
9. What do you want to earn five years from now?
10. What do you really want to do in life?

When we look at these questions more closely, we see that they cluster around specific themes. The first group is taken from the Barbara Walters school of interviewing. The idea behind questions 1, 3, and 4 is that by asking semi-insightful, self-evaluative questions, you can get a sense of the *real* candidate. This approach might make for a good episode of *20/20,* but it doesn't glean useful information about what the candidate would *really* be like on the job.

Take question 3, about the candidate's greatest strengths and weaknesses. "What do you really gain by asking that?" Huffcutt pointed out, "Who's going to tell you their true weaknesses? I'm not going to say, 'Well, you know, sometimes I stay out too late at night drinking and I'm late for work.' Who's going to say that?" As Huffcutt pointed out, "Applicants would likely have prepared for these types of questions and thought about them and developed a standard, pat answer. They're going to say something that sounds good but doesn't really portray a weakness: 'Sometimes I try to do things too well' or 'Sometimes I take my work too seriously.' "

Likewise, question 1 ("Why should I hire you?") is the equivalent of Walters asking a presidential candidate, "Why should we elect you?" If the question sounds rehearsed, so will the answer. "Obviously, any applicant worth their salt would come up with a nice answer for that," said Huffcutt with a shrug. Question 4 ("How would you describe your-self?") is "another one that's not going to do much." Stating that you're an enthusiastic, hardworking team player doesn't carry much predictive value about your ability to carry out and complete tasks. At its core, the problem with the Barbara Walters constellation is that the questions elicit prepackaged responses that don't really tell us anything about the candidate's actual skills.

The second group, composed of questions 2, 9, and 10, requires candidates to gaze into the future. But unless they're applying for a job at a psychic hotline, their predictions carry little weight. Even more problematic is that applicants can be—shall we say—less than forthcoming about their true plans—a little like the blind date who assures you that their current dead-end job is "just a stepping stone." Look at question 2, about what you see yourself doing in five years. As Huffcutt pointed out, "Everybody is going to come up with a nice-sounding answer: 'I want to be advancing in the company; I want to be working toward higher levels.' Everyone is going to say something that sounds deep."

The final cluster, questions 5, 7, and 8, takes the opposite approach and turns the interviewer into a historian. The thing is, though, when people revisit the past they often reconstruct it. Questions like number 7 ("Why did you decide to seek a job with our company?") invite artful responses.

"Once again, who's going to give a truthful answer? 'I'm desperate, the bills are piling up, I need a job, and you have an opening,'" Huffcutt asked. Instead, "they're going to come up with some nice-sounding answer."

And the winner (by default) is unassuming question 6 ("What do you know about our company?"). "That can actually be a decent question," explained Huffcutt. "That gets into whether they took the time to research your company, which can be a good sign—at least better than the previous questions." Number 6 is still not the best of questions, but it does provide *some* helpful information.

All of the other top ten questions invite a performance by the candidate: "I work too hard . . . I'm a team player who enjoys a good challenge . . . My life's dream is to work for your company . . . in this exact job." Yeah, that's the ticket.

Although everyone from the lowliest worker to the CEO knows that these performance charades are going on, hiring managers are attracted to the first-date format, thinking that a good conversation will allow their instincts to guide them to the right candidate. "There is a strong feeling," Huffcutt explained, "that you can't achieve accuracy in selection without going through the interview." We want to really sniff out that perfect candidate and get the sensation that, yes, this is the right person for the job.

The reason managers can err so easily is that, in addition to ignoring objective data, they focus on and give too much credence to irrelevant factors, which is the second trap we all fall into when making a judgment. It's a trap familiar to anyone who's ever bought a bottle of wine solely because of the attractiveness of the label or picked an accountant based on the appearance of his office.

Interestingly, the purveyors of act-now, special-offer junk mail can shed light on this behavior. Take what happened in South Africa when a consumer lending bank wanted to push personal loans to fifty thousand of its customers. Working together with a team of economists, the bank crafted several variations on the same basic loan offer letter. The different versions were randomly assigned to recipients and mailed off without any indication that the letters were part of an experiment.

The letters included different interest rates (ranging from 3.25% to 7.75% per *month*); some featured a comparison to a competitor's rate; others a giveaway ([Win one of] TEN CELL PHONES UP FOR GRABS EACH MONTH!); and still others a photo of either a man's or a woman's pleasant, smiling face.

Now, you'd think that the customer would evaluate the offer based purely on interest rate and the specific terms of the loan. Marketing gimmicks such as competitor comparisons, giveaway offers, and fanciful photos shouldn't be part of the calculation. Indeed, the comparison to a competitor's offer didn't really affect the would-be customers. Similarly, throwing in an opportunity to win a cell phone didn't have much of an overall effect. The unexpected effect kicked in with the least relevant variation: the inclusion of a picture of the smiling face in the corner. Men who received a picture of one of four smiling *women* were much more likely to sign up for the loan than were the men who received a picture of a smiling *man*. According to the study, the magnitude of this effect is "about as much as dropping the interest rate 4.5 percentage points." Obviously, having a picture of a pretty woman on a letter doesn't make for a better financial offer, but researchers speculated that the men were attracted to the woman and therefore signed up for the loan.

Let's take a step back here. It's unlikely that any man would consciously sign up for a higher-interest loan just because the offer letter had a picture of a woman on it. But just like the college freshmen who misdiagnosed the longevity of their relationships because they ignored valuable information about the quality of their relationships, the loan customers made diagnostic errors in evaluating the attractiveness of the loan because they didn't focus on the important data.

Imagine how many buying decisions we make for similarly irrelevant reasons—do we really think that we'll get a better deal or product from a company whose ad features a spokes-gecko or a "priceless" slogan?

Swayed by the picture of the woman, the South African bank customers were prone to diagnose the loan offer as attractive, in the same way that the MIT students were swayed by the description of the substitute professor as "warm" and NBA teams were swayed by a player's draft order.

Huffcutt's work on job interviews shed an interesting light on one of the more intriguing aspects of the diagnosis bias, one that we might consider dubbing the "mirror, mirror" effect. When we conduct job interviews, said Huffcutt, "we often base the image of the ideal candidate on ourselves. Somebody comes in who's similar to us, and we're going to click; we're probably going to want to hire them." But, of course, there's no proof that just because potential employees are similar to their manager, they'll be a better fit for the company. In fact, there's a compelling case to be made that managers would be better off hiring someone *unlike* them— so that where the manager falls short, the new hire can pick up the slack.

Still, managers have a difficult time turning their backs on the "first-date" job interview. "Everybody thinks they have this ability to see an applicant and make a great decision, truly understand them," explained Huffcutt. "Everybody thinks they can do that, and that's part of the problem. It's hard to convince somebody that they're not doing as well as they think."

This tendency is by no means limited to managers who do the hiring. We all diagnose when encountering a person or situation for the first time, and study after study shows we're not very good at it. And yet, whether we're interviewing a potential candidate or entering a new relationship, time and again we overestimate our ability to form an objective opinion.

If we can't overcome the diagnosis bias outright, we can take a cue from mythology and adopt Odysseus's strategy. Knowing that he wouldn't be able to help but follow the sirens' song, jump from the ship, and drown, he had his crew tie him to the mast.

When it comes to interviews, managers need to restrain themselves from delving into first-date questions and focus instead on specific past experience and "job-related hypothetical scenarios," said Huffcutt. It's the Joe Friday, just-the-facts-ma'am approach. The idea is to focus on relevant data and squelch any questions that invite the candidate to predict the future, reconstruct the past, or ponder life's big questions. It's all about the important information. What kind of accounting software are you familiar with? What experience do you have running PR campaigns? How would you reduce inefficiencies on the assembly line?

Because they confine managers to specifics, these structured interviews fare much better than their unstructured counterparts. The meta-analysis showed that "Joe Friday" interviews are *six times* more effective than first-date interviews at predicting a candidate's job performance.

But even then interviews aren't that great as a predictive tool, because some people simply know how to sell themselves better than others. As counterintuitive as it sounds, you don't need interviews at all. Research shows that an aptitude test predicts performance just as well as a structured interview.

"But then again," Huffcutt pointed out, "everybody expects an interview." Huffcutt's solution is to turn the process on its head. "Given that the applicant is expecting an interview," he offered, "the ideal system is to use the higher accuracy techniques up front to make your decision—things like mental ability tests, work samples." Then, "when you've identified your top candidates," he advised, "you use an unstructured interview to really sell them on taking the job, get them excited about the company. You can use it for some very useful things, just not for the hiring decision itself."

The point is, when we're in the position to make a diagnosis, we *all* become overly confident in our predictive abilities and overly optimistic about the future. Like the students in rocky relationships who believed love would prevail, we often ignore all evidence that contradicts what we want to believe.

While the Odysseus approach might help us avoid asking the kinds of questions that lead us to incorrectly diagnose a person or situation, Huffcutt makes it clear that it's harder to overcome this sway than we might think.

When we asked him whether his own department had made any changes in its hiring procedures based on his research, Huffcutt smiled. "That's a great question," he said, "and the answer is no. I've made some suggestions on how we can do better on interviews, but so far they haven't been taken."

Chapter ⁵

The BIPOLAR EPIDEMIC and the CHAMELEON EFFECT

A psychiatric outbreak.

↓ ↓ ↓ ↓ ↓
Sugar pills and Prozac.

↓ ↓ ↓ ↓
Tricking Israeli army commanders.

↓ ↓ ↓
How to sound beautiful.

↓ ↓
How old do you feel?

↓
The love bridge.

t had the makings of an epidemic. From 1994 to 2003 the number of children diagnosed with bipolar disorder—a condition characterized by cycles of devastating hopelessness and despair followed by times of ecstatic excitement—had skyrocketed. In 1994 only twenty-five of every hundred thousand American kids under the age of nineteen were diagnosed as bipolar. But by 2003 the number of cases had shot up by a staggering *forty times*. A doubling of this rare but serious condition would have been newsworthy in its own right, but a fortyfold increase made it clear *something* was going on. The question was what.

One explanation is that there was a surge in the number of kids suffering from the disorder. But the diagnosis of 800,000 children in 2003 alone, compared with 20,000 per year just a decade earlier, signaled a radical change—a fundamental shift, perhaps, in the process of growing up. But no such change had been identified. Moreover, because bipolar disorder involves a heightened risk of suicide, if its occurrence had increased, we'd expect to see a corresponding spike in suicide and attempted suicide rates among young people. Over this same period, though, suicide rates among America's children didn't rise at all—in fact, they went *down* by 23 percent.

Another explanation is that the number of kids with bipolar disorder had always been large, but that in the last decade more parents had begun to seek psychiatric help for their children. The problem with this theory is that if there had been a massive stampede to psychiatrists, it stands to reason that diagnoses of disorders other than bipolar would have increased as well. But there was no such surge.

And this brings us to the third possible explanation: if the number of children suffering from bipolar disorder hadn't increased, and the number of parents seeking psychiatric help for their kids hadn't increased, maybe all that had changed was the number of children being *diagnosed.* Not only does our exploration of this theory take us deeper into the two diagnosis traps we explored in the last chapter, it also uncovers a new and powerful trap that affects both the person with the bias and the person being diagnosed.

It turns out that even the medical community is not immune to the lure of the diagnosis bias. As the job interviewers taught us, one of the traps in diagnosing is that we tend to rely on arbitrary information. To understand how this force contributed to the bipolar epidemic, we must cross an ocean and travel back in time to the tumultuous world of pre–World War II Germany. There a psychiatrist named Emil Kraepelin was developing the first categorization scheme for mental disorders. Instead of relying on objective, scientific data, Kraepelin used his own intuitive judgment to arrive at the diagnostic scheme. Some of the labels he developed are still used today, including manic-depressive disorder, also known as bipolar disorder. Some of his other diagnoses, however, are more obscure and, frankly, unnerving—such as his category of "individuals with distinctly hysterical traits," which included "dreamers and poets, swindlers and Jews."

Nonetheless, psychiatrists found Kraepelin's diagnostic system to be a useful tool (he's regarded as the father of modern psychiatry) because it created an analog to the medical model of diagnosing diseases. If a patient visits a physician and complains of a sore throat, headache, and fever, the doctor can do a quick examination, diagnose strep throat, and administer the prescribed remedy. Similarly, under Kraepelin's system, a patient who sees a psychiatrist and exhibits symptoms of bipolar disorder can be diagnosed and assigned a course of treatment, be it therapy or medication. This medical model of diagnosis has proven popular with psychiatrists up through the present day.

In 1980 the new edition of the *Diagnostic and Statistical Manual of Mental Disorders* (DSM-III) broadened the definition of bipolar disorder to include individuals with less pronounced symptoms. No longer did the diagnosis require previous hospitalization for a manic episode. The new diagnostic now included such commonplace descriptors as "feel[ing] sad or empty"; "appear[ing] tearful"; exhibiting "fatigue," "indecision," or "insomnia"; being "more talkative than usual"; suffering from "distractibility"; or having "inflated self-esteem." Even individuals who met only some of these criteria could now be included under the bipolar umbrella.

On top of that, as British psychiatrist David Healy explained, in the 1990s pharmaceutical companies increasingly began to draw attention to this formerly rare and relatively unknown condition. Their campaign included the publication of new journals, the establishment of bipolar societies and annual conferences, television commercials for new treatments, and frequent workshops for mental health providers. During that time it was difficult for either parents or therapists to avoid hearing talk of bipolar disorder. What followed, said Dr. Healy, was a snowball effect. The more bipolar disorder was placed in the spotlight, the more clinicians were exposed to it, the higher the diagnosis rate climbed, which in turn led to further diagnosing. Factor in the new symptom standards for the illness, and the bipolar epidemic became so widespread that a Massachusetts hospital treated groups of preschoolers. Healy reported that even a two-year-old has been diagnosed with the disorder.

Now, the bipolar designation was arbitrary for a few reasons: Kraepelin had relied on his own perceptions, rather than on hard science, when categorizing the mental disorders; the

DSM-III broadened his original definition in 1980; and pharmaceutical marketing campaigns since then had attempted to bring more people into the fold. Primed to be on the lookout for bipolar disorder, psychiatrists started seeing it everywhere they looked. What many of them failed to recognize was that they had fallen into one of the traps of the diagnosis bias—arbitrarily assigning labels.

On its own, relying on arbitrary information causes enough problems, but this inclination is further complicated by the other trap of diagnosis: our tendency to ignore objective data that contradicts our initial diagnosis. To gain a deeper understanding of how this trap plays out, we talked with psychologist Bruce Wampold. Dr. Wampold is the kind of man who believes in empirical, quantitative evidence and objective data. He used his degree in mathematics and his psychological training to analyze what it is that makes psychotherapy work. His adherence to quantitative evidence meant that Wampold had to rely on large enough sets of data to make sure he was capturing all the relevant factors. It was only after taking into account every relevant scientific study on the effectiveness of psychotherapy that he began his meta-analysis.

The typical study that Wampold reviewed and analyzed looked something like this: A group of real-life patients who had sought therapy for a variety of reasons were randomly placed with different therapists, some of whom subscribed to a "medical diagnosis" theoretical model, and others of whom didn't. After the period of therapy ended, the clients were questioned about their lives and emotional states. They were asked whether their concerns had been alleviated and what their overall experience of therapy had been. Replications and variations of this experiment conducted with thousands of clients and hundreds of therapists produced a rich data set for Wampold. When he crunched the numbers, the results were surprising.

Wampold's findings showed that there were three distinct elements that made a psychotherapist successful. The first and most straightforward was talent. Just as there are good and bad managers, some therapists are more skilled than others. Some of the clinicians—regardless of theoretical orientation—stood out as highly effective and successful in treating their clients. The second element Wampold identified is what's called "therapeutic alliance"—the quality of the relationship the practitioner formed with the client. Therapists who had good relationships with their clients tended to have more positive results than those who didn't. The third factor was whether the studies allowed the therapists to use the method of therapy with which they felt most comfortable.

Surprisingly, diagnosis didn't figure into the equation one way or the other. That is, clients who were treated by a therapist who used the medical model were no better or worse off than their counterparts who saw practitioners who *didn't* use the medical model. As Wampold told us when we interviewed him, "diagnosis is irrelevant; it doesn't matter what the diagnosis is. You can go through the diagnoses—depression, panic, PTSD—and it doesn't matter. The whole notion of certain treatments for specific disorders falls apart." That is, "it's not the particular treatment that's making the difference; it's the ability of the therapist to work with the patient, creating a collaborative bond."

To be clear, Wampold is not claiming that psychotherapy isn't effective. His meta-analysis actually found that it had very positive mental health effects. Neither does he believe that therapists who subscribe to the medical model don't do a good job. His comprehensive research simply points out that the diagnostic model doesn't have any therapeutic advantage in and of itself.

Now, returning to the apparent epidemic of bipolar disorder, one could argue that despite aggressive diagnosing, children were benefiting from being prescribed medications for bipolar disorder. Indeed, officials from the Centers for Disease Control have argued that the introduction of selective serotonin reuptake inhibitors (SSRIs) such as Prozac, Paxil, Celexa, and Zoloft during the 1990s was the reason for the reduction in suicide rates. As the argument goes, children treated with SSRIs were less likely to feel depressed and commit suicide.

But a closer look at the data reveals a different picture. In 2002 a group of researchers analyzed all FDA medical and statistical data about the efficacy of SSRIs. They looked at "47 randomized placebo controlled short-term efficacy trials" conducted on the major SSRI drugs. Their conclusion stunned the psychiatric community. It turned out that when all the studies were aggregated and all the data meticulously analyzed, SSRIs were no more clinically effective than placebos in making patients—either kids or adults—feel better. That is, sugar pills and Prozac had about the same therapeutic effect.

Dr. David Antonuccio, professor of psychiatry and behavioral sciences at the University of Nevada, explained to us, "When it comes to SSRIs and children, only three out of the sixteen randomized control trials they had for kids showed a positive result. *Only three out of sixteen.* And of course there is also the risk of serious side effects."

Although the hard data had shown that the medical model of diagnosing served no therapeutic purpose (Wampold's study was published in 1997) and that the SSRI drugs are clinically ineffective, psychiatrists nevertheless kept diagnosing and prescribing. Once even the most seasoned professionals begin diagnosing, it's very hard to stop.

But there's another aspect to diagnosis we have yet to explore—its effects on the person being diagnosed. What about those kids who have been diagnosed as bipolar? What are the potential effects of such a diagnosis? To investigate this dynamic and uncover the third and most surprising trap of diagnosis, let's head to Israel, where 105 soldiers were about to participate in a grueling fifteen-week commander training program. It was a rigorous and intense process, requiring harsh physical training, mental concentration, and sixteen-hour workdays.

The would-be commanders didn't know it, but this particular course was going to be different from any to date. Before this session's classes started, psychologist Dov Eden informed the training officers leading the program that the army had accumulated comprehensive data on each of the trainees, including, Eden explained, "psychological test scores, sociometric data from the previous course, and ratings by previous commanders."

Based on this comprehensive information, Eden told the officers, each soldier had been classified into one of three "command potential" (CP) categories: "high," "regular," and "unknown" (due to insufficient information). Trainees from each classification were divided equally into the four trainee classes. "You will copy each trainee's CP," Eden told the officers, "into his personal record. You are requested to learn your trainees' names and their predicted CP by the beginning of the course."

The trainees, of course, had no idea that any of this was going on. And the officers didn't know that the so-called command potential, along with all the supporting data, was completely bogus. Scores were randomly assigned to the trainees and had nothing to do with their intelligence, past performance, or ability.

Nonetheless, when Eden returned fifteen weeks later, he discovered something remarkable. At the end of the course, the soldiers took a paper-and-pencil test that measured their new knowledge of "combat tactics, topography, standard operating procedures, and such practical skills as navigation and accuracy of weapon firing." This test wasn't rigged; it was part of normal procedure, a standardized assessment all soldiers took at the end of their training. But this is where the effects of assigning soldiers to the different command potential categories became apparent. The soldiers whom the training officers *thought* had a high CP score performed much better on the test (scoring an average of 79.98) than their "unknown" and "regular" counterparts (who scored 72.43 and 65.18, respectively). Simply being labeled, however arbitrarily, as having high leadership potential translated directly into actual improved ability—improved by a staggering 22.7 percent. Remember, neither the trainers nor the trainees had any idea what was going on. Without realizing it, the trainees had taken on the characteristics of the diagnoses ascribed to them.

This kind of phenomenon is by no means limited to the military. A meta-analysis conducted by psychologists at SUNY Albany suggested that these same diagnostic effects operate in the workplace. If you've ever been fortunate enough to work for a boss who values and believes in you, you'll know that you tend to rise to meet the high expectations set for you. On the other hand, there's nothing that will make you feel more incompetent and demoralized than a supervisor who is convinced you don't have what it takes.

The same phenomenon can occur when a psychologist or psychiatrist assigns a label to a client, be it bipolar disorder, anxiety, or depression. As Wampold explained, one of the problems inherent in diagnoses is that "there's pressure to make everything fit with that diagnosis, so once that diagnosis has been made, all the behaviors and decisions become confirmatory." When a child who has been branded as bipolar appears "tearful" or feels "sad or empty," these emotions get interpreted as part of the condition. When we are labeled, explained psychologist Franz Epting, "it's easy to start acting it out as a way of being in the world." We fit into the mold created by the diagnosis. "And then it becomes quite a tangle between what's *really* going on with us versus what we have been labeled with."

In other words, this molding process becomes self-perpetuating: when we take on characteristics assigned to us, the diagnosis is reinforced and reaffirmed. Take a look at what happened with the Israeli soldiers and officers. When Eden informed the trainers that the command potential scores had actually been fabricated and assigned randomly, they staunchly disagreed. In a desperate attempt to prove their point, they offered up evidence that the high-potential soldiers indeed performed better on the exit exams. This, of course, is circular logic. The exit tests confirmed the initial diagnosis; the trainees had merely molded their abilities to the diagnoses ascribed to them.

And this is the third trap of diagnosis: when we brand or label people, they take on the characteristics of the diagnosis. In psychological circles, this mirroring of expectations is known as the Pygmalion effect (describing how we take on positive traits assigned to us by someone else) and the Golem effect (describing how we take on negative traits). But let's use "chameleon effect" as our catchall term. This phenomenon helps to explain why fifty-one women waiting for the phone to ring had a lot in common with the soldiers in the Israeli commander training study. The women had signed up for a study on communication; all they knew about it was that they would be having a short conversation with a randomly selected man. When the phone finally rang, the women engaged in seemingly ordinary chitchat—they talked about the weather and their college majors, the kinds of things you'd expect a couple of strangers to discuss. But unbeknownst to the women, they were engaged in a hidden dance.

The prelude to the dance had begun a few minutes earlier. The men on the other end of the line had also signed up for a communication study. But unlike the women, each man, before calling the woman, had received a "biographical information form" and a snapshot of her. What the men didn't know was that although the bios were accurate, the pictures were not. In fact, they were photos of completely different women, specially selected by the researchers beforehand. Half of these fake photos were of very pretty women, while the other half were of women who were more ordinary in appearance. Each bio was randomly assigned one of the photos.

You don't have to be a psychologist to guess that while the men gave the bios a quick read, they took a good, hard look at the photos. After reviewing the bio and the photo—but before actually talking to his assigned partner—each man was handed an "Impression Formation Questionnaire," which asked him to rate his expectations about her.

The results of the survey were telling. Regardless of what

the bios said, men who saw pictures of pretty women expected to interact with "sociable, poised, humorous, and socially adept women." The other group of men—the ones who thought they'd be talking to less attractive partners—thought the women would be "unsociable, awkward, serious, and socially inept."

Once each man had formed an opinion, it was hard for him to see the woman in any other light. And, as you can imagine, the men brought these biases into their phone conversations.

Meanwhile, the women were still sitting alone in their rooms. They had no idea that the men had been shown pictures—real or otherwise. When they were connected with the men, they simply engaged in casual chitchat.

And this is where the experiment *really* began. The researchers recorded the calls, then edited out the men's side of the conversations. The resulting clips, containing only the women's voices, were played to a third, independent group of twelve ordinary people, who knew nothing at all about the study and had never met any of the other participants. This fresh group was completely unaware of any biases the men may have held.

Listening to *just* the women's side of the conversations, this jury was asked to evaluate each woman using the same Impression Formation Questionnaire the men had filled out earlier.

Remarkably, without knowing it, the jury members cut in on the mysterious dance that had taken place between the men and the women. They attributed the same traits to the women based on their *voices alone* that the men had attributed to them based on their (fake) *photos*.

How did the jury come to the same conclusion? After all, they never met any of the participants, saw any of the snapshots, or were told about the men's biases. They didn't get to listen to the men speak and were completely in the dark about the nature of the study.

The answer lies with the subtle power of the chameleon effect. Remember that before the men had exchanged a single word with the "beautiful" women, they already thought of them as socially graceful, funny, composed, and collected.

Once the men formed this opinion, it affected every aspect of how they interacted with the women. Imagine if you were talking on the phone to someone whom you believed to be attractive. You'd likely be more engaged, listen more actively, and generally find yourself more immersed in the interaction.

When the "beautiful" women spoke with their mysterious strangers, they couldn't help but react to the cues the men were sending. Without realizing it, they took on the characteristics that the men had expected them to have. The researchers explained, "What had initially been reality in the minds of the men had now become reality in the behavior of the women." The women unconsciously picked up on the "beautiful" opinion the men had of them and acted accordingly. In other words, being thought of as beautiful made the women actually think of themselves as beautiful and exhibit "beauty" in their conversations.

Now, who hasn't walked a little taller or smiled a little brighter after being told how beautiful they look? But does the chameleon effect simply change our self-perception temporarily, or can it actually have long-term effects? New research from Yale indicates that diagnosis can indeed have a lasting effect on our health.

In Hartford, Connecticut, folks at a senior living center took a break from their regular activities to participate in a special hearing test administered by the Yale researchers. The seniors put on a pair of headphones that played a sequence of three ascending pitches for each ear. Each time the seniors heard a tone, they were supposed to raise their hand. Raise your hand after every tone and you get a perfect score of 6. Miss four of the six tones and you only earn a score of 2 out of 6, which means your hearing is fairly impaired. Given that everyone tested was over the age of seventy, it wasn't surprising that the average score was just 3.53.

Next the seniors were asked to perform a task that seemed completely unrelated to the hearing test. "When you think of an old person," they were asked, "what are the first five words or phrases that come to mind?"

The researchers noted how each person responded, and categorized each answer on two separate scales: one from very positive (e.g., "compassionate") to very negative (e.g., "feeble"), and another from external (e.g., "white hair") to internal (e.g., "experienced").

With two seemingly disparate sets of data—the hearing test and the attitude profile—in hand, the first phase of the study was complete. The hidden connection between the data was revealed three years later, when the same seniors were invited back to take the hearing test again.

Time had taken its toll, and, unsurprisingly, the average hearing score went down. But not all participants' hearing had deteriorated equally. Far worse off were those individuals who three years earlier had relied mostly on negative and external descriptors to describe old age. Even after statistically isolating the other factors that would diminish hearing (age, medical condition, etc.), the researchers found these external and negative perceptions of aging were responsible, on average, for a whopping 0.7-point drop in a person's hearing test score—the equivalent of the effect of eight years of normal aging alone—in just three years. In order to make sure that the senior citizens' self-diagnoses had affected hearing, and not the other way around, the researchers looked at those participants who had received a perfect score on the first hearing test. They found that among individuals who expressed negative and external stereotypes of old age, even those who had had perfect hearing scores the first time around were just as likely to experience diminished hearing as those who had started out with poor hearing.

Negative and external feelings about old age, in other words, can actually make people *physically* age faster. And the effect is not limited to hearing alone. Similar studies have found that negative stereotypes about aging contribute to memory loss and cardiovascular weakness, and even reduce overall life expectancy by an average of 7.5 years.

These studies reveal that psychology and physiology are inextricably connected in ways that no one imagined. To explore this dynamic more deeply, let's go to Capilano Canyon, a place whose beauty exemplifies the Pacific Northwest. Set against a mountainous backdrop, the area's lush old-growth rain forest is split by a dramatic canyon where the Capilano River flows. One of Vancouver's most renowned attractions, Capilano Canyon draws tourists and locals alike.

Nestled within these woods is a small but sturdy wooden bridge. Elevated ten feet off the ground, made of solid cedar, and bordered by guardrails, it offers a secure way across the stream.

A little farther up the canyon lies the Capilano suspension bridge. Built in 1889, this shaky rope structure spans 450 feet and hovers 230 feet above the ground. As wind blows down the canyon, the bridge sways, causing even the most sure-footed hikers to feel a little weak in the knees.

Little did the hikers taking in the scenery on one particular day know that the suspension bridge also had the power to sway their thinking.

At various times throughout the day, researchers had a young female assistant wait at the end of one bridge or the other. All the assistant knew about the research was that she was to adhere to a set of specific protocols. She was instructed to approach men between the ages of eighteen and thirty-five, one at a time, as they stepped off the end of each bridge. She would speak briefly to each man, following a scripted story—that she was a psychology student conducting a study on "the effects of exposure to scenic attractions on creative expression."

The assistant would then ask each man to fill out a short survey. When he was finished, she would offer to tell him about the study when she had a little bit more time. With that, she'd tear off a corner of the survey, jot down her name and number, and hand over the scrap of paper. Most of the men happily accepted the number and hiked off into the sunset.

The researchers also sent a young male assistant, armed with the same instructions, to approach men crossing each bridge. He gave the same spiel about a psychology study and likewise offered his telephone number should participants have any further questions. But unlike his female colleague, this assistant was repeatedly turned down by the subjects, who said "Thanks, but no thanks" to the offer. Over the next few days, only three curious guys called him up.

The female assistant's phone, on the other hand, started ringing right away and didn't stop. But what was interesting was *who* called her. Of the sixteen men who crossed the secure, wooden bridge, only two called. However, half of the eighteen men who crossed the suspension bridge called.

It's not likely that the men who called had developed a sudden interest in the psychology of creative expression. More likely, they had developed an interest in the psychology *assistant.* But had she miraculously become prettier or more attractive when talking to the men who crossed the suspension bridge? Why were those men so much more likely to call? The answer, the researchers concluded, was based on the relative shakiness of the two bridges.

Imagine walking across a rope bridge suspended hundreds of feet above a canyon. With each step, the bridge feels flimsier and less stable. You hold your breath; your heart rate increases; beads of sweat appear on your forehead. Physiologically speaking, the adrenaline rush you experience in such a situation is the same feeling of excitement you experience when you develop a crush on someone.

When the men who crossed the wooden bridge saw the research assistant, most of them looked at her and saw just that, a studious research assistant. But for the men who crossed the rope bridge, anxiety and adrenaline translated into a heightened romantic interest in the assistant. Their physiological reactions affected their perceptions. But could there be an alternative explanation? Could the nature of the bridges have acted as a filter of sorts, determining what type of men crossed them?

To test the possibility that the men who crossed the suspension bridge might simply be more courageous and daring than the group who crossed the wooden bridge, and thus more likely to take a chance on calling the assistant, the researchers went back to Capilano to conduct a follow-up study. In this second study, they stationed the female assistant only at the end of the suspension bridge. She approached some of the men right after they crossed; with others, before approaching them she waited for ten minutes after they had finished crossing. If the men who used the suspension bridge were indeed self-selecting brave souls, you'd expect both groups to call the assistant up in equal numbers, regardless of when she approached them. But the researchers confirmed the earlier results: the men who met the assistant when they had just crossed the bridge were much more likely to call than the ones who had been approached ten minutes later, when their anxiety had subsided and their adrenaline levels had gone down. The bridge's ability to enhance the men's romantic attraction earned it the moniker "the love bridge" within the psychological community.

We're constantly sending and receiving cues and subtle messages to and from one another—swaying and being swayed, even if our rational brain hasn't been let in on the secret. As these studies illustrate, we can't help but take on the characteristics others ascribe to us. There's a hidden dance at work within even the most seemingly straightforward interactions—and in this way, we're all psychological chameleons.

Chapter 6

In FRANCE, the SUN REVOLVES AROUND the EARTH

Who wants to trick a millionaire?

Splitting the pie.

Sentimental car dealers.

The talking cure for felons and venture capitalists.

Russian justice.

The rational Machiguenga.

ips puckered, Henri looked like he had just swallowed a spoonful of spoiled crème brûlée. He kept blinking, as if he could wish away the foul taste in his mouth. In the background, the music grew increasingly ominous.

The day had started out on an unusually hopeful note for Henri. Against the odds, he was selected from among thousands of hopefuls to be a participant in *Qui veut gagner des millions*, the French version of the game show *Who Wants to Be a Millionaire*. As Henri sat down in the tall chair onstage, the lights dimmed and host Jean-Pierre Foucault introduced the contestant and his girlfriend, Sophie, who was cheering him on from the audience.

Regardless of the country it's shot in, *Who Wants to Be a Millionaire* follows the same rules: contestants answer multiple-choice questions that grow progressively more difficult as the amount of money at stake increases. The first few questions are always gimmes, such as

Which family member did Red Riding Hood go and visit?
A. Her mother
B. Her sister
C. Her grandmother
D. Her second cousin, twice removed

They progress to more obscure trivia, such as "How many sailors accompanied Columbus on his voyage from Spain to the New World?" If contestants run into trouble, they can use one of three lifelines: call a friend for help, narrow down the answer choices, or poll the audience.

Henri had done well on the first few questions, but everything changed when the host asked him, "Qu'est-ce qui gravite autour de la terre?"—that is, "What revolves around the earth?"

Henri looked down in concentration as the answer choices were read aloud: (A) The moon, (B) The sun, (C) Mars, and (D) Venus. Henri reread the question out loud and mulled the choices over in his head. As the ominous music continued to play, he bit his lip. Seeing the contestant's puzzlement turn into genuine consternation, the host offered some advice: "Take your time, and if you have any doubts, use a lifeline."

Needing all the help he could get, Henri decided to invoke

his "ask the audience" lifeline. You'd think that Henri was smart to poll the audience. After all, even if some people get the answer wrong, in the aggregate the audience is usually right. But Henri was about to learn the hard way that our irrational perceptions of what's fair can dramatically sway our decision making.

"OK, audience, please use your answer pads," instructed the host. "Please answer this question for Henri . . . What revolves around the earth? If you know, please answer, and if you don't know, please abstain. (A) The moon, (B) The sun, (C) Mars, (D) Venus. You must vote now. Thank you!"

As the audience voted, the camera focused on Henri's girlfriend, dressed in a green sweater and fashionable red eyeglasses, looking utterly bewildered as to why her boyfriend couldn't come up with the right answer by himself. Then the camera panned across the French audience, capturing the dismay on their faces—a sign that they had made a diagnostic decision about Henri.

To say that Henri was no Galileo would be an understatement. Whether because he had slept through his elementary school science classes or because he was overcome with nervousness under the spotlight, Henri was stumped.

When the audience's answers were revealed, Henri took a deep breath, and swallowed hard: so much was on the line—he had to get this question right to stay in the game. As you might expect, no one in the audience voted for the answer that Venus revolved around the earth. For whatever reason, though, 2 percent voted for Mars. And then came the strange part. "If you allow me," said the host, "it is perhaps my own opinion, but the result is quite divided." Only 42 percent of the audience voted for the right answer, the moon. A full 56 percent voted for the sun revolving around the earth.

Henri was dumbfounded, and at this point we might ask whether something is horribly wrong with the French educational system. But it wasn't ignorance that the audience was exhibiting.

As we delve into what happened in France, we'll uncover our next psychological undercurrent—one that affects interactions from the boardroom to the jailhouse to the playground. It begins with a German experiment that anyone who had to share things as a kid can relate to. Researchers in Berlin placed a random pair of strangers in separate rooms. Each participant was told that he or she had been paired with a partner, whose identity would not be revealed. The pair would be given a combined sum of $10—but it was up to them to decide how to split it. The catch, though, was that the participants couldn't talk to each other, flip a coin, or enter into negotiation. Instead, one person was randomly chosen to decide how to split the money.

The splitting participant could divvy up the money any way he or she wanted. The receiving partner was then presented with the offer and had to decide whether to accept it or not. If the receiving partner accepted, both participants would collect their shares. If he or she rejected the offer, *both* parties would leave empty-handed.

This game would be played only once, so the participants

would be given no second chance. Furthermore, the participants were told that after the round was over, they would remain anonymous, going their separate ways.

Let's put ourselves for a moment in the shoes of the person deciding how to divvy up the sum. Most of us would probably opt to share the pot equally. Indeed, when it was time to make their choices, the majority of participants did decide to divide the sum right down the middle, so that each person would get $5. And all of the receiving partners who were presented with this offer accepted it.

The interesting part is what happened when the people deciding on the split gave themselves more than half. As you can imagine, their partners felt indignant. But were they indignant enough to walk away from the money? The answer, a vast majority of the time, was a resounding yes. Rather than accept the money that had been offered, most participants who were presented with an unfair split rejected it, opting instead to walk away empty-handed.

Now, from a purely rational perspective, it would have made sense for the receiving partners to accept *any* offer. After all, *some* money is better than *no* money. Two dollars, while not as good as five, is still better than zero. Regardless of the logic of such arguments, though, the overwhelming majority of partners who were presented with an unfair deal rejected the offer. They went home empty-handed but with the feeling that justice had been served.

What's more, their willingness to walk away from the deal when the split was uneven wasn't affected by the amount of money that was offered. When the same experiment was repeated with $100 instead of $10, participants were no more likely to accept an inequitable split.

What the study demonstrates is our deep-rooted belief in fairness and the great lengths to which we'll go to defend it. It was this adherence to the rules of fairness that swayed the French *Who Wants to Be a Millionaire* audience. Did Henri, who didn't know basic astronomy, really deserve a million euros? To the French audience, the answer—by a 56 percent to 42 percent vote—was a resounding no. They *deliberately* chose the wrong answer because it didn't seem fair to them for Henri to progress in the game with their help when he couldn't even answer such an easy question.

When Henri followed the audience's wrong answer, you could hear the spectators' muffled laughter. To them, giving the undeserving contestant the right answer would have been like allowing the uneven splitter to walk away with a disproportionate amount of money; it just wouldn't be fair.

But what if Henri had been someone the audience members expected less of—a first grader, for example? Would they have been as harsh? A variation of the "splitter" experiment sheds interesting light on this distinction. Participants in this study were presented with the same rules, except that instead of pairing up with another person, they were told they would be partnered with a computer, and that the computer would choose how to split the money. When the computer made "unfair" offers, the partners didn't balk. They were willing to accept an uneven split in the computer's favor, even though they would have rejected the same offer coming from a real person.

In other words, when it comes to fairness, it's the *process*, not the *outcome*, that causes us to react irrationally. This is called *procedural justice*. We don't expect a computer to be fair—but we do expect people to be.

Consider what would happen if we participated in a similar experiment where the person making the split was allowed to communicate with us. Imagine if he told us he was having financial difficulties and could really use the extra cash. We'd probably be willing to settle for less than half. Having been given a good reason for the inequitable split, we'd be less likely to feel that we were being taken advantage of and would be more likely to accept the offer.

But even the most calculating professionals are swayed by fairness. When you think of car dealers, you certainly wouldn't associate them with the notion of fairness. But despite their reputation for oily salesmanship and bilking consumers, in fact they're often the ones being taken to the cleaners—by auto manufacturers. Most car dealerships are relatively small operations and have little pricing power compared to the auto manufacturers. If you're a Ford dealer, for example, then Ford Motor Company is your only supplier; they control pricing and can dictate what your inventory will be. The dealers regularly pay high prices and get stuck with poor inventory—models that are difficult to sell but that the manufacturer needs to move.

When researchers talked to car dealers, they discovered

that the dealers evaluated their relationships with manufacturers in a surprisingly irrational way. A nationwide survey of car dealers revealed that rather than focusing solely on the results of their transactions with the manufacturers (Did I overpay? Did I receive high-quality inventory?), the dealers cared more about how the manufacturers *behaved* toward them. According to the research, what mattered to the dealers wasn't just whether they felt they got a good deal; they evaluated transactions by such seemingly insignificant details as whether the manufacturers "[took] pains to learn the local conditions under which dealers operate," acted in a "polite and well-mannered" fashion, and "treat[ed] dealers with respect." These fairness factors proved more important than the underlying economic numbers to the dealers' overall level of satisfaction with the outcome.

The researchers concluded that auto manufacturers and business managers alike "place too great an importance on margins and outcomes" when what was clearly more important to the customer was the perceived fairness of the process. They recommended that all managers—regardless of industry—put greater "effort, energy, investment, and patience" into nurturing the relationship. As the car dealer study suggests, how we are treated—the fairness of the procedure—has as much to do with our satisfaction as the ultimate outcome.

What is especially interesting about the issue of fairness is how important it is for people to feel they have a voice. A group of researchers asked hundreds of felons from Baltimore,

Detroit, and Phoenix to fill out a survey. These men had been convicted of crimes ranging from drug possession to fraud to armed robbery. The first part of the survey consisted of factual questions, such as the nature of their conviction and the length of their prison sentence. In part two, the survey moved on to questions about perceptions of fairness: How were you treated? How did you like the judge? Were the lawyers nice to you?

All of the survey questions fell into one of two categories: focusing either on the specific outcome—in this case a fine, probation, or prison time—or on how fair the process seemed—how the respondents perceived their journey through the legal system.

When researchers tabulated and analyzed the results, they found a peculiar pattern. As we'd expect, in evaluating the fairness of their trial, respondents placed a lot of weight on the outcome. Someone who got off with a light sentence naturally thought the trial was more fair than a guy who got the maximum sentence.

But it turns out that regardless of the crime they committed or the punishment they received, respondents placed nearly as much weight on the process as they did on the outcome.

One of the factors weighed most heavily by respondents was how much time their lawyer spent with them. The more time he or she spent with them, the more satisfied the respondents were with the ultimate outcome. Now, you'd think that the results would have been the opposite: a convicted felon who got stuck with a long sentence, especially after spending time with his attorney, would be angry. But it turns out that the behavior of his lawyer made a huge difference. In other words, although the outcome might be exactly the same, when we don't get to voice our concerns, we perceive the overall fairness of the experience quite differently.

The need to be heard, it turns out, isn't limited to just convicted felons. As you walk up Sand Hill Road in Menlo Park, California, with its modest-looking two-story office buildings, you don't notice anything particularly glitzy about the place. But on closer inspection, and after a couple of Ferraris go speeding by, you realize the affluence of the area. In these offices some of the nation's biggest high-tech companies had their start.

Sitting in their plush offices, venture capitalists in Silicon Valley and elsewhere around the country were asked about the entrepreneurial endeavors they had backed. Although the specific questions differed from those asked of the convicts, they fell into the same two general categories: outcome and process. The survey included specific questions about their dealings with entrepreneurs, such as "To what extent did the CEO provide you with timely feedback on the performance of the venture?" and "To what extent did the CEO keep you up to date on the performance of the venture?"

You'd expect the venture capitalists, or VCs, to be more analytical and detached in their reasoning than the felons. Simply put, a good investment is one that makes you money.

But when we look at the VCs' responses, it's clear that they, too, placed disproportionate weight on whether they felt their voices had been heard.

In analyzing the results, the researchers noticed that "timely feedback from an entrepreneur led investors to feel the entrepreneur was fairer, to trust the entrepreneur more, to be more supportive to the entrepreneur's strategic decisions, and to monitor the venture less frequently." If the investment's financial return is analogous to a prisoner's sentence—an objectively measurable result—the company's CEO is like the defense lawyer. A CEO who kept in touch gave the VCs a much more favorable impression of the underlying venture than did a CEO who was less communicative.

But this overemphasis on communication could be detrimental to a venture capitalist hoping to earn a good return on an investment. The VC-entrepreneur relationship is one in which it really *is* all about the money, and the frequency with which a CEO stays in touch with a VC has virtually no bearing on the success of the venture. A VC's evaluation of a venture should be only about the bottom line—how well the company is doing. For all he or she knows, the CEO who is uncommunicative might be the very one who is busy working night and day to help his start-up make it.

While the sway of procedural justice and our desire to have our voices heard are important to us all—whether we're car dealers, criminals, or venture capitalists—*how* we actually define fairness varies dramatically from culture to culture. Say that in the example of *Who Wants to Be a Millionaire* Henri changed his name to Henry and competed in front of an American audience. American audiences are almost certain to help out a contestant, regardless of his apparent abilities; data shows that in the United States, the "ask the audience" lifeline results in the correct answer more than 90 percent of the time.

When *Who Wants to Be a Millionaire* was introduced in Russia, though, the production team noticed that the audiences there would often give the wrong answer—and not just to confused souls like Henri. Russian audiences didn't discriminate—they deliberately misled both smart and less smart contestants alike. In fact, Russian audiences were so likely to give the wrong answer that contestants learned to be wary of the "ask the audience" lifeline.

When we contacted the *Who Wants to Be a Millionaire* production team for an explanation of the Russian phenomenon, they were just as perplexed. But Geoffrey Hosking, an expert in Russian history, had some interesting insights. We caught up with Hosking during his last week as a visiting professor at Princeton, as he was preparing to return to England, where he is on the faculty at University College London. Hosking first became fascinated with Russian culture during the time of Khrushchev; he is especially interested in why socialism was ultimately unsuccessful in Russia. Little did he ever imagine that his research would one day help explain the peculiarities of *Who Wants to Be a Millionaire*.

To solve the mystery of what prompted Russian audiences

to give wrong answers, Hosking took us back in time to peasant villages in the Russian countryside. Before the twentieth century, Hosking explained, peasant communities were governed by a principle of "joint responsibility." Everyone in the community acted together—whether paying taxes, supplying conscripts to the army, keeping peace in the community, or apprehending criminals. The peasants grew up expecting to lend one another a hand.

As the country became more industrial under the Soviet regime, people brought the old country ways to the city. Although life in communal Soviet apartments was cramped and difficult, Hosking explained, it was common for people to lend one another money and small items such as kitchen implements or matches. "It was fairly trivial stuff," he said, "and of course you find that a lot in other communities, not just Russian—but I think in Russia it was more systematic and expected." This attitude also prevailed at factories, where "Russians were constantly responsible for each other's lives."

But the same interdependent community that had your back could also turn against you if you stood out or were seen as different. In Hosking's view, this proclivity stemmed from the perception that "people who departed from the norm could be dangerous to the whole community—whether they were very rich or very poor. Either way, there was a tendency to seek the center and to resent people who were misfits."

And that, explained Hosking, is the key. "If people became very poor they were obviously a burden on the rest of the community. If they became rich it probably meant they were up to no good: they were criminals or did things which endangered the community."

This view of wealth is in direct opposition to Western attitudes toward wealth. "On the whole," Hosking reflected, "Americans regard it as justified if someone becomes rich. Now in Russia, the oligarchs"—a select group of entrepreneurs who found a way to make quick money after the Soviet collapse—"all achieved their wealth by means which were of dubious regard at best. That's the first thing that Russians resent. And secondly I think they resent the very fact that these people have become so much richer than everyone else."

From this perspective, it is clear that the *Who Wants to Be a Millionaire* audiences in Russia see contestants as trying to get rich on the backs of the audience members—and why should they contribute to such unfair behavior?

In their own ways, Henri and the Russian contestants violate a core pillar of their respective cultures' notions of fairness. What's fair in Moscow isn't necessarily fair in Paris or Berlin. As the world economy becomes more global, the differences between cultural interpretations of fairness become increasingly important.

Researcher Joseph Henrich decided to test the cultural universality of fairness. To begin with, Henrich replicated the money-splitting experiment among UCLA graduate students. He decided to use a dollar amount that he knew would be significant to students, and came up with $160, which translated to 2.3 days' worth of work at the grad students' standard university wage of $9 an hour. The rules of Henrich's experiment were exactly the same as those of the original study: you only play once, and you never find out who you were partnered up with.

As in the original study, the most common split offered in the UCLA study was 50/50, which the receiving partner always accepted. After the game was over, Henrich interviewed the participants to see what they had been thinking as they considered their offers. The same word came up again and again: fairness. "I thought that if I offered less than half," participants said, "my partner wouldn't accept the offer." And it turns out that the participants deciding on the split were right. Asked whether they would have accepted an 80/20 split—that is, an offer of $32—virtually all of the partners scoffed. "That would be unfair," they protested. They'd rather go home empty-handed. Some even went so far as to say that they would have categorically rejected *any* offer that was less than 50 percent.

Next, Henrich took his experiment on the road, heading to one of the most remote places on earth, deep into the Peruvian Amazon to visit the Machiguenga tribe. Eight hours from the nearest major city, the Machiguenga have been isolated from modern society for centuries. They live in small villages, but each family is self-sufficient, making its own tools and growing and gathering its own food.

Henrich brought along a translator who spoke a dialect of Arawakan, the native language. Next, he figured out what sum would be the equivalent of 2.3 days of work for the Machiguenga. Because the Machiguenga don't have their own currency, Henrich looked at what they earned from their occasional work for logging and oil companies that hired local labor. Their pay for 2.3 days of work came to twenty Peruvian soles.

Using that sum as the amount to be divided, Henrich carefully explained the rules of the game to the Machiguenga. But here in the Amazon, the game took a very different turn.

Unlike the UCLA participants—or, for that matter, participants from Japan, Indonesia, and Israel—the Machiguenga who made the split on average offered incredibly low sums to their partners. While the most common offer at UCLA was a 50/50 split, most Machiguenga offered an 85/15 split, favoring the person making the offer.

Even more strikingly, unlike the UCLA partners, who reacted to such lowball offers with indignation, when the Machiguenga partners were presented with these lopsided splits they nearly always chose to accept the offer. In so doing they were adhering remarkably closely to a rational economic model: from a purely objective, utilitarian perspective, it's logical to accept *any* offer rather than end up with nothing.

When interviewed afterward, the Machiguenga who accepted the offers laid out their reasoning. "Several individuals," explained Henrich, "made it clear that they would always accept any money, regardless of how much the proposer [splitter] was getting." Rather than viewing themselves as being treated unfairly by the offering partner, "they seemed to feel it was just bad luck that they were responders [choosers] and not proposers." The Machiguenga choosers viewed any offer as a generous gift. And those splitting the pie didn't see why they should give up half of their "winnings" to someone who was lucky just to get anything.

Some tribe members did make a 50/50 offer. When Henrich interviewed them, he found that each and every one of these people had spent significant time living among modern Westerners and felt the 50/50 split was the fair thing to do.

In the end, the Machiguenga are no more rational than are the UCLA students; they simply have a different perception of what's fair. In Russia it's not fair for one person to get rich. In America it's only fair if the splitter presents an even-steven offer. And in the Amazon jungle it's finders keepers.

We don't typically think of fairness as an irrational force, but it dramatically affects our perceptions and sways our thinking.

We've all been in situations where we had to negotiate a position. From an objective, logical perspective, it would make sense to focus strictly on the issue at hand: the offer we're presenting or the price we're asking for. But by talking through our reasons for that price or position, explaining how we arrived at it, and communicating what we feel is the fair thing to do, we can enjoy the same benefits as the attorneys who spent time with their clients and the entrepreneurs who talked frequently with their investors.

When we're busy completing a project at work, rather than assuming the final product speaks for itself, it's good to remember to regularly engage and update members of our team during the process. Similarly, when we travel to another country we should keep in mind that as we exchange currency, we also must shift our notions of fairness. As it turns out, because of these fairness sways, whether we're dealing with an auto dealer or a Machiguenga, it's not always true that what's fair is fair.

Chapter ⁷

↓

COMPENSATION
and COCAINE

Switzerland's toxic conundrum.

The GMAT rebels.

↓↓↓↓

The power of the pleasure center.

↓↓↓

Hijacking altruism.

↓↓

Fast times at "Commie High."

↓

The anticipation factor.

Whether they're Fortune 500 CEOs or high school principals, managers are always looking for ways to better motivate people. But is there a hidden side effect of bonuses and incentives meant to spur performance? What are the unintended consequences of offering people a financial carrot? To get a unique angle on the relationship between motivation and reward, let's travel to the University of Zurich, where researchers made some surprising findings.

Switzerland conjures up images of idyllic green pastures, snowy mountain ranges, and men in lederhosen blowing alpenhorns. The last thing that comes to mind is a mound of containers filled with toxic sludge.

In the 1940s, alarmed by the atrocities of World War II,

Switzerland's political leaders began developing a nuclear program. In typical Swiss fashion, the program priorities soon shifted to the more peaceful goal of creating nuclear power: five plants now provide about 40 percent of Switzerland's electricity. The country has a relatively clean energy program, but with any nuclear power comes nuclear waste— waste that has to go *somewhere*.

In 1993 the Swiss government identified two small towns as potential nuclear waste depositories, but they didn't know how the townspeople would react. Would they be outraged? Or, understanding the importance of the nation's nuclear energy program, would they "take one for the team"?

Two University of Zurich researchers were equally curious and decided to try to get some answers to this question. They asked the residents of the towns: "Suppose that the National Cooperative for the Storage of Radioactive Waste (NAGRA), after completing exploratory drilling, proposed to build the repository for low- and midlevel radioactive waste in your hometown. Federal experts examined this proposition, and the federal parliament decides to build the repository in your community." In a town hall meeting, the townspeople were asked whether they would accept this proposition or reject it.

Naturally, many people were frightened by the prospect of having the waste facility so close to their homes. But at the same time, whether out of social obligation, a feeling of national pride, or just a sense that it was the fair thing to do, 50.8 percent of respondents agreed to put themselves at risk for the common good. The other half of the respondents, however—those who said they would oppose the facility—still represented a significant obstacle for the government.

To see if this problem could be resolved, the researchers tested out a seemingly rational solution to bring the nuclear waste dump opponents on board. They talked to a new group of individuals from the same community and presented them with the same scenario, but added, "Moreover, the parliament decides to compensate all residents of the host community with 5,000 francs [about $2,175] per year and per person . . . financed by all taxpayers in Switzerland." Once again they were asked, in a town hall meeting, would they accept this proposition or reject it?

Now, from an economic perspective, a monetary incentive should make the proposition of living close to a nuclear waste storage facility easier to swallow. Indeed, we naturally assume that the best way to get someone to do something unpleasant or difficult is to offer some kind of financial incentive. It's why employers give bonuses when their employees take on more challenging or time-consuming work and why parents tie their children's allowances to performance of specific chores. Along this line of reasoning, the higher the compensation, the more likely it should be that people would do what you were paying them for.

Regardless of how much money is actually offered, though, rationally speaking, *any* amount of money should be better than nothing at all. That is, the $2,175 the Swiss researchers proposed might not be enough to convince *all* residents, but it should win over at least some of those who were opposed.

But that's not what happened.

For some reason, when the researchers introduced financial compensation into the equation, the percentage of people who said they would accept the proposition not only didn't increase—it *fell* by half. Instead of being motivated by the financial incentive, the townspeople were swayed to reject the nuclear dump en masse: only 24.6 percent of the people who were presented with the monetary offer agreed to have the nuclear dump close to their town (compared with the 50.8 percent who agreed when no money was offered). In addition to contradicting the laws of economic theory, this response just doesn't make sense.

Even when the researchers sweetened the deal to $4,350— and then again to $6,525—the locals remained firm in their opposition. Only a *single* respondent, in fact, changed his mind and accepted the offer when more money was put on the table.

Managers, parents, and, of course, economists have long operated under the assumption that monetary incentives increase motivation. But psychologists are beginning to discover that the connection between the two is trickier than it first appears. To understand what was really going on in Switzerland, we need to look into a paradoxical aspect of financial compensation, one that illuminates the strange relationship between monetary incentives and two very different parts of our brain.

Our first insight into this mysterious relationship can be found at an Israeli university where forty students sat with number 2 pencils in hand, preparing to take a mock version of the Graduate Management Aptitude Test (GMAT), the entrance exam used by most business schools.

Now, these Israeli students weren't actually applying to business school; they were taking the GMAT as part of a psychological study. Though they knew a high score on the mock test wouldn't result in admission to any MBA program, the volunteers were encouraged to do their best anyway.

Next the researchers brought in a separate group of forty students and asked them to complete the same test—but they added a concrete reward: for every right answer, a student would get 2.5 cents—not exactly enough to retire on, but better than nothing—which is what the first group of students received.

Check out the list of the actual student scores, ranked from highest to lowest. See if you can spot the surprising pattern.

Scores (out of a possible 50 points)

Students receiving no compensation	Students receiving 2.5 cents per correct answer
49	50
48	44
48	44
45	43
42	40

42	39
42	36
40	35
37	35
37	35
37	34
37	34
36	32
36	32
36	31
35	30
34	26
34	26
34	26
31	26
31	24
31	23
31	23
29	22
29	21
24	21
23	21
23	19
23	19
22	13
22	11
20	8
20	0

18	0
7	0
3	0
0	0
0	0
0	0
0	0

At first, the two columns look pretty similar. But the most interesting numbers are found down toward the bottom. Of the forty participants who weren't paid anything, four scored a zero on the test. Because the exam was multiple choice, getting a zero by dumb luck is virtually impossible. More likely, the four students simply thumbed their noses at the researchers. You pay me nothing, these rebels must have thought while filling the Scantron sheet with mockingly artistic designs, you get nothing in return.

But the group of paid participants had twice as many zeros. Now, you'd think that the opposite would be true: payment, after all, should act as an incentive to perform better. This is where the paradox witnessed in the Swiss countryside comes in. In each situation, the money effectively seemed to serve as a *dis*incentive: paid townspeople were *less* willing to host the dump, and compensated test takers *underperformed* on the exam.

When you look at the top 50 percent of performers in each group of test takers side by side, you see that the unpaid students *still* consistently beat out their paid counterparts, with an average score of 39 to the paid students' 34.9. In fact, looking across the board at all the scores, the students who didn't get a penny performed better than their paid counterparts, with an average score of 28.4, compared to the paid test takers' average of 23.1.

Economists can debate the reasons that such financial rewards backfire. But researchers at the National Institutes of Health (NIH) have been able to pinpoint the neurophysiology behind this paradox.

The NIH researchers placed participants in a specially modified MRI machine fitted with a computer monitor and a simple joystick. Lying inside the machine, the subjects played a video game reminiscent of the Atari era. At the start of each round of the game, either a circle, a square, or a triangle would appear on the screen. Each shape held a unique meaning. A circle meant that if you succeeded in completing an upcoming task—zapping a figure as it appeared on the screen—you'd earn a monetary reward. Different circles corresponded to different rewards. An empty circle was worth twenty cents. If the circle had a line through it, it meant that $1 was up for grabs; two lines meant a $5 reward.

When the subjects saw a square instead of a circle, they braced themselves for potentially bad news. The object of the game would be the same—zap the figure—except that *failing* to do so would result in a penalty of twenty cents, $1, or $5.

If the participants saw a triangle, it meant that no money

was on the line. Regardless of whether they hit the target or not, they would neither lose nor gain any money on that round.

While the participants were playing the game, they were shown a running tab of their earnings and losses. Meanwhile, the scientists monitored their brain activity. The scientists noticed that every time a circle or a square appeared—that is, every time there was money to be gained or lost—a certain part of the brain lit up. This region, which remained dormant when a triangle was shown (and no money was on the line), is called the *nucleus accumbens.*

The nucleus accumbens is, evolutionarily speaking, one of the most primitive parts of the brain, one that has traditionally been associated with our "wild side": it's the area of the brain that experiences the thrill of going out on a hot date, that sparks sports fans' exuberance when their team pulls out a last-minute victory, and that seeks out the excitement of Las Vegas. Scientists call this region the pleasure center because it is associated with the high that results from drugs, sex, and gambling.

At its most extreme, the pleasure center drives addiction. A drug like cocaine, for example, triggers the nucleus accumbens to release dopamine, which creates a feeling of contentment and ecstasy. The reason cocaine is so addictive is that the pleasure center goes into overdrive and the threshold for excitement climbs higher and higher. The MRI study surprised the researchers because it revealed that the pleasure center is also where we react to financial compensation.

And the more money there is on the line, the more the pleasure center lights up. A monetary reward is—biologically speaking—like a tiny line of cocaine.

Now, compare this reaction with our neurological reaction to altruistic behavior. In 2006, a few years after the NIH study, Duke scientists asked subjects to play a similar Atari-style video game, but instead of earning money for themselves, the participants were told that the better their score, the more money would be donated to charity.

In the MRI images, the pleasure center remained quiet throughout the game. But a completely different region of the brain, called the *posterior superior temporal sulcus,* kept lighting up. This is the same part of the brain responsible for social interactions—how we perceive others, how we relate, and how we form bonds. To make sure that the participants were reacting to altruism and not just to the act of playing a video game, they were also scanned while they watched a computer playing the game with the same charitable results. Despite the fact that the participants were just observers, the posterior superior temporal sulcus—what we'll call the "altruism center"—was hard at work.

Taken together, the findings of the Swiss nuclear depository survey and the Israeli GMAT study shed new light on the relationship between these two parts of the brain. Unlike, say, the parts of our brain that control movement and speech, the pleasure center and the altruism center cannot both function at the same time: either one or the other is in control. If the two brain centers functioned concurrently, then in the Swiss survey you would expect a compounding effect—that is, the percentage of townspeople who agreed to host the nuclear dump would have grown in accordance with the increase of the stipend. But that didn't happen. In the first half of the study—when no money was offered—the altruism center took charge, as people weighed the danger of having a nuclear dump nearby against the opportunity to help their country. The moment money was introduced, on the other hand, the entire situation got processed differently. The pleasure center took over, and in people's minds the choice came down to the dangers of the dump on one side and making a "quick franc" on the other. But the 5,000-franc stipend was much too low to excite the pleasure center.

The same thing happened with the GMAT takers. The moment monetary incentives were introduced, the altruistic motivation (completing the task to help out the researchers) waned, and money became the reason to proceed. But with such a small reward for the pleasure center, the students were more prone to slack off.

It's as if we have two "engines" running in our brains that can't operate simultaneously. We can approach a task either altruistically or from a self-interested perspective. The two different engines run on different fuels and also need different amounts of those fuels to fire up. It doesn't take much to fuel the altruism center: all you need is the sense that you're helping someone or making a positive impact. But the pleasure center seems to need a lot more—2.5 cents per right answer or a 5,000-franc stipend for agreeing to tolerate a nuclear dump site just isn't enough.

This intersection of economics, biology, and psychology regularly plays out in our everyday lives. Suppose a friend calls you and says he needs help moving. You might grumble a bit, but most of us would show up on a Saturday to help out. But what if your friend asked the same favor and offered to pay you $10 for your trouble? Chances are you'd decide that that small amount of cash wasn't worth a day of back-breaking labor, and you might remind your friend about the existence of *professional* movers. Likewise, imagine facing a deadline and desperately needing a coworker to stay until ten o'clock at night to help with the project. Your coworker would be more likely to stay late and pitch in if you explained your predicament and asked for a favor, rather than offering to pay her $15 for her time.

But it's about more than just simple favors. This finding should be of interest not only to those looking for help with an unpleasant task, but also to those running charities or holding fund-raisers. As anyone who has listened to an NPR or PBS pledge drive knows, not only are your donations rewarded with the knowledge that you're helping to keep public radio or TV in business, but you usually also score a free book, tote bag, or DVD in appreciation of your generosity. Yet the research we have been exploring suggests that this kind of payment may undermine our initial altruistic motivations.

It turns out that when the pleasure and altruism centers go head to head, the pleasure center seems to have the ability to hijack the altruism center. Let's take a look at how this neurological kidnapping plays out in a small magnet school in Michigan.

Community High School in Ann Arbor was founded in 1972 as the city's first alternative education school. The eclectic student body, combined with the school's unofficial mascot, the AntiZebra—a rainbow-colored creature who sported stars instead of stripes—earned the school the widely used nickname "Commie High."

From its inception, Community High was a place of few rules. Those that were in place—such as the mandatory wearing of shoes—were routinely overlooked. The high school had always been rich with opportunities for intellectual and creative freedom, and students were continually encouraged to develop their own unique strengths. As for the teachers, their starting salary in 1996 was $22,848. The disparity between a heavy workload and a low salary illustrates these professionals' dedication and commitment to helping students become well-rounded individuals. Indeed, Community High had a long waiting list to get in—new students literally had to line up for blocks in order to secure a spot in the school.

As the school's popularity soared, an opportunity arose to secure independence from the union and its regulations: a new state law allowed schools to operate more independently if they tried out new, innovative programs. And so, to gain this independence, Community High decided to start a pilot program. Although the faculty could not easily identify an urgent problem that needed solving, the school had to launch *some* new project. So, in true Community High fashion, the teachers and administrators convened and brainstormed.

In the course of their brainstorming the teachers recognized that students basically fell into two groups: those who were highly motivated and regularly came to class and those who were less enthusiastic and took advantage of the loose rules to skip classes. The goal of the pilot project would be to reverse the trend of skipping classes, improve overall attendance, and, in the process, increase student performance (the idea being that if you're not in school, it's difficult to learn). In order to evaluate attendance, on a random day in the last week of each semester teachers whose classes had at least 80 percent of their students in attendance would be rewarded with a salary bonus that equaled roughly 12 percent of their annual salary.

Now, remember, the school had adopted the attendance incentive merely as a way of implementing a pilot project requirement. Teachers had not demanded higher compensation, and Community High's attendance problems were not beyond the norm. Still, a few years into the program, the classroom inspections had shown that course completion had improved from 51 percent to 72 percent. The pilot seemed like an obvious success.

But a closer investigation revealed that the program was not as fruitful as it first appeared. For one thing, although the *completion* rate had gone up, the *attendance* rate had remained constant, falling just a tad from 59 percent to 58.62 percent. This means that although students were more likely to remain enrolled in a class, their attendance habits were no better than before the pilot study was launched. The most surprising finding, though, was what had happened to the average cumulative student GPA: it had taken a nosedive from 2.71 to 2.18.

During this period, academic standards at Community High hadn't changed, and the overall makeup of the student body remained the same. Moreover, GPA scores at a nearby school held steady over the same time period, indicating that the Community High figures were not simply part of a broader district trend. The decrease in average GPA pointed to a troubling conclusion: students weren't learning as much.

When researchers from the W. E. Upjohn Institute studied these figures and interviewed administrators and teachers, they gained an interesting insight. The researchers' analysis revealed that the teachers had shifted their focus. Once the pilot study was introduced, in order to secure their bonuses the teachers began concentrating their efforts on enticing students to show up who would otherwise have cut class. That is, rather than pulling a *Stand and Deliver* or a *Mr. Holland's Opus* and inspiring all students to achieve their true potential, the teachers followed a very different path.

Without anybody realizing it, the lure of a salary bonus

had pitted the teachers' pleasure centers against their altruism centers. All of a sudden the teachers had a bonus carrot dangling in front of them. Instead of focusing on teaching their students, they began chasing after the reward. To keep the students coming back to class they "included activities such as more field trips and in-class parties"—probably not what they had in mind when they entered the profession.

The Community High teachers didn't give up on their values or consciously lower their standards. It's just that the pleasure center has a way of sneaking up on us. Before we even know it, we've veered off the path we had originally planned. How does the pleasure center take over? Anton Souvorov, an economist at the University of Toulouse, has shown through an elaborate mathematical model that a reward can trigger an addictive response. Not only does our response to a monetary reward resemble our response to a drug like cocaine, but so does our drive to attain the reward. The Community High teachers exhibited the same types of behaviors as addicts seeking to get high, albeit to a much lesser extent: they became fixated on a reward and unknowingly altered their standards, goals, and conduct in the process.

Neuropsychologists have shown that activities associated with addictive substances and those associated with monetary rewards are both processed by the pleasure center. Because monetary incentives present such a strong allure to us, they distort our thinking. At Community High, what initially was created as a rational incentive program to increase productivity yielded out-of-character behavior with counter-productive results. Slowly but surely, the pleasure center overrode its altruistic counterpart.

Now, the problem isn't with rewards per se. It's only when you dangle the *possibility* of a reward ahead of time—creating a quid pro quo situation—that these destructive effects arise. An extensive review and analysis of motivation studies found that the prospect of a reward excites the pleasure center even more than the attainment of the reward itself. Taking a kid to Disneyland because she won the science fair is one thing, but telling her ahead of time, "If you enter the fair and win it, I'll take you to Disneyland," is another. It's that *anticipation* factor that drives the addictive behavior and suppresses the altruism center.

And it's true not just with children. Everywhere we look we see efforts to provide concrete financial incentives: from compensating star teachers whose students do well on standardized tests to giving tax credits to people who house Hurricane Katrina refugees. Of course, these individuals deserve recognition for their efforts. The problem with offering incentives, though, is that they carry a lot of baggage with them. For Swiss townspeople, Israeli students, and American high school teachers alike, throwing money into the mix diminished altruistic motivation and introduced unexpected behavior.

Chapter ⁸

DISSENTING JUSTICE

The Supreme Court conference.

Peer pressure and Coke-bottle glasses.

Ferris Bueller and the blocker.

"We are not focusing on the name you give to potatoes."

The captain is not God.

Not just thinking out loud.

Justice has been served.

Something strange happens when you put people in groups. They take on new roles, form "in group" alliances, get swept up by extreme stances, and succumb to peer pressure. In a group setting, the reasonableness of our thinking can be distorted and compromised. So it's not surprising that the hidden sways we have discussed so far reveal themselves just as prominently within a group setting. And nowhere are group dynamics more speculated about than within the marble walls of the highest court of the land.

The nine justices of the U.S. Supreme Court are aware that their every minute action and statement will be scrutinized—and amidst this scrutiny these lifetime appointees have to figure out a way of working together in the most efficient and productive manner. But just how exactly do group dynamics affect the decisions of the Supreme Court?

We spoke with Justice Stephen Breyer to better understand the procedures underlying the decision of a case. In talking to Breyer, what emerged was that the Court has found a way of circumventing a powerful psychological force that surfaces in nearly every group interaction.

To see how this happens, we'll look in on an important meeting called the "conference." This is the first time when all the justices convene in the same room to discuss the merits of the case before them. This conference is a justices-only meeting: no clerks, no audience, no outsiders.

But before we step inside, in order to get a true appreciation of the conference and just how much time and effort goes into the process of making a ruling, Breyer takes us back a few weeks, to the moment when a brief first lands on his desk.

The work starts with sifting through many different legal opinions. Breyer painted the picture: "First I get copies of briefs [memoranda] of maybe thirty to fifty pages each. And I usually have between ten and twenty briefs in a typical case." The briefs are submitted by the parties to the case and by supporters of one side or the other. As he reads each one, it's tough to remain neutral. "Now, all the time I have a very tentative hypothesis, but then I'm very open to being changed," he said. "I don't mind at all if I change, so I might go back and forth several times as I read it. I might read the government [brief] quite quickly because the government has good lawyers, and then I'll go through the amicus briefs. As I'm reading the briefs, I talk to my law clerks about them. Before the oral argument, I've read the brief, I've talked to my law clerk, my law clerk has written a memo, and then I have another conversation with my law clerk. And all that time I'm trying to make up my mind and I switch around and try different theories out." This back-and-forth process allows Breyer to distill all the information before formulating his stance. "And everyone [on the Court]," he noted, "has some process like that."

Once this is done, the justices are ready for the next stage, the week of oral arguments. The justices are not yet formally debating the case among themselves. "We hear the arguments and we're simply to ask questions," Breyer explained. "We ask questions of the parties—it's really not for them to make their argument at all; we already know their arguments. We're really asking questions about points that bother us."

Then it's time to start deciding the case. The justices may have shared memos with one another beforehand or talked informally, but the purpose here is to voice and discuss their opinions. By the time the conference convenes, the justices have had a chance to look at all sides, think the matter over, discuss troublesome points with their law clerks, query both sides, and hear their colleagues' questions.

The conference is purposely structured and has been run in essentially the same way since the 1800s. "In the conference, we go around the table in order of seniority, from the chief justice down to the most recent appointment," Breyer explained, "and everybody speaks once before anybody speaks twice." This ensures that every opinion is represented. "Each person might spend five minutes per case . . . They're trying to explain their reasons for which direction they're leaning. And everybody writes down what everybody else says. And then there'll be some discussion back and forth afterwards. And on the basis of that discussion—which is a preliminary discussion—it's fairly clear how the Court is likely to break down."

The group dynamic that the conference unintentionally avoids was first empirically studied by Solomon Asch in a landmark psychology experiment. This study not only illuminates what goes on in the Supreme Court, but also explains how the role played by a single individual can shift an entire group's opinion.

In Asch's study each participant was placed in a room with several other people. The participants were told they would be tested for visual acuity. The task seemed simple enough: the group was shown three straight lines of varying lengths, and each person was asked to determine which of the three lines matched a fourth line. It was pretty straightforward; the lengths were so glaringly different that you certainly didn't need a magnifying glass or a ruler.

But what the participant didn't know was that the other "subjects" in the room were really actors, and all of them had been instructed to give the same wrong answer. As the actors called out their erroneous answers one by one, the real participant was bewildered. But something strange happened: rather than stick to their guns, most participants began to doubt themselves and their lone dissenting opinion. What if I misunderstood something, or what if I've been looking at the lines from a weird angle? Time and again, they figured that it was best to go along with the group—and save themselves the embarrassment of being odd man out. Indeed, 75 percent of subjects joined the group in giving the wrong answer in at least one round.

Now, it's easy to dismiss the study participants as being too easily manipulated. But regardless of how independent-minded and steadfast we may think we are, we're all tempted at times to align ourselves with a group. We may worry that if we voice an unpopular viewpoint others will doubt our intelligence, taste, or competence. Or we may just not want to make waves. The challenge is to know when to speak up.

Breyer explained that even when the thought "Oh, I'm the only one" arises, he'll speak up, saying something like, "I actually don't agree, but I'll swallow it because there's no point writing a dissent in this. I don't feel *that* strongly about it." He added, "If I'm all by myself, I have to feel pretty strongly before I write a dissent." This reasoning makes perfect sense. If justices were to write a formal dissent every time they disagreed on a small point, the Court would come to a standstill. But the fact that a dissenter speaks up can make all the difference.

As Asch found, although the sway of group conformity is incredibly strong, it depends on unanimity for its power. In a variation of the line study, Asch ran the experiment exactly as before (an unsuspecting participant, a room full of actors giving the wrong answer), but this time he added a single actor who gave the right answer. This lone dissenting voice was enough to break the spell, as it "gave permission" to the real participant to break ranks with the other members of the group. In almost all cases, when a dissenter spoke up, the participant flew in the face of the group and gave the correct response. The really interesting thing, though, is that the dissenting actor didn't even need to give the *right* answer to inspire the real participant to speak up with the correct response; all it took to break the sway was for someone to give an answer that was *different* from the majority.

To prove how powerful the dissenter—even an incompetent one—really is, a clever experiment was conducted. In this variation, administered by psychologist Vernon Allen, a participant was once again placed in a group made up of actors and asked to answer simple questions. But in this version each participant was told that before the start of the study he would have to fill out a self-assessment survey alone in a small office. After five minutes, a researcher knocked on the door and told the participant that due to a shortage of rooms, he would have to share the space with another subject (who was in reality—you guessed it—a paid actor).

The most striking thing about the actor was the eyeglasses he wore. As Allen details in the study, the glasses were custom-made by a local optometrist and fitted "with extremely thick lenses that distorted the wearer's eyes, and gave the impression of severely limited visual ability." In this case, "extremely thick" is an understatement: the lenses were so Coke-bottle-like that they had to be ground down in the middle "to allow enough normal central vision to prevent the confederate's experiencing headache and eyestrain."

As if that weren't enough, to really drive home the point of the actor's "visual impairment," the actor and a researcher engaged in a pre-scripted conversation. "Excuse me, but does this test require long-distance vision?" the actor asked apologetically. When the researcher affirmed that yes, it did, the actor explained, "I have very limited eyesight"—as if that were a surprise to anyone—"and I can only see up-close objects." Showing concern, the experimenter asked the actor to read an easily legible sign on the wall. After straining and squinting to make out the words, the actor, alas, failed. Point made.

The researcher explained that he needed all five people for the study, claiming the testing apparatus did not work with fewer than five subjects. He invited the actor to participate, stating, "Just sit in anyway, as long as you are here. Since you won't be able to see the questions, answer any way you want; randomly, maybe. I won't record your answers."

But the actor, thick glasses and all, still enabled participants to escape from the sway of the group. Ninety-seven percent of participants conformed to the group when there was no dissenter present, but only 64 percent conformed when the visually impaired confederate was among them giving a different—but equally wrong—answer. Obviously, we wouldn't expect a clearly incompetent dissenter to turn around as many participants as would a competent dissenter, but it's important to note that the presence of a dissenter—any dissenter, no matter how incompetent—still made it possible for a large segment of participants to deviate from the majority and give the right answer.

The power of the dissenter, as we'll soon see, plays out not only in the Supreme Court, but also in international diplomacy and airline safety. But before we see how, it's important to understand the full power of the psychological dynamics underlying this force. To do so, we turn to a family therapist. David Kantor, a Boston-based family therapist, led what might very well have been the first incarnation of reality TV. In an effort to study how schizophrenia manifests in family systems, Kantor set up cameras in various rooms of people's houses, then pored over hours of footage of ordinary folks' lives. Although Kantor's research didn't tell him much about schizophrenia, he did detect a pattern that emerged again and again within every group dynamic, regardless of whether schizophrenia was a factor.

In analyzing the tapes of the families he studied, Kantor found that family members traded off playing the same four distinct roles. The first role was that of the *initiator*: the person who always has ideas, likes to start projects, and advocates for new ways of moving forward. Think of someone like Matthew Broderick's character, Ferris Bueller, in *Ferris Bueller's Day Off*. The entire movie is about Ferris's new, creative ideas for something fun to do: let's ditch school, take a vintage car out for a joyride, sneak into a fancy restaurant, attend a baseball game, and star in a parade while we're at it. When you're in the same room with a Ferris Bueller type, it's hard not to get excited about whatever new project or idea he has in mind. You can always count on initiators to come up with new ideas; they aren't necessarily the life of the party, but they're definitely the ones who suggest having a party in the first place.

If initiators are represented by Ferris Bueller, their opposites—*blockers*—are like Ferris's friend Cameron. Ferris wants to take a joyride; Cameron is afraid of getting caught. Ferris wants to go to a nice lunch; Cameron points out that they don't have a reservation. Whatever new idea the initiator comes up with, the blocker finds fault with it. "Let's go to Disneyland!" exclaims the initiator. "No, it's too expensive," retorts the blocker. "Let's start a new company!" "Most fail within the first year." If hanging out with Ferris Bueller makes us want to go out and do something fun, spending a minute with Cameron makes us reluctant to do anything. Of course, it's easy to think of blockers as pure curmudgeons. But as we'll soon see, they play a vital role in maintaining balance within a group.

Initiators and blockers are bound to lock horns, which is when the *supporter* steps in, taking one side or the other. If there's a decision to be made, you can bet on the supporter siding with either the initiator or the blocker. The fourth role, that of the *observer*, stays fairly neutral and tends to merely comment on what's going on: "It seems we're having a disagreement about whether or not to go to Disneyland."

Most of the tension in the group lies between the initiator and the blocker. Initiators are all about making new things happen. They have a wealth of fresh ideas. They might be wildly optimistic and have a tendency to rush to action, but their creativity, energy, and drive can be instrumental when it comes to innovation. In contrast, blockers question the merit or wisdom of new decisions. Instead of merrily going along for the ride, they raise points about the potential harmful consequences that might follow.

It's easy to see why people and organizations are naturally attracted to initiators. They bring in fresh energy and new ideas, and for them the sky is always the limit. It's equally easy to see why those same people and organizations would want to steer clear of blockers.

Think of how American politicians and media, for example, reacted to the French during the days leading up to the second Iraq war. At the time, taking on the role of initiator, the U.S. administration made countless arguments to convince politicians and foreign nations to join America in war. White House personnel motivated, energized, and pushed forward—and, before long, managed to get public opinion on their side.

But when the president tried to get a UN resolution passed in support of the war in Iraq, French foreign minister Dominique de Villepin tried to block the measure, firmly announcing, "We will not allow a resolution to pass that authorizes resorting to force." Likewise, when Bush wanted to push forward and go in to search for weapons of mass destruction, President Jacques Chirac decreed "total confidence" in the UN inspectors doing the job without further intervention. And when the United States was getting ready to attack, de Villepin warned instead about "the North Korean regime ... It's in no way better than Iraq's and has weapons of mass destruction, in particular nuclear ones which aren't hypothetical, but, regrettably, definitely exist."

The French were quickly branded as obstructionists, and Congress got so upset that it actually passed a resolution officially renaming the Capitol cafeteria's french fries "freedom fries." In true blocker fashion, the French embassy retorted, "We are at a very serious moment dealing with very serious issues, and we are not focusing on the name you give to potatoes."

Now, the French made an argument that—in retrospect—should have merited more careful attention. But because they so conveniently fit the role of the blocker, the French were simply seen as a thorn in Bush's side.

As tempting as it is to dismiss them, though, blockers do, in fact, play a vital role in maintaining balance in a group. A blocker functions as the brakes that prevent the group from going down a potentially disastrous path. Even if the blocker's opinion is wrong, at least it adds a perspective to the debate—giving others an opportunity to look at things in a different light.

Breyer explained how the role of the blocker serves a necessary function in the Supreme Court: "If somebody is going to write a dissent . . . they have a point, they have some kind of point they're trying to make. Quite often the opinion [of the majority] is changed somewhat in response to comments and opinions [of the dissenters]. Occasionally—maybe once or twice a year—the whole Court shifts."

Even when dissenters don't have enough votes to change the Court's opinion, they still affect the process. "It makes the other person take account of the point. They have to answer it or they have to take it into account," Breyer said.

"Last year," Breyer recalled, "I disagreed very strongly in this case involving segregation or desegregation or affirmative action. How did I show I was feeling so strongly? I wrote a seventy-seven-page dissent—which I never do. Never. The longest I had previously written was probably about twenty pages. So that was unusual, and then I spoke for twenty minutes from the bench, which was *very* unusual, and I knew it was unusual. So there are structured ways of saying if you think that there's something that's wrong."

Although Breyer knew that the Court was unlikely to change its mind, by voicing his views he put his arguments on the record, forced other justices to respond to them, and provided a springboard for Congress to create new laws.

There's no question that dissenters in a group setting do make the process messier, and blockers are not always given much of a voice. "In many European countries," explained Breyer, courts "don't publish dissenting opinions. [Judges] can disagree, but they only have one opinion, because they want people to think that the law is what it is—no argument with it. It's true in Belgium; it's true in the EU."

It's easy to understand the desire to present a unified front. But as Breyer pointed out, the end result—in this case, the Supreme Court's majority opinion—is actually improved by dissent. "The thing about writing a dissent," Breyer reflected, "is it's actually a pain in the neck for the person who is writing the [majority] opinion . . . and suddenly [has] to deal with this dissent." The majority has to revise its opinion in response to points raised by the dissenters, then the dissenters rebut, and on and on it goes. As Breyer put it, "People keep writing and writing and writing." But the process serves an important function. "How is that helping? Well, it's helping because it makes it a better opinion. Because people [justices] have to think through all the rejections."

As Breyer pointed out, "People have different views on this. Some people, like [former Chief Justice] Rehnquist, thought it was a waste of time to dissent. He didn't like to dissent. And sometimes he hardly bothered to answer a dissent. Other people, like Justice Scalia, they'll answer. They don't like anything to go out with an argument on the other side that hasn't been answered."

Blocking might not be pleasant—for anyone involved—but it's a necessary component of healthy group dynamics—one that can literally save lives.

Think back to Captain Van Zanten's decision to take off from Tenerife airport without tower clearance. The accident that occurred sent shockwaves through the aviation world. In the aftermath of the crash, agencies scrutinized cockpit recordings from every plane crash and near miss over the years. Seventy percent were determined to be the result of human error, and the majority of those errors had to do with team dynamics. Listen, for instance, to the final seconds of the cockpit recording of Van Zanten's flight.

When Van Zanten put his hand on the throttle and revved up the engines, the first officer instinctively tried to stop him: "Wait a minute. We don't have ATC clearance."

Van Zanten agreed, but seemed irritated at the attempt to thwart or delay him. "I know that," he responded. "Go ahead and ask."

What's striking is that the copilot starts to dissent but is immediately rebuffed. Indeed, when Van Zanten tries for the second time to take off, the first officer keeps quiet. And without the voice of the blocker, a deadly sequence of events unfolds.

NASA's research into plane crashes ultimately helped revolutionize aeronautical procedures. A new model for cockpit interaction was born: Crew Resource Management (CRM), which teaches pilots, among other skills, how to be effective blockers. We interviewed Dr. Barbara Kanki, a psychologist who was recruited by NASA to work on CRM at the Ames Research Center because of her expertise in nonverbal communications. "I knew nothing about aviation, space, or the military," Kanki reflected about her early days working for NASA.

But her expertise fit right in with NASA's effort to improve airline safety. "Up till then," Kanki explained, the standard explanations for crashes relied on physical causes. "You had a plane crash because something broke or the pilot flew into the mountain—not exploring what was underneath the problem." The question of *how* a crew ended up in such disastrous situations intrigued Kanki. When researchers evaluated pilot performance on a mission simulation, according to Kanki, they found that "performance differences did not seem to be tied to technical skills. It seemed more to do with management skills. And that was the turning point."

Thanks to researchers like Kanki, the aviation field has been transformed. Looking back at the pre-Tenerife years, Southwest Airlines captain Lex Brockington explained, "In the airline industry there was a time when the captain was almighty, in charge of everything, almost godlike. The captain was making a decision and everyone else was scared to overrule him and wouldn't open their mouths."

Van Zanten was a celebrated captain. Not only would questioning his judgment have been embarrassing, it would have been tantamount to mutiny. How could you criticize a call made by the head of safety at KLM?

But CRM has changed these dynamics. "When I came into Southwest Airlines," Brockington explained, "there was a big push to get around these human-error mistakes. CRM is distinctly designed to get away from that 'the captain is the man' view. Now, the captain is still ultimately in charge of the airplane. But nowadays it's not like the captain is God.

Even when pilots interview for a job, they give them scenarios and they tell them, there's a first officer next to you, the dispatch (the person who puts together all the paperwork and flight planning), and so on." Pilots are trained to communicate effectively and accept feedback, and crew members are taught to speak up when they see that their superior officer is about to make a mistake.

Captain Brockington likes to take it even a step further. "I like to vocalize my thoughts. I think out loud. That way the person sitting next to me always knows what I'm thinking. And if the copilot can detect a flaw in my thought pattern, he or she is more apt to speak up. They don't say you have to do that, but I think it's a good idea."

Brockington gave us a case in point. "Let's say you're cruising along and you have a lot of thunderstorms out there, you've got weather building up, you're heading to a certain airfield, and you're getting close enough to actually see some of these storms develop or the radar points them out. Now you're thinking, 'Hey, I've got weather building up. I'm looking at the wind; it looks like it's moving in that direction. If it gets that way, we're going to start looking at the weather, find some other alternate bases we can go to. If we have to hold in a holding pattern, do we have enough gas?' "

Because the presence of a strong initiator can quell a blocker, Brockington consciously takes on the role of an observer. "Now, I can sit there and not say anything," he explained, "and all of a sudden we go into holding patterns and the first officer knows nothing about what I'm doing. I just made the decision and off we went, versus saying exactly what I said to you." Brockington's method of thinking out loud makes it easier for the first officer to weigh in with a different point of view or challenge the captain when necessary.

At Southwest, they really push this culture of teamwork. "We only hire people who are very friendly and outgoing people," Brockington said. The crew and officers stay at the same hotel and socialize together, as well. "We invite the crew to come down. If you feel the captain is approachable, you're certainly more apt to speak up if you have a concern." Brockington tells his crew, "We all make mistakes, so I really want you to speak up if you have a problem. If you see something that you don't like, it won't hurt my feelings."

When Brockington goes in for his annual CRM course, one of the instructors he might get is Captain Cathy Dees. She teaches CRM to new hires and a refresher course for current Southwest pilots. When pilots spot a departure from safety procedures, they are *trained* to challenge the captain. The challenge takes the form of three steps that all Southwest pilots know by heart. "The first step," Dees said, "is to state the facts"—for example, "Our approach speed is off." If that's ineffective, the next step is to "challenge." According to Dees, research has shown that "generally the best way to challenge someone is to use their first name and add a quantifier to the fact. 'Mike, are you going to make it on this approach? Check your altitude.'" That will get the captain's attention and bring him or her out of the tunnel vision he or she may be experiencing. "It's important to state the fact without being condescending," she said.

If these two procedures fail, the third step is to "take action. If someone were flying an unstable approach—that means they were approaching the runway and they were perhaps a little too high or too fast, or not in a condition to make a normal landing—we would want them to go around," Dees explained. The action Dees advises would be to get on the radio and say, for example, " 'Southwest 1 going around, we're too high.' And once you say something on the radio, the tower controller will cancel your landing clearance. And that way the action takes place without physically fighting over equipment in the airplane, which might aggravate the person flying."

More often than not, the first two steps are enough to get a captain's attention; there is rarely a need for the first officer to take action. The training emphasizes the need for the blocker to speak up and for the person in charge to listen and communicate effectively.

This freedom to give feedback and voice concerns—and the willingness of those in charge to tolerate dissent—is just as important in a boardroom, where a costly mistake can be averted by being open to dissent from blockers in the group. Accordingly, it's not just pilots who have benefited from CRM training. The medical community is also responding to human-error failures by adapting aviation's approach to crew coordination. The Agency for Healthcare Research and Quality is supporting research at the University of Texas to apply aviation safety practices and training concepts to medicine, particularly in operating rooms and emergency rooms.

CRM training is also being used in industrial settings, such as offshore drilling operations and nuclear power plants. The training helps workers in control rooms and emergency command centers avoid making operational errors that could lead to accidents.

Whatever the situation, be it the cockpit or the conference room, a dissenting voice can seem, well, annoying. And yet, as frustrating as it can be to encounter blockers, their opinions are absolutely essential to keeping groups balanced. It's natural to want to dismiss a blocker's naysaying, but as we've seen, a dissenting voice—even an incompetent one—can often act as the dam that holds back a flood of irrational behavior.

Epilogue

Swimming with the riptide.

The power of the long view.

Zen economics.

Propositional thinking.

One man's trash is one woman's masterpiece.

A cable guy, a banker, and a pharmaceutical rep.

The real devil's advocate.

Perched above the beach, a tube of sunscreen in one hand and a whistle in the other, lifeguards are trained to watch out for the greatest danger associated with swimming in the ocean. The cause of 80 percent of near drownings, this threat isn't clearly visible at first glance; instead it lurks unseen.

When underwater sandbars form near the shore, they act as dams, keeping water from flowing back to the ocean. The pressure builds, ultimately breaking the sandbar and creating a rip current as the water pours through the breach. Anyone unfortunate enough to be in the riptide's path will be dragged away from the shore.

One's natural reaction, of course, is to try to swim *against* the current and back toward the beach. But even strong swimmers are no match for the current's force. As any lifeguard can tell you, the best way to escape the pull of a riptide is to swim parallel to the shore until you escape the current's path.

Similarly, when it comes to psychological undercurrents, the best way to counter them isn't necessarily to follow our natural instincts. That's what makes avoiding these invisible forces so challenging—sometimes it's our instincts that cause us to be swayed in the first place.

But there are antidotes that we can use to avoid getting carried away by these currents. Our quest for a way to overcome our irrational aversion to loss led us back to Jordan Walters, the financial adviser from Smith Barney. Jordan offered an example that illuminates his perspective on overcoming this psychological force: "Let's say you're traveling on a long trip and you have a flat tire," Jordan began. After fixing the tire, you have two choices: you can look for shortcuts to make up the lost time and completely rearrange your trip, or you can continue on your way and accept that you're running behind schedule. Jordan advocates the latter, "longview" method: You might be a little late, but "you're on your way again and you still know where you're going." Rearranging your trip on the fly, on the other hand, can get you thoroughly lost.

When things go wrong, we can either apply a short-term, Band-Aid solution or remember that in the grand scheme of things it's only a minor misstep. Having a long-term plan—and not casting it aside—is the key to dealing with our fear of loss.

"Our clients," explained Jordan, "are really in it for long-term capital accumulation and preservation." The challenge is not to allow short-term fluctuations—a "flat tire," if you will—to get in the way of one's long-term plan.

The same is true in our everyday lives. "You won't believe what just happened to me," our friend Erin recently told us. The day before, we had talked to her about our findings on loss aversion, about how it skews and distorts our thinking and judgment. She told us she had been sitting in her car on a congested street in San Francisco. "This idiot in front of me," she complained, "wouldn't move. The light turned green, and he just sat there." Without even thinking about it, Erin had her foot on the gas pedal, ready to swerve into the oncoming traffic lane to pass the guy. But just as she was about to carry out the maneuver, she thought of what we had told her about Jordan. "I realized I was being loss averse, trying to avoid losing time, and I thought, 'What am I doing?'" Instead of reacting to a short-term impulse (trying to save a few seconds), she took a long-term view (realizing that those few seconds weren't worth putting her life in danger).

Our natural tendency to avoid the pain of loss is most likely to distort our thinking when we place too much importance on short-term goals. When we adopt the long view, on the other hand, immediate potential losses don't seem as menacing.

Seeing firsthand how powerful and detrimental snap judgments can be, Jordan decided to teach his kids the value of long-term thinking. "I created an investment game," he told us, "that looks at the longer term." Jordan was reacting to the way in which schools introduce children to investing. "If you look at the schools and their investment games, the difficulty is that they have to work with a semester: a short time horizon. So you're given a certain amount of hypothetical money, you pick a few companies, see who wins at the end of a few months. But there's a problem with that in that you're looking at a very short-term window rather than at a full market cycle. You're looking at a market that could melt in three months or surge in three months, and you really haven't looked at the company's fundamentals. So what I did is take away the time barriers."

Jordan spent time with his children helping them evaluate companies in sectors they would be familiar with—toy manufacturers, food makers, restaurant chains—and purchase select stocks. But his focus was not so much on which companies they chose as on the time horizon involved. And how often do Jordan's kids check the prices of their stocks? "They follow the stocks on an annual basis," he says. Once a year—loooooooong term.

If looking far into the future is the way to avoid the faulty decision making that can result from loss aversion, the antidote to getting swept up in commitment—the force that keeps us from giving up on a project even though it's clearly failing—is to don Zen Buddhist glasses and learn to let go of the past. There's a point where we have to accept that what's done is done, and it's better to shift direction than to dig ourselves deeper into a hole.

The "letting go of the past" strategy holds true whether you're a government official financing a dead-end public works project—because so much has already been invested in it—or a marketing manager continuing to support a failed campaign because you don't want to be seen as a quitter. It just doesn't make rational sense to stay aboard a sinking ship. As one venture capitalist told us about managing investment expectations, "Sometimes you just have to know when to shoot it in the head."

In his book *Only the Paranoid Survive,* Andy Grove, former CEO of Intel, tells the story of how in 1985 he and Intel cofounder Gordon Moore decided to get out of the memory chip business and focus all their resources on the emerging field of microprocessors. At the time, their core business was memory chips. As Grove explained, "Our priorities were formed by our identity; after all, memories *were* us." But Intel had been losing money on memory chips for some time, as a result of the entry of high-quality, low-priced, mass-produced Japanese chips. Clearly, Intel needed to do something. Grove related, "I was in my office with Intel's chairman and CEO, Gordon Moore, and we were discussing our quandary. Our mood was downbeat. I looked out the window at the Ferris wheel of the Great America amusement park revolving in the distance, then I turned back to Gordon and I asked, 'If we got kicked out and the board brought in a new CEO, what do you think he would do?' Gordon answered without hesitation. 'He would get us out of memories.' I stared at him, numb, then said, 'Why shouldn't you and I walk out the door, come back, and do it ourselves?' " That was how Intel overcame the sway of commitment and made its momentous decision to concentrate on microprocessors, paving the way for the company to become one of the greatest success stories in American business.

When we find ourselves unsure about whether or not to continue a particular approach, it's useful to ask, "If I were just arriving on the scene and were given the choice to either jump into this project as it stands now or pass on it, would I choose to jump in?" If the answer is no, then chances are we've been swayed by the hidden force of commitment. Making a clean break might feel uncomfortable, but it could be in our best interest.

Avoiding the next stream also requires a Zen-like approach. The best strategy for dealing with the distorted thinking that can result from value attribution is to be mindful and observe things for what they are, not just for what they appear to be. You have to be prepared to accept that your initial impressions might be wrong.

Simply realizing that we're making judgments based on assumptions about a situation or a person's value can free us from this sway. Remember the SoBe experiment, where people who drank the cheapo SoBe performed worse on a mental acuity test than did those who drank a full-priced version of the exact same drink? In a variation of that study the researchers ran the experiment as before, but this time they asked the participants before the test whether they thought the price they had been charged for the drink would affect their concentration. Now, if the answers to these questions seem obvious, that's the point. The researchers wanted the participants to think about the fact that the price of the drink had nothing to do with its potency. Indeed, those students who received the cheapo SoBe *and* had to answer this question experienced no decrease in their mental acuity scores, performing just as well as their counterparts who received the full-priced drink.

In similar fashion, Elizabeth Gibson had to fight her natural inclination toward value attribution when she was walking down a street on Manhattan's Upper West Side and spied a piece of art wedged between two garbage bags. She was tempted to walk away, but then she stopped to reflect about the art. "I had a real debate with myself," Gibson told the *New York Times*. "I almost left it there," she said. "It was so overpowering, yet it had a cheap frame." So Gibson took it home, where she hung it on her wall. Years later she discovered the true provenance of the painting. Known as *Tres Personajes*, it had been painted by renowned Mexican artist Rufino Tamayo. The painting had been stolen and later discarded. Had Gibson come along twenty minutes later, it would have already been picked up by the garbage collectors. Instead, the painting was auctioned by Sotheby's for over a million dollars. Had any of the other pedestrians who passed by known that this piece belonged in a museum, they would certainly have snatched it up. Instead, they evaluated it by its surroundings and cheap-looking frame and passed it by.

Whether we're shopping at a clearance outlet or a chic boutique, we sometimes need to fight our tendency to consciously dismiss an item because of its price. Instead, we should ask ourselves, "If I got this item as a gift, would I like it? If it cost \$1—or \$1,000—how would my perception of it shift?" The more we become aware of the factors affecting the perceived value of a person or object, the less likely we are to be swayed by value attribution.

But not all sways are so easily vanquished. It's virtually impossible for us not to make judgments about people and situations. We judge, or diagnose, the world around us (and, in turn, get diagnosed) all the time. In the case of job interviews, we can reduce our tendency toward the diagnosis bias by instituting regimented structures that force us to focus on objective data. But what about instances where we can't follow a script or we don't have access to hard data? Is there a practical way to reduce the bias that comes with diagnosis?

Psychologist Franz Epting suggests that we can overcome our tendency to succumb to the diagnosis bias through what's called "personal construct theory." One of the main principles of this theory is that we make diagnostic errors when we narrow down our field of possibilities and zero in on a single interpretation of a situation or person. All of us have certain lenses, or constructs, that we use to sift through the endless flow of information we encounter. For example, when we meet new people we may judge them on whether they dress well or poorly, whether their shoes are polished or not, whether they seem to be liberal or conservative, whether they are religious or secular, hip or nerdy. These constructs are useful insofar as they help us to quickly assess a situation and form a temporary hypothesis about how to react. Forming initial opinions is one of the ways in which we try to make sense of the world given limited time or information. But we have to be careful not to rely too much on such preemptive judgments, as they can short-circuit a more nuanced evaluation. They can narrow our perceptions and make us more apt to get swayed by a hasty diagnosis.

What personal construct theory teaches us is to remain flexible and examine things from different perspectives. Epting explained that this approach is called "propositional thinking." It's all about keeping evaluations tentative instead of certain, learning to be comfortable with complex, sometimes contradictory information, and taking your time and considering things from different angles before coming to a conclusion. It can be as straightforward as coming up with a kind of self-imposed "waiting period" before making a diagnostic judgment.

When it comes to the fairness sway, our emotional reaction can be just as intractable and difficult to set aside. One way to counter the fairness sway is to try to weigh things objectively and not succumb to emotional maneuvers or moral judgments (Would I rather achieve my goals or teach the other person a lesson?). But what can we do in situations where our actions are being evaluated based on how fair others perceive them to be?

One answer comes from research conducted at Duke University. The results of the study sound like the beginning of a bad joke: What do a cable guy, a banker, and a pharmaceutical representative have in common? Researcher Jack Greenberg studied how employees from these different sectors perceived their performance evaluations. He found that regardless of the industry, it was incredibly important for employees to feel that they were active participants in the evaluation process. The employees were more likely to feel that the process was fair when supervisors solicited their input prior to an evaluation and used it during the process; when there was two-way communication during the evaluation interview; and when the employees had the chance to challenge or rebut an evaluation. In other words, if the employees were *involved* in their evaluation, they felt it was fairer. Another study found the same to be true of employees' perceptions of pay raise decisions.

When we make decisions or take actions that will affect others, keeping them involved will help ensure that they feel the process is fair. It's important to keep others apprised of our decision-making process—to communicate what we're thinking: "I know this is a tricky situation; I'm not sure what to do myself. I think the best course of action is to do such-and-such." Voicing our own discomfort or uncertainty shifts the focus to the situation at hand. A potentially divisive situation can be transformed into a collaborative effort, allowing people to evaluate the facts objectively, rather than be swayed by the sense that the process was unfair.

Just as communicating our process is important, so is giving voice to the dissenter. In group situations, the presence of a blocker can actually make the decision-making process more rational and less likely to go off the tracks. It gives us a new appreciation for someone who tends to play "devil's advocate." The term originated in the Vatican to refer to a priest designated to argue against a papal nominee. The priest assigned to represent the devil's position, so to speak, brought balance to the debate. Although no one is likely to win a popularity contest by playing the devil's advocate, businesses would do well to respect a dissenting opinion—if not straight-out encourage someone to take on such a role. The dissenter, of course, is as likely to be wrong as anybody else, but the discussion of the points made by the dissenter can add perspective to the debate.

Living in a time when we can predict hurricanes, treat diseases with complex medical interventions, map the universe, and reap the benefits of systematized business approaches, it's easy to forget that under the surface we humans are still influenced by irrational psychological forces that can undermine a logical perspective on the world around us. The fact is, all of us are swayed at times by factors that have nothing to do with logic or reason. From NBA coaches to heads of state, from managers looking to hire a job applicant to trained psychiatrists studying why we act the way we do, each of us brings a variety of different experiences, emotions, and perceptions to our thinking. It is only by recognizing and understanding the hidden world of sways that we can hope to weaken their influence and curb their power over our thinking and our lives.

Acknowledgments

When Liz Hazelton moved to Doubleday, we could only hope that fate would reunite us. Liz's dedication, spirit, and enthusiasm are unparalleled, and we couldn't have asked for a better team at Currency/Doubleday. We're grateful to Roger Scholl for his editorial expertise, commitment to excellence, and continual direction and encouragement; Sarah Rainone for her thoughtful feedback, fresh ideas, and unwavering support through the process; Talia Krohn for her editorial contributions; Michael Palgon for his strategic thinking; Nicole Dewey for nailing the subtitle; Meredith McGinnis for her endless supply of creative ideas; and Louise Quayle for her hard work on our behalf.

This book wouldn't have materialized without the continual support of our fantastic agent, Jennifer Gates. We're grateful for the invaluable advice we received from Esmond Harmsworth and Mary Beth Chappell, as well as for Rachel Sussman's pinch-hitting.

Thanks to Larry Leson for being the best speaking agent we could ask for and for making the finest gazpacho in the world.

Speaking of the finest, this book wouldn't have sounded half as good without Hilary Roberts, and we wouldn't have looked half as good without Josyn Herce.

We're indebted to the many experts who shared their stories, knowledge, and experience with us: Justice Stephen Breyer for his thoughtful reflections; Steve Spurrier for taking time out during spring training (and Rita Ricard for arranging the interview); Jordan Walters for his sage advice; Dan Ariely for his insights and ideas; Franz Epting for providing clarity and wisdom; Dean Falk for her precision and passion; Bruce Wampold for his articulate explanations; Lex Brockington for his view from the helm of a 737; Cathy Dees for her enlightening explanations; Barbara Kanki for her informative history of CRM; Allen Huffcutt for his sharp and entertaining analyses; Marco Gemignani for his views on cultural dynamics; Becca Levy for discussing her research with us; Eric Johnson for helping us navigate the economic waters; David Antonuccio for illuminating a complex subject; Geoffrey Hosking for offering cultural insights; Adele Barker for her fascinating stories; Max Bazerman for his helpful insights; Saar Gur for his venture capitalist perspective; Toni Vaughn Heineman for her enthusiasm and passion; Tammy Johns and Mara Swan for their wisdom about hiring practices; "Dr. Hastings" and the other physicians we spoke with for providing a fascinating window into the medical world; Shani Harmon for illuminating Kantor's group roles; and Alex Olhovich for inspiring new ideas.

We're also grateful to all the people who have supported us through this process: Denise Egri (wielder of the red pencil); Auren Hoffman (don); Noah Kagan (initiator); Dina Kaplan (New York catalyst); Juliette Powell (power diva); Pete Sims (author/thinker); Michael Breyer (courtroom connector); Josh Rosenblum (intellectual at large); Andreea Nicoara (genius/translator); Noah Brier (marketing guru); Sara Olsen (cheerleader); Dave Wallack (strategist); Dave Blatte (monk); Marc Blatte (novelist); Jeanne Neary (shiksa goddess); Marianne Manilov (organizer extraordinaire); John and Alison Roberts (editors/proofreaders); the ESi crew (WebEOCers); Cort Worthington (creative counsel); René Wong (advertising genius/El Paso holdout); Pablo Pazmino (doctor/human rights student activist); Pam and Roy Webb (critical thinkers); Mark Schlosberg (do-gooder); Matt Miller (scientific adviser); the Lischinsky family (sounding boards); Kyle Bach (consigliere); and Mom and Dad (parents).

Thanks also to musician Jason Kleinberg for providing the fiddle music on our Web site, and to John Hoffsis and Craig Sakowitz for lending their voices. New York accommodations provided by Corey Modeste and Peter Fleischer.

Notes

The names of the medical doctors and patients in this section have been changed.

Chapter 1

10 **The passengers aboard KLM Flight 4805:** Macarthur Job and Matthew Tesch describe the chain of events leading up to the Tenerife air collision in *Air Disasters: Volume 1* (Fyshwick, Australia: Aerospace Publications, 1994), pages 165–80. PBS's *NOVA* program "The Deadliest Plane Crash" offers a documentary perspective on the disaster. Information about the *NOVA* episode, as well as a link to the cockpit recorder transcript, can be found at http://www.pbs.org/wgbh/nova/planecrash.

17 **egg sales in southern California:** Daniel Putler's egg study, "Incorporating Reference Price Effects into a Theory of Consumer Choice," was published in *Marketing Science* 11 (1992): 287–309.

You may need to refresh your calculus and advanced economics theory before reading Putler's study, as it is geared to the academic reader and contains advanced mathematical formulas and graphs.

19 **orange juice shoppers in Indiana:** The orange juice study that replicated Putler's egg findings, "Modeling Loss Aversion and Reference Dependence Effects on Brand Choice," was authored by Bruce Hardie, Eric Johnson, and Peter Fader and published in *Marketing Science* 12 (1993): 378–94. We found *Advances in Behavioral Economics,* edited by Colin Camerer, George Loewenstein, and Matthew Rabin (New York: Russel Sage Foundation, 2004), to be a great source for examples of loss aversion, including the egg and orange juice studies.

19 **when we sign up for a new phone service:** "Mental Accounting Matters" by Richard Thaler (chapter 3 of Camerer, Loewenstein, and Rabin, eds., *Advances in Behavioral Economics*) describes telephone customers' preference for a flat-rate fee—including a reference to Kenneth Train Press's *Optimal Regulation* (Cambridge, Mass.: MIT, 1991), p. 211—and contains a footnote about the AOL flat-rate-pricing chain of events.

20 **AOL stumbled upon this same phenomenon:** The interview with AOL CEO Steve Case about the flat-rate-pricing shift appeared in the *Washington Post* on December 9, 1997. The article is titled "A Conversation with Stephen M. Case, CEO of America Online."

22 **Jordan Walters:** All identifying client details in the Jordan Walters interview have been changed to preserve client anonymity.

Chapter 2

30 **"twenty-dollar auction":** Information about Max Bazerman's auction of a $20 bill can be found in his book *Judgment in Managerial Decision Making* (New York: John Wiley & Sons, 2002), pages 79–80. When we talked to Bazerman, we learned that he now

performs a $100 version of the auction for executives. This auction goes up in $5 increments. But the higher stakes don't prevent enthusiastic bidding. Bazerman originally got the idea for the auction from Martin Shubik's "The Dollar Auction Game: A Paradox in Noncooperative Behavior and Escalation," which can be found in the *Journal of Conflict Resolution* 15 (1971): 109–11.

33 **LBJ was surely the hands-down winner:** We found helpful information about LBJ in Robert Dallek's *Flawed Giant: Lyndon Johnson and His Times, 1961–1973* (New York: Oxford University Press, 1999); and Doris Kearns Goodwin's *Lyndon Johnson and the American Dream* (New York: Harper & Row, 1976). All LBJ quotes in this chapter were taken from his public speeches, recorded conversations he had with his staff, or information he provided to his biographer, Doris Kearns Goodwin.

37 **George W. Bush's remarks about Iraq:** All George W. Bush quotes are taken from public speeches he gave during his presidency.

38 **Nobel Prize–winning economist Daniel Kahneman:** Daniel Kahneman and Jonathan Renshon applied behavioral economic dynamics to politics and war in their article "Why Hawks Win," published in the January/February 2007 issue of *Foreign Policy.* The article can be found in its entirety at http://www.foreignpolicy.com/story/cms.php?story_id=3660.

Chapter 3

42 **Dr. Dean Falk, an anthropology professor and forensic expert:** Our knowledge of *Homo floresiensis,* the evolutionary island effect, Brodmann area 10, and the anthropological disputes about the discovery came from an interview with Dr. Dean Falk.

45 **a precocious young Dutch student named Eugene Dubois:** You can learn more about Eugene Dubois from Pat Shipman's *The*

Man Who Found the Missing Link (New York: Simon & Schuster, 2001).

49 **journey beneath the streets of Washington, D.C.:** You can read more about Joshua Bell's performance in the Washington, D.C., metro station in Gene Weingarten's article, "Pearls Before Breakfast," which appeared in the *Washington Post* on April 8, 2007. The article and a video segment of the performance are available at http://www.washingtonpost.com/wp-dyn/content/article/2007/04/04/AR2007040401721.html.

52 **that is, until Charles Dawson came along:** The Piltdown hoax is detailed in several books, including John Evangelist Walsh's *Unraveling Piltdown* (New York: Random House, 1996).

55 **a clever experiment using SoBe Adrenaline Rush:** The SoBe study was conducted by Baba Shiv, Ziv Carmon, and Dan Ariely. Titled "Placebo Effects of Marketing Actions: Consumers May Get What They Pay For," it was published in the *Journal of Marketing Research* 42 (2005): 383–93.

57 **Ohio State theater department's productions:** We learned of the Ohio State University discounted theater ticket phenomenon from "The Psychology of Sunk Cost," by Hal Arkes and Catherine Blumer, published in *Organizational Behavior and Human Decision Processes* 35 (1985): 124–40.

62 **modern anthropologists from universities and museums:** The scientific debate surrounding *Homo floresiensis* has continued to unfold since our interview with Dr. Falk. In September 2007 a new study analyzing the wrist bones of the Hobbit revealed that they are different and distinct from human bone structures, cementing the likelihood that *Homo floresiensis* is indeed its own separate—and fascinating—species. To learn more about the studies investigating *Homo floresiensis,* see D. Falk, C. Hildebolt, K. Smith, M. J. Morwood, T. Sutikna, P. Brown, Jatmiko, E. W. Saptomo,

B. Brunsden, and F. Prior, "The Brain of LB1, *Homo floresiensis,*" *Science* 308 (2005): 242–45; D. Falk, C. Hildebolt, K. Smith, M. J. Morwood, T. Sutikna, Jatmiko, E. W. Saptomo, B. Brunsden, and F. Prior, "Response to Comment on "The Brain of LB1, *Homo floresiensis,*" *Science* 312 (2006): 999; T. Jacob, E. Indriati, R. P. Soejono, K. Hsu, D. W. Frayer, R. B. Eckhardt, A. J. Kuperavage, A. Thorne, and M. Henneberg, "Pygmoid Australomelanesian *Homo sapiens* Skeletal Remains from Liang Bua, Flores: Population Affinities and Pathological Abnormalities," *Proceedings of the National Academy of Sciences* 103 (2006): 13421–26; Z. Laron, L. Kornreich, and I. Hershkovitz, "For Debate: Did the Small-Bodied Hominids from Flores (Indonesia) Suffer from a Molecular Defect in the Growth Hormone Receptor Gene (Laron Syndrome)?" *Pediatric Endocrinology Reviews* 3 (2006): 345–46; M. Tocheri, C. Orr, S. G. Larson, T. Sutikna, Jatmiko, E. W. Saptomo, R. A. Due, T. Djubiantono, M. J. Morwood, and W. L. Jungers, "The Primitive Wrist of *Homo floresiensis* and Its Implications for Hominin Evolution," *Science* 317 (2007): 1743–45.

Chapter 4

68 **Buried within this mountain of data:** The NBA draft order study was authored by Barry M. Staw and Ha Hoang. The researchers used an empirical methodology called *factor analysis* to analyze players' statistics and distill the data into three distinct categories of related elements: quickness, toughness, and scoring. They then ran a regression analysis to evaluate the significance of draft order picks on a player's career. The study was published in *Administrative Science Quarterly* 40 (1995): 474–94.

71 **the students of Economics 70:** Harold H. Kelley of the University of Michigan authored the experiment about the "warm"

professor. It is titled "The Warm-Cold Variable in First Impression of Persons" and published in the *Journal of Personality* 18, no. 4 (1950): 431–39.

75 Professor Allen Huffcutt: We interviewed Allen Huffcutt of Bradley University about his knowledge and research relating to employment interviews. He is currently working on a new research-based conceptual model with colleagues Phil Roth and John Kammeyer-Mueller that attempts to improve our understanding of, among other things, how a candidate's performance shapes interview decisions.

77 daydreaming about their girlfriend or boyfriend: Tara K. MacDonald and Michael Ross conducted the college freshman dating experiment. It is titled "Assessing the Accuracy of Predictions About Dating Relationships: How and Why Do Lovers' Predictions Differ from Those Made by Observers?" and was published in *Personality and Social Psychology Bulletin* 25 (1999): 1417–29.

84 in South Africa when a consumer lending bank: The data about the bank loan offer variables is described in a June 17, 2005, working paper titled "What's Psychology Worth? A Field Experiment in the Consumer Credit Market," by Marianne Bertrand, Dean Karlan, Sendhil Mullainathan, Eldar Shafir, and Jonathan Zinman. It is available at http://www.princeton.edu/~rpds/downloads/Shafir_2006What's%20Psych%20Worth_%20South%20Africa.pdf.

Chapter 5

90 It had the makings of an epidemic: The analysis of the data that revealed the fortyfold increase in bipolar diagnoses is found in "National Trends in the Outpatient Diagnosis and Treatment of Bipolar Disorder in Youth," by Carmen Moreno, Gonzalo Laje, Carlos Blanco, Huiping Jiang, Andrew Schmidt, and Mark Olfson. It was published in the *Archives of General Psychiatry* 64 (2007): 1032–69.

92 **a psychiatrist named Emil Kraepelin:** Information about Emil Kraepelin's methodology and deviation from scientific protocol can be found in Michael Shepherd's "The Two Faces of Emil Kraepelin," published in the *British Journal of Psychiatry* 167 (1995): 174–83.

93 **pharmaceutical companies increasingly began to draw attention:** Dr. David Healy's article "The Latest Mania: Selling Bipolar Disorder" provides an overview of the events leading to the exponential increase in the diagnosis of bipolar disorder. It was published in *PLoS Medicine* 3 (2006): 185. It can be viewed in its entirety at http://www.pubmedcentral.nih.gov/articlerender.fcgi?tool=pubmed&pubmedid=16597178.

94 **who believes in empirical, quantitative evidence:** Bruce Wampold's research about the factors responsible for effective psychotherapy is presented in his book *The Great Psychotherapy Debate: Models, Methods, and Findings* (Mahwah, NJ: Lawrence Erlbaum Associates, 2001). In the book, Wampold compares the medical model of therapy with what he calls the *contextual model* and shows that the vast majority of the assumptions underlying the medical model are not empirically supported. Because Wampold's research underscores the importance of the client-clinician working relationship, he encourages prospective clients to seek a competent practitioner with whom they feel comfortable and whose therapeutic style and approach match their preferences.

97 **sugar pills and Prozac had about the same therapeutic effect:** As part of our investigation into the bipolar diagnosis and the medical model, we spoke with Dr. David Antonuccio, professor of psychiatry and behavioral sciences at the University of Nevada. Antonuccio and two of his colleagues, David Burns and William

Danton, reviewed studies that examined the effectiveness of SSRI antidepressant drugs, and they authored an article titled "Antidepressants: A Triumph of Marketing Over Science?" It was published in the electronic journal *Prevention and Treatment* 5 (2002), available at http://www.antidepressantsfacts.com/2002-07-15-Antonuccio-therapy-vs-med.htm. One of the meta-analytical studies they examined analyzed FDA data on clinical drug trials. This study, titled "The Emperor's New Drugs: An Analysis of Antidepressant Medication Data Submitted to the U.S. Food and Drug Administration," was written by Irving Kirsch, Thomas Moore, Alan Scoboria, and Sarah Nicholls. It was published in the electronic journal *Prevention and Treatment* 5 (2002).

97 **The would-be commanders didn't know:** Dov Eden and Abraham Shani wrote about the army officers' diagnoses of their trainees and the reciprocal effect that followed in "Pygmalion Goes to Boot Camp: Expectancy, Leadership, and Trainee Performance." It was published in the *Journal of Applied Psychology* 67 (1982): 194–99.

99 **A meta-analysis conducted by psychologists at SUNY Albany:** A meta-analysis conducted by Nicole Kierein and Michael Gold found that managers' perceptions of their workers influence productivity levels. The study, titled "Pygmalion in Work Organizations: A Meta-Analysis," was published in the *Journal of Organizational Behavior* 21 (2000): 913–28.

101 **fifty-one women waiting for the phone to ring:** The study about the women who were perceived as sounding beautiful is titled "Social Perception and Interpersonal Behavior: On the Self-Fulfilling Nature of Social Stereotypes." It was authored by Mark Snyder, Elizabeth Decker Tank, and Ellen Bercheid and published in the *Journal of Personality and Social Psychology* 35 (1977): 656–66.

104 **New research from Yale:** "Hearing Decline Predicted by

Elders' Stereotypes," authored by Becca Levy, Martin Slade, and Thomas Gill, was published in the *Journal of Gerontology: Psychological Sciences* 61B (2006): 82–88.

105 **And the effect is not limited to hearing alone:** Becca Levy has published articles about aging and longevity ("Longevity Increased by Positive Self-Perceptions of Aging," by Becca Levy, Martin Slade, Suzanne Kunkel, and Stanislav Kasl, published in the *Journal of Personality and Social Psychology* 83 [2002]: 261–70); functional health ("Longitudinal Benefit of Positive Self-Perceptions of Aging on Functional Health," by Becca Levy, Martin Slade, and Stanislav Kasl, published in the *Journal of Gerontology: Psychological Sciences* 56B [2002]: 409–17); and improved memory ("Improving Memory in Old Age Through Implicit Self-Stereotypes," by Becca Levy, published in the *Journal of Personality and Social Psychology* 71 [1996]: 1092–1107).

106 **the Capilano suspension bridge:** To learn more about the research involving the young men who misinterpreted their feelings toward a research assistant, see "Attraction Under Conditions of High Anxiety," by Donald Dutton and Arthur Aron. It was published in the *Journal of Personality and Social Psychology* 30 (1974): 510–17.

Chapter 6

115 **The pair would be given a combined sum of $10:** The pioneering study examining the roles of the two players in the ultimatum games was authored by Werner Guth, Rolf Schmittberger, and Bernd Swarze. Titled "An Experimental Analysis of Ultimatum Bargaining," the study was published in the *Journal of Economic Behavior and Organization* 3 (1982): 367–88.

118 **When you think of car dealers:** "The Effects of Supplier Fairness on Vulnerable Resellers" was written by Nirmalya Kumar,

Lisa Scheer, and Jan-Benedict Steenkamp. It was published in the *Journal of Marketing Research* 32 (1995): 54–65.

120 **A group of researchers asked hundreds of felons:** The study about procedural fairness and convicted felons, titled "Procedural Justice in Felony Cases," is by Jonathan Casper, Tom Tyler, and Bonnie Fisher. It was published in *Law and Society Review* 22 (1988): 483–508.

121 **Sitting in their plush offices, venture capitalists:** The venture capitalist study, titled "Procedural Justice in Entrepreneur-Investor Relations," is by Harry Sapienza and M. Audrey Korsgaard. It was published in the *Academy of Management Journal* 39 (1996): 544–74.

123 **Geoffrey Hosking, an expert in Russian history:** Geoffrey Hosking has authored numerous books about the Russian people and their history, including *Russia and the Russians: A History* (Cambridge, Mass.: Belknap Press, 2003); and *Rulers and Victims: The Russians in the Soviet Union* (Cambridge, Mass.: Belknap Press, 2006).

In learning about Russian culture, we had the pleasure of interviewing Dr. Adele Barker, a professor at the University of Arizona and editor of *Consuming Russia: Popular Culture, Sex, and Society Since Gorbachev* (Durham, NC: Duke University Press, 1999). She told us the following story, which exemplifies the cultural contrast between Western values and life during the Soviet era: "It was the middle of winter, like minus a million degrees. I was sitting on a bus, and across from me was a little old lady, and I looked at her and then a couple of minutes later I looked at her again and I smiled. And she didn't smile back, but it wasn't unusual. And when she got up to get off, she came up to me and she said in Russian—I'll never forget it—'Young lady,' she said, 'here we do not smile.' And it meant two things: one, there's nothing to smile about, but two, you don't know me and I don't know you and we don't do that. We don't do that. Because you don't know with whom you're having business, as they say in Russian. There isn't the same sort of chattiness with strangers in Russia as there is in the States."

125 **the differences between cultural interpretations of fairness:** Joseph Henrich's study about the Machiguenga is found in "Does Culture Matter in Economic Behavior? Ultimatum Game Bargaining Among the Machiguenga of the Peruvian Amazon," published in the *American Economic Review* 90 (2000): 973–79.

Chapter 7

133 **Two University of Zurich researchers were equally curious:** The Swiss nuclear incentive study, titled "The Cost of Price Incentives: An Empirical Analysis of Motivation Crowding-Out," was conducted by Bruno S. Frey and Felix Oberholzer-Gee. It was published in the *American Economic Review* 87 (1997): 746–55.

136 **forty students sat with number 2 pencils:** The GMAT study conducted in Haifa, Israel, can be found in Uri Gneezy and Aldo Rustichini's "Pay Enough or Don't Pay at All," published in the *Quarterly Journal of Economics* 115 (2000): 791–810.

139 **to pinpoint the neurophysiology behind this paradox:** Brian Knutson is one of the pioneers of neuroeconomics, an emerging field that investigates the various regions of the brain associated with decision making. You can read about the role of the nucleus accumbens in "Anticipation of Increasing Monetary Reward Selectively Recruits Nucleus Accumbens," by Brian Knutson, Charles Adams, Grace Fong, and Daniel Hommer. The study was published in the *Journal of Neuroscience* 21 (2001): 1–5.

141 **our neurological reaction to altruistic behavior:** The study exploring the neurological aspects of altruism is titled "Altruism Is

Associated with an Increased Neural Response to Agency." It was conducted by Dharol Tankersley, Jill Stowe, and Scott A. Huettel and published in *Nature Neuroscience* 10 (2007): 150–51.

144 **a small magnet school in Michigan:** To find out more about the results of the pilot study conducted at Community High School, see "Teacher Performance Incentives and Student Outcomes," by Randall Eberts, Kevin Hollenbeck, and Joe Stone, published in the *Journal of Human Resources* 37 (2002): 913–27.

147 **a reward can trigger an addictive response:** The economics paper suggesting that rewards are addictive, "Addiction to Rewards," was written in 2003 by Anton Souvorov at the University of Toulouse.

148 **It's only when you dangle the *possibility:*** The meta-analysis study suggesting that rewards interfere with intrinsic motivation when they are presented in a quid pro quo fashion is titled "Extrinsic Rewards and Intrinsic Motivation in Education: Reconsidered Once Again." Authored by Edward L. Deci, Richard Koestner, and Richard M. Ryan, it was published in *Review of Educational Research* 71 (2001): 1–27.

Chapter 8

153 **In Asch's study:** Solomon Asch's classic study about the pressure to conform to a group was published in *Groups, Leadership, and Men*, edited by Harold Guetzkow (Pittsburgh: Carnegie Press, 1951). Asch's chapter, titled "Effects of Group Pressure upon the Modification and Distortion of Judgment," appears on pages 177–90.

154 **it depends on unanimity for its power:** Asch's study about the freeing effect of a dissenter is titled "Opinions and Social Pressure." It was published in *Scientific American* 193 (1955): 31–35.

155 **the dissenter—even an incompetent one:** Vernon Allen and John Levine conducted the study featuring the visually im-

paired actor. Their study is titled "Social Support and Conformity: The Role of Independent Assessment of Reality." It was published in the *Journal of Experimental Social Psychology* 7 (1971): 48–58.

163 **NASA's research into plane crashes:** Barbara Kanki, who works for NASA Ames, is the coeditor (together with Earl Wiener and Robert Helmreich) of *Cockpit Resource Management* (San Diego: Academic Press, 1995), a resource book that describes the application, philosophy, and history of CRM.

Epilogue

172 **sitting in her car on a congested street:** Our fast-driving friend "Erin" (a.k.a. Speedy Gonzales) asked that her real identity be concealed; she was afraid that this book could be used against her if she ever gets into an accident. We hope she continues to heed Jordan Walters's advice and reforms her driving habits.

179 **The results of the study sound like the beginning of a bad joke:** To learn more about how fairness operates in the workplace, read "Determinants of Perceived Fairness of Performance Evaluations," by Jerald Greenberg, published in the *Journal of Applied Psychology* 71 (1986): 340–42.

You can also read "Effects of Procedural and Distributive Justice on Reactions to Pay Raise Decisions," by Robert Folger and Mary Konovsky, published in the *Academy of Management Journal* 32 (1989): 115–30.

Index

Index

Index

Index

Index

Index